D0971345

MERLIN'S
BONES

MERLIN'S BONES

FRED SABERHAGEN

A TOM DOHERTY ASSOCIATES BOOK
NEW YORK

MERLIN'S BONES

Copyright © 1995 by Fred Saberhagen

A Tor Book
Published by Tom Doherty Associates, Inc.
175 Fifth Avenue
New York, N.Y. 10010

Tor® is a registered trademark of Tom Doherty Associates, Inc.

Design by Lynn Newmark

ISBN 0-312-85563-X

Printed in the United States of America

MERLIN'S
BONES

ONE

✍ Amby ✍

I t was midnight, cold and wet, when a friend came running, staggering breathless into our shabby little camp, to gasp out the terrifying news that we were being hunted by Comorre the Cursed and his whole army. The name of the runner who thus saved our lives was unknown to us at the time, but the sincerity of the warning was unmistakable.

Looking back, I am still impressed by the courage we displayed, poor outcasts that we were, all seven of us who had been camped together. We all had some idea of what Comorre was like—an evaluation based only on hearsay, though it was to prove terribly accurate—and we could readily imagine what the Cursed One might decree as punishment for poor fools who had held him up to ridicule. And yet, despite our terror, none of us collapsed in hysterics, and we all remained together.

Even now, remembering those days after a truly remarkable length of time—and, I hope, some gain in wisdom—even now I wonder that most of us did not panic and scatter wildly in our flight. In that case the luckier ones might have drowned individually in bogs and streams, or fallen over cliffs, while the unlucky would have been rounded up by our pursuers. I doubt that any of us would have survived for more than a day or two. Possibly we were constrained to stay together by some strand of magic, too subtle for me to detect at the time. If so, the question of whose magic it might have been is a profound one.

Some of us could certainly have traveled faster on foot than our old wagon could roll behind our two lame oxen—but no, we took the time to break camp in an organized way, not abandoning our belongings. Through all the late hours of the night we plodded willingly along beside the wagon. Bran's young wife Jandree was the only one who rode the whole way, along with whoever happened to be driving. Sometimes Maud was in the wagon too, to care for her.

Young Jandree lay wrapped in ragged blankets, swaying and jolting with the bumps in the road, clutching her swollen belly and praying semiconsciously to all the gods whose names she could remember. She was full nine months pregnant at the time, actually going into labor, and therefore had no choice regarding means of transportation. Bran, her husband, was fiercely determined to stay with his wife in her time of trial, and the rest of us had come to depend heavily on Bran. No doubt much of our apparent courage could be explained by the fact that each of us was mortally afraid of being left alone.

As I have said, we all were poor outcasts, each in his or her own way. Each had been brought into Bran's company by some unique chain of accidents. As a group we had been together most of the winter, traveling more or less at random up and down the land. Some of us, Flagon-dry and Maud and Ivald, had, like the oxen, seen better days. Jandree and Vivian were young adults, by the standards of the time, Bran on the verge of middle age. I was only ten years old and had not seen very many days at all.

We were a troupe, and for the most part we worked well together. I have since been witness to many performances much worse than ours, some of them on fine elaborate stages. In some ways we were genuinely talented. Among us we played the roles of mountebanks and jugglers, singers and horn-tootlers, drumbeaters and dancers, storytellers and fortune-tellers and would-be magicians. We had been stopping and starting and dawdling our way back and forth across the countryside, earning enough in food and coin to keep ourselves going, depending for the most part on Bran to tell us what was going to happen next and tell us what we ought to do—and then suddenly, one midnight just past the end of winter, after being roused out of our camp at the edge of a poor village, we were all fighting to control our panic, and fleeing for our lives.

At least the weather was no worse than wet and blustery, not the fierce, deadly cold it might have been.

The one small advantage we thought we possessed over our pursuers—and, with the stories about Comorre in mind, we did not doubt that there would be pursuit—was that the land would probably be unfamiliar to them. Comorre the Cursed and most of his soldiers came from Brittany across the sea, from whence they had been drawn, like other tyrants and would-be conquerors, by the news of Arthur's death. Comorre was already calling himself a king, and his hope was to carve out and hold a kingdom for himself.

Jandree, I think, must have been twenty years old that spring, give or take no more than a year. She was fair-haired, as were most of our crew, with wide blue eyes that more often than not made her look a little frightened, and a generous womanly body. There was something out of the ordinary, truly beautiful, about her. Her singing voice was lovely. Looking back as best I can through the eyes of my ten-year-old self, I remember her as a good companion when she was not in pain. Jandree of course was the chief reason why Bran insisted so fiercely on keeping the wagon and the oxen. Though he would have been stubborn about giving up the wagon in any case; it would also be vitally useful again when we had got far enough away from Comorre to think of stopping to put on a show.

Bran was a sturdily built, middle-sized man who looked to be thirty or perhaps a little less. His fair hair and beard both had a tendency to curl. At some point in the past his nose had been broken, but notwithstanding that, his face could be whatever kind of face he was required to present at the moment. He was a juggler and singer and storyteller who had seen the little band accumulate around him, while he, effortlessly and even somewhat reluctantly, became its leader. He was generally quick with a clever word—sometimes, as with his little jokes about Comorre's watery eyes and bad teeth, too quick for his own good.

Next let me mention spare-bodied, one-handed Ivald. Ivald had come, by what precise route I never learned, from somewhere in the wave-pounded, cold-bitten land of the Northmen. He spoke our language with a notable accent and blamed the loss of his left hand and wrist on an encounter in his homeland with a berserker—a warrior maddened by the worship of Wodan. Whatever the details of that encounter years ago—I never learned them all—it had left Ivald almost dead, permanently maimed, and his family wiped out. Ivald's face and body were eroded with the scar tissue of many wounds, his eyes were a washed-out blue, his hair and scraggly beard as gray as ice at the end of winter, though he was really only a few years older than Bran.

In the months and days before the midnight warning that sent us fleeing for our lives, Ivald contributed to our common cause chiefly by doing a comic juggling act, that of a one-handed man perpetually surprised that he could never juggle more than two balls or cups or knives at best, and kept perpetually dropping things. A large segment of our audiences never failed to be enormously amused. Ivald also had a way with oxen and other animals, and had trained a dog to take part in his act, counting numbers with barks and head nods. When the dog died he started trying to teach one of the oxen.

Let Maud be number four in my roll call of our party. She had been with Bran and Jandree longer than almost any of the rest of us. Stocky and graying, almost toothless but still energetic, she was a mother figure to the rest of us. She sewed up our shoes and clothing, told our fortunes, and cooked our food. She concocted medicines when necessary, and on the night we were forced to flee she rode part of the time in the wagon with Jandree, expecting soon to preside at the delivery of an infant.

Then there was Vivian. Let me assign her number five—at ten I was somewhat too young to appreciate her properly. That spring Vivian was fifteen, tall among the women of those times, her hair an intriguing reddish blond, eyes green, her body thin but not too thin to display a woman's curves. Vivian did erotic dances—more or less erotic, depending on the audience—and helped out when we tried to introduce an element of magic into the proceedings. She could go into an actual trance on short notice—sometimes. At other times she only pretended to do so, or thought she was doing so, and was easily induced to behave hysterically. The dream of her young life was to become a real enchantress, and indeed she had some talent along those lines, but needed a good teacher, which she had never had. Viv was the newest member of the troupe, having joined about a month after I was brought aboard. Before that, she said, she had been a postulant at one of the earliest Christian convents in the land. This I supposed gave her a certain kinship with my mother, who had had some similar experience in a nunnery, though it seemed unlikely that the two had ever met.

Let number six be Flagon-dry, a potbellied hulk of a man who from time to time, when we were trying to entertain an audience, performed feats of strength. Flagon-dry (his name had come to him in early manhood, he said, from his determination to leave no liquid in the bottom of a cup or drinking horn) was large and dark, and physically strong—but, looking back, I think not all *that* strong. Many of his feats he accomplished by trickery, such as substituting a horseshoe of lead or tin for one of iron, before he strained and grunted and bent the metal in his bare hands. He had exotic tattoos over most of his body. He was about Maud's age or slightly older, going bald and with his remaining hair twisted into a single pigtail in the back. Like Maud he was missing a number of teeth. When Flagon-dry let his gray beard grow, as he usually did, it gave him a certain air of massive authority and sometimes helped him convince the credulous that he was a wizard—which he certainly was not. He claimed to have spent part of his youth enrolled in a Roman legion, before the last of them had taken ship for other lands.

I cannot very well get on much further in this tale without saying a little about myself—I have been putting off the attempt, for reasons having very little to do with modesty, and that is why I now appear as number seven.

Bran and his people all called me Amby, which may have

been short for Ambrose or Ambrosius. The diminutive was what my mother had called me, and was doubtless the only name I was able to give them when they first took me in from near-starvation at the roadside. My height was average and, despite my brush with serious hunger, I was solidly built and rather muscular for a ten-year-old. In my rare early confrontations with a mirror I beheld blue eyes, dark hair with a tendency to curl. A fatherless boy was I—at least my mother had frequently called me so, in tones of pity. By the time I was ten I could remember my dead mother only vaguely. Whatever combination of fate and accident had brought me into existence had blessed me with quick hands, quick wits—and certain other gifts, of which more later. At the same time, fate had given me less fear of the world than was good for my chances of survival. In return for being rescued from the roadside, I served Bran and his group by routinely doing a hundred chores and errands, helping the juggler and the would-be magicians; and once or twice, when a sufficient crowd had gathered for a performance, I had functioned effectively as a self-taught pickpocket. This enterprising theft did not become a habit, for when I thought to share the results, Bran did not appear particularly pleased.

At the time of our flight from Comorre, much about my own origins remained mysterious to me. Vague and undigested in the back of my mind lay the knowledge that at some time before my memories began, my mother had been expelled from a Christian convent, for some reason I had never been told. Later in life I heard stories of how she had supposedly been visited in the convent by a mysterious, handsome lover. There was no doubt about the fact that my mother had given me a crucifix to wear, hung it around my neck on a leather thong when I was an infant, and for some reason I had it fixed in my mind that she had had that image from my father. The crucifix was of Roman or African origin (it was hard to determine which), carved from some unidentifiable kind of horn, and when it was hung around my neck was already polished by wear, in a way suggesting it was very old.

*　*　*

During the months since I had joined Bran's minstrel troupe, our wandering trail had crisscrossed the land over a distance of several hundred miles. Then came the ill-starred night when in one of our performances in a small village Bran had started to make fun of Comorre—of that murderer's bad teeth and watery, teary eyes and deceptive air of general debility. We had thought the tyrant-invader a safe distance away, but unluckily for us there had been a witness who, according to our guardian angel, thought to curry favor with Comorre by reporting our transgression. Offenses seemingly milder than ours had in the past been more than enough to arouse his deadly anger.

Nothing was easier on that first night of our flight than for us to lose our way in darkness, and that was exactly what we did. Nevertheless we pushed on desperately. If we kept moving, there was at least a chance of our putting a safe distance between ourselves and our pursuers before dawn. Once a well-placed flash of distant lightning revealed to us his mounted men, who at the time were still hundreds of yards away, and fortunately just in the act of taking the wrong road. But our two old oxen with their broken hooves, and our ramshackle wagon with its wobbling wheels, left a distinctive trail, and we could not expect that the hunters would stay with their wrong turning very far.

It was some time after midnight when the road we had been following took an unexpected angle, and we found the direction in which we had been expecting to go completely blocked. We had come in the darkness to the top of a cliff overlooking the unseen sea—a high cliff to judge by the sound of the surf below. Bran and Ivald debated briefly and uselessly as to how we might have lost our way.

We had had no intention or expectation of being as close to the sea as this—but here we were. Our despair became almost paralyzing when we realized that we had managed to get ourselves boxed in on a peninsula, no more than half a mile long and extremely narrow. An occasional lightning flash confirmed the terrible fact: we were indeed quite thoroughly trapped, with arms of the ocean to our right and to our left, and Comorre's people somewhere behind us. But with the stars all well hidden by thick clouds, finding directions had become a guessing game, and we must have taken a wrong turn a long way back.

There was only the one road to be seen, the scant track we were already following, and I do not think anyone even suggested that we should turn back. We knew with a nightmarish certainty that Comorre's people were behind us, that by now they must have found their way back to the proper road, and that they were certain to be coming after us at dawn, when they would again be able to read the tracks of our two oxen and the wagon.

It is a measure of our desperation that the next thing we began to hope for was to find a boat. The wind and intermittent rain—unfortunately not yet enough rain to wash away tracks—indicated that the ocean when we reached it would be dangerously rough. Still, it would be better to drown than to be captured. The stories of what Comorre did to those who offended him were not easily forgotten.

Exhausted, we pushed on. But our efforts brought us to no beach or boats, but only back to the rough edge of a cliff—and then, when the winding of the road turned us away from that, we almost at once skimmed the brink of another cliff no more than a stone's throw from the first. Our peninsula was narrowing with an ugly swiftness that suggested that its extremity could not be far ahead.

And now, when we peered in that direction, lightning began to show us what appeared to be some kind of fortified outpost. Here was a small complex of buildings standing with the tip of the peninsula at their back, behind an outer wall thrown clear across our little tongue of land.

Roman construction, Flagon-dry muttered, as if he were trying to sound normal and matter-of-fact: a casual traveler commenting on the sights. Bran, disputing out of habit and without much force, argued that it did not look all that Roman.

Again came lightning, like the smiting together of gargantuan flint and steel by playful gods. This time the explosion in the atmosphere fell on our landward side, the quick glare washing over us to reveal a stark landscape of rock and sea—and giving us a better look at the outpost and its wall. There, just ahead across the narrowest neck of the peninsula, where the land was no more than thirty yards or so in width, stretched a stone barrier some ten or twelve feet high—very smoothly, professionally built, out of keeping with the rough landscape. In front of the wall a shallow ditch had been somehow dug and broken out of the rocky ground, adding three feet or so to the height.

Lightning played again, and the appearance of the stonework altered drastically in the abrupt alternation of light and shadow from one flash to the next. In fact the change in perception was quite mundane and natural—as mundane as lightning ever can be—yet somehow it keyed in my mother's old warnings against the witchcraft and enchantment in the world. From her I had picked up the attitude that magic was a tricky and fascinating business, sometimes irresistible though deadly dangerous for the unwary.

At these repeated revelations of that wall I underwent a stabbing conviction, irrational but sharp and certain, that it was only the outward indication of some vitally important boundary, otherwise invisible.

Who or what might be waiting for us—for me in particular—beyond that border, I could not imagine. But whatever was there could not wholly belong to the same world in which I had lived my short years to date.

TWO

❧ Interlude ❧

An intermittent rain came pelting almost horizontally onto the speeding windshield, the wet streaks adding a liquid tremor to the green glowing symbols of the satnav screen so conveniently reflected on the glass. The single occupant of the old car was observing that display with intense interest, without for a moment taking his eyes from the road. The rapidly changing numbers of the satnav informed the driver of the precise moment-to-moment location of his vehicle, a reading accurate to within less than a second of latitude and longitude.

The driver's face, faintly visible in the glow of instruments, and now and then sharply illuminated by passing headlights, had a somewhat haggard and ascetic look. There were moments when he looked thirty years of age, longer intervals when he appeared to be over forty. He was dressed in a dark business suit, shielded by a transparent raincoat, with a dark hat beside him on the right front seat.

He had reached the last leg of a long journey, begun at short notice and in haste. He had expected to encounter few helpful signs on this winding two-lane road, and this prediction had proved well founded. The Antrobus Foundation did not encourage casual visitors; an understandable attitude, the driver thought. They must be chronically besieged by crackpots.

Even before beginning his long journey through this alien

countryside, the lone traveler had been reasonably sure that it would be concluded in the dark. Still, the hour was not quite as late as he had feared; the embers of an early December sunset, spectacular a few minutes ago, were fading rapidly in rain but not quite gone.

His mind absorbed in matters of life and death, the man in the car was speeding to confront a woman he had never seen or spoken to, and who was certainly going to believe him mad when he revealed the true purpose of his visit . . . unless, of course, she had by then been subjected to other encounters of a nature to prove beyond all doubt that the world was much more complex than she had believed.

Tonight such evidence would very likely be provided.

The narrow concrete, cracked in many places, gleaming and slippery with drizzle, did not appear to have been resurfaced since the 1990s. The automobile's safety systems, doubtless taking the state of the roadway into account, considered the driver's speed excessive and occasionally admonished him with electronic beeps.

Pressured by his sense of urgency, the driver for the third time in the last ten kilometers attempted to telephone the woman he was so eager to encounter. He had to talk to Dr. Elaine Brusen, though he would not be able to tell her the truth, or anything near the truth—not at first. But it was necessary to begin—the sooner the better—to prepare her for revelations now sure to come.

The driver's hands were both firmly on the wheel when he began to hear the distant, repeated ringing. On this fourth attempt the phone was (at last!) answered by a living human. The distant chiming abruptly ceased, and an unfamiliar female voice—he had no way to be sure that it was Dr. Brusen's—sounded in the cabin of the speeding car.

"Hello?" The voice conveyed the impression of a person habitually pleasant, but just now afflicted by both surprise and irritation.

"Hello, Dr. Brusen?"

"Yes, who's this? I'm very busy."

"I appreciate that, Doctor. My name is Fisher, and I've been trying for several hours to reach you on a matter of great importance. We need to talk about some of the special problems that must be interfering seriously with your work tonight."

"I'm sorry, I don't have time now." There was a puzzled pause. "What do you know about my problems?"

"I know something of their causes."

A longer pause, in which the speeding tires inexorably hummed. Puzzlement had quickly devolved into suspicion. "How did you get this number?"

"I realize that it's the private line inside your laboratory, Doctor. In fact your security, electronic and otherwise, is one of the things I most need to talk to you about. I really must see you in person. I'm on my way now, and I'll be in the parking lot outside your lab in about ten minutes." As he spoke, Fisher juggled the wheel dexterously, negotiating slippery curves. And he continued to watch the shifting, reflected satnav numbers, counting down.

"Impossible! You can't get in here. Who did you say you were?"

"My name is Fisher," the caller repeated patiently. He spelled it, slowly, in his precise and colorless English. "I know that doesn't mean anything to you yet. I promise a full explanation when I see you."

He paused, listening to humming silence. At least she had not yet hung up on him. Before she should decide to do so, he pressed on: "Meanwhile, if you should have any trouble—if any new difficulty should arise, particularly if it seems threatening—return my call, at this number, right away. I assume your phone has a caller ID turned on?"

Her breath puffed in a sigh of exasperation. "I tell you I can't be bothered with all this! Good night."

And the connection was broken.

Silence, but for the faint noise of speeding tires on degraded pavement. The automobile, like so many of those built after the first decade of the twenty-first century, ran whisperingly quiet, on an engine that burned no fossil fuels, and a drivetrain and tires of designed materials.

* * *

Fisher was not surprised at being cut off on the phone. Poor
Elaine! He felt he knew the woman well enough to talk to her on
a first-name basis. He had to keep reminding himself that really
she was almost a stranger to him—and he, of course, a total stranger to her. But even had he not known her at all he would have
felt sorry for her.

She must be having a difficult night of it already, finding herself unexpectedly isolated from the rest of the world, actually
alone in the building now, her equipment probably behaving er-
ratically from time to time—naturally such difficulties would be
enough to upset her. Because as yet she could have no idea of the
real problems that were going to descend on her in the next few
hours.

At last his headlights picked up, on the right, an unmarked side
road that Fisher judged must be the one he wanted; satnav had
predicted the moment of its appearance almost to the second.

A few yards down the turnoff was a sign:

ANTROBUS FOUNDATION
20 KM/HR
VISITORS MUST STOP AT GATE

And there was the laboratory ahead.

Fisher had not been near this building, nor even in this part of
the world, for a long time. Still, the shape of the massive stone
edifice, marked with a few lighted windows and now faintly visible in the backwash of lights from its grounds and parking lot,
awoke old chords of memory. It was so familiar that he had to
steel himself against a pang of some soft and inappropriate emotion. As he continued up the winding drive, he did a hasty mental
review of the various means he might employ to approach the
true goal of his visit.

Sixty or seventy meters along the drive, halfway between the
highway and the looming converted mansion, a three-meter

metal fence loomed up, and the road split to pass on both sides of a small central gatehouse. The gate was raised, and the little building was lighted, with bright exterior lamps over the stop sign where the visitor was supposed to halt. Fisher slowed almost to a stop, gazing into the bright interior. Obviously this checkpoint was supposed to be manned. The absence of any guard strongly suggested that things had progressed further in the wrong direction than the visitor had hoped.

As Fisher drove slowly in through the unattended gate, he raised his gaze to the scattering of lighted windows high in the dark stone wall. She would be up there, behind one of those.

> *On either side the river lie*
> *Long fields of barley and of rye*
> *That clothe the wold and meet the sky*
> *And thro' the field the road runs by*
> *To many tower'd Camelot . . .*

Someone's idea of a joke, thought Elaine Brusen sourly, studying the verse that had just popped up on her computer screen. Either one of the in-house programmers was carrying his or her idea of humor much too far, or a virus had sneaked in past all the defenses. Like most of the lab's computers, the machine before her at the moment was tied into a net. That, of course, did not mean it should be possible for crackpot humor to come through at some joker's whim, interfering with business.

Yet there were the words, black as dark ink against the subtle ivory of the glowing screen.

Here in the laboratory, things tonight had been going quietly, if not very successfully, for Elaine Brusen. Her day's work, begun at about nine in the morning, had prolonged itself into an unscheduled night shift; but that in itself was almost routine. Several peculiarities in the behavior of both hardware and software had appeared today. None had been particularly noteworthy in itself, but taken together they hinted that something out of the ordinary might be going on.

The chiming of the phone on her private line, a rare event in these days when she had deliberately tried to arrange seclusion, had contributed to her growing sense of the unusual. And only minutes after she had hung up on the unknown man calling himself Fisher, she had been forced to admit to herself that, strange as it seemed, it was quite possible that for the rest of the night she was going to be entirely alone in the whole building. The people normally present in the stockroom and in test lab (maybe someone from down there could at least end this absurd poetry crosstalk) were no more to be found than those in Security or Communications. Calls to their personal phone numbers went mysteriously unanswered.

She might have worried more than she did, had not her work almost continuously demanded her attention. In the other room, her private net of big parallel processors, forming most of the hypostator's vital organs, had things moving forward swiftly on the holostage. Another iteration or two, and the product would be something more than a mere image.

Yet Elaine was unable to focus entirely on the job. When, in response to some faint, perhaps imaginary, sound from outside, she put her face right against the glass of one of the lab windows, she could see the gate, and almost all the parking lot. Though she could not see the whole interior of the little booth at the entrance to the lot, she had the impression that no guard was on duty there.

As she moved away from the window there crowded in upon her the memories of other strange events and discrepancies, each minor in itself, that had popped up, in desultory fashion, over the past week. She could no longer explain the total of them as mere coincidence. It was as if someone else were interfering deliberately with her work. All right, she admitted to herself, a paranoid idea; but there it was.

The newly arrived visitor, running his gaze over the building before him, observed that it had lasted well. It had been built around the time when the nineteenth century rolled over into the twentieth as the private home of the eccentric multimillionaire John Antrobus. The converted mansion was almost entirely dark. Only here and there a few windows glowed, random and indirect signs of life.

Then, before disappearing for good on an African expedition that seemed ill-advised, the builder had endowed the Antrobus Foundation, and bequeathed to it his strange mansion. His intent, codified in the exacting provisions of his will, had been that the chief business of the foundation, by which he evidently meant its key research, would be conducted at the site.

The parking lot held spaces for almost a hundred vehicles, and at this hour of this night almost all of them were empty. A discreet small spotlight now appeared focused on one visitor's space, automatically selected for him by the lab's security system. Doubtless the same system, if still functioning normally, had already recorded his car's license, and despite the many spaces empty wanted to exercise precise control over what space the newcomer was to occupy.

Well, the security system was no doubt ingenious, state-of-the-art for the second decade of the twenty-first century. But tonight it was certain to be overmatched.

Two other vehicles were already in the lot. One of these was a small new auto that he judged must belong to Elaine Brusen. As Fisher eased his car to a stop, he stared, with no great surprise but with a certain sense of doom, at the other machine. This was a large ambulance, a looming converted van, last year's or possibly this year's model. It was parked, lightless and unmoving, straddling three of the spaces nearest the building, those normally reserved for handicapped or privileged folk. The van had backed in and stood facing the exit, the closed rear doors toward the building, as if expecting to receive or deposit a patient here, then make a quick departure.

Fisher hardly took his eyes from the ambulance as he parked his own car some twenty yards away and slowly dismounted. Standing, he leaned on a cane—the implement was curved, particularly at the upper end, but certainly not a conventional crutch. It did not look as if it would be comfortable in the armpit. Actually it looked more like a kind of hiking stick, tough unvarnished oak.

Standing at his full height, Elaine's visitor was wiry and moderately tall. An air of energy made him look somewhat younger than he had while slouched in the driver's seat. Black eyes and black unruly hair stood out against skin that had once been very fair but now looked unfashionably and unhealthily weathered.

Rain still fell, thinly and relentlessly. Fisher delayed putting on his dark hat long enough to look up at a region in the northwestern sky where a few stars were visible. Stars were impressive, as always, no matter from what time or place one looked at them. He would have liked to look at tonight's moon as well, before proceeding with his business, but clouds allowed no chance of that. Still, his face indicated that he found some reassurance in what he saw in the sky.

After absentmindedly making sure that his car was locked, he limped steadily, neither hurrying nor hesitating, straight toward the ambulance. At each step he leaned on his stick, whose appearance sometimes changed suddenly when it fell into shadow from the glaring lamps illuminating the parking lot. There were moments when, seen in starlight only, it might have been a broken staff, or perhaps the shaft, now bladeless, of a bent and broken spear.

The windows of the silent van were quite opaque with wet and darkness, and Fisher could not be sure at first that there was anyone inside. These days it was difficult to tell by simply listening whether a vehicle's engine was running or not. But at the moment the condition of the engine probably did not matter. Without hesitation he raised the curved end of his ambiguous but useful stick and rapped sharply on the driver's glass.

Immediately the window was rolled down the breadth of a hand, and the shadowy image of a woman's head, topped by dark, smooth hair, became visible in the interior darkness. A suggestion of jewelry, gleaming darkly red, was visible, as well as a high collar at her throat.

"How is he?" Fisher asked, in a language very different from the modern English he had used on the phone. He stretched his neck a bit and squinted, doing what he could to look inside the vehicle. In the rear compartment of the ambulance he thought he could just make out a human form stretched at full length, attended by shadowy figures. He thought he recognized one or two of those figures also, and nodded a silent greeting that was not returned.

"He is as expected." The voice of the woman in the driver's seat was low and soft—it was not always so. Still it carried a sense of great smoldering anger and great purpose.

"I wish him well," Fisher said.

"I think you do not."

"Truly, I pray for his recovery."

"Meanwhile doing your best to prevent it. You pray for a miracle, then."

He let it pass. With a small motion of eyes and head, he indicated the dark wall above them, with its lighted windows. "The woman in the building is still alone?"

"I would like her to remain that way a little longer. Until I am quite ready to go in."

"I'm going in there now." It was a firm declaration. "I intend to talk to her, if possible before you do."

The voice from inside the ambulance was thin and icy and remote. "I have told you what I would like. You have been warned."

Making a stubborn effort to repress an involuntary shiver, Fisher thought that he succeeded. He shook his head. "I am not your enemy. One who is your enemy is doubtless speeding on his way here now—but you must know that as well as I do."

Receiving no response, the man began to turn away, and then swung back. "Have you communicated with her?" He raised his eyes toward a lighted window.

"Not yet."

"Does she know this vehicle is sitting here, marked as an ambulance?"

No answer.

"If she does know it's here in her parking lot, what do you suppose she thinks it's doing?"

"You will have to ask her about that—if you are really going in."

"I will ask."

* * *

At last the limping visitor did turn, and moved away as steadily and unevenly as he had approached, leaning on his stick.

He was distracted, as he approached the front door of the building, by an improbable vision caught in the corner of his eye, the swift and sinuous movement of something large as a human being, but traveling on all fours.

Pivoting on his cane, Fisher whirled briefly to look back, not at the spot where the creature had vanished, but at the darkened ambulance.

As he turned quickly, he caught another glimpse of some great beast capering between him and the rainy sky, sliding over a high concrete wall, vanishing behind the slab-sided bulk of a trash collector.

But the wounded, limping Fisher had the power to cope quite well with events on that level of strangeness. In a moment he had faced away from the van again and was going on about his business.

He reached the main doorway, surrounded by cheerful exterior lighting that struck him as incongruous. Disregarding the several notices in large print, all demonstrating a lack of hospitality, he pushed a button beside the door, applying in the most mundane way for admittance.

He had to push the button four more times, and was leaning on it almost continuously before the irritated voice of Elaine Brusen at last responded on the building's intercom.

"Fisher here, Dr. Brusen. I repeat that I must see you."

Her voice rasped louder at him through the speaker. "Go away! Kindly stop bothering me. Good night!"

Silence again. Fisher faced the fact that it was going to be necessary for him to do something to several locks, and probably more than one alarm, to gain admission. He took a moment to gather himself mentally, then managed what had to be done with a single, sharp rap of his oaken stick against the metal door, accompanied by a commanding phrase. At once locks sprang obediently open, while alarms remained silent—all accomplished at the cost of a certain drain of psychic energy, and a wave of weariness.

Shaking his head in an effort to overcome the latter, the visitor pulled open the door and stalked in, the sounds of his entrance echoing back through dark and empty corridors. Eschewing elevators despite the difficulty with his leg, he hobbled ahead through deep gloom. Up the curve of a broad marble stair, obviously a relic of the days when this had been a private mansion and old Antrobus himself had been in residence. Yes, good old Antrobus. Several things about the place, echoes and memories, gave the visitor an eerie feeling.

One floor up, he left the familiar stairway, limping away down a broad corridor. Here, with a little light coming out from under doors, it was easier to see where he was going.

In one of those lighted rooms ahead, Dr. Elaine Brusen was alone, doubtless still grappling doggedly with her job. Probably she had not realized that she and her laboratory were being ruthlessly cut off from the rest of her familiar world. She would not be expecting him; he could only hope she wouldn't scream when he appeared.

Well, whether he intruded on the hardworking scientist or not, she would not be alone for long.

THREE

❧ *Amby* ❧

In a state of utter misery our little band maintained a stumbling progress through the darkness and the rain. We measured our gains in painful yards along the wretched road, all mud between its jutting rocks. The voice of Bran, who was leading the oxen, monotonously rose and fell, delivering curses against the impulse that had caused him—he freely admitted that he was more at fault than anyone else, and had already asked our pardon—to make sport of Comorre and thus arouse the tyrant's deadly anger.

The rest of us were mostly silent, except for the helpless cries of Jandree, sounding in time with the jolting of the wagon. We had all forgiven Bran, and could not have imagined doing otherwise. Our fear, compounded by exhaustion, had degenerated into something like despair when the smell of the sea, brought to us by the wind in our faces, suddenly grew stronger. And at the same time the road, seeming as confused as we were but like us doing its best to keep from plunging over a cliff, turned abruptly to our left.

Bran and Flagon-dry and Maud—who stuck her head out of the covered wagon for the purpose—started arguing fiercely with each other, shouting above the wind, elaborating their slightly different ideas concerning our one remaining hope: maybe, if we could somehow find our way down to the water, there would be a boat, even one large enough to hold us all. Possibly we could find two craft tied up together somewhere. And it was true that sometimes people kept boats hidden in the most unexpected places along a riverbank or coast. It was even conceivable that if we found a boat the wind and waves would let us use it. The strength of the wind, and the ominous sound made by the waves on the invisible rocks below, indicated that tonight the ocean would be dangerously rough at best, but I am sure we were all in silent agreement that it would be better to drown than to fall, alive, into the hands of the Cursed One.

Exhausted, pushing on in frantic slowness along the dangerous cliff-top road, more than one of us stumbled and came near tottering over the edge. But we could see no road or even path that might lead down to the possibility of beach and boats. The road we were on—by now it had degenerated to a mere track, obviously seldom used—was bringing us ever closer to the small cluster of unfinished-looking buildings ahead. But first we had to face the uncompromising wall that cut in front of them, all the way across the narrow peninsula. In my perception that barrier had now settled down to look more or less solid and ordinary—it was, after all, only made of stones. Behind the outer wall loomed a large house, or manor, surmounted by the beginnings of a watch-tower that in its nascent stage reached a ragged half-story above the level where the roof of the main building seemed likely to take shape—if the structure was ever going to be given a proper roof. The uneven top of the tower, like that of the wall, showed signs that construction had been suspended for the winter—at the edges could be discerned the plastered covering of straw and dung, hardened by time and cold, meant to protect against the penetration of water.

The more closely we approached this half-built wall (stones and straw and a little horse manure on top, nothing mystical at all), the higher it rose in our perspective, and the less we could see of the buildings and whatever else lay beyond.

In that direction, the peninsula rose even farther as it continued to narrow, ending at last, some forty or fifty yards beyond the visible construction, in a sharp, rocky promontory. This extremity of land was only very dimly visible even in the lightning, which had now moved farther off. Whatever might be up there at the termination of solid earth, whether there were more buildings or only more rocks, it was impossible to tell.

Obviously someone had seen in this rocky tongue of land a good site for a fortified outpost, braced against assault with the sea at its back.

Bran interrupted his cursing long enough to repeat: "Not Roman construction. Blocks seem of the wrong size for that." At first that seemed a safe enough opinion; many years had passed since the Romans constructed anything in our land.

"It is, though. Roman." Flagon-dry was not reluctant to contradict our leader. None of us was, when we thought we knew what we were talking about. "Look at the way those stones are cut and fitted."

Really it seemed unlikely that any of us could see clearly any details of those stones. But Bran at the moment had neither the will nor the energy for an extended argument, and conversation ceased. The wagon, wheels squeaking and straining, labored forward on the uneven track. Ivald, who happened to be driving the oxen at the moment, pounded the weary animals with a stick.

Far below us, but only a few yards to right and left, and still invisible in darkness, the sea rushed in against the rocks, and thundered sullenly, and drained away. Behind us, going back as far as our ears could reach along the faint unbranching road we had been following, the night was ominously still.

By now we were so close to that road-blocking wall that any sentry on its uneven top who was even moderately alert must surely have discovered us. Near the center of its length the stony barrier thickened into two pylons, each a higher, thicker reach of the same construction. But—startling sight!—between these bastions, in the very middle of the wall's length, gaped a dark emptiness of space. Evidently the gate that had to be there, and must normally have been closed at night against intruders, was instead standing open, a sign either of insanely confident hospitality or monumental carelessness.

One thing we could determine as we drew nearer was that the buildings ahead, even though they were only partially complete, were not deserted. The faint smell of wood smoke drifted to us on the wet sea wind, and in that portion of the scene framed by the open gateway I could see two or three orange chinks or reflection of the firelight from inside one of the buildings.

The inviting gateway looked just about wide enough to accommodate our wagon—but Ivald allowed the weary oxen to halt just outside.

For the moment none of us quite dared to enter.

Military outpost, private stronghold, religious community, or fortified manor—whatever the nature of the compound whose threshold we were about to cross, no one inside it seemed to be on guard.

As the wagon stopped, Bran and Flagon-dry, silently and as if by mutual agreement, went forward. Flagon-dry had a hand on his dagger, the biggest weapon any of us possessed.

The two men advanced, calling out hesitantly and fearfully, announcing their presence at almost every stride. With Bran a step in the lead, they went in through the open gateway and soon after vanished from our sight.

One-handed Ivald had climbed to the high driver's seat, and perched there, watching, his nose dripping cold rain. Meanwhile Vivian and I were cowering under the wagon, getting out of the rain for a little while at least. Intermittently we could hear Flagon-dry and Bran talking to each other in the darkened yard beyond the wall. Then one of them pounded heavily, with what sounded like a dagger hilt, upon something wooden in the soggy darkness. When no response was forthcoming, one of our men must have pulled on a knob or handle, for abruptly, with a faint booming noise of broken closure, the door swung out, releasing a modest flood of the fire- or torchlight into the night, revealing hints of a flagged dooryard.

Bran's voice, carrying clearly to us outside the gate, once more called boldly. "Hello, inside the house?"

No answer.

"Hello? Damnation, don't tell me no one's here."

Bran and Flagon-dry's presence and their hailing, repeated in the three or four languages they could command between them, evoked no reaction from whoever had so recently lit that fire and those torches. Presently Bran turned and called back to the rest of us, and Ivald leaped down and led the oxen in through the open gate, stopping the wagon in the middle of the paved yard. Vivian and I followed on foot.

Bran addressed us all with his voice of authority. "We're going indoors. We must have shelter somewhere; we're perishing out here."

None of us needed to be coaxed. Jandree, in one of the intervals between her convulsing labor pains, was lifted out from under the leaky wagon cover, and then borne blinking and moaning and wet into what had to be the great hall of the central building, an edifice of modest size, at least in its present state of incompletion. The part that had been finished was certainly solidly and comfortably made. We all came crowding in, dripping and gaping, making a wretched little crowd just inside the undefended entrance, gazing at tile floors and plastered walls, a high, beamed roof.

I have said the house was of modest size, but that was by the standards of manors and castles. Even though incomplete, it was bigger than all but one or two of the buildings I had ever seen up to that time, and therefore impressive to my ten-year-old self by size alone. The hall was two stories high, and proportionately long and broad. The rectangular table in the center did not really dominate the room, but was still large enough for a score of folk to have found seats around it—had there been a score of chairs, instead of less than half that many. At each side of the great room a fire roared in a stone hearth, and on each of the long walls two torches, spaced to spread their light, burned in wall sconces. At the far end, opposite the entry where we gathered, an impressive set of double doors, patinated bronze or copper, stood closed, the knob of each door set with a handgrip in the shape of a heavy metal ring.

The room could not have been deserted for more than about a quarter of an hour. Near the fire at the far end, a medium-sized pig, skinned and gutted but retaining head and feet, hung spitted and slow-roasting, very nearly done to judge by the hunger-making smell that drifted through the room, mingling with wood smoke and other aromas less easily identifiable.

And the table was set, with clean plates and platters, flagons of clear water and of wine, a small wooden cask that turned out to contain mead, and an odd assortment of painted earthenware cups and crystal goblets. Bread and other food had been set out, as if for a meal that had never quite begun. A bowl of fruit held shapes and colors that I had never before associated with things to be eaten.

It was some time before any of us noticed that there were just seven chairs at the table. One, somewhat larger than the others, stood at the end farthest from the entry, proclaiming that the head, while three were spaced irregularly along each of the long sides.

And at each of the seven place settings, which were grouped toward one end of the long board, were fine utensils, plates and knives and spoons of excellent workmanship. The clean plates were actually of metal instead of wood, some of silver and some even of gold.

I remember clearly how I gaped in wonder at drinking vessels of horn and dishes of Roman glass, decorated with strange animals in red and yellow and green. They were in fact the first glass (other than a few badly made, distorting mirrors) that I had ever seen.

For a few moments we all stumbled about just inside the door, surveying this inviting assembly of wonders and dripping puddles of rainwater on the tiled floor. At any moment the rightful owners of this room, the intended consumers of this magnificent food and drink, would burst in, armed and raging, and fall upon us—for some reason I pictured them accompanied by savage dogs. They would drive us back out into the storm to perish, to be eaten by the dogs, those of us they did not kill on sight . . . but moment after moment passed, and those outraged people did not appear.

Our hesitation was an uneasy state that could not last long, not with fire to warm us near at hand and the aroma of roast pig to madden us with hunger.

Wordlessly Bran took the initiative, half leading, half carrying a groaning Jandree toward a substantial couch at one side of the room. Then Flagon-dry went rushing down to the far end of the hall. Drawing his dagger, he stabbed the hot greasy pig as a way of establishing a grip on it. Evidently the spit had not been rotated for several minutes, and the meaty carcass was starting to scorch on one side. Yanking it away from the fire, Flagon-dry threw it heavily into a cleared space on the long table, toward that end.

Bran meanwhile had gone down the length of the hall and was now pounding firmly on the closed double doors at the far end. Looking at them closely now, I saw that the knob of each door was a bronze lion's head, the pull-ring hanging loosely in the lion's teeth.

Bran waited only briefly for an answer before he gripped one of the large rings in each hand and yanked on them. Looking past him as the doors boomed part way open, I saw a darkened hall of large but indeterminate size, tenanted by a big table and other shadowy furniture, but evidently not by human beings.

After a moment, Bran pushed the two doors almost shut again and turned his back to them.

"No one in there," he said, and turned his worried gaze back to Jandree. Then he fixed his eye of command on me. "Amby, take the oxen to the stable—it must be behind the house. At least they can be warmed and fed." That settled it—we were here to stay, for the remainder of the night anyway, for good or ill, whether we survived or died.

I made no protest, but I did not omit to grab one of the small loaves of soft, white bread from the great table and stuff it under my shirt to save it from the worst of the rain when I had to go outdoors again. Flagon-dry, already chewing like some predatory animal upon a greasy chunk of pork, came with me, I suppose on the theory that the crazed or terrified inhabitants of the house might have taken shelter in the stable or some other outbuilding. Or at least that someone might be there, a witness from whom we might learn the reason why the house seemed to have been abandoned minutes before our arrival.

Flagon-dry helped me unyoke the oxen. Then, mumbling

more to himself than to me, he shouldered the heavy wooden ox-yoke and carried it along to the stable, while I led the footsore animals.

The stable proved to be handily accessible, even as Bran had predicted, built within a few yards of the rear of the house. It was modest in size but quite complete, a large, plain, solid structure with nothing overtly mysterious about it—except perhaps how amply it had been provisioned. There were several empty stalls, as well as three or four occupied by horses and a milk cow or two. There our own long-suffering animals could be rubbed dry and fed, from overflowing bins of grain and fodder.

But no one was hiding in the stable. Flagon-dry, pitchfork in hand, poked his way up into a hayloft to make sure. Then he cataloged a number of things that the gods could do to him if the room we had just been in was really the great hall of any kind of proper manor house—or if this house was Roman-built. Too many things were strange about the place, made it too different from any castle or manor that he'd ever seen.

Flagon-dry stabbed with the long tines of his fork into a pile of hay, moving thoughtfully as if he wanted to try out how things worked in this strange place. There were no stable hands hiding in the hay pile. Somewhere above and out of sight, rainwater gurgled, running through broad copper-sheathed drains (we had glimpsed them from outside), channeling the flow from unfinished but crudely waterproofed rooftops into cisterns, as if this miniature stronghold were stocking itself against a siege.

Tending our animals, and leaving them in stalls with food available, took only a few minutes, but I had gobbled my loaf of bread long before we were done. A covered walkway led us from the stable to a rear entrance of the house—also unlocked and unbarred. This way led us in through the kitchen, which was large and well equipped, with fires banked in two stoves, and on a counter more bread freshly baked, still warm from the oven. A fresh loaf, bigger than the one I had just eaten, came back with me through a side door to the great hall, where despite the depredations of my hungry comrades I found what looked like as much food as ever still available on the table and the hearth. Maud had carved a portion of the roast pig in more civilized fashion, so inviting chunks and slices of roast pork lay now in a huge silver platter, surrounded on the table by a welter of discarded bones and grease.

Bran and Vivian had helped Jandree into dry clothing, which, they told me, was plentiful, in many sizes and styles, in the upstairs bedrooms. The object of their attention, looking not much better for the change, now lay amid dry blankets on a couch at the end of the hall. Old Maud and young Vivian were intermittently in attendance on her.

Immediately I slid into one of the side chairs at the table and began to eat, gobbling bread and fruit and meat.

With my hunger dulled, if not completely satisfied, I decided to explore. I was not particularly interested in discovering shoes—though my own had worn through miles ago—or in replacing my rags with newer clothing, except for reasons of warmth. To me, strangeness was always interesting in itself, and whatever else might be true of this house, it was exceeding strange. Carrying with me the last of my second sandwich of bread and pork, I walked through some of the other rooms, first on the ground floor and then on that just above, and gaped with more or less comprehension at their contents.

The broad main stairs, beginning in an alcove opposite the front entrance, climbed one floor and then cut off abruptly against a temporary roof of planking, upon which rain now drummed with a hollow sound. But no water came leaking through that barrier, or through the finished, plastered ceilings of the bedrooms that occupied most of the completed upper floor. Candles, or hearth fires, or both, were burning in all the upper rooms. Warm quarters for the traveling entertainers tonight—if ever we dared to go to sleep.

The folk who normally occupied these chambers were certainly wealthy—no special vision was required to see that. The house boasted many distinctly separated rooms, far more than I had ever seen in one building before.

The resonant voice of Flagon-dry drifted up from the hall

below, grumbling that a proper Roman villa would have had a central heating system.

Garments, seemingly enough to clothe a village—a prosperous village—were indeed available for the taking, spilling out of chests and wardrobes in four or five upstairs rooms whose doors were open. Almost all of what was visible impressed my unsophisticated self as finery.

Most of the doors upstairs were carved and decorated, and just one of them was tightly closed. I gave no thought to trying to open it, because even in my childhood few doors were totally closed to me. When I stood in that strange house and faced those wooden panels and closed my eyes, I could see behind my lids certain things about the room behind the barrier. It contained a number of intriguing tall racks or cabinets, holding many complicated objects whose nature I could not yet discern. Some people moved there, men and women I had never seen before. I was perfectly certain that the folk I glimpsed were not present behind the door while I was looking at it—but they had inhabited this chamber at one time. Or perhaps they were going to occupy it in the future. The images were blurred, jumping with magic whose vitality and strangeness were unlike any I had ever experienced before.

Easily the most vivid and notable among the people in these visions was the one whom I thought of, from the moment I first saw her, as the Jeweled Lady. Something was different, unique, about her; slowly I realized that she had probably never been in this house at all, and perhaps was never going to be.

And as I looked at her, I could see her more clearly than any of the others. She was no older than Jandree, or at least she looked no older, but she was nothing like Bran's wife in any other way. Raven-haired and slender, and of a pale-skinned, exotic beauty, adorned with pearls and diamonds and a huge, dully gleaming red gem at her throat, and with furs and fabrics that I could not have named. My Jeweled Lady reclined gracefully upon a couch of silken draperies, inside a sunny room whose walls were plastered white. A giant, tawny cat in a jeweled collar, some kind of panther or lioness, though I knew not those names at the time, reclined sleekly at her feet. All unaware of my scrutiny, the Jeweled Lady was gazing into a great round crystal that rested on a stand beside her couch. And I knew, with the knowledge that is given in dreams, that she was intent upon some vision of her own.

And then it seemed that something in her private magic was suddenly successful, and the gaze of those black eyes fastened upon me. There was triumph in them, and an eager questioning.

Her voice was as silent as the closed door from whence it issued, and the lips of her image did not move, but yet the words and even the tones came clearly through, so that I felt I should know this lady's voice if ever I were to hear it in the normal way.

Where are the Bones? Young lad, where are they?

Bones? I had no doubt that that was the word, the concept, the lady wanted to communicate; but she might, for all I knew, have meant the skeletal leftovers from our roasted pork downstairs. I opened my mouth, but could not answer, either aloud or in any other way.

But the lady was impatient, and she was not going to let me off as easily as that. Her demands became imperious, though still her fine lips did not move.

Who are you, boy? And tell me, what have you to do with Merlin?

Of course I recognized that name—everyone had heard the stories of King Arthur's mighty wizard. But she might as well have asked me what I had to do with the Man in the Moon.

When the Jeweled Lady saw that her latest question had availed her nothing, she smiled her most kindly smile, one that would have looked well on the face of her lioness, and tried a softer tack.

What is your name, my child? Where are you?—I can't see you clearly. And in my vision she leaned a little closer, peering carefully. *Perhaps you are standing on the very rocks wherein old Merlin's Bones are buried?*

The great cat also turned its eyes of a startling yellow in my direction, as if it might be able to see me better than its mistress could. The beast showed no particular anger or excitement, but drew all its four feet underneath its body, as if preparing to pounce across the gulf between us and catch me and bring me back. But that abyss was far too great for any pouncing cat to leap, even if it were able to disregard the wooden door between. Without being especially fearful I tore my gaze from the blank panels and turned away. Immediately I knew a grateful sense that the contact was securely broken, the Jeweled Lady and her dangerous pet once more at an enormous distance.

Some instinct warned me, rightly or wrongly, to keep silent about the lady behind the door—anyway, I knew that if the door were opened she would not be there. Now I could see the magic swirling inside that apartment, smell it as strong as burnt pork and wood smoke, though on a very different level of perception. What was to me a strong signal left my companions almost totally unaffected. Flagon-dry passing me in the upstairs hallway, on a mission to seek out some new clothes for himself, only glanced at me with mild curiosity and walked on, all unaware of what was engaging my attention. Vivian, who came along on a similar mission a moment later, was sensitive enough to be aware of something strange behind the door—I saw her frown—but the distraction was not enough to stop her in her search for garments.

I have said that there were hallways. They ran both upstairs and down, connecting rooms, and any hallway at all was an unusual feature in any house or castle, even the grandest, of the time. The sheer common sense, the obvious gain in convenience and privacy, of such a scheme delighted me when I began to think about it.

The upstairs corridor from which doors opened into bedchambers was broad, as if part of some grander castle. I moved along it, briefly entering some rooms, only glancing into others. In the wardrobe of the third chamber that I entered, I did discover shirts and trousers that would fit me, along with more than one warm jacket. There were even clean linen undergarments, all of a proper size. Here too were several pairs of shoes only a little larger than my present footwear, through which my toes protruded.

Looking about the room, which was comfortably furnished

with bed, chairs, and table, I noted a few more items of boy-sized clothing strewn carelessly about. There were even scaled-down weapons, short sword and short spear hung on the wall; I handled these and put them back. Even peaceful toys: there was a kite, with a cloth dragon's tail, and in the bottom of the wardrobe lay ice skates with blades of carved and polished bone, which might have fit the well-shod feet of the young heir to a wealthy family.

Still shivering intermittently with wet cold despite the fire in this room's hearth, I stripped off my own soggy, dirty rags, threw them into a corner of the room, and then jumped as a simultaneous sharp movement caught the corner of my eye. It was only a mirror—a wood-framed glass, tall as a man, standing against a wall. As I have mentioned, I had seen looking glasses before, and indeed remembered my mother gazing at her tired reflection in a small one. Now I studied the transformation of my pale form in the glass as I put on my new stolen garments, all warm and dry. In a few moments, I was clad excellently well. A prosperous merchant's or landowner's son, or even a prince's heir, I thought, might look like this.

Suddenly I wondered, as if the idea had never occurred to me before, just who I was.

Then in an instant my blood chilled, and I stood motionless. It was no longer my own face looking back at me from the mirror, but the wrinkled and haggard countenance of an old man, no one I had ever seen before. His figure, simply dressed in a plain dark robe, stood facing me. He was tall, I thought, but slightly hunched. His eyes under their great bushy brows were restlessly alive, filled with an energy that made it hard for me to notice any attribute as common as mere color—and also made it hard for me to tear my own gaze free. Those compelling eyes had weary pouches under them. The old man's unkempt hair and beard were almost white.

His bearded lips were moving silently, and I knew he wanted urgently to talk to me, and that it was within my power, if I allowed myself to listen, to hear his words.

This was frightening, because it was different from, more intense than, any other vision I had ever experienced. And then the old man looking out at me from the mirror spoke my name, thus making the business more frightening still.

His eyes were on me with a frightening intentness, and I allowed myself to hear what he said next.

You are the one called Amby.

"Yes sir."

There followed a substantial pause, while the old man rubbed his forehead, as if he were trying to reorganize his thoughts. *I had forgotten . . . what you looked like.*

It is no very uncommon thing for a child to encounter an adult who seems to recognize him, while at the same time the adult remains a stranger to the short, blurred memory of childhood. No doubt this man was someone who had known my mother, who had seen me when I was small. I could think of no immediate reply, but I began to feel slightly more at ease.

The old man leaned forward a little, bracing himself with hands on knees, as if to get closer to me. *Certain people, dangerous people,* he said, *are going to ask you questions about my bones. You must be careful what you tell them.*

"Sir?"

I am Merlin. And he straightened his bent body, as much as possible. He rubbed his head again, in that uncertain way. *I had forgotten that you would not know my name. I am Merlin, and my bones must be allowed to rest in peace.*

Strange visions, as I have already said, were nothing new to me. Few such apparitions in themselves had power to frighten me. But the number of them in this house, and their special vividness, made them unsettling. Instead of listening to the old man any more I turned from the mirror and ran out of the room.

FOUR

✤ *Interlude* ✤

In the three years she had been working at the Antrobus Foundation, Dr. Elaine Brusen had developed a healthy respect for the quality of the electronic security systems and other hardware guarding her laboratory. Her assessment of the people charged with operating those systems was less favorable. Still she was surprised that tonight's persistent caller had been allowed to get as far as the front door, and astonished that he been able to invade the building. What was the matter with Security today?

Fisher's presence in her workspace was the culmination of a series of weird happenings, none seemingly important in itself, that had taken place over the last several days. Tonight, after dismissing her unwanted caller on the intercom, Elaine had yielded to a feeling of things gone awry, and had several times risen to look uneasily out of the windows of her lab. When her view of the parking lot showed her two unfamiliar vehicles besides her own, one of them inexplicably an ambulance, her first assumption was that the mysterious Fisher had something to do with this invasion.

Then, only a minute after she had denied the intruder entrance, she glanced up to discover the figure of an unfamiliar man standing in the doorway.

She was seated at the keyboard of her computer, struggling with technical problems, chief among them at the moment the anonymous, invasive poetry that refused to go away. This chamber, like the holostage room next door, was large. Modern lighting had been installed in the high ceiling above stone walls.

Except for the presence of a small handful of assistants and support staff for several hours daily, Elaine for the past three days had been living almost in isolation in this and a few nearby rooms, working and occasionally sleeping in the same building, only once going home to her apartment. Among the functions now served by the old house was that of conference center. It was a rambling place, three stories high and so big as to be vaguely castlelike. There were bedrooms, meant to house the occasional important visitor or overworked employee, and a small kitchen. Ordinarily support groups of office and technical helpers were on hand, along with some security people and a housekeeping staff equal in skill if not in numbers to that of a good hotel. Currently, as Elaine was just beginning to realize, every employee except herself was absent; now that the matter was forced on her attention, she could remember hearing some of the reasons, and they had individually seemed good and sufficient.

But now their total effect was certainly ominous.

And of course, Security—it was impossible that they could all have been given the night off.

Much of this ran through Elaine's mind in an instant, when she looked up and was startled by Fisher's presence. He had come in so easily, evidently not delayed at all by thick doors and high-tech security.

Tonight's visitor, getting his first look at Dr. Elaine Brusen face-to-face, decided that she looked at least as haggard as he did, and besides that, more overworked.

She returned Fisher's gaze coldly; obviously she was upset, but still more angry than frightened. "I'm surprised that the guard let you in."

"There is no guard on duty at the moment, Dr. Brusen." He spoke English clearly and fluently, but with some hard-to-define accent lurking in the background.

A few moments passed while Elaine considered that statement. The more she thought about the history of the Security staff, the more she found it not totally unbelievable.

Trying to avoid appearing shocked or frightened, she protested again that she was too busy to talk to anyone. Then, trying to get a handle on the situation somehow, she added: "Have you anything to do with that ambulance out in the parking lot?"

"I've no direct connection with it, no. But it is one of the things I wanted to talk to you about."

"Is there someone in it?"

"If you mean a patient, yes. Along with several attendants."

"What patient?" Dr. Brusen's voice grew querulous. "I don't understand at all; why should an ambulance have brought anyone here?"

He gestured, conveying ambiguity with an expressive hand. The other gripped his staff. "It's a long story, and I certainly don't know all of it. But I'll be glad to furnish as much explanation as I can."

"I've told you, I'm too busy tonight."

He ignored this reply. His gaze moved past her, probing into the laboratory, estimating things in his own way. His stick tapped once on the hard floor.

"You and your colleagues call your new device—I suppose it's in the next room?—you call it the hypostator."

"What do you know about that?" Sharply.

"You hope—perhaps believe—that the Nobel prize for physics lies within your grasp. That the hypostator will bring you to the brink of being able to alter, to re-create—not virtual, but fundamental, reality."

"If you've been talking to some of the other people who work here—"

"I have not. You are currently testing the range of your equipment. Are you having unexpected trouble reaching certain geographical locations?"

Elaine was silent for a time, considering how to respond. Fisher's question showed a frightening familiarity with the facts. Her work, truly a pioneering advance into the nature of space and time and matter, had been for some days now approaching a crucial point.

"Are you a scientist?" she demanded.

"In the broad sense, I try to be. If 'science' means knowledge— May I sit down?" He gestured vaguely; several chairs were spaced about the room.

Elaine hesitated over several sharp replies, then changed her mind. "Of course, sit down." She would feel less uncomfortable that way than with him standing, almost looming over her.

Her visitor tossed his hat on a table and without removing his coat dropped gratefully into a chair, at a reassuring distance from Elaine and her most precious equipment. "An unusual building," he commented, looking round him at high walls and ceiling, while his palms thumped gently on the chair arms. He had left his cane, or walking stick, leaning against a table, within easy reach. "But I rather like it."

"So do I. But most people think the design is rather eccentric." Elaine hesitated. The intruder at least spoke rationally; it seemed to her that an inordinately long time had passed since she had talked in a meaningful way with anyone, about anything but the mere mechanics of her work. She asked: "You know the history of the foundation?"

Fisher nodded. "Building and land acquired by the bequest of an eccentric billionaire, a little past the middle of the twentieth century. Thus did the Antrobus Foundation come into being— and what is its purpose?"

"Our charter says the foundation is established and endowed to investigate the nature of reality."

"How much do you know about the founder?" he asked.

Elaine blinked. "John Antrobus? Very little, actually. Except that he has been dead for decades."

Fisher nodded again, as if he had just been confirming a minor point for his own satisfaction. Then he surprised Elaine by saying: "I met him, many years ago."

"Here?"

"Yes."

"And worked for him?"

Fisher seemed to consider that idea.

"But of course—he must have been before your time." Elaine made a helpless gesture. "Mr. Fisher—or is it Dr.—?"

"Either way."

This acknowledgment of academic standing reassured Elaine to some extent. "I'm sorry, but I still don't quite understand who you are. What your business is here now, with the foundation or with me. And how did you get this phone number?"

"Dr. Brusen, a great many people, some in the far corners of the world, are interested in your work here. I represent some of them. I do mean to go into that, later—first, may I ask if you consider your work here safe?"

She blinked again. "We have a full environmental clearance, if that's what you're concerned about."

Fisher shook his head. "I had in mind something more fundamental. Do you know whether the scientists and administrators involved in this project have ever engaged in a serious discussion among themselves as to the possible dangers to the world at large posed by their work?"

A distracting thought seemed to occur belatedly to Elaine. "Are you a journalist? One of those media people? If so, I don't have a story for you yet."

The visitor changed position slightly, easing his sore leg. "No, I'm not looking for a story. I would prefer to tell you one, instead. As for my business, you might say I represent the stockholders."

"Who are they?"

"The investors. Those who have their lives tied up in your project."

"Their lives? Oh, I suppose you mean their life savings, in Antrobus Securities and so on. I'm no expert in the terms of the endowment. If financial matters are your concern, you'll have to talk to someone else."

Fisher only smiled. "As long as I'm here, I'd really like to see what the hypostator looks like."

He was suddenly out of his chair, staff in hand, and limping straight for the door to the next room. Elaine jumped up, too. Uttering lively protests, she attempted to head her visitor off.

To no avail; Fisher had the door already open.

Beyond was a hexagonal room, twenty feet between opposite walls. High, windowless, stone-walled, softly lighted from above. In the center, occupying about half the total area, a knee-high circular dais supported the holostage itself. This device was now, as usual when in operation, invisible inside its own display.

"I presume," said Fisher, pointing with his stick, "that what we see running now is a kind of stage-saver program?"

"That's right."

The stage-saver program was impressive in itself; when the display had received no meaningful input for two minutes, it protected the stage-space from erosion by gradually building up a skyline of skyscrapers at night, thousands of twinkling windows, making a three-dimensional vision of a city that was impossibly huge and gracious and inviting, as well as being totally imaginary.

The oaken stick now shifted, pointing toward the back of the room, where stacked metal cabinets, one heavily shielded, occupied an entire wall. Overhead a jungle canopy of cables arced up from those cabinets and down again, disappearing in the illusory night sky above the holostage. "And back there's what you call the hypostator. I've seen your preliminary reports. Don't be alarmed—I have no intention of interfering. I wish you'd tell me, though—under the cover of your stage-saver program, what scene is the hypostator building?"

Elaine took thought. Her visitor, though uninvited and unwelcome, was polite and well behaved. And the more she looked at him, the older she thought he was. For whatever reason, she almost always felt more comfortable with older men than with people in any other category. "Stonehenge."

"Interesting." Fisher, unsurprised, only nodded slightly. "I asked you earlier whether there was any trouble obtaining the necessary geographical reach—?"

"No. It's not as if we're actually transporting anything between our model site and here. That won't be possible. But going as far afield as Salisbury Plain illustrates the beauty of the process—or one of the beauties: the fact that our distance here from the template area doesn't really matter that much."

As the visitor turned back to face Elaine, his knee suddenly threatened to give way. He slipped and grimaced and clutched his cane.

"Can you manage all right on that leg? Why don't you come back into the computer room and sit down?"

"I'm all right, thanks." Obligingly he turned his back on the display and limped toward the door. "I hope to be walking normally soon."

"Skiing accident?" Trying to be bright and cheerful.

"No, not exactly." He paused, then with a wry smile added: "A little mishap with a sharp blade."

"Goodness." The word sounded flat. Fisher could sense that the pendulum was abruptly swinging the other way; his unwilling hostess was becoming distrustful again, increasingly uncertain of whether she ought to be afraid.

Fisher had no trouble understanding such a reaction, and he smiled reassuringly as they moved back into the computer room, where he resumed his seat. "It's all right. I can still get around pretty well."

Elaine nodded slowly, closed the door on the display room. "Excuse me for a moment," she said, returning to her own chair. "There's something I'd like to check up on." Then as smoothly and casually as possible Elaine picked up the nearest phone and silently punched in the number for Security. When in fifteen seconds there was no response, she tried another number, calling outside the building.

Fisher observed her actions without speaking, or moving to interfere; he was reassuringly tolerant of her obvious efforts to tell someone that he was here, to check up on him somehow. He allowed her to discover for herself that no matter what button she pushed, what voice-commands she gave the phone, it wouldn't work. The instrument wasn't totally dead, but it produced nothing but a melange of strange unhelpful sounds. Upon its little screen there appeared only an enigmatic logo, no more familiar than the sounds. A red banner bearing a golden lion rampant, like some medieval shield.

She hung up the phone.

And in a moment the four or five little screens in the room had flickered in unison and were showing something else:

> *But who hath seen her wave her hand?*
> *Or at the casement seen her stand?*
> *Or is she known in all the land?*
> *The Lady of Shalott?*

"Oh damn." Pointing an accusing finger at the nearest display of neatly lettered verse, she turned suspiciously to Fisher. "I don't suppose you know anything about this?"

"I must admit I do." Fisher blinked apologetically. He gripped his stick firmly. "Tennyson," he said.

Elaine's anger grew. "So you are somehow responsible for this . . . for the phones not working? For these words, appearing on my screens?"

Trying to look appropriately contrite, he made a little bow. "I thought a few verses of Tennyson might help me to make a point in our discussion. As a way of leading gradually into a certain subject."

"Then I would like to ask you to cause Tennyson or whoever it is to disappear again. To put things back to normal."

"I'm afraid that's not possible at the moment."

"Dr. Fisher. Can you tell me just who it is you represent?"

"I can try." He offered what he hoped was a disarming smile. He twisted at his staff as if in nervousness. "I'd like to hear more about your work first."

Elaine, without quite knowing how her anger had been deflected, found herself talking. Her work—she was really rather obsessed with her work, proud of it, and had to struggle to keep from explaining it enthusiastically to every visitor—was focused on the nature of spacetime, as approached and defined by science and technology.

"I prefer the term hypostatic reality for the subject of this investigation. The metaphysical questions I prefer to leave to the metaphysicians."

* * *

While the pair were in the midst of this discussion, they noticed
that the verse on the computer screens had changed again:

> *There she weaves by night and day*
> *A magic web with colours gay.*
> *She has heard a whisper say,*
> *A curse is on her if she stay*
> *To look down to Camelot.*
> *She knows not what the curse may be,*
> *And so she weaveth steadily,*
> *And little other care hath she,*
> *The Lady of Shalott.*

"Weaving," said Elaine, struck by something apposite. "Actually, it is a kind of weaving, I suppose."

She proceeded to elaborate. In this case the threads that
would form the warp and woof of the new fabric were micro-
beams of tunneling particles, violating the normal status of spacetime millions of times a second. One result of the new technology
was the creation of some really exotic particles—"and of more
than particles. We have one theorist who holds that what the hypostator forms is a kind of miniature bubble-universe. The implications keep getting broader and broader. I suppose we may wind
up, among other things, testing the theory of cosmological infla-
tion."

Fisher, who had been listening intently, was impressed. "You
mean, how was the universe created?"

"Right. There is space, and there is time, and there are the
rules of the game. Out of these comes everything else. All the
complications."

The visitor was frankly awed—or perhaps only tried to give
that impression. "If your machine is leading you in among those
questions, then I should think there'd be a million things you'd
want to try to do with it. And others you'd be afraid that someone
else would try."

She nodded. "I've already thought of several I'd like to try.
And you're right, many others are rather frightening. I'm some-

what concerned that our endowment requires us to go public with everything we discover."

The visitor posed the question of whether such experiments could be dangerous to the world as a whole, or to that part of it relatively close to the particle accelerator.

Elaine commented that scientists tended to think, even worry, about such questions more than the rest of the world suspected. When anything really new was about to be tried, the physicists and mathematicians involved frequently held an informal meeting—carefully and privately organized without publicity, of course—to raise and debate such questions among themselves.

"Off the record, I can assure you that something of the kind has happened at more than one new particle accelerator. But as far as I know, not one of these conferences has ever concluded that any experiment represented a real danger to the world."

"In fact," she concluded, "such discussions assessing risk seemed to have become a kind of informal tradition. It seems to have started with the construction of the first atomic pile at the University of Chicago in 1942."

"But the people conducting the experiment do feel better for having had the discussion among themselves," Fisher commented.

"I'm sure they do."

"And so far they've always been right?"

"We're still here, aren't we?"

"Yes." Fisher nodded, smiled, and seemed to come to a decision. "I'd really like to take a closer look at what you're doing. I don't mean that you should put on a special demonstration, anything like that. Just whatever you happen to have going at the moment. Under the stage-saver program."

Reluctantly Elaine allowed herself to be persuaded. Soon she and her visitor were back in the display room.

She touched a control and instantly the imaginary modern city vanished. Stonehenge, the real place, where dawn would soon be breaking, was onstage.

"How beautiful," Elaine commented impulsively.

"Yes. But as a matter of fact there is something else, at another geographical location, I'd like to see. And I think your machine here might make the viewing possible. Hopefully even more than viewing."

"Yes?"

"Yes—Camelot."

The young woman nodded to herself, confirming in her own mind that at least this request had some congruence with the crazy verses on her computer screens. But she could still summon up a hope that he was joking. "King Arthur's place, you mean?"

"Yes." The look on Fisher's pale, somewhat haggard face was not humorous, she thought, but rather expressive of deep yearning.

Elaine, feeling a faint stirring at the roots of her hair, especially up the back of her neck, gently cleared her throat. "Well—you see, we do know how to connect with Stonehenge. Where to look for it in geographical coordinates—in Salisbury Plain, near the middle of England. Where are you going to look for Camelot?"

"I could furnish you with some satnav coordinates to try. There would be no guarantee of immediate success."

"Well, it's a bit out of my field, but I do seem to remember reading that King Arthur is now considered to have been some kind of real fifth-century cavalry leader. One of the last defenders of Roman Britain against the barbarians, or something of the sort?"

The visitor smiled at last. "Something of the sort."

"What happened to him?"

"Actually that rather brings us round toward the purpose of my visit." Fisher paused for a deep breath. "I had news of him only a little while before I came in here."

"Oh?" Again the tentative, hopeful smile. Waiting, hoping, for the whimsical remark.

"Yes. He's in the ambulance." Confronted now by a look of total blankness, Fisher amplified, with a nod of his head toward the window: "The one out in the parking lot."

"King Arthur."

"Yes."

"King Arthur's out there now, in this parking lot."

The visitor nodded.

"Dr. Fisher—if that's really your name—"

"Please." Fisher lifted a gentle but inflexible-looking hand. "You have seen for yourself there's an ambulance. For the moment, don't worry about the identity of the patient. The important point is that there are truly dangerous people out there with him. Whatever you may think about the truth of the matter, *they* firmly believe that your newly operational equipment offers the possibility of saving King Arthur's life and eventually restoring him to his throne." Again he smiled gently. "Have I mentioned yet that you have become world famous? In certain circles?"

"Dr. Fisher, you really must excuse me." Elaine got to her feet. Her voice was suddenly bright and brittle. "I'm very busy, and now I have to ask you to leave."

"But you see, I'm not the one you have to worry about." With a slight nod in the direction of the parking lot, Fisher indicated where the real threat lay. "I'm in here now, and I haven't done you any harm. I've said I won't interfere with your work. I won't hurt you, I never will. But soon *they* will be ready to come in. And they'll get in as easily as I did. You'll be safer if I'm with you when they arrive."

Elaine drew two rapid breaths. "You refuse to leave?"

"Absolutely. Why don't you show me something else of what your hypostator can do? While we wait to see what happens next. Or let's just sit here and talk about it, if you don't want to let me back in there with your most valuable equipment."

Dr. Brusen was making a conscious effort to control her breathing. "How did you get in here? Without setting off alarms?"

"Magic was involved," her visitor said softly.

"Oh?" She uttered a small, brittle sound. "Is Merlin out there too?"

"You're humoring me, Dr. Brusen. But I don't mind. Merlin is not involved in tonight's business as an active magician. Instead he is the subject of a certain inquiry. Or rather, his bones are."

"Really? I always enjoyed the stories . . ." A distant light came into Elaine's eyes, and something in her attitude shifted subtly. "Do you know what?"

"What?" Fisher forced himself to sit back, relaxed, his hands clasped behind his head. His staff as always was in easy reach.

"For a long time—for years, ever since I began to grow up—I've been thinking I'd like a chance to meet Merlin."

"Why?" Deeply interested, closely attentive, her listener leaned forward.

"Because, in all the stories, he controls vast powers, and yet he always seems so confident. I'd like to ask him how he did it."

Fisher's dark brows knit together. "*Shouldn't* vast power give one a feeling of confidence—?"

"You'd think so, wouldn't you? But if one is sane, it doesn't seem to work that way. In real life, it seems to me, the more powerful one becomes, the more one has to worry about." Then she added thoughtfully: "Maybe he wasn't sane."

Fisher brought his hands down to the chair arms, awarding his hostess a light seated bow. "A perceptive answer. I'd say he's sane. But he's not always very good at answering questions." The lean man's expression had sobered. "As for meeting him—well, God be with us both."

"What was that?"

A tapping sound, repeated irregularly, followed by a dry trickle. Fisher looked up to the ceiling, then toward the next room.

Elaine reached the door before he did, looked in, paused in horror. Stonehenge had disappeared, to be replaced by cloudy turbulence. It was as if a fine, dry powder was being ejected in handfuls from the display, to fall and dust the floor with grayness. The tapping sound was made by the ejection—seemingly from nowhere at all—of larger bits and pieces of . . . something.

Except that it seemed to be coming from, or through, the display on the holostage, the source of the intruding material was hard to find. Along with delicate snowflakes of dust came heavier fragments of stone, and bits of wood, bouncing and clattering from walls and floor.

There were strange violent noises, some electrical pyrotechnics that sent Elaine hurrying for the power switches on the cabinets at the rear of the room. But before she reached them, the huge display had flickered and returned to its normal condition. Stonehenge was back; the ejection of material had stopped.

But there was no doubt that it had happened. The whole hexagonal floor was littered.

"What—?" The woman's voice was ragged with bewilderment.

Slowly she realized that the debris on the floor contained bits of color, bright red and white. It looked like—it looked like organic flesh and bone, bloody red and stark white, at least those fragments that had not been burnt or put through some other desiccating process.

"Is that bone? It looks like bone." A note of hysteria was creeping in.

Fisher, bending over to look closely, appeared to be intensely, intellectually interested. "I certainly believe so . . . yes. Human bone!" He pronounced the last two words with triumphant emphasis.

A moment later the visitor had pounced eagerly upon the rubbish. His lean, nervous hands were busy, sifting dirt to find more fragments. On finding some, he went poking eagerly with his cane, at once-white fragments charred and shattered—only to sit back, a moment later, trying to hide his disappointment.

Elaine could only stare in wonder at this behavior.

"Too fresh," the visitor muttered now, like some insane cannibal disappointed in a restaurant. "These bones are far too fresh."

Still Elaine could see no opening by which the strange accumulation might have fallen into the laboratory from outside. There was only the one door, and some holes in the walls for power conduits and air ducts. It was hard to imagine how the material could be entering the chamber by any of these routes.

But several kilograms of—ominous rubbish—had been brought in from somewhere—as if through the stone walls of the lab.

"Matter transport of some kind? But that can't be . . . the hypostator doesn't . . ."

"Oh, yes it can. We expected that." Fisher was down on the floor, scrambling awkwardly, impeded by his stiff knee, to recover and sift the newly arrived fragments and splinters. Elaine saw with a feeling of faintness that some of the sharp-edged white chips appeared so fresh as to be oozing blood.

Then she cried out. Fisher, down on all fours at the moment, turned his head to see what had startled her. Both stared at the four figures crowded in the doorway. A slender, dark-haired, dark-clad woman, with a great red jewel at her throat, stood flanked by two men. At her feet crouched a giant, tawny cat.

FIVE

✸ Amby ✸

D arting back down the central stairs, I rejoined Bran and my other companions. By now they had gathered again in the great hall, where there was warmth and light and food. Without being able to give myself any good reason for doing so, I refrained from mentioning either of my recent visions. Anyway, those peerings into strange distances had not alerted me to any immediate peril. And I thought it doubtful that my friends, aware of my propensity to see strange things, and intent upon enjoying their new clothes and food and warmth, would give them much attention. When I came downstairs they took little notice of my changed appearance, for most of them looked different too, and for the same reason.

Vivian was the most radically transformed, and the sight of her distracted me from thoughts of magic visions. She had been led, either by magic or instinct, to some remarkable finery. Especially I noticed her new green dress of some exotic fabric, which I later learned was called silk. Also she had found somewhere a small hand-mirror, framed in a green material that I later learned was jade. This she was holding at arm's length, the better to admire her new clothes. I noticed there were new rings on Vivian's fingers, and in her ears.

Ivald had eaten, for he was sitting at the table in front of a greasy trencher, which still held a few crumbs of bread and meat.

There was an empty wine cup, too. He had been hungry like the rest of us, but obviously once his belly was satisfied his next thought had not been about clothes. Still in his old garments, still slowly dripping rain, he was staring thoughtfully across the room at Jandree where she lay quiet on the great couch, at the moment either asleep or unconscious. It was neither a lustful nor a loving look. Instead Ivald's wasted face appeared worried, as if it were on him rather than on Bran that the responsibility lay for deciding how to take care of all of us, including the helpless woman.

Suddenly the one-armed man pushed back his chair and got to his feet. In a rasping voice that had given up on trying to hide its fear he demanded of us all: "Where is everyone? I mean, where are all those worthy folk who must live here?"

Naturally the same question had been in all our minds, but no one had been able to imagine a satisfactory answer. Even Bran only looked at the questioner and away again, toward the tall double doors opposite the entry. I noticed that they had been pushed tightly closed again, shutting out the darkness of the room beyond.

"They're gone," said Vivian at last, neatly summing up all we really understood about our situation. She was sitting, in her captured finery, on one side of the long spacious table, her small feet in new shoes on the seat of a chair. "Maybe we frightened them and they ran off. But they'll be back." She giggled hopelessly. "Well, at least we'll have had a last meal before they kill us, and we'll die dry and warm." She spoke the last sentence with her mouth full.

Ivald poured himself another cup of wine and drank it quickly. There was urgency in his rough voice. "What I must know is, *are* they coming back?"

Flagon-dry shrugged. "Of course they are, sooner or later. Probably sooner. No one's going to abandon a place like this, are they, and everything that's in it?"

Maud joined in. "Aye, they must be coming back, and soon. It would make no sense for them to run off into the rainy night, just leaving everything, like . . . like . . ." She seemed to be able to think of no helpful comparison, and smacked her lips over another sip of wine. "And why should they run?" She looked around the company and giggled harshly. "No one could be afraid of us."

The one-armed man was staring into his empty cup. "What if—?"

"What if what?" Bran was at the table, in one of the smaller chairs, with his feet in new boots up on another. He was sitting back now in a proprietary attitude, picking his teeth with a splinter, but we who knew him well could see that he was far from relaxed. On her couch behind him his wife groaned fitfully.

"This place . . ." Now it seemed that Ivald could hardly speak, for the fear that some new idea had engendered in him. He made an awkward gesture with a tight fist. "What if it belongs to Comorre, or to one of his vassals?"

That was indeed a terrifying thought, and it froze us all momentarily. But soon Bran pointed out that our persecutor's emblem, which we knew was a boar's head, was nowhere visible. And, when we came to consider the matter, it was hard to imagine Comorre or any of his lieutenants ever allowing a gate to stand open in the middle of the night, let alone abandoning a stronghold as well provisioned and rich in loot as this.

"Why should it belong to Comorre?" demanded Bran.

"I don't know." Ivald's fist came softly down on the table. "Because that is how . . . that is how the world is. Such people are wealthy and powerful, and possess fine things."

"Bah. He hasn't been long enough in the land to furnish a place like this."

"But long enough to capture one."

Bran had no answer for that. He thought for a moment and got to his feet. Having seen Jandree settled as comfortably as was possible in the circumstances, he insisted on making a thorough exploration of the house. He listened intently to what information Flagon-dry and I could give him about the stables and other outbuildings, and decided that they could wait until morning.

For my part, I had had enough of the upstairs with its flaring magic, enough of the strange, attractive woman who peered at me through a closed door, and of the visionary old man in the mirror. Enough of magical images intruding themselves upon me, even

though the people they represented were really somewhere else—
if they were still alive at all. At least I had had enough for the
time being, and so I chose not to take part in the exploration.

But Bran, as soon as he discovered that one of the upstairs
doors was locked—it was, of course, the same door through which
I had seen the Jeweled Lady—called downstairs for me to come
up and put my special talents to use.

Still reluctant to tell the company about my recent visions, I
took up my position in front of the locked door and gazed at it in
silence. For the moment there was nothing to be seen.

Bran braced his hands on his knees and bent beside me, bringing his head on a level with mine while I stared. "Is anyone in
there, Amby?" he asked me softly. Meanwhile Vivian moved forward past me, pulled back her red-gold hair, and put her pink ear
to the paneled wood.

I was scarcely listening. There was strong magic behind those
carven panels, or there had been. But I continued to be certain
that no one was there, in the here-and-now practical sense that
Bran meant. Probably my Jeweled Lady had never been physically
present in this house. Currently the visionary stage was empty.
Anyway, as Maud had suggested, it was hard to picture the
wealthy owners of a place like this just cowering out of sight, hiding under a bed or in a closet, terrified by our invasion. They
would have to be timid and feeble indeed if *we* could scare them
so.

Vivian, with little patience, soon shrugged and gave up listening.

"No," I ventured at last, still staring at the door. "No, I'm
sure. There's nobody in there." I paused before adding: "Not
now."

"Well, then." Bran paused, evidently seeing from my manner
that matters were not quite that simple. "Is there anything in
there . . . that we ought to see? Or ought to have?"

I understood his meaning, or I thought I did. The room behind the door still seemed crowded with the high racks, or cabinets, but what they held was only a mysterious blur. "I don't
know, Bran. I don't think so."

That was good enough for Bran. He was ready to turn away, but Flagon-dry had come along and now began urging that we ought to break down the silent door and discover why it had been locked. But Bran only looked at me, shrugged, and walked on. He had learned to trust my ideas and suggestions in certain matters, more than I had yet learned to trust them myself; there were plenty of other things about our new quarters to occupy his attention.

The house was large enough that anything like a comprehensive exploration required at least a quarter of an hour. I suppose we spent a little longer than that, one of us remaining always with Jandree. At one point, when we were about halfway through, Bran remarked in a thoughtful voice that there were no rooms for servants. But Flagon-dry only snorted that the servants, as in many other houses, doubtless slept on the floor, or in one of the outbuildings we had not yet examined.

When we all looked into the darkened ground-floor hall behind the double doors, it proved to be round in shape, and so large that even when we brought in candles the chamber remained shadowy and badly lighted, so much so that I began to wonder to myself if magic were involved. If so, the spells must be so subtle and superior that at first look I was not directly aware of them. We tended to trip over things and bump into furniture as we tried to perform an inspection in the gloom.

Occupying the center of the chamber stood a vast circular table. Even at age ten I was struck by the impractical size of it, the solid breadth of the table's top so great that most of its area would be well out of reach of even tall, long-armed men around the rim. I bent, peering into the dimness beneath to see more table legs than I could conveniently count, spaced all around the rim and also running in lines like spokes to and from the center. This immense piece of furniture was surrounded by a dozen or more chairs, carved in the same style. Most of these chairs were draped in fine white linen cloths, while a couple stood uncovered.

In the gloom only one side door to the great circular hall was immediately visible, standing ajar and leading to a kind of armory or guardroom, long and narrow and almost windowless. Stacked casually in a corner of this room were furled banners, most of them wrapped round short poles. As if, Flagon-dry commented in a low voice, they were meant to be carried into battle. We unwrapped several and looked at them, and all bore emblems whose meanings I could not have guessed, except that they were not Comorre's. The guardroom was dim, like the great circular hall, but was not so big that our candles failed to illuminate it.

In yet another, smaller room, opening from the guardroom through an inconspicuous door, we discovered a flag or pennant bearing the device of a great golden cat on a red field, which Bran said he recognized as that of Arthur, or Artos.

At that time I had never seen a lion, even in a picture, but the image recalled to me the bosses on the double doors of the main entrance to the circular hall, as well as the creature I had seen accompanying the Jeweled Lady.

Bran unfurled yet another flag by candlelight, and then just sat where he was, gazing at another banner, bearing a red dragon on a green background.

In the armory there was also a red dragon helmet, of fine, even futuristic (though at the time I did not know that word) workmanship in enameled steel.

It was Ivald who suggested an explanation. More than likely Arthur, like other kings and rulers, had used several heraldic devices during his life. Often such a change was made to avoid confusion with other leaders who had used the same or very similar ones.

Flagon-dry demanded: "Are you telling us that Arthur was the lord here?"

"I don't see why it's impossible. Arthur had other castles than Camelot, did he not?"

"This is hardly a castle."

"Well, other houses, then."

Argument died out quickly. We were all frightened, though we tried to avoid showing it, and all reluctant to utter every thought that passed through our minds.

* * *

Also in the guardroom or armory off the Hall of the Round Table, we opened chests, cabinets, and closets to discover an impressive cache of weapons and armor. These were valuable items, of awesome workmanship and fine materials.

The quantity was great enough to have equipped a company of men, perhaps forty or fifty; bows and arrows and throwing spears and pikes and lances, swords and daggers and shields and helms, all of a most catholic variety of styles of workmanship. There were solidly built bunks, stacked two and three high, for twenty men or even thirty, and a mess hall of modest size, with its own door leading back into the kitchen.

Trying yet another door, we entered another large room, a kind of adjunct to the armory, and had a scare that threatened to launch us into panicked flight, because our first impression was that ten or a dozen men were waiting for us in silent ambush.

Flagon-dry was so startled at the sight when he entered the room that he knocked down the nearest figure with a blow from the sword he had just picked up, so that the empty thing fell and came apart with a crashing and clanging fit to wake the dead.

Moments later, inspecting the situation in relative calm, we saw suits of full-metal armor, each standing on its own small rack, so that the room appeared almost full of standing armored men. Each hollow suit, from visored helmet to metal toes, was composed of dozens of pieces cunningly hinged and riveted to fit together, so that the complete set would encase a man's whole body; none of us had ever seen the like before.

"How could a man move, let alone fight, in one of these?" he asked a few moments later, wonderingly, holding an arm of one of the things and making the dead joints move.

"He'd need to be a strong man."

Someone thought that men were never meant to really wear such stuff; the truth had to be that they were magically animated.

We moved uneasily away, picturing the empty suits grabbing up weapons and striking us down, fearful of somehow activating the spell.

"And what are those?" Later I was to learn that the strange weapons were jousting lances, stacked in racks against the wall.

And shields of metal. There was even armor for horses—more pieces of steel whose purpose eluded us until we saw one piece in the outlined metal shape of a horse's head.

At the back of the house we came upon a shed housing a forge, cold and silent now, where armor no doubt could be made.

Spreading his thick arms, Flagon-dry inquired, almost reverently, of the world: "What house have we entered?"

But none of us with him could give him an answer.

We concluded our inspection with the feeling that we had at least looked into all the rooms, with the exception of the one locked upstairs chamber. Outside, rain alternately drizzled and poured, a comfortable sound when one is warm and dry indoors.

Except for Jandree, who was again crying uncontrollably in bursts, and Bran, who suffered with her, we were all finding it difficult to stay awake. And I am sure we would have slept, except that none of us really dared to do so. The dawn could be no more than an hour or two away at most, and even if for some strange reason the rightful inhabitants of this stronghold were unwilling or unable to come back, surely Comorre had not changed his plans regarding us. Our pursuers had not given up. Their arrival at the open gate could be delayed no more than a few hours.

Vivian wondered aloud: "Ought we to shut the gate?"

Flagon-dry shrugged his heavy shoulders. "What good will that do? The owners will only be all the more angry at us when they return."

"How could they be any more angry than they're already going to be? Or we could tell them it blew shut. Or that we closed it to keep dangerous intruders out."

That line of discussion seemed to lead nowhere. There was a pause before Bran commented: "Comorre and his people are strangers in this part of the country, too."

"How does that help us?" Maud wanted to know.

"Just that they probably don't know whose place this is, any more than we do."

"So what?"

Bran spoke steadily. He sounded almost completely worn

down, but still doggedly determined, not defeated or hopeless. "Well, one thing we *cannot* do is run from them any longer. Not until we get some rest. Even if we weren't trapped here at the end of the land, with the sea ready to swallow us, all of us are on our last legs." He looked over his shoulder at the figure on the rumpled couch. "Jandree can't even walk across the room. The oxen will quit on us, or die under the yoke."

No one could argue with those facts, and the rest of us murmured or nodded agreement. Then we sat looking back at Bran, waiting again for him to save us.

The speaker paused to look at each of us in turn. "And another thing we cannot do, even if we shut the gate, is keep out more than half a dozen men or so, if they decide they want to come over the wall. It would be nice if our hosts had finished the wall to its proper height last building season; if it were twenty feet high, an attacker would have to think about ropes or scaling ladders, and maybe things would be different. But, as matters stand . . ."

Rain swirled down the chimney, hissing in one of the hearth fires, which were burning a little lower but had not died. Not many alternatives were left.

Moving as if with a sudden access of energy, Bran jumped up from his chair and pitched another small log into the fireplace. Flame tongues grappled hungrily with their new food, sank in their rounded fangs of orange and blue. He turned, dusting his hands—suddenly fastidious in his new clothes—and smilingly confronted us with his conclusion.

"But we had better shut the gate. Suppose Comorre arrives and finds us in possession—how will he know that *we* are not the rightful occupants?"

"*Us?*" Flagon-dry roared the word in disbelief.

Bran stage-gestured dramatically, spreading his arms wide. "Why not? We'll all be wearing decent clothes, for once. And I don't suppose Comorre, or anyone among his followers, knows what we look like—except that I, as the leader, have probably been described to him."

Flagon-dry groaned. The rest of us sat or stood or lay cushioned on rugs and pillows, waiting to be told what to believe.

Bran pressed on. "But I can look like anything I want, I'm good at that. He probably doesn't even know exactly how many are in our troupe. He won't expect to find poor traveling players wearing enameled helmets and gemmed diadems. He won't expect them to be standing in rich robes atop a fortified wall. Nor to have weapons in their hands, and be haughtily looking down at him from behind a closed gate. Hey? *That* should throw him off the track!"

I suppose our response was as enthusiastic as could be expected, given our weariness. A group of us were on our way out to see that the gate was closed when Bran, who was walking in our midst, suddenly demanded: "What about the wagon tracks? Do they show, approaching the gate from outside?"

Bran and Flagon-dry and Ivald and I went running out the front door and across the courtyard and peered out at the last few yards of road, looking for our own tracks, but the rain, though now almost stopped, had already washed those signs away.

The sight of the familiar wagon standing in the courtyard gave our leader a new idea. That ancient conveyance was long overdue for a total breakdown, especially after the last few hours of hard travel. All four wheels had wobbled ominously on their axles. One wheel had lost its metal rim shortly after midnight, and the other three were threatening to fall off.

"Here's a thought!" Bran had eaten again, and his voice had regained a little energy. "We're going to push our wagon over the cliff."

"What?" That was Flagon-dry.

Ivald had a quicker understanding. "Where?"

"Shove it over the edge, outside the gate. Let Comorre find some pieces of it there when he comes looking. Evidence that we all went over in the storm. Our bodies have been washed away."

I shivered at the thought, but still agreed with the others that our leader's idea was an excellent one. Four of us pushed and dragged the lumbering vehicle out through the gate again. Bran and Ivald scrambled through the wagon one last time, removing anything in the way of cherished personal effects—very little fell into that category—as well as several items that we would find it hard to do without if and when we went onstage again—as we would no doubt do if we survived our visit to this ominously comfortable house. And if we somehow, sometime, reached the point of being able to once more put on a performance. There were tambourines, panpipe and reed pipe, a fiddle and a harp, Flagondry's lead horseshoes, and a few other oddments.

Then we moved the wagon to the most convenient spot on the edge of the cliff and heaved. There followed an epoch, satisfactorily long, of near-silence before we heard a dull and distant crashing and splintering. It was a very brief and minor sound against the untiring utterance of the sea.

Retreating to the courtyard again, we closed the gate behind us. The mass of bronze-sheathed oaken timbers swung to with a satisfying thud. After letting the two heavy bars down into place—each needed two men to handle it—we retreated into the house.

It was very late at night, while some of the adults were still arguing about this, and the still-unbreathing baby was still fighting its own life-or-death struggle to be born, when I fell asleep tangled in a kind of rug on the warm hearth, not far from the low fire. At least I started to fall asleep, then jerked awake with a sudden inward shock. I must have cried out, for my friends all turned to look at me.

It had been my old man of the mirror again, the one who had said he was Merlin, looming out of nowhere in my dream, and this time I had thought I heard him crying out in terrible, overpowering urgency.

. . . *bones, bones, bones* . . .

The rest was garbled. Something about bones, and danger. I thought the visionary speaker was trying to wake me up, to send me a warning, hurl a message to me from a great distance. But the message failed in incoherence. His wordless cries were indistinct, blurred in my mind by the closer and more immediate shrieks of the woman giving birth.

Looking back at my brief experience of the world, I could not remember ever knowing an old man. Certainly, before entering this house, I had never known this one. He might have known my mother, seen me as a baby, but now he came intruding as a stranger into my life.

"Amby's dreaming," Vivian commented in an interval between the regular screams issuing from Jandree. They all knew that I was given to strange, vivid dreams.

She smiled at me wanly, doing her best to be reassuring, and the others nodded. And then Vivian, as she sometimes still did out of habit, marked herself with the sign of the cross.

SIX

J andree's long labor came to an end at dawn. Despite the renewed screams of the woman in torment, I in my exhaustion had once more fallen asleep curled by the hearth. I awakened only a little after the event, to be informed that the infant had entered the world and had already gone out of it again.

"Birth-strangled," as Maud explained to me in a stage whisper.

"What?"

"The baby's dead. The cord was twisted around its little neck." She walked along the table, economically blowing out some scented candles that Vivian had found somewhere and had lighted before dawn.

"Oh." At the time I had no real understanding of umbilical cords, and very little about birth, except for what I had seen, on a couple of earlier occasions, of the basic raw and bloody fact.

Jandree, huddled under coverings on the couch, looked to me as if she had lost a great deal of weight. She was drained in body and mind, her hair damp strings, face very pale. She was only intermittently conscious, and at least to my inexperienced eye she looked as if she might be dying herself. Maud, though she certainly needed sleep herself, stayed with the sufferer, patiently doing and saying the things that kindly, helping women always say and do when others are in trouble. There had been another change of bedsheets and clothing, and the bloody ones hurled away into a corner of the room.

Jandree kept picking up the baby's body again and again, refusing to be separated from it. Until Vivian, also being helpful as was often her habit, for the third or fourth time pried the small, still form of the infant out of the mother's arms, then handed it, still wrapped in a luxurious towel, to me. I suppose Vivian had no reason for doing so other than that I happened to be standing near and she was hoping I would somehow get rid of the burden.

Bran, who had not slept, was sitting exhausted on a chair near the couch. His face looked as if death had defeated him, too.

I looked at the little bluish face on the small body I was holding, and on impulse stroked the bald and wrinkled scalp. It was not the first death I had seen by any means, not even the first dead baby, but it struck me as terrible, and I had no idea of what to say, though at the same time I felt a great yearning to be of help.

I looked up to see Bran approaching, in his hand a small cup that he had filled with water from a carafe at the table. With a few words and a gesture or two, he showed me how he wanted me to hold the dead infant, while he poured the Christian water on its head and murmured Latin words. It was the first baptism I could remember seeing, and though the simple ritual gave me no sense of magic, I was impressed. Bran turned away, and set the cup back carefully on the table, and went to stand staring at nothing.

Maud and Vivian had just finished cleaning Jandree up—again—and getting her settled amid clean bedding, and were giving her water to drink, along with sympathy, when I felt a feeble stirring in my arms, and heard a faint cry. This was followed in an instant by a determined squirming, and a strong yell, lusty and demanding.

With the infant, now a healthy pink, alive after all, and installed at its weeping mother's breast, its shaken parents murmured to each other about a name, but I think were afraid to give one.

Maud and Vivian began trading muttered recriminations as to which of them had been so sure that the baby was dead.

Bran, worn out by a seesaw of emotion but now a father after all, fell asleep slumped in a softly cushioned chair, without having made any decision as to what we ought to be doing about the deadly danger we all still faced. Knowing what we knew of Comorre, there was no reason to think that his people had given up the pursuit.

Our leader being effectively absent, snoring faintly, gave the rest of us a chance at decision-making—if we wished to try. Jandree currently was even less able than her husband to talk intelligently, and I was a child, extraordinarily useful at spying things out, but not to be trusted making choices. So Maud, Vivian, and Ivald sat at the table with Flagon-dry, who was the only one who looked as if he might be attempting, or at least pretending, to come up with some kind of plan.

The other members of the impromptu council tended to be easily distracted. "All these fine things," said Vivian, looking dreamy, running her hands down over her green dress. "Do you know?" She yawned. "I wonder if this house *was* Camelot?"

Everyone had heard a hundred marvelous stories describing the magnificence of style and wealth enjoyed by King Arthur and his court before the fall. The tales told of gold and jewels, fine glass and ivory and amber and all the rest. And then there were the mysterious banners, the fine armor and weapons we had discovered . . .

Maud snorted. "Silly goose! This house is new, so new it's still being built. And Camelot was much bigger."

"Were you ever there? Did you ever see it?" Vivian's voice was small, ready to be awed.

"No, not I." The older woman vigorously shook her head. "But everyone knows it was much bigger and finer than this house." She looked about and sniffed. "Though even this house is much too fine for the likes of us to live in."

Vivian turned her gaze to Bran, and spoke before she remembered that he was asleep. "Bran, did you ever see it?"

Our leader looked up, startled out of dreams. "What?"

"Sorry I woke you. Camelot, we're talking about. King Arthur's castle and the town around it."

Bran, already staring off into the distance again, shook his head and silently mouthed the one word: *No.* His eyes sagged shut again.

"We're only humble folk," said Flagon-dry. "All of us." He frowned, swirling wine in the cup in his big hand, but he made no attempt to empty the vessel rapidly.

"Of course." Vivian looked down with pride at the sleeves of her new stolen dress. "But . . . but even at Arthur's court they must have had entertainers in from time to time. I'd love to see it!"

The older woman laughed. "Maybe they did, but you never will. Camelot was destroyed, just after Arthur died." Maud often discussed catastrophes in a way, a tone, that made it seem she relished them.

"Was it? How do you know?" Vivian was a tenacious dreamer.

"Everyone says so." Maud always considered that a clinching argument.

"How was it destroyed?"

"Burned, I suppose. Any kind of house or fortress will burn, if you get inside it and set fire to the wooden parts."

"But you had never been there? Never seen the place?"

"Just told you I never did. No. I don't suppose that many have. Is that other wine any sweeter than this? Maybe I should try some of that."

"There you are! You don't really know." Vivian seized whatever she could get in the way of minor triumph. "Maybe the walls of Camelot still stand. I'd like to see it. And who's to say that he's really dead?"

"*Arthur?*" Maud snorted again, and smiled. "He's dead dead dead, little one. He was all cut to little bits in a battle."

As if prodded by the mention of someone being cut to little bits, Ivald muttered something and got to his feet. The one-armed man had fallen asleep at the table for a little while, head pillowed on his whole arm. He had been steadily consuming wine, and seemed to be growing increasingly ill at ease, as if with some presentiment of disaster. Now he turned and hurried out of the room. Ivald was still clad in his own old worn-out garments, the only one of our group who had not yet helped himself to a change of wardrobe.

"Fearful as a woman," Flagon-dry grumbled, shaking his head. He belched roast pork, and more exotic food. "No wonder he had to flee the Northland. Men there can't get away with acting like that. Maybe he'll come back to do the cooking and the laundry."

A minute or two passed and Ivald did not come back.

"Run after him, Amby," Maud told me, a woman sounding no more fearful than Flagon-dry himself. "See what he's up to. Likely he's only in the privy throwing up. Ate too much, drank too much, too quick, on an empty stomach."

I nodded, and went to investigate. No mature judgment was required to grasp the fact that Ivald was behaving out of character. He might be womanish in some ways, I thought, and he was certainly not a warrior type, but neither was he ordinarily given to fits of panic, or to heavy drinking. We had a right to know whether in his wine-soaked anxiety the one-armed man was going to do something crazy that might create new problems for us all.

Ivald was not to be found in the deserted kitchen, or in the little armory shed. Nor in the stable, nor in the privy farther back. As I stepped urgently but sleepily out into the light of early morning to continue my search among the odd gray shapes of rock that filled the tongue of land out to its end, I could faintly hear through open doors and narrow windows the voices of the three people who were awake in the great hall behind me. Flagon-dry and Maud and Vivian were trying to work out some plan by which we could bluff Comorre's people, or anyone else who showed up at the gate, by pretending that we were the rightful occupants of this place.

"—whatever this place may be," Maud concluded. I could picture her looking about mistrustfully.

Flagon-dry, who always tried to maintain some reputation as an expert on Roman matters (and on a great many other subjects), maintained that the most likely purpose of this complex of buildings was to contain, defend, and support some small crypt or temple, probably an oracle.

Maud was doubtful about this, but Flagon-dry continued to insist that the place was too luxurious for a mere military outpost, and too remote from towns and villagers and cultivated fields to be some landowner's manor house. Nor did it seem to have housed a community dedicated to any religion, new or old, that he had ever heard of—none of the rooms looked like dormitories or cells, and the impression given by the distribution of clothing and other articles was that men and women had shared certain bedrooms.

What was left? An oracle!

Flagon-dry's assertive voice faded as I moved farther away from the house, looking for Ivald among the labyrinth of tall rocks.

Flagon-dry was soon to be proved right about the oracle—but in fact matters were more complex than any of us imagined.

Only a couple of dozen strides behind the house, and a few yards from the other outbuildings (later, there turned out to be no real servants' quarters among them—but by the time we made sure of that, we were past wondering about servants), I came upon a roof-less shell of a building, surrounded and almost hidden by tall rocks. It would have been possible at first glance to think this structure was unfinished, too, but a second look indicated that its incompleteness had another cause. It was in fact a ruin, much older looking than any of the other buildings nearby. Even when whole, the chapel (for so I quickly came to think of it) had been much smaller than the house, smaller even than the great hall in which we had found shelter, perhaps only ten strides long by half that distance wide. Last night's rain still puddled on the stone floor. The walls had once been plastered and bore some indica-tions that the little building had been a Christian church or chapel—I had seen the cross often enough before, in other places, and indeed was wearing a much smaller, horn-carved version of the same device upon a chain around my neck, the only gift I could remember getting from my mother. But in this chapel crosses had been molded into plaster or carved out of stone or wood or horn, some bearing the image of the Crucified Man and others not, some still intact while others had been broken.

It appeared that after the little building had been all knocked apart and ruined, an older kind of shrine had been erected, or reinstated, on the site. Looking at what was left of the walls, I was unable to decide in my own mind which god had been here first.

Other symbols, less familiar to me, were present, too. A bronze stag, as someone told me later, was definitely a Wodan symbol. The raven and the wolf were here, and they also belonged to the dark, one-eyed god of the Northmen.

A buzz of flies, sounding eager and hungry so early in the spring, and a sweetish stench indicated the presence of some kind of meaty offal. Perhaps blood had been ritually spilled here and splashed about, not long ago; the long rain made it hard to tell. I wondered if it was human blood. Everyone had heard stories of human sacrifice, carried out by druids, among others, but I had never seen anything bigger than a pigeon killed in ritual.

Ivald was sitting on the bare stone floor in the middle of the little chapel, staring at the wall, his glassy gaze aimed in the general direction of one or more of the religious symbols. I couldn't tell which deity, old Wodan or Christ, the relative newcomer from far-off lands, was the recipient of his intense concentration—maybe there was a third candidate, lost somewhere in the markings on the wall. The one-armed man, his upper body swaying slightly, looked so strange that I almost feared to approach him, and only watched from a distance for a little while.

When at last I deliberately made a small noise, scuffing the wet stone floor with one of my new shoes, Ivald gave a start and became aware of my presence.

He shifted his position and turned and looked around until he saw me. "Amby," he said then. But nothing changed in his face, his voice was remote, and after the one word he once more fell silent.

"Yes," I said. "Are you all right?"

Ivald was staring at me in a way that made me edge back a

little toward the gap in the ruined wall that once had been a doorway.

"Ivald," I repeated. "Are you all—?"

His voice was hoarse. "When Comorre catches up with us . . ."

"Yes?" Fear, a contagion of Ivald's terrible fear, suddenly made it hard to get any words out of my throat.

The Northman raised his large, pale fist, and I saw that it was trembling. "Do you know what he does to children? What he's going to do to you?"

"No," I breathed.

"To the baby, too. Better if it had never started breathing. Know what he'll do to all of us?"

I wanted to turn and run, but it seemed that my limbs would not obey.

"Do you know?"

Wordlessly I shook my head.

Ivald's voice held me as if by magic, but the power in it was not magic. Rather it was fear, deeper and older than the eldest spells. "I heard what he did to a village that had angered him. His men took the village children . . ." His voice stopped as if it had run into an obstacle. His haunted eyes bored into me. "I can't watch that," he added simply, as if he were commenting on some elementary fact. He repeated: "I can't watch such things happen anymore." Now it was the same, matter-of-fact voice in which he might have told me: "I only have one hand, and can't juggle three balls at the same time."

Cold dread had now penetrated my very bones, and I could find nothing to say. Tearing myself away at last, leaving Ivald in the chapel, I went uneasily back to make my report to the others.

SEVEN

ran was vaguely interested when I told him about my discovery of the chapel. He was relieved to hear that Ivald had not done anything desperate and did not appear to be on the verge of doing so. Before our leader went to look at either Ivald or the chapel, he established a schedule for the rest of us by which one of us would always be keeping watch, from atop the wall or the little half-built tower atop the house, against the possibility of Comorre's people coming up the road and taking us unawares. By now the sun had been up for an hour, and we began to hope that they had given up the pursuit after all.

Having arranged an informal roster of sentries, and having seen Vivian go out to take the first shift, Bran asked me to show him the building I called a chapel. I led him out among the wooden outbuildings and the towering rocks that came crowding up close to the rear of the big house, like giants who were somehow eager to take part in its construction.

We found Ivald huddled now in a corner of the ruin that I had decided must be a chapel. He was still sitting on the floor, weeping like a woman, shamelessly, softly and hopelessly. Bran in his quietly compelling voice urged the one-armed man to get hold of himself, and soon persuaded him to come back to the house with the rest of us.

* * *

After that we all, except Jandree and Ivald—who had fallen asleep at the long table, his head on his arm—took turns as lookout, either on the wall or atop the watchtower. Around midmorning Flagon-dry, the current lookout, let out a piercing whistle.

Five of us were soon gathered on the raw, unfinished top of the wall to stare. A glint of armor and a bright speckling of banners half a mile away soon turned into a column of horse and foot, dull brown and gray with here and there a spot of brightness or color, advancing over a road that was too wet from last night's rain to yield a cloud of dust.

Now the worst had happened: our terrible pursuers had really caught up with us. In a quarter of an hour or so they had deployed themselves in a formation only a few yards in front of our wall and gate, scores of mounted men, some in chain mail, most all of them armed with spears and shields, bows and slings and knives, and a few long swords. There was the boar's head banner, wet and drooping. A crowd, made up of less materially successful warriors and hangers-on, followed on foot. Comorre's effective fighting force was evidently about two hundred strong, an impressive army for those days in our land.

The bronze-sheathed gate, which had looked and felt so comfortingly massive earlier, now seemed a futile, childish thing. Of course the gate, however strong, and the long, low wall, virtually unmanned by defenders, were not going to keep an army of active soldiers from forcing their way into the compound. Not if their commander decided to order the attempt. As I think I have mentioned before, the barrier in most places was no more than about twelve feet high, not counting the lowering of the ground level by the ditch in front of it. The stonework was almost equally thick, suggesting that its finished height was planned to be considerably more. But as matters stood, a nimble attacker standing on a horse's back, or otherwise improvising a short ladder, would be on top of the wall in a moment if no determined defender knocked him back. And the problems of defense were made worse by the fact that no real parapets existed on the unfinished wall, though in two or three places the masonry rose higher along the outer face, offering irregular shelter for a few defenders. Elsewhere, anyone standing atop the wall would be nakedly exposed to attackers' missiles.

Anyway, I didn't think matters were actually going to come to an attack. One of the soldiers would demand in a commanding voice that the gate be opened, and we would have no choice but to obey.

Would we? Well, maybe.

Bran had now put on an impressive helmet—although not the one bearing the red dragon—and a cloak, which made a profound transformation in his appearance. Thus equipped, he went up a short flight of stone steps to the wall-walk, and appeared, leaning with folded arms upon a breast-high informal parapet, its top surfaced for the winter with a hardened coating of horse manure and straw, to hold a dialogue with the men who were sitting their horses just outside our gate.

We relied on the unfinished wall to explain why we displayed no flag.

There were three men approaching. One of the two subordinate officers was a Northman, wearing a distinctive long-sleeved woolen coat.

The captain of the troop was impressive in his own way, his head encased in an iron helmet with flanges that partially protected his face while allowing him good vision. He had a sword strapped at his waist—swords at that time were comparatively rare weapons—with a throwing-spear slung on his back, over a vest of some hairy animal skin. His saddle, as I recall, was fitted with stirrups, which were also something of an innovation.

He hailed us—hailed the two men visible, Bran and Flagon-dry, who was also in borrowed finery, doing his best to look solemn and important. Flagon-dry was carrying an impressive ceremonial spear, and made a believable-looking captain of the guard.

The man on the horse rode closer and introduced himself respectfully. "I am Dreon, captain in the service of Comorre of Brittany." Whether he had come from across the sea or not, his deep voice sounded with a good command of our language.

"I am Hamond, humble servant of the oracle." Bran's voice was perfectly confident, and the made-up name had come out of his mouth without a moment's hesitation—no doubt he'd had it ready for some time. He also fabricated a name, which I admit I do not remember now, for Flagon-dry, and introduced him, too.

Down in the courtyard, invisible to the troops outside the wall, Vivian, after whispered consultation with Maud, was putting on over her green dress a rich vermilion cloak and headdress, borrowed like the rest of our new clothes from the house's seemingly inexhaustible store of finery. This was not the garb of an exotic dancer, or of the lady of a manor, or even of a woman of the nobility. Vivian seemed to have become a priestess. She had also marked her face, neck, and arms with painted symbols that might, for all we knew, have had some mystic meaning.

In another moment she had joined Bran and Flagon-dry on the wall. At once all the faces outside the wall were turned our way. At first the great mass of soldiers stared with reflex wolfishness at the slender, flame-haired girl. But her haughty look and bearing, even more than her fine garments, soon froze them into attitudes of silent, grudging respect.

Obviously this Dreon, like the Romans who'd come this way so many years before him, was wary of druids, or of anyone who gave a hint of possessing similar powers. The men on horseback blinked up at the helmeted figures confronting them—they needed to look up only slightly, because the top of our wall was not very high in front of them, with Bran and Flagon-dry standing almost within spear thrust, and necessarily exposed to missiles.

The captain considered them carefully. Next he cast a long look to right and left along the thirty yards or so of wall. It was a disquieting action, as if, I thought, he might be estimating how long a front he might have on which to attack, and we to defend.

At last Dreon raised his face again to the men atop the wall and asked: "What oracle might that be, soothsayer?"

Bran chose that moment for one of his impressive, well-timed pauses. If I had not heard his quick-witted responses time and again during the winter just passed, putting down hecklers and threateners in countless country fairs and manor yards and villages, I might have thought him at a loss for a good answer. Looking away from his interrogator, as if he were taking a silent inventory of the oracle's assets before he revealed its name, he allowed his eyes to rest briefly on haughty Vivian, then on stout, impressive Flagon-dry—and lastly on me. I was a totally insignificant figure, and probably would have been omitted from Bran's survey except that I was in view, and I appeared too well dressed and too idle to be a servant.

Then Bran opened his mouth, but what reply he had in mind to give we never learned. For I was seized at that moment by one of those impulses to which most folk yield once in a lifetime, or, if they are lucky, never.

"The Oracle of Merlin's Bones!" I piped up.

I am sure that Bran, like everyone else present, myself included, was taken by surprise at this announcement. But when that happened to Bran he was not one to betray the fact, and gallantly and cleverly he played along. "You've heard the story?" he inquired blithely, turning to the captain. At the same time Bran raised an eyebrow, all ready to be astonished if Dreon should confess ignorance.

Dreon appeared a very stolid type, not much interested in whether strangers thought him ignorant or not. "The story, sir?"

"Why yes, the story. How the greatest magician in the world, not all that many years ago, fell madly in love with a beautiful and mysterious young woman—as old men, like young ones, will dote upon young women sometimes—and how he was betrayed by her, when she tired of old Merlin and turned against him the very spells she'd wheedled out of him? How she confined him by magic, so that he must lie forever under a great rock?"

"We've all heard that," said the captain, looking and sounding not much impressed, allowing himself to be distracted by his restless horse.

"Behold the very rock!" said Bran, pointing firmly though not overdramatically to the promontory almost directly behind him. "Beneath it Merlin is confined!"

Dreon grunted something and looked almost bored. His two officers sat their horses silently.

Bran was determined to impress them. "The great magician's bones lie moldering for all time beneath those stones. Once deprived of Merlin's help, neither Arthur nor Camelot could stand. In a few years they—"

"We've heard all about that, too." Dreon cuffed his horse on the ear, and at last it stood still, quivering. "It seems to me that if Arthur missed his great adviser so much, he ought to have come here and asked advice of your oracle."

Bran did not even blink. "Why, he did just that, good sir. Of course he did." Gloomily our leader shook his head. "Oh, would that our late king had *followed* the advice, once given!"

The conversation went on a little longer. Our side, with Bran doing most of the talking, naturally kept on about what a famous and successful oracle this was. But I thought it was largely wasted effort, because none of Comorre's people now doubted that. To me, Bran and Flagon-dry's claims and explanations soon started to sound awkward, and even a touch uncertain. Meanwhile, our caller at the gate and his fellow officers, though remaining confident, became a shade more deferential. Listening, I got the confusing impression that Dreon and his colleagues outside the gate now had a better idea of who we were supposed to be than we did ourselves—as if, once Merlin's bones had been brought into the discussion, the situation had somehow fallen into place for them.

Once Bran shot a quick glance at me. His face was almost expressionless, but I got the distinct impression that at the first good opportunity he was going to grab me by my new collar or my greasy hair and question me: What private knowledge did I possess about Merlin, or Merlin's blasted bones, and why had I brought them into the discussion? Evidently Bran wished the situation was as clear to him as it now appeared to be to Comorre's captain.

Dreon meanwhile was methodically getting around to the object of his visit, asking Bran and Flagon-dry whether any of the servants or managers of the oracle had seen anything of a small group of mountebanks traveling with a wagon.

Bran looked at us, his visible companions, one by one, and this time received blank looks in return. "There are no entertainers here," he assured the captain solemnly, and a trifle coldly. "Itinerant or otherwise." Gradually I had come to understand that Bran must have received somewhere the kind of education rich men expected to obtain for their sons. He could come up with a big word when he chose, boldly throwing in morsels of Latin from time to time.

He added haughtily: "We do not welcome carnivals."

"Of course not, sir." And Dreon smiled faintly. "Anyway, it's not exactly songs and dances that we expect to get out of these people when we find them. Not happy singing, anyway. Oh, they may do some yelling and jumping about, because they are to be made to burn and bleed for certain crimes they have committed."

Just as Dreon spoke of yelling, the baby cried loudly somewhere inside the house, and the common domestic sound seemed to confirm how thoroughly we were established as proprietors. Where there were babies there had to be mothers, and where there were mothers, men. For all our visitors could tell, our unfinished wall might well conceal a small army of guards, all heavily armed and ready to defend to the death their wives and children, not to mention their oracle and its precious soothsayers and attendants.

Flagon-dry, the very image of bearded authority, cleared his throat and suggested: "Captain, are you certain that these minstrels, or whatever they are, came this way? You followed them out on this peninsula?"

"Oh yes. Quite certain. We followed their trail."

"Well then, have you thought that they might be hiding among the rocks at the bottom of the cliffs, outside our walls? There are not many other places they could have gone. You may search down there, if you wish." It was a gracious granting of permission.

It was at about this point that Ivald—why, I do not know, unless he was irresistibly drawn to see the enemy—appeared for the first time on the wall. In an effort to help our deception, he like the others was now wearing some shoulder furs, and some ornament on his head.

When Ivald showed himself, the officer sitting his roan horse on Dreon's left, a fellow Northman, got a look at him, and immediately drew himself up in his saddle. A moment later Ivald noticed the man, and their eyes met. And locked.

For the space of two or three breaths, neither said anything. Then the man outside announced stiffly: "You are Thrain; I recognize you." The accent with which he spoke our language sounded much like Ivald's. His tone was strange. Only later did I realize that I had seen a brave man struggling with sudden terror, a breath of midnight come into the middle of the day.

"Thrain is dead," said Ivald, after a pause. He was standing motionless and staring back woodenly at the other, as if he were looking at his own death. And I would not have recognized his voice, which for some reason had gone an octave lower.

The man on the roan horse shook his head. "Thrain, the grave-breaker. Buried once, maybe, but not dead." He drew a deep breath, in the manner of one about to enter a place where courage is required, and made a sign fending off the evil eye, and added something in his own language, to which Ivald did not respond.

Then the man on the horse raised his voice louder, speaking in our tongue. He was a warrior, and an officer leading warriors, and could do no less than advance, even if he was terrified. "I say you are Thrain the Grave-Breaker. The berserk!" That last word was unknown to me then.

There was a silence, marred only by the whinnying and shifting of horses.

"That man is dead," Ivald repeated at last. He turned, with an abstracted look upon his face, and went down the short stone stair from the rampart to the interior courtyard. Once his hand groped at the wall, and I thought he was moving almost as one blind.

Dreon had listened to this exchange without comment. Presently he excused himself and his men, politely enough, from the parley, and the three rode back among their men.

Meanwhile I went down inside the wall again to look silently at Ivald, who was sitting at the refectory table, staring at the wall and pouring wine with a hand that trembled. I had several questions that seemed urgent, but I dared not ask them.

Shortly after the parley broke up, we observed that Dreon had set his men the task of exploring down the cliffs outside the walls, looking for some sign of their quarry there.

After dispatching a squad on that mission, the captain came back to the gate, this time alone, and requested to be allowed in, with another detachment, to search for the fugitive entertainers. "King Comorre will expect me to see with my own eyes that they are not here."

Bran stalled him off coolly. "That is not possible just now, Captain."

"Then when, sir, will it be possible?"

"That is hard to say." Bran went on to explain that just now was a particularly bad season for any outsiders being allowed into the oracle for any reason.

Dreon did not press the issue. But neither did he order his men to move on.

Bran sent me to climb the high rocks behind the manor, to see if I could observe any other troop movements. I was still puzzling over Ivald.

The morning was keen and clear in the aftermath of last night's wind and rain. Gulls cried, and the banners held by the troops outside had dried and were snapping briskly in the sea breeze. In an hour or so Comorre's searching troops, getting themselves splashed by waves along the sand and shingle, had some success. We could hear from their yelling back and forth that they had promptly located the wreckage of the wagon, but had found no bodies either of people or of draft animals. Soon some of the men were climbing back up the cliff, carrying bits and pieces of debris, loose wheel rims and broken wood, to show their officers. All of us hoped in silent desperation that they would soon respectfully turn their backs on our little stronghold and ride away, bearing with them some fragments of the smashed wagon and whatever might have been left of its contents, as evidence that the people they were trying to find had been mangled in a fall and all the bodies washed out to sea.

From time to time Dreon, now standing fifty yards away, turned his head to gaze in our direction. To me this action had a suspicious look, as if he were far from convinced that we had not given the entertainers sanctuary. I doubt that he ever entertained a glimmering of the truth—that would have been too fantastic.

Later, with Jandree still hardly able to get out of bed, and Flagondry for the time standing as the lone guard on the wall, the five remaining members of our troupe withdrew into the central hall of the house. There, occupying chairs at the long table, we discussed these matters hastily and urgently among ourselves.

EIGHT

O ur conference in the hall came to no real conclusion—because Bran had fallen into one of his contemplative moods, a state in which he responded to every question with a grunt, and was obviously not ready to give us the decision we required. Every few minutes Vivian or I ran out nervously to exchange a few words with Flagon-dry, who still stood sentry, or to take a direct look over the wall. Every time any of us looked, there were Dreon and his soldiers. Instead of going away as we kept devoutly praying, the small army obstinately remained outside our gate.

Meanwhile it seemed that every member of our group except Bran, and Ivald, who was still withdrawn, kept pestering me, demanding to know what had possessed me to break into the fine web of deception that Bran had been spinning so successfully. Maud even claimed, on the basis of no evidence that I could see, that my absurd proclamation about the oracle's name threatened fatal complications for us all. Had I any reason to think that Merlin's bones were really buried under the nearby rocks?

Seeing that I must now give some explanation, but wanting to go over the matter as few times as possible, I waited until I had the attention of a majority of my colleagues before I offered: "Well, I saw something a little while ago."

Maud was the first to pounce. "Saw something? What?"

I did my best to explain, to an attentive audience, about the Jeweled Lady behind the door. For the time being I kept silent about my other vivid vision, the old man in the mirror. Somehow I had a vague feeling that the old man ought to be protected. But I tried to repeat what the lady had said to me, to reconstruct word for word her demands to be told the location of the bones.

"Merlin's bones?"

"Well, she *did* say something about Merlin; I think maybe about his being in the rocks . . ."

"It was Bran who said that, later!"

I was silent.

"Amby, are you telling us the truth? You really had one of your visions, and this woman in the vision actually said something about Merlin's bones?" Maud was ready to shake me, I could tell, but I took care to keep edging out of her reach.

"Yes, it's the truth. She was . . . looking at me, from somewhere. And she asked me something about bones—about where they were. And then she said something about Merlin after that."

"Asking you? Then she could see you."

"Yes, I told you. She could see me, as long as I was looking at her."

Maud was aggrieved. "Why didn't you speak up sooner about this vision? If you really had one?"

"I have a lot of visions, and I didn't know what to say. Anyway, you were all busy getting new clothes and things." I fear my tone was not respectful. Maud would have cuffed me had I not dodged away.

Then, thinking that I had better get all necessary revelations over with at once if possible, I mentioned the old man in the mirror, and was subjected to another round of questioning.

I have said that everyone but Bran seemed to be annoyed with me. Now in an especially thoughtful mode, our leader asked me no questions, but from time to time darted a sharp glance in my direction, and this silent scrutiny worried me more than the others' harassment.

Not that any of us could really tell whether our cause had been helped or hurt by our claiming possession of the remains of a dead magician. Near-despair swept over us—over me at least—as we saw Comorre's men starting their cooking fires and setting up an encampment, at the center of which stood a small tent in which there seemed to be just about room for the captain, unlike his troops, to sleep in out of the weather. A few men led all the horses inland to look for forage while Dreon entered his tent and the rest made themselves at home in the open.

Flagon-dry, when I visited him on the rampart, grumbled that they were not setting up their camp in the proper Roman fashion. I think he was almost ready to walk out through the gate and show them how.

I suppose, if it had not been for the impossibility of moving quickly and stealthily with Jandree and her infant, some of us would have voted to devise some kind of plan to sneak out of the compound in the dead of night—but as matters stood such an escape was impossible. Anyway, at dusk Comorre's troops established a picket line clear across the width of the peninsula, paralleling our outer wall at a distance of a hundred feet or so. They also lighted several well-spaced watch fires. In some ways this army appeared to be as well organized as that of the Romans must have been. I thought I might possibly have been able to sneak my way between the fires and get clear, but for others any such scheme was obviously hopeless.

Flagon-dry in his grumbling way remarked that at least the place was amply provisioned for a siege, with dozens of chickens and pigs neatly penned up in back, and storerooms holding more grain than we were ever going to use, and dried vegetables and fruit. I had heard the rain barrels gurgling full on the night of our arrival. The roofs of the smaller buildings—some of them were finished—and the unfinished upper surfaces of the sprawling house all drained into barrels or cisterns. In this climate there was no more hope that a besieged garrison would die of thirst than that they would succumb to sunburn.

Dreon, when he came back to sit his horse outside our gate for another talk, was noncommittally willing, at least for the moment, to accept Bran's refusal of admittance. The captain was evidently content to wait for orders, or for the arrival of Comorre himself, before he took any direct action. The ominous inference was that the Cursed One's arrival lay in the near future.

Meanwhile we were wondering if we dared attempt to provide either the credulous captain or his evil master with a prophecy, in hopes of getting rid of them that way.

Some of us—particularly Ivald, who returned temporarily from the chapel to spend another interval with us—were horrified, stunned at the very idea of facing our enemy so boldly. Doubtless this oracle housed genuine powers of some kind—what punishment might they inflict upon us?

Bran, though, when he roused himself from his brown study and began talking freely to us again, said he was seriously considering the idea of manufacturing and delivering prophecies. Slowly he brought the others into a willingness to try.

He now proposed to tell Dreon that the oracle was available for consultation—but he, Bran, would have to query the oracle himself to discover when the most accurate predictions could be expected for such eminent visitors.

Practical Maud demanded: "What sort of prediction would you give him?"

"I? None. Because fortunately we have Vivian." Bran scratched his bearded chin. "She could make a very convincing pythoness."

Vivian's eyes were huge. "What's that?"

"A woman possessed by a soothsaying spirit."

The girl was obviously both intrigued and frightened by the idea of daring such a performance. She pondered it a while, then asked: "But what *would* I tell . . . that one, if he came?"

"What message to devise for King Comorre? We'll have to be careful, naturally. But it shouldn't be too difficult to come up with something that would get him and all his people moving away from us . . . hmm." Bran nodded slowly.

Ivald spent but little time with the rest of us. He had stopped consuming wine—or at least had slowed down his consumption drastically—but his mental condition seemed to be deteriorating, perhaps under the continued stress of our virtual imprisonment.

He was eating very little if anything, and he seemed not to be sleeping at all. At first I thought it good that he was drinking less, but then I began to wonder. It was as if stronger powers than old Bacchus had him in their grip. Hour after hour, day and night, he spent in the ruined chapel, where the symbols of the contending gods looked down as implacably as the stones of the walls.

It began to worry me, so that I went to Bran with questions. "Bran, what's a berserk?"

Perhaps Bran had been expecting to be asked that question, for he had an answer ready. "A madman, possessed by Wodan. Who becomes a terrible fighter."

"Oh." I pondered. "Should we ask Ivald what that man meant, who called him by some other name—Thrain, that was what it sounded like, right?"

"You ask him, Amby, if you want."

But I was still afraid, and did not ask.

On this our second morning in the stronghold, I went somewhat belatedly to milk the two cows in the stable. There was plenty of feed for the animals in lofts and bins, a fortunate state of affairs because on our rocky bit of land there was no pasture into which they could be turned out.

Vivian presently joined me, and while I milked, she gathered eggs from the adjoining roosts of barnyard fowl. And we talked over our situation. She asked me if I had done anything with the baby to make it live.

I thought that a strange question. "No. What could I have done?"

In the kitchen, fire still burned in one stove while the others looked clean, though I had never seen anyone adding wood or removing ashes, and the smell of fresh bread filled the air. Who had prepared the dough and baked it? In the early morning I saw Maud and Vivian in the kitchen eyeing each other rather nervously, each of them denying that she had made the bread.

We had now been long enough in the house, without visible servants, that domestic chores ought to have been piling up. But somehow the jobs that no one felt like doing seemed to simply disappear—for example, the dirty laundry and other debris we had thrown about so carelessly. The corners of all the rooms, into which we tended to toss unwanted objects, were nevertheless as clean and bare as they had been when we arrived. Meanwhile clean sheets and towels and clothes were still plentifully available whenever we looked for them in chests and closets. Whenever I took notice of the long table in the hall, it was clean and orderly, with no trace of greasy spills or even crumbs. What was left of the roast pork of yesterday, or two days ago, and there was quite a bit, still looked and smelled and tasted fresh, though it had simply lain on a platter in the hall, where you might have expected it to dry out or perhaps to spoil.

At certain moments, especially when I was considering these matters, I thought I could hear a subdued murmuring, like the voices of well-trained and quiet servants. The sound was always in the next room, but I knew that if I went to look there would be no one.

After delivering the morning harvest of milk and eggs to the kitchen I went out again, with Bran's approval, but mainly following my own urge to explore. I was increasingly aware of, and intrigued by, tantalizing, intriguing hints of magic in the air, subtle but powerful, saturating the unfinished construction, flowing in the rocks around all the buildings. In a way it was like the feeling that precedes the winter's first serious fall of snow.

I went to investigate the high rocks at the tip of the promontory. Bran had said that if I climbed up there I ought to see what I could see, especially whether there was any sign of reinforcements for Comorre, or of some other army.

For a moment I thought that some of the rocks around the house were marching figures, like giants come to finish building the manor or perhaps to fight in its defense.

On this clear morning I was granted a good view of sea and land for miles in every direction.

I saw nothing new in Comorre's camp, but did accomplish one practical observation—after a nimble scrambling round the ragged pinnacle of land, and a good look at what lay below, I decided that there was no way up these cliffs inside the wall, and no way down them without long ropes. The sheer rock faces, or as much as I could see of them by peering precariously over the brink, appeared to have been laboriously scraped and smoothed, doubtless by men working on scaffolds. When I stared at those sheer rocks I thought I could envision some of the elaborate tricks of slings and scaffolding that had been used to make sure that no attacker was ever going to climb them. Yesterday Dreon's men, working on the cliffs outside the wall, had had considerable difficulty in clambering up and down—at least one had fallen to his death in the sea, which came right up to the base of the cliffs—but these rock faces on the narrowing flanks of the peninsula inside the wall were worse. I felt confident in reporting to Bran that there was no way by which an invader could come up against us from the shore.

The highest rock, jutting up at the very end of the tongue of land, overtopped by several yards the house's highest surfaces, unfinished under their plastering of dung and straw. I could see the land-horizon over the tower's top. Looking landward, I beheld no distant armies, or indeed anything in particular except the land itself, still gray and dun brown with winter. Looking out to sea, I saw no ships, not even fishing craft.

When I started down from the high rock, something prompted me to take a slightly different route, and I came down at a small natural amphitheater, three or four concentric tiers of flat-topped rocks for seats, curving rounds of a giant's stair, beside the dark triangular entrance to a cave of unknown depth. Both amphitheater and cave entrance were almost surrounded by towering slabs of rock, so that one might have moved in a routine way through the house and its immediate surroundings indefinitely without ever discovering them.

Vivian had found her way to the place by some different route and occupied one of the lower seats, as if waiting for me.

She was staring into the dark entrance, marveling at the cave. "I wonder how deep it goes. It might be useful as a hiding place, and if things don't go just right we might be glad to have one."

I had no trouble at all, given the scent of magic that surrounded this little circle of worn rocks, in identifying it as the place where an oracle must have functioned, delivering answers and prophecies. When I stared at the empty space, and let my eyelids close, I could dimly apprehend a vast swarm of human images moving there, and hear faint echoes of a thousand voices, mostly ancient. For me the experience was similar to regarding the locked door of the upstairs room in the manor, save that out here in the open air a much vaster perspective of time and space lay open to my inspection.

What I have called the natural amphitheater was small and crude, big enough for perhaps fifteen people, or at the most twenty, to sit or stand as audience on the rocks that surrounded on three sides a small, flat, open space. The mouth of the cave made the fourth side of the oracle's stage, and the dark opening naturally made the place look suitably mysterious.

But there was much more to the site than what could be scanned by ordinary eyesight. The longer I remained there the more things revealed themselves to me. Just standing in the little circle of rocks was enough to make me nervous, and I dared not allow my gaze to rest for very long on any of the worn places on the stones; the phantoms evoked, the sign and scent of violence and fear, were too disturbing.

And when I faced the cave mouth directly I was brought to a sudden halt. Peering in and down, trying to pierce the dimness with my special, inward sight, I became aware of what I vaguely perceived as a great mother lode of magic, buried somewhere down deep inside the cliff. It was a sobering experience, and I expected that if I got much closer to whatever was down there, it would be frightening.

For a moment I hesitated, irresolute. Part of me was ready, eager, to step in and begin an exploration of this fascinating place. But some more cautious component of my nature whispered that such an attempt had better wait.

"Amby? What's wrong?"

I shook my head. *Wrong* was not exactly the right word. What I perceived might not be necessarily dangerous, might in itself be something true and proper. Yet it was unsettling, like the unexpected sight or smell of some great beast. Standing in that entrance, I received intimations of a powerful, unique presence lurking, or buried, among the rocks below.

Vivian in this instance allowed herself to be guided by me, as she was beginning to learn to do in matters of magic.

Prudently, subdued if not exactly frightened, we soon went back to the house to report.

Bran was not much surprised when we told him of the cave—we had already come to the conclusion that the place where we'd found refuge must be an oracle. Nor was he much surprised to hear from me that there was genuine magic aplenty down below—he had learned to rely on my perception in such matters. He was curious enough to want a look at the site where prophecies and pronouncements must have been delivered, but at the moment he was standing his shift of sentry duty on the wall. He suggested that Viv and I examine the cave, using reasonable caution, to see if it might do as an emergency hiding place.

Vivian was intrigued, and had become at least as determined to investigate as I was. She came back with me to look into the cave.

NINE

This time I did not hesitate, but went straight in, and on doing so I noticed how well worn was the entrance path, the rock itself eroded and smoothed into a shallow trench by many feet. Vivian, still standing just outside, commented that people must have been following this path down into the cave for a long, long time.

"For more than ten years?" I asked.

She blinked at me. "For much longer than that. Look at how the stones are worn!"

"Then I guess maybe this's *not* Merlin's oracle." Vivian frowned at me, and I amplified: "Everyone says he's only been dead about ten years, Viv." All the stories I had heard, while varying widely in some other particulars, agreed on that.

"Amby, I'm going to ask you once more, and I want you to tell me the truth—why did you suddenly bring up the name of Merlin when Bran looked at you, there on the wall?"

"I told you before, Viv. The Jeweled Lady said his name, and then later it just popped into my mind."

This time Vivian seemed to believe me, and sat down on a rock to give the subject serious consideration. "Well, he *might* be buried here for all we know. What might have happened is that *now* it is his place, his oracle—where his spirit answers questions. But fifty years ago, or a hundred years, some other power must have ruled here, and given prophecies—and maybe there was yet another one, a thousand years before that."

After a pause, she asked me: "Exactly where would Merlin's bones be, if they were here?"

As soon as that question was put to me, it seemed to me that I could answer it. But for the moment I said nothing.

A few moments later, she had joined me inside the cave. We stood there holding hands, our eyes closed. It was an uncanny feeling—we both began to get stronger and stronger intimations of an ominous and overwhelming presence, somewhere down inside the earth.

At last we went hand in hand down into the cave exploring. According to all the stories, Arthur in the last years of his reign had sorely missed his exotic, powerful counselor. And to judge by the worn look of the stones around the cave entrance and stone seats of the amphitheater, this place had seen crowds, marching throngs of people, for a long, long time, had been an oracle of some kind much longer than Merlin had been gone. Prophecies must have been uttered here in the years when the Roman presence in the land was strong, and doubtless other prophecies a long time before the Romans had arrived, great Caesar himself at their head. Preceding Rome had been long druid years, stretching into centuries. And back again beyond those, these same rocks had stood here listening to conjurations made in other tongues, in the remote age of whatever powers had ruled here before such people as druids came to be.

Ten years, though then a lifetime's span for me, was nothing. Listening, as we began that long descent, I thought I could hear an ancient whisper, and a laugh.

On our last passage through the house Vivian had picked up a torch—taking one of the spare ones that were used in wall sconces in the great hall—but on entering the cave we soon realized that we might have been able to do without it. When we shielded our eyes as much as possible against the daylight behind us, we saw that coming up from below was other light, greenish and watery and indirect, sufficient for us to find the well-worn path. The cave, we realized, must be open somehow to the daylight down near the level of the sea. Also a fresh, faint breeze rose up in our faces.

Touching the worn rocks, looking at them and smelling them—you will understand that I do not mean sniffing at them with my nose like a hound, but sampling a psychic essence—I received an inward confirmation that this use for the little amphitheater was very old.

"Amby?" Vivian's voice was intrigued. I was standing with my eyes closed again, sniffing. Secure inside my lids, I could almost see and hear the priests and priestesses standing here—see them almost clearly enough to have described them. Vivian was right, there had been a long, long chain of them, stretching back through time. Here and there the chain was broken, but after each break it began again, sometimes in service to a different god.

But here, at a point that I was later able to locate as about halfway between the top and bottom of the cave, was something very different from the rest. Here, at the entrance to a very small side passage, was the thing I had sensed while still standing on the surface that now seemed so far above. We had come upon the locus of an occult shock. Here was a break in mundane space and time, a foreign body embedded in reality, like a wasp or a spider in amber. At this point the explorer ran into a glowing and restless imprisonment, transcending those phantom lines of comparatively ordinary historical priests and priestesses and fortunetellers.

I could not protest that I had not been warned. I had known when I stood in the upper entrance to the cave, and perhaps even before that, that something far out of the ordinary lay below. This encapsulation was a kind of singularity in psychic space. It marked the entrance to a branching passage leading to, or around, the very place . . . the very rock . . .

"*Amby?*"

I don't know whether I replied to Vivian or not. After a long moment I felt faint and had to sit down. But I was not to be allowed the luxury of unconsciousness, and soon was on my feet again. There was a fascination to this place, like that of biting on a sore tooth. I *had* to go into the side passage, groping my way forward by myself.

"Amby, what is it? Come back! Don't get lost!"

Her hand was on my arm, but I jerked free. "I won't!" I shouted back.

The sudden impulse that had claimed me took me off the well-worn path, out of the faint light from the upper entrance, and the watery green light, fainter still, arising from below. Flanking the side path were two upright outcroppings, shaped (or was their shaping only an illusion?) like miniature guardian dragons or griffins, and I knew—somehow—that the way I had to travel lay in the dark and narrow gap between them.

Here were no signs of ancient winding pilgrimages, no smoothing of the rock by endlessly repeated wear on sides or floor. Not many human beings—if any—had ever entered here. It was a tight fit even for my small body, between the almost-touching sides of the twisting passage. Far too tight, I thought, for a fully grown man to have come this way.

Yet I knew, I could sense, that here *he* was, somehow right in here with me, my old man of the mirror, the old man with whom—I was beginning to know it now, with a conviction deeper than logic—with whom my destiny was inextricably bound up. In the darkness there was no way I could see where I was going, but with full confidence I groped my way ahead.

I was not in the least afraid. Somewhere in here I was going to find *him*. And, though I did not know why, the act of finding him suddenly loomed up like the most important thing I'd ever done in my whole life.

Within a minute of leaving Vivian, I had worked my way into a branch of the inner cave whose only access had been almost entirely sealed off by great heavy stones, stacked one upon another. Yet now there was light again, at least for me. I could see that these stones, denser and harder, were a poor match with the surrounding rock. But on the other hand it appeared impossible, at first glance, that they could have been conveyed in here from the outside world.

At irregular intervals Vivian's voice sounded from some remote distance, calling my name again, and each time I heard her voice I raised my own, abstractedly, telling her that I was all right, that I would rejoin her in a little while. At first, as if she thought this would discourage me, she announced that she was refusing to try to follow me into the side passage. Then I could tell that she had made the attempt, only to discover that she was physically just a little too big to fit in. And she tried to get me to come back to her at once. But I insisted upon exploring. And in a way she, with her deep interest in magic, was glad that I insisted on going on.

We had thrown our torch away, but I now wished that I had it.

At the center, a circular passage had been cut—or somehow *blown*, as craftsmen do with molten glass—into the deep rock, surrounding the innermost mystery. As if the rock had once been no more than sea froth, swirled and wafted into place, to harden once more into something like dark granite. On the sides were images, which did not appear to have been carved, but rather shaped or cast from molten rock, as in some titan's foundry. But they were not human images, nor the likeness of any animals that I had ever seen.

Going round and round this tunneled circle in the deep rock, I persisted in my search for what seemed a long time, until I could identify, see and touch, the actual rocks where the little that was left of the old man's body was now to be found.

Just as my hands made contact with that surface, I thought there came an ominous tremor through the rock. Vivian must have felt it too, for she again called after me.

And I heard other voices, long lost and buried in the rock. Inhuman voices permeating all the stone around me, roaring soundlessly, muttering, laughing, howling . . .

Never had I seen or even imagined any place like this. How had I got in here? How would I get out? Reality seemed to go swirling here. I was not dizzy, but I could see and feel that the world was. My eyes and hands alike told me that the very substance of these stones had gone unstable with the burden of what they were trying to conceal.

And now I had no doubt at all that *he* was in there, imprisoned in the very stones. Letting my eyelids close again, I had no difficulty in picturing him, very much as I had glimpsed him in the mirror. My old man, shouting silently with the pain and desperation of his imprisonment . . .

"Are you Merlin?" I whispered the words urgently, leaning with my forehead against the rock.

I am, I have already told you who I am. When this actual waking-world communication reached me, it held no tone of hurt or desperation, as his voice had in my dream, but rather of tenderness and patience. I felt the words, I understood them clearly, but they did not reach me through my ears.

"Yes . . . I knew." But I had wanted to make absolutely sure. I wondered whether I should try to tell Merlin about the Jeweled Lady and her questions; maybe later, I decided. Then I remembered the stories about Merlin, the ones that everybody knew. "You want to get out."

Yes. Then there was a moment of weakness, of confusion, a change of intention, and this surprised me. *No. For me to escape this confinement is not possible.*

Continuing to picture the old man as I had seen him in the mirror, I pushed from my mind the terrible image of a crushed and mangled skeleton. That came only from my imagination. I wanted to ask him whether he was dead or alive, but somehow that seemed discourteous. Instead I inquired: "Can I see you?"

No.

For a moment I felt lost; why was I here at all? Feeling desperately inadequate, I asked: "Can I do something for you, then?"

The mangled skeleton (the image created by my fear would not go away) was speaking. *You can do many things for me, my boy. In fact you must do them.*

"What?"

With your help, and that of others, I am going to rebuild Camelot, and see a new king crowned, to sit in Arthur's seat. But you must not reveal these things to anyone. Not yet.

"I want to see you," I persisted at last.

Have you a mirror? Use a mirror, and you can see me. But I must warn you, you may not like what you see.

"I don't mind." Having lived with my gift for most of my conscious life, I was not particularly timid about what I saw.

And there may be danger. The worst might happen if my enemies should discover where I am.

That reminded me. "There was a lady . . . in a vision I saw a lady, who looked into a crystal, and asked me where you were."

But you could not tell her.

"That's right, I could not."

And suddenly I was frightened, and I began to withdraw.

The bodiless wizard's voice pursued me, shouting at me, but when I heard upsetting things I stopped my ears, because I did not want to hear . . . and I continued to work my way back out through the narrow passage.

After a timeless struggle through near-darkness, I rejoined Vivian. She frowned, and told me I looked pale, and asked me what had happened.

"Nothing." Nothing, I meant, that I was just then capable of discussing. My fear had passed. For the time being, I was determined to keep the secret of Merlin's presence in the rocks. Perhaps I wanted to spare Vivian from an immediate fright, which I was certain was uncalled for.

She was not entirely satisfied. "Do you want to go back up, Amby?"

I turned my head, this way and that, sniffed at the cool air rising out of almost-darkness. "No. We should go down."

"Why?" Apprehensively she looked in that direction.

"There's nothing we have to worry about down there—I don't think. I mean, I think all the—the real magic—is here at this level."

"What do you mean, real magic? What sort?"

"I don't know. The . . . oracle, in the rocks. It isn't going to bother us, if we don't bother it."

My companion asked a few more questions, but I remained reluctant to tell her what I had seen and done in among the rocks, and that I had not been alone in there. Vivian was disturbed, but still fascinated, and she soon agreed that we ought to go down farther.

I asked her if she had a mirror I could borrow.

"What do you want that for?"

"Never mind. I'll tell you later."

Our descent was for the most part quite uninteresting, taking us perhaps fully two hundred feet below the upper entrance, to the bottom of the cave at sea level. The main path was well worn, and clearly visible all the way, though in several places side channels and corridors went off, none of them much marked by use.

When we had at last descended all the way to the bottom, Vivian and I discovered that the lowest portion of the cave floor made a ledge that lay at high tide only a foot or two above the level of the sea. A tiny arm of ocean, less than a dozen yards in width and only about twice as long, came right in, its chill green surface rocking slightly, like that of water in a tub, in sympathy with today's light surf outside.

I crouched down and put my hand into the cold water, bright with the sunlight flowing through it from outside the cave. This lower entrance was all flooded now, but there was—or there would be when the tide and waves were right—an opening sufficient to allow the passage of a good-sized boat, from this safe hidden little harbor to the open sea, or back again.

Someone had built—partially built, and partially carved out—a real dock here once—maybe, over the centuries, many times more than once. Traces of the old wood still showed, gnarled and waterlogged, though most of it had rotted away, and the most recent users of the facility had made do with just the stone shelf.

There were three boats tied up here in the wavering watery daylight, and one of them was by far the largest, bigger than the other two put together. This long, narrow, deckless craft was the first of its kind that I had ever seen, though I had heard so many stories that I had no trouble recognizing the type. It was in fact a longboat of the kind that Northmen used, more than forty feet in length, with space for twenty oars—I counted ten on a side. Without at first realizing any of the implications of its presence, I took note of the fact that the craft was seriously damaged, as if by a heavy blow from a large rock, the long narrow strakes caved in under one gunwale.

Beside me I heard the sharp little intake of Vivian's breath as she turned around. My special vision had given me no warning, but I knew from painful experience that such special powers as I possessed could be useless, or worse than useless, against mundane dangers.

Not five yards away, a man garbed in the chain-mail shirt of a fighting Northman, and wearing shaped leggings like Ivald's old ones, and a sheepskin cloak, stood on the stone shelf holding a shield of painted hide, and a leveled spear, and watching us. He had come out, in perfect silence, from somewhere in the darkness among the rocks behind us, and now he was blocking our retreat.

TEN

Moments later, a dozen additional Northmen, all but one of them armed and garbed much like the first, had emerged from their concealment in the deeper shadows of the cave to confront us where we were standing near the little dock and the glowing water. I had never seen such men before, but I had no trouble recognizing their kind from stories, and a wave of fear shot through me. In a moment one of them had seized me by the arms, and two others grabbed Vivian.

Vivian was still wearing the priestess's garb she had earlier put on, and with great presence of mind she spoke in that character, forbidding the intruders, on pain of serious occult punishment, to touch either one of us.

Whether their leader accepted this threat at face value, or whether it was only that he considered us obviously harmless, I don't know, but in the next moment he made a decisive gesture, commanding that we be released.

There was never any doubt as to who was giving orders. The leader was the first man we had seen, a handsome, broad-shouldered young warrior with black hair, large enough to tower above his fellows. He soon introduced himself to Vivian as Hakon. His second in command—the unarmed man whose dress did not match that of the others—was Guthorm.

This Guthorm wore a horned helmet, which I soon learned

was the sign of a Norse magician. He wore robes instead of trousers, and was heavily tattooed about the face and on what I could see of his arms.

All the Northmen spoke our language to some extent, though most of them understood it better than they spoke it. When Vivian claimed occult authority they laughed irreverently. But I thought that they pretended to be more skeptical than they actually were, because they not only released us but stood back a pace or two.

In a few moments we were conversing on what seemed almost friendly terms. Hakon from the moment he saw her treated Vivian with some respect. He scarcely noticed me, and I assumed he took me for her page, or some other insignificant attendant.

With fluent words and animated gestures he told us how, during last night's rough weather, he and his boatload of followers, thirteen men in all, had managed in their longboat to make a safe landfall at the sea-level entrance to our cave. They had steered into the cave in a desperate attempt to keep their boat from being smashed to pieces on the rocks, and had been successful enough to save their lives.

Indeed, Hakon's seagoing boat—he spoke of her affectionately as the *Short Serpent*—had been practically forced into the cave by waves and wind, being damaged on the rocks in the process.

Guthorm spoke up at this point to say that last night's events had convinced him that some magical force had been acting to compel him and his men to this place, and wanted them to stay.

Hakon's ship, now lying bow-down in shallow water, was intermittently grating on the bottom, only kept afloat at all by being tied to a bronze ring in the stone dock. It was a raiding longboat, the first of its kind that I had ever actually seen, though I had heard descriptions of them, and stories of the terror such men and vessels brought to peaceful farms and villages. I had already counted twenty seats for rowers. The name, *Short Serpent*, was marked in runes—at that time I could not read them—on the gunwale.

The tiny harbor held a couple of other craft, too small and

otherwise inappropriate for this band of adventurers, who therefore paid them no attention.

The Northmen told us they had been intermittently exploring in the cave since their arrival, and had more than once climbed up through the cave as high as the upper entrance. But they had decided to wait until night fell again before venturing out in that direction. Actually nothing had prevented Hakon and his followers from climbing all the way up through the cave and reaching the house while it presumably stood empty, before our arrival. But through some quirk of fate, or luck, or perhaps the intervention of some greater power, the privilege of first entry to the house had been reserved for our ragtag group of entertainers.

Every man in Hakon's group, except Guthorm, held a short spear ready, and on the left arm of each spear-carrier was a painted shield of tough hide. Thus prepared, they began the ascent out of the cave with us. Every few steps, as it seemed to me, one of them turned his head to warn Vivian and myself what would happen if we did not tell them the truth about who we were and what was going on up above.

I could only look helplessly at Vivian. She for her part did not hesitate for a moment, but repeated in a ringing voice that she was Vivian, speaker and servant of the oracle. Obviously she had been practicing, rehearsing in her own mind the effort to deceive Comorre, but the Northmen of course did not know this and were impressed by the swift certainty of her response.

Vivian glared boldly at the men, and in a voice that only quavered once, warned them that they had already profaned the temple of Merlin's Oracle by laying hands on her. Yet if they treated her with respect from now on, they might be able to avoid punishment.

I said hardly a word, but stayed close to Vivian and played my humble role of page.

We were well on our way up to the surface when Vivian admitted—or remarked, as if it were of little importance—that at the moment we, the servants of the oracle, were besieged in our walled compound. Well, I thought, it would hardly have been possible to keep that fact a secret.

"Besieged? Well, it's not surprising that someone has built a fort out on such a tongue of land. But who is reckless enough to attack such a world-famous establishment?" Hakon was grinning by the time he finished, and I couldn't tell whether he believed half, or perhaps none at all, of what we had been telling him about the oracle.

"An invader," said Vivian, calmly and thoughtfully, "whose destruction the oracle has already predicted—so that it is assured, no matter how he may struggle to avoid his punishment."

"Hmm. And how large an army has the invader brought to this siege?"

"Maybe a hundred men. Maybe a few more. It doesn't matter."

"Ho, doesn't it? What's this impudent invader's name? And how many men are there on your side, fighting to defend the walls?"

Vivian shrugged with elaborate indifference. "His name's Comorre—not that it matters. It hasn't actually come to fighting yet." She paused, looking at Guthorm. "I didn't know," she added, "that Northmen going viking carried druids with them."

Hakon only laughed. Guthorm, speaking reluctantly, as if he had difficulty deciding what attitude to take toward this strange seeress of this strange oracle, explained that he was not truly a member of Hakon's band at all, but had joined them only a few days ago.

He added: "I am an emissary of King Vortigern."

No doubt both Vivian and I looked blank. The name of Vortigern meant nothing to either of us; this was not necessarily strange, for at the time there might have been, within two hundred miles of where we stood, thirty men calling themselves king of this or that.

As we continued to ascend the path, it was easy to see, by the way the Horned One frowned and looked about him, that he too was aware—though not nearly as thoroughly as I was—of Old Merlin's presence in the nearby rocks.

The fact that the Northmen and the druid were with us made little difference in my own awareness of the presence of the old man who had told me he was Merlin. Once more I could feel him almost within reach as we climbed up through the cave. As I passed the entrance to the little side passage I hesitated momentarily, and thought of darting away in that direction. But as I looked that way I got the impression that the dark mouth of the narrow, twisting tunnel had closed up, so that now even a child could not have squeezed into it. When one of the Northmen shoved me forward I went meekly on.

The druid also paused briefly, as if sensing something out of the ordinary, when we passed those special rocks wherein, according to my privileged information, all that was mortal—and perhaps something that was not—of the great wizard Merlin had been somehow sandwiched. Guthorm frowned, and several of the Northmen hesitated. But they were all well-traveled men, though young, and presently moved along, making routine signs that were supposed to offer some protection against bad magic.

Shortly after that we regained the surface. More than a dozen Northmen, blinking, followed Vivian and myself out into the sunlit amphitheater of the oracle and stood there looking suspiciously about them, now and then menacing the air with short jabs and gestures of their spears.

On emerging from the amphitheater we almost immediately met Bran, who had started out to look for Vivian and me, and was naturally dismayed to see our unexpected escort.

Bran, and later the others, were astonished to see Vivian and me returning in the company of Hakon and his fellows, who had literally sprung up out of the earth. Vivian continued to speak to the newcomers in her idea of elegant speech, using the lofty, remote tones that she supposed a priestess ought to use, and meanwhile I said hardly a word. I watched Bran eagerly as soon as he came into sight, in hopes that he would give me a clue as to what my new role was to be.

Bran and the other members of our troupe all grasped the essentials of the situation with reassuring quickness and played along. If some of them seemed confused at first, why that was only to be expected when more than a dozen armed men turned up on the doorstep, well within what we had come to think of as our protective wall.

Soon Bran was performing introductions. He named us all, himself included, by our true names—that was simpler than suddenly thrusting unfamiliar aliases upon us, and these alien newcomers could have no idea that our proper names belonged to a troupe of traveling entertainers. Bran of course awarded himself the title of high priest of this facility, and introduced Jandree—when Hakon finally saw her—as his revered consort. Vivian and I were both assigned the roles of what might now be called sensitives, channels through which the power of the oracle spoke to mere humanity. Flagon-dry and Maud, as could be seen from the elegance of their apparel, were also functionaries worthy of respect. This was established by the way the high priest spoke to them, but their duties were left undefined. Ivald was out of sight for the time being, in his chapel as usual I supposed, and Bran was probably relieved that our visitors' encounter with him could be postponed.

Bran and the rest of us, who had made ourselves the new proprietors of the Oracle of Merlin's Bones, were of course now locked into our roles by the presence of the Northmen. No longer having to ourselves the space inside the walls, we former fugitives, having posed as seers, could hardly admit that we were only frauds.

Now Hakon boldly demanded that the seeress provide him with a prophecy.

Vivian coolly put him off, saying that the conditions were not favorable just now.

When the man we had known as Ivald, attracted by the strange voices, came to see what was going on, he was as surprised as the rest of us had been to see the new arrivals. But soon he was exchanging a few words with them in some incomprehensible Norse dialect.

Meanwhile I watched our one-armed comic juggler, wondering. This man had been a berserk? A maddened warrior? We had never given Ivald a title, but had we done so it must have been the Harmless. Since I had known him he had never demonstrated anything but fear and loathing when the subject of martial matters came up. On the other hand I had more than once seen him take an interest in babies and small children in the village audiences, petting them and trying to make them laugh.

And now we had to explain convincingly to the Northmen about the Oracle of Merlin's Bones.

For several years before Bran, and we who were his followers, reached Merlin's Rock, the world had been full of reports of how Arthur had fallen in battle. The stories were compounded with rumors, often conflicting, of the final fate of the late king and his court. The Northmen even in their own distant land had known of Arthur—we supposed at the time that everyone in the world must be familiar with that name—and they had heard several versions of these tales, just as we had.

There were also various stories concerning Merlin, but these agreed at least on one essential fact: his sad fate at the hands of the treacherous young woman who'd used his own magic to put him away under the ground.

The tales regarding Arthur varied wildly, even on points one would have thought essential. Some mourned the fact that he was irretrievably dead. Others blithely denied the great king's mortality, maintaining that he had been carried badly wounded from the field and borne off to some remote place of safety, where he would eventually be healed, and from whence he had promised to return.

One narrative gave it as certain that the king had been baptized a Christian. Another provided vivid details of how he had utterly rejected that alien creed. Yet another affirmed that Arthur's nephew Mordred, who some said was really his bastard son, had fought at the king's side and had fallen trying to defend him. Not so, said others; Mordred and Arthur had led opposing forces, and had slain each other with simultaneous strokes of spear and sword.

It seemed that no one in the land, at least no member of a band of wandering entertainers, or of pillaging Vikings either, could be certain of the truth regarding King Arthur's fate—except that he was unquestionably gone. No one doubted the existence of the fortified city of Camelot, but its location was hazy, to say the least.

"Who was Merlin?" I asked this question of Bran as soon as I could do so out of hearing of the Northmen. There had been moments in my past relationship with Bran when I had convinced myself that he knew everything.

Bran in his thoughtful way refused to give me any quick answer to my query. But Maud had heard me ask, and she was never wary of quick answers.

Maud was washing her hands at a kitchen sink, which was fed by a water pipe from a cistern just below the unfinished roof. "He's dead now—or some say, confined by magic under a rock. Everyone knows that."

"Bran, when he was telling the story, said under a rock."

"So the story goes. Well, Old Fool Merlin doted on a young wench, as men very often do, and she wheedled from him the secrets of his magic, and served him in that way. Nimue was her name, if I remember right."

"All right, Maud, I know he's supposed to be stuck under a rock now; all the stories say that. But I mean who *was* he? I know he was a great wizard, and that he served King Arthur, but . . ."

"Who was King Arthur's wizard?" Maud paused in her current task of rinsing out the baby's napkins. I suppose, though it did not occur to me at the time, that this house of magic would have supplied enough clean cloths to render this task unnecessary—but it seems likely to me now that Maud when she was nervous simply wanted to keep busy.

She gave me a stare of disbelief, as if to say that no one could have lived ten years and still be so unfamiliar with the world as not to know the essentials of the story of Merlin and King Arthur.

And at first she seemed at a loss to provide a proper answer. No way to decide where to start in giving me the catalog of confirmed Merlin miracles. It was as if I had asked her how to tell which way was up.

Well, I did already know most of the miracle stories, the ones that everybody knew. What I wanted now was to learn what sort of man it had been who worked the miracles, and what he had been trying to accomplish in his life; but at the age of ten I lacked the words and the force to convey this distinction.

"A miracle worker, Merlin was!" Maud burst out at last. "If he'd been with Arthur at the last battle, then they'd have won. We'd not see the likes of Mordred trying to rule, or Comorre here in our land."

Then her expression changed, and she fixed me with a fierce glare. "And where did you get the idea to say that this was the Oracle of Merlin's Bones? I never heard of any such place."

Naturally that meant that its existence was virtually impossible. And I in turn could give no better answer than before.

Guthorm, self-proclaimed emissary of Vortigern the King, showed some relief on meeting Bran, evidently convinced that at last he had met a true colleague in the person of this high priest. The druid explained his mission to Bran, and told how his magical arts of divination had led him to throw in his lot with the Northmen. Some might dispute whether the late Arthur was really dead or not, but Bran and others in our group knew full well that Vortigern—old Vortigern, the Vortigern—had died more than half a century ago.

Neither Bran nor any of the rest of us thought the druid really meant he had been sent by a king who had been dead for sixty years.

Bran, conferring later with his own people, told us that the name "Vortigern" meant something like "high chief."

"Maybe some new ruler has claimed that title now."

"Maybe."

The tattooed man in the horned helmet let us all know that he was seeking a certain Fatherless Boy, whose magical value to

Vortigern had been foretold—and that I seemed to meet the qualifications.

Hakon and his men had hardly been in the house long enough to think of sheathing their swords and putting down their spears when something happened to cause them to ready their weapons again: a distant shout announced the arrival of Comorre himself outside our gates.

The voice of the man who had brought his army hunting us was high and thin, and carried clearly. Its accents were strange and terrible, like those of a man pretending, in jest, to be frightened. The effect was sharpened by a ghastly laugh.

The first words we heard clearly in Comorre's quavering tones were a demand that the gates be opened, and control of the oracle surrendered.

ELEVEN

C omorre's presence at our gate, his call for admittance, drove every other concern out of our thoughts. Bran had to mount the wall and deal with the situation immediately.

All of us in Bran's old group were dreadfully curious about the Cursed One. Most of the Northmen seemed to have heard of him too, and climbed up on the wall at several places, to gaze at his army, with, as I thought, various degrees of professional regard and envy.

In my case fear was the chief motive. I climbed to the broad, uneven top of the unfinished wall and peered out anxiously past one of the few available parapet corners of raised masonry to get a look at the monster. There was no need for anyone to point him out to me; the actions of the other men outside, as well as his distinctive clothing and golden ornaments, left no doubt as to which one was the leader. Indeed, the king, if he had any real claim to such a title, did appear ugly, and at first glance ineffectual, being a little under the average height. His hair and beard were prematurely gray, his eyes watery, and his mouth had a way of twisting to one side, especially when he attempted to laugh or smile.

Comorre had brought with him only a small number of additional men, his personal escort, so that his army outside our walls was not much increased. But now, in the center of the somewhat enlarged camp, a silken pavilion had been erected. It was the first shelter of its kind that I had ever seen, dwarfing the little tent of Captain Dreon, which had been moved to give King Comorre the highest ground. I gaped, supposing such a splendidly decorated device truly worthy of a king.

So far Bran had bravely kept the gate closed—though perhaps greater bravery would have been needed to open it. How long the Cursed One would submit to being balked in this fashion was something none of us could guess.

And Comorre openly announced that he had come to get a look at Merlin's Bones.

From his seat on an impressive horse, he smiled his twisted smile up at Bran on the low wall. "You have told my faithful captain, Dreon, that those important relics are here."

"That is true, Your Majesty." Bran, solemnly bowing, awarded the intruder the royal form of address.

"Then I suppose you can show them to me, High Priest, when I come in?"

"I regret, Majesty, that is not possible. The Bones are buried deeply, and not even we, who serve the oracle most intimately, can actually see them."

"An unsurpassed oracle, yours must be—you really should consult your own power there, High Priest, on the question of my being admitted. Now don't tell me that you have done so? A true and faithful oracle could not have advised you to keep me waiting outside your gate."

"Perhaps the honor would be too great for our humble establishment. In any case, the meaning is unequivocal."

At that Comorre grew angry. "If it did that, it is no oracle at all, and anyone who says it is deserves punishment! I will return to talk with you again, High Priest." And he reined his horse away, breaking off the conference for the time being.

At least, I thought, the subject of Merlin's Bones had distracted our persecutor from his search for impudent minstrels—we could at least hope that those unfortunate wretches had been completely forgotten.

Now the Northmen, looking about them in the broad yard between the outer defensive wall and the manor house, were increasingly surprised to see no visible defenders but ourselves.

"Where are your fighting men? Your guards?" Hakon at last demanded, looking suspiciously about him.

Bran was ready for the question. "Until now, none has been necessary. And now that the need has arisen, you are here."

Hakon digested this slowly. Then he looked round at his men as if inviting them to join him in appreciating the joke. "You expect us, a dozen men, to defend you—this long, half-built wall—against an army?"

"It is obvious to me," said Bran, "that you have been sent here for that purpose. And I can promise that you will find our defense a profitable enterprise."

Hakon scratched his head. "I have to admit, High Priest, that it was a strange series of events, storms, and coincidences that brought us here. Some power out of the ordinary must have been responsible."

Our leader nodded graciously and invited the Northmen into the big house. They accepted politely enough, leaving a sentry on the wall, but crossed the threshold with weapons still drawn. Once inside, the armed men eventually put their spears and swords away, but continued to look suspiciously about, took care never to become widely separated, and instinctively guarded each other's backs. I think this was partly because some of them were simply unused to houses. But also the more sophisticated among our visitors, including Hakon himself, had been immediately struck by the total absence of common servants.

When their leader mentioned that he was puzzled by the missing menials, Bran reacted calmly, explaining that all the servants had recently been dismissed, in obedience to an inexplicable command of the oracle.

Hakon seemed to accept this explanation. But like Bran, some hours earlier, he was very firm about wanting to inspect the entire house. That was all right with Bran, because our great secret, that of our identities, was not susceptible to being discovered by a search.

The locked door upstairs now was no longer locked. When Hakon went to pull it open, the door yielded as easily as if it had never been locked at all.

None of us said anything for a long moment. Then Bran, pausing before he stepped over the threshold of the room behind the door, breathed: "It is a library."

That word was new to me. And the thing itself was a sight so strange that I had no trouble believing that the place must have belonged to King Arthur's peerless wizard. The tall racks and cabinets of my vision, now that my physical eyes could see them, turned out to be bookshelves, something I had never seen before.

Eventually I looked away from the stacked books long enough to notice other things. What struck me with the greatest force was that there was perpetual light in that library, day and night, shining out into the upstairs corridor whenever the door was open. Sunlight, though indirect when the day was cloudy, entered through high, broad windows, and also through glass panels set into the ceiling itself. I think that none of us, either Bran's people or Hakon's, had ever seen the like before. I remember noticing, even in the midst of my wonder at the books, that the polished wooden floor was gently worn, as if by many years of use.

The room contained a profusion of lamps and candles, most of which, as we discovered later, lighted themselves automatically at dusk, neat small flames springing into being to make up for the diminution of natural light. Later I noticed that some of these lamp flames burned perpetually, day and night, never running out of oil, though they were never refilled—at least not by human hands.

The obvious magic investing the whole room, compounded by the strangeness of the many scrolls and stacks of paper, was enough to keep most of Hakon's men out of the library after their first brief look, and some of them flatly refused to enter.

The library was cozily furnished with hearths and rugs and hangings to keep it warm, and with comfortable chairs and writing stands. But in my eyes the most remarkable thing about it, stranger than magical light and heat, was still the maze of shelves, lining every wall, and free-standing in much of the space between walls—the endless shelves and their burden of uncountable books.

The array of packed shelves went clear up to a ceiling that was higher than tall Hakon could reach. Here and there along the aisles between bookcases were footstools and even ladders to give access to the higher levels.

When I, curious as usual, went exploring into the labyrinth of shelves, it soon became evident that the room was much larger than any of the others on this floor, so large indeed that its farther reaches were still out of sight. Here and there were scholars' nooks, chairs and lamps and writing tables, some of these last piled with scrolls and stacks of blank paper, equipped with inkwells and pens. I remember being at first unsure of the purpose of these last implements.

Most of the books, in particular those shelved nearest the door where we had entered, were on scrolls of parchment or paper. Others in the room's remoter reaches were stacks of flat paper bound between flat covers.

I pulled out a scroll of modest size from one of the lower shelves and unrolled it awkwardly, spreading it atop one of the many unused desks. The paper was covered with methodical small handwriting, applied in black ink with a quill pen. I was pleased to discover that I could puzzle out some of the simpler words, my mother having taught me the basic skills of reading before she died.

Hakon, never one to be made timid by new things, had pulled out a scroll too, but had not unrolled it. Instead he was shaking the tubed paper tentatively in his fist, as if he thought it might be some kind of club. "What are all these?" he demanded.

"Books," said another voice. I wondered to see that Bran was now gazing about him with awe, as if we were in the chapel of his god. He dropped his voice to a whisper so that Hakon would not hear. "Whose house," he asked, reverentially, as if the question had never come up before, "whose house have we come into?"

If the library held any answer to that question, it was not immediately obvious, and we did not take the time to search. In a few minutes we moved on, without sounding the farthest depths of the tall maze of shelves.

On the threshold, I looked back, promising myself to investigate this mystery when other matters had become less pressing.

When we reached the armory the Northmen shook themselves, as if wanting to be free of spells, and stood a little taller. Here they were in their element, and the trove of books and other less manly matters upstairs was instantly forgotten. They moved forward with grunts of appreciation. They goggled, as we had, at the ingeniously jointed suits of armor, and some expressed their disdain at such cowardly devices. But it was clear that they lusted after some of the keen-edged, hard-steel weapons.

Bran did not fail to notice, and generously handed out the weapons as gifts. Noting the fierce look of satisfaction in the eyes of the recipients, I felt sure, from that moment, that we were going to be defended.

After leaving the armory, our continuing reconnaissance brought us to the upstairs bedroom where Jandree had now relocated herself and her infant—it was less drafty there, she said. Bran's wife was still weak, able to do little more than lie on a couch and nurse her infant.

Bran had sent me running ahead to warn Jandree of what was coming, thus giving her a chance to prepare the role of wife of the high priest. I found her completely alone except for the baby, as she was so often during these hours. She listened with round blue eyes to my description of the intruders, and my assurances that so far they seemed harmless. After that she seemed to relish the prospect. Jandree propped herself up among elaborate pillows, hastily combed her hair, and wrapped a fine silk robe around her shoulders.

The young commander of the Northmen had demonstrated little more than a businesslike interest in the attractive Vivian. But even I noted that his attention was much more firmly caught when he first met Jandree, though the latter was only starting to recover from the ravages of a difficult childbirth.

The infant had begun to cry again, and the mother was nursing it when the strangers entered. When Jandree looked up her eyes seemed to go straight to those of Hakon, and to be caught by them.

"Greetings, Lady." He made a little bow. "You need not fear me, or my men, though we come into your presence armed."

"I do not fear you," Jandree told him, quickly and quite naturally. "You are welcome here."

Hakon gazed at her a few more seconds, then gestured to his men, who were gawking from behind him, that they need not bother to search this room. When he was going out, Hakon lingered for a moment in the doorway, his eyes fixed on those of the woman on the couch, and I thought for a moment that he would speak again—but then he went on out.

As the day wore on, Bran took every opportunity he could to fire meaningful glances at his old comrades. Each time the message was plain: "One thing we must not let any of these people do is suspect for a moment that we are not who we are pretending to be." That he thought it necessary to remind us showed that he was rattled.

Flagon-dry and Hakon were standing side by side, looking out over the parapet. Flagon-dry commented gloomily that probably no one in the land could raise a bigger army than this one now camped at our gate.

I had been listening to the druid. "What about King Vortigern?"

The only reply I got from Flagon-dry was a strange look; perhaps Hakon knew the political history of the last century just as well as Flagon-dry did.

Comorre himself, on horseback and attended by a herald, was once again approaching our gate. It was time we answered his demand to receive a prophecy. He was not in a mood to be simply put off.

"High Priest, if you have heard some story about my searching for certain minstrels who are within your compound, and that causes you to be so obstinate, there is a misunderstanding. My only wish is for these show-people to perform for me. I have in mind to see them do a little dance. To give me a song or two. No more than that."

Bran replied that he would consult the oracle. Comorre accepted that, and once again we had gained a little time.

Most of the crew of Northmen had so far remained out of Comorre's sight, behind our wall. They were testing their sharp new weapons on bits of timber in the courtyard, and were beginning to establish themselves in this house, even as we, Bran's people, were fast coming to think of the manor as our own. Soon after the Northmen entered the house, some of them began to display an open interest in the valuables that were casually on display. Dozens of pieces of gold and silver tableware, knives and spoons and cups and plates, as well as a few items actually studded with jewels, were visible in the great hall, on the long table and some nearby sideboards. Our guests' interest in such objects was casual, compared to their craving for the fine weapons. For the time being they were content to let this lesser loot alone. After all, a Northman's chief concern when away from home was normally the amount of loot he might acquire and how readily such gains could be converted into usable wealth. The only valuable treasure to be found in a foreign land was that which could be carried away.

Hakon and his men made faces of contempt at the soft beds, except for one or two who bounced on them with loud bawdy remarks. Later, when it came time to sleep, at least one Northman remained always on guard, while the rest lay stretched or curled like animals on the floor, the whole crew keeping in one or two rooms.

The nameless officer in Comorre's force who had recognized Ivald had obviously spread the word among his companions about Thrain the Berserk, for when Ivald appeared on the wall again, the faces that turned toward him from outside wore expressions of caution if not exactly of respect.

We in Bran's troupe still did not clearly understand why this should be so. When we tried to ask Ivald what was going on, he put us off with short answers. His manner was gloomy and fatalistic.

The purported emissary of King Vortigern continued to take an interest in me; though some of my companions, and some of the Northmen, agreed that this fellow was mad for claiming to have come from Vortigern a month ago.

Hakon told us that he had been led by certain signs and omens to allow the druid to join his party, when they had first met, somewhere along the coast.

As the day of the Northmen's arrival wore on, the members of our little group of former fugitives frequently took advantage of opportunities to exchange meaningful glances with one other. We dared not relax for a moment, and felt ourselves caught in the middle, between the barbarians within the gates and those without.

As far as we could tell, none of them as yet had even suspected that we were impostors.

With Bran at his heartiest and most convincing, I think that on that first day none of the Northmen doubted for a moment that we were the rightful proprietors of this shrine/oracle, and Bran himself its high priest, or chief soothsayer—our leader had them convinced that we were the heirs of Merlin himself and would be the mouthpieces through which that great wizard continued to utter prophecies.

When Bran had concluded his last nerve-racking speech of the afternoon to these dangerous men, and retired to an upstairs room where he could be alone with his wife and babe, he almost collapsed from the strain.

Trying to satisfy our curiosity, Vivian and I went together to look for Ivald, and found him once more in the chapel. This time he was thoroughly soaked in wine, head pillowed on an emptied wineskin. When we tried to rouse him, he muttered about having heard some Christian idea that wine could be turned into blood.

When we got him to his feet, he drunkenly tried to juggle several objects—a cross from one of the niches in the wall, a dagger, an empty flask—with one hand. The result surprised no one, except perhaps Ivald himself.

Ivald's fear seemed to have a wider focus than merely his own fate. He continued to express his concern about my fate as a child if Comorre should conquer us, and that of Jandree and her baby. He groaned at the unbearable thought that we and the others might be butchered or sacrificed.

I got the impression that Ivald really was not worried about us, as much as about himself—he thought he could not stand to be exposed to such happenings again.

Vivian had more sensitivity to magic than anyone in the house except me, more than anyone else I could remember ever meeting at that time. Certainly she was well aware of the presence of the old man under the rock. At the time she had, if possible, even less understanding of that presence than I did. Nor had she nearly as clear an idea as I did of what the man was like behind the magic we detected.

Naturally she was curious from the start about the remnant of the old man under the rock. She feared what little she could perceive of him, even as he began to fascinate her—but she found me nonthreatening and had developed a genuine liking for me.

She would stroke my hair sometimes, or let her hand rest on my shoulder, and I think it was on that day that I began in my childish way to fall in love with her.

Hakon climbed the wall at dusk and once more surveyed Comorre's army, then casually announced that he thought the fighting would start before long. After arranging for double sentries through the night, he sent some of his men back down into the cave to stow away their newly gathered treasure, and to guard their damaged longboat, as well as the couple of smaller craft that might conceivably be used in an emergency evacuation. Hakon thought the *Short Serpent* was repairable, given the proper tools and wood, and some of his men had doggedly searched the house and grounds, so well equipped in other ways, for usable materials. None could be found.

* * *

Bran, dining with our guests in the central hall, calmly assured the newcomers that this was only further evidence of the power of our predictions—the soldiers, like the servants, had been dismissed, on the instructions of the oracle. The powers that ruled on Merlin's Rock had been calmly confident that no warriors would be needed until he, Bran, and his men had arrived. Truly the Northmen been sent here by fate, or by the gods, to fill that need against the army outside!

Hakon, who was no fool though no deep-thinker, raised an eyebrow at this argument. He remarked that, given the odds, the oracle had made an embarrassingly high estimate of his and his men's fighting abilities.

Then he added: "What scale of pay does your oracle have in mind to offer us?" Free prophecies, it seemed, were not going to be enough.

I seemed to recall that when our midnight flight began, our entire treasury had consisted of three or four small copper coins our leader happened to have in his pocket. But Bran remained unruffled.

"Since you and your men are here with us, Sir Hakon, and cannot very well leave, and since this bandit leader Comorre is likely to be angry with you for that alone, it might seem that no other wages than your own survival would be necessary. But we can in fact do much better than that."

I wondered whether Bran had come upon a trove of coin somewhere; in this house such a find would have been no great surprise. But then I remembered the golden dishes.

Hakon nodded slowly. "Tell me something about this Comorre. Whenever I'm going to fight a man, I like first to know him as well as possible. I know Comorre claims to be a king, but he's certainly ugly enough to be a bandit."

Bran shrugged. It was the elegant gesture of a high priest or other aristocrat. "I'll tell you what I can. But the man is really a stranger to us as well—outside of the fact that his chief joy seems to be in torturing helpless victims. We may consult the oracle, if it is important to know more about him."

"I'd like to ask your oracle some things, but I think I'll not use up a prophecy to find out about Comorre. Maybe you can't tell me much about him, but you ought to be able to answer one question—why is he your enemy?"

Our leader answered thoughtfully. "Well, I suppose he has come to the mistaken conclusion that we are his. To begin with, the oracle has not given him satisfaction, and he doesn't understand that we are only its servants, not its masters. For another thing, he suspects that we are sheltering some unhappy wretches, a certain band of traveling entertainers that he is minded to skin alive."

"Entertainers?" Hakon frowned in honest puzzlement. "Why should one who calls himself a king bother with punishing such folk?"

Bran shrugged again. "For some reason he doesn't like them. Maybe they gave him a poor performance. I tell you, friend Hakon, kings and bandits have at least one thing in common: they feel little need to give us lesser mortals reasons for anything they do."

The Northman smiled faintly, and then nodded thoughtfully. "I've noticed that. Anyway, where are these entertainers? Possibly they know something about the enemy that would be useful for me to know. You needn't be afraid I'll tell him where they are."

High Priest Bran looked bored. "It's not our business to search for menials, any more than for mice. You've been through the cave, and the house—have you or your men discovered such people anywhere?"

"No."

Our leader smiled. "Anyway, I suspect that the real reason we are besieged has little to do with itinerant performers. The fact is that, having seen our snug little stronghold from the outside, Comorre the Ugly now wants it for himself. It will be up to us to prove that we can defend our holdings."

"And can you?"

"With your help, friend Hakon, I believe we can. Again I say, that is why you were sent to us."

Hakon thought for a while. Then he asked: "Just how much do prophecies generally cost, hereabouts?"

"The usual price need not concern you. For our noble defenders, there is no cost."

And individual prophecies for all the Northmen were arranged, then and there. Vivian, hovering convincingly on the edge of trance as she took personal charge of investigating Hakon's future, prophesied not only victory, but a long life and great wealth for him and his men, if they fought on our behalf.

"I see wealthy farms in the north country," she intoned. "Rich fields of hay, and many cattle—and they all belong to you."

Hakon's men were listening eagerly. "More than one farm apiece?"

"Three . . . four of them, at least. For each of you. And I see three fishing boats, equipped with strong new nets, making a good catch . . ."

And so it went on. I could see that Vivian's words, and an occasional fluttering of the lashes of her entrancing eyes, soon had most of the Northmen all but persuaded that to stake their lives in defense of the oracle and its deserving staff would be no more than their basic duty.

TWELVE

That evening Bran and Hakon sat at the rectangular table in the central hall, sipping strong red wine from silver cups. Their heads were close together, but they were making no particular effort at secrecy. I could overhear them concluding a deal involving all the silver and gold utensils. If the house was overrun by Comorre's army, obviously these eminently portable treasures would go to the attackers and not to Hakon's crew, who now acquired a real stake in its defense. As soon as the deal had been concluded with a handshake, several of Hakon's men started tying the stuff into bundles using curtains and blankets. We who were Bran's followers watched, with a lack of anxiety that must have impressed the Northmen, as the plates and goblets, clean or dirty, from the table and cupboards in the great hall, vanished into those crude containers. Meanwhile Bran told jokes and stories that made the Northmen laugh—except for Guthorm, who stood in the background, impatiently disapproving, not of the commerce in treasure but of the levity.

Don't worry, was the message I thought we onlookers conveyed by our attitude—*Don't worry about our reaction. Help yourselves to our treasure. We who are privileged to serve such an important, infallible oracle as this one will be able to replenish our riches anytime we choose.*

* * *

Hakon detailed three or four of his men to carry the compactly heavy sacks down deep into the cave, and hide them there, for safekeeping, among the labyrinth of rocks.

Meanwhile, the druid who had come with the Northmen entered the great hall and conferred anxiously with Bran and Hakon. I could overhear and see enough to know that I was the subject of this discussion. When Bran saw that I was listening, he called me over, to be present while my fate was being discussed.

The Horned One, as Vivian and I had begun to call him between ourselves, gave every indication of being much concerned for my life and health. He was determined, whatever else happened, to bring me away in one piece, so that I could be taken to Vortigern.

When Guthorm had gone off somewhere, Bran talked to me alone. "What do you think of this, Amby? The fellow says there's a king who's taken an interest in you, though he's never seen you."

"A king? Not Comorre, I hope."

"No, I don't think so." Bran shook his head. "There's every indication that he's talking about someone else altogether."

"And this king wants me to come to him?"

"So Guthorm says."

"Why?"

"I've no idea, Amby. I could try to guess, but I don't know."

"Then I don't know what to think, Bran."

My leader, with more than enough other problems to worry about, scratched his head. "And when this druid says 'King Vortigern'—well, I don't know what to think about that, either."

"Why?"

"There was a real king by that name. But he died years before any of us was born."

Vivian came up with the explanation that I was wanted by Vortigern as a magical consultant of some kind, and favored my going on those terms. But the whole discussion seemed unreal.

Bran would have been willing to turn me, or anyone else, over to the Northmen (or even to Comorre) if he thought he could save his wife and his own child by doing so. Bran would also be willing to get away with his wife and child, if that should prove possible, saving them and leaving the rest of us to our fate.

Looking back, I cannot blame him.

At a word from Hakon, the Northmen began wearing a succession of different uniforms, borrowed from a large selection in our ground-floor armory, while taking their turns at sentry duty on the wall. Thus we hoped to give the impression that we had more men than we really did.

Comorre came back to the gate for yet another conference, this one conducted by torchlight. It appeared that, rather than suffer losses in a direct assault, thereby weakening his army, the Cursed One would much prefer to be invited in, with a few men, to consult the oracle. Considering the situation from Comorre's point of view, there was no profit to be seen in attacking a twelve-foot wall unnecessarily. Especially when the attackers could not be sure about the true number of defenders.

Flagon-dry shook his head and commented in an aside: "Once he's inside the gate, and able to look the situation over, he can take whatever steps he wants—summon an attack, with a yell, or whistle."

Bran offered to allow the would-be king in through the gate, provided he brought no more than two or three soldiers. But Comorre was unwilling to trust himself with such a small bodyguard amid an undetermined number of Northmen and strange magicians, and held out for a dozen of his own troops as escort.

The oracle, of course, found such a large number of intruders unacceptable.

Meanwhile, in intervals of private discussion, Hakon disputed tactics with Bran and swore that neither he nor his men would lift a finger to help us if we were stupid enough to allow Comorre the Cursed and even a small number of bodyguards in through our gate, to let him confirm with his own eyes how undermanned our defenses really were.

* * *

The point was moot. Bran continued to forbid entry to any substantial number of Comorre's troops, and once more the Cursed One withdrew. The hours dragged on, and the general feeling among us was that the chances of our being attacked were rapidly increasing. Bran and Hakon, having concluded their agreement over the valuables, formalized the alliance with a handshake. Even with the Northmen on our side the odds would be something like ten to one in favor of the attackers. Bran's hope was that Hakon's boatload of enthusiastic raiders, men who cheerfully accepted that the business of their lives was going to be fighting and dying, could repel at least a first attack, inflict enough damage to make the enemy think twice and turn away.

Meanwhile, Ivald's periodic reemergences into our society were quite brief. He continued spending most of his time in the ruined chapel, where the symbols of at least two different religions (as well as an increasing number of emptied jugs and wineskins) contended silently for his attention and his loyalty. I perceived nothing magical about these symbols in themselves.

Bran and Hakon, the latter developing a curiosity about Ivald, went to have a talk with Ivald. Hakon suggested that the one-armed man, who seemed to be having a spiritual crisis, should pray to Thor for help.

"Oh, don't get me wrong, Wodan is fine—just the thing for kings and wizards and berserks." Hakon looked at Bran. "And this Jesus who died on a cross may be fine, too, for all I know—if you don't mind helping your enemies, a tactic I understand he recommends. But I always say, for the ordinary man, like you and me, one who just tries to get along without doing anything heroic, Thor's the best choice. Among the northern gods, at least."

Ivald looked at his fellow Northman, saying nothing.

Hakon was not content to let it go. "In war, Thor's hammer's at least the equal of any other weapon of gods or men. Right?"

"Have you seen it?" Ivald demanded suddenly.

Hakon blinked. "What's that?"

"Thor's hammer. Have you ever seen it, heard it, felt it?"

Hakon looked at Bran, who for once had no good answer either. And Ivald—or Thrain—smiled bitterly and shook his head, dismissing Thor.

The men who were trying to counsel him exchanged troubled glances—this wasn't good.

Ivald now seemed to be only waiting, resigned. He was willing to come back to rejoin the rest of us.

Bran at last had a question: "Ivald. Will you arm yourself, if it comes to fighting, and join us on the wall? We're going to need every man."

Ivald squinted at the questioner. " 'If'?"

"Oh, all right then—when it does. You're right, it doesn't look like a fight can be avoided. I'm hoping that if we turn them back once, they'll be ready to talk some more."

For ninety-nine out of a hundred Northmen, it would have been an insult to ask such a question, suggesting that he might prefer to sit out a battle merely because he lacked one arm—or worse, because the thought of fighting turned him queasy in advance. But Ivald did not appear to be insulted.

"Oh aye, oh aye, I'll fight." Ivald's voice was surprisingly calm. But it sounded like the calm that comes when hope is gone.

We thought that we and the Northmen did a good job of concealing the smallness of their numbers from the attacking army—until the fighting actually started.

Ivald, sober enough to take his turn at watching on the wall, once more exchanged looks with his old enemy or acquaintance who was now a member of the army outside the gate. Chance decreed that I should be also on the wall when this happened.

Neither man seemed surprised to behold the other; it was as if both understood that their fate had brought them together again.

"Do you know him, Ivald?" I asked—a rather stupid question—when the silent confrontation was over.

Ivald answered without looking at me. "Yes. I know him. He was one of those who fought against me in the north country."

"Did he go berserk?" something prompted me to ask.

Ivald was silent for so long that I thought he was not going to answer. At last he said: "No, not he."

I was growing very tired and sleepy, but felt uncomfortable with the relative isolation and soft beds offered by the rooms upstairs— the magic lurking in the strangeness of Merlin's library was not conducive to sound slumber, either. And besides, from the way the druid looked at me, I half suspected him of wanting to get me into one of those upstairs beds. This was an unjustified suspicion, as matters turned out, but such things had happened to me in my year of beggary, before I attached myself to Bran. For these reasons I had fallen asleep in a more or less public corner of the great hall.

In the grayness before dawn, I felt myself jerked awake, knocked out of a recurrent dream of the Old Man shouting, by a loud noise in the waking world. Jumping up, I beheld a face contorted and unrecognizable, that of a man who had just burst in through the front door to give the alarm. It took me a moment to realize that this was Ivald—or Thrain.

The one-armed man was gripping an ax in his white-knuckled hand and had slung two or three spears on his back as alternate weapons. He had the strap of a shield looped on his wrist also, and had come to me—all the men were busy—for help in strapping the shield to his arm stump. This he conveyed to me entirely by gestures. Terrifyingly, it was as if he had suddenly lost the power of speech—he only grunted, and groaned. Somehow I understood, without being told, that he had reconsecrated himself to Wodan.

Outside the windows, the clamor of a fight had started, and day was struggling to be born. My fingers fumbled with the unfamiliar strap and buckle. But before I could get the difficult thing accomplished, he raised his head, as if listening—then bellowed some words I could not understand, pulled away, and ran out of the house.

I followed him at once, compelled to see what was going on.

Ivald—or Thrain—had dashed across the courtyard, headed

for the wall. I saw him biting his own arm stump until blood spurted anew from the scarred flesh. An inhuman sound, an animal groaning and roaring, was now issuing, almost without pause, from Ivald's mouth.

Comorre's men who had been foraging with their horses in the inland woods, a quarter of a mile from the house, had evidently been secretly making ladders there as well. When the attack started, troops brought out of concealment half a dozen of these crude scaling devices and carried them forward to lean against the wall at widely separated points.

A couple of Hakon's men had been watching alertly from their respective positions atop the wall, and they sounded the alarm immediately, before any ladders could actually be put in place. Still, some of the enemy, jumping and climbing from horses' backs, were atop the wall at two or three places before Hakon's men who had been sleeping in the courtyard could get into position to oppose them. It is easy to see, with my current advantage of long hindsight, that defending a fortification was not the type of warfare to which the Northmen were accustomed.

After dashing out of the front door, I ran back and forth across the courtyard, wanting to see the fighting. Bran and Flagon-dry were now atop the wall and wielding weapons. But the druid caught up with me, grabbed me, and pulled me back into the house. His intention was to drag me to safety, out of the house by the back way, through the kitchen, and thus toward the upper entrance of the cave. But I tore free of his grasp and ran out again into the courtyard.

Maud caught up with me there, and she and the druid together pulled me away to a place of relative safety, this time around one of the front corners of the house. Here I was still near enough to the fighting to see a great deal of it. We three spectators pulled our heads back when the occasional flung spear or other missile came clanging near. At times the sound of missiles striking on walls and roofs and earth became continuous, like hail. There was a steady roar of sound in the bright air, more than a hundred voices screaming all at once. I had witnessed brawls before, in street and tavern, but never, never, anything like this.

For what seemed a long time, I could not take my eyes from Ivald. I saw him seize an enemy's shield in his teeth and wrench it out of his way. At the very start of the fight, he swung his ax to knock one opponent back off the wall, then ran at amazing speed along the rampart to slay a second, who died, I verily believe, before the body of the first had time to hit the ground outside. Then I began to see with my own eyes, not in a vision but in the world of solid flesh and bones, things even more difficult to believe. One-handed, Thrain/Ivald seized the top of the nearest scaling ladder; I saw Thrain pull the ladder, with the full weight of a climbing warrior aboard, free of the ground. One-handed he shook it, as a terrier might shake a rat, so that the body of the attacker was separated from his shield and weapons, and all flew free. Then Ivald smashed the ladder to pieces with a single blow against the parapet. Retaining in his hand the largest fragment, a sturdy pole some nine or ten feet long, he used it alternately as a flail, then a quarterstaff, then a pike, jabbing and pounding attackers down from the next ladder, and the next. Those whose armor would not break were beaten to pulp inside it. Enemy swords and spears stuck in the thick wood, and were wrenched out of their owners' hands.

He killed or maimed at least a dozen opponents in hand-to-hand fighting.

The list of Thrain/Ivald's victims included his old enemy from the old country, who accepted their new encounter as fated. I had little doubt then, and have none now, that the enemy would have attained their objective with that first hard rush, certainly with the second—had it not been for Ivald—or for Thrain.

When Ivald's ladder-log was splintered into uselessness at the fourth blow or the fifth, he grabbed up another weapon—there were now plenty lying about. I saw him skewer one man on a spear, the blade piercing armor and sticking in the body immovably at first, until Ivald with his one hand lifted blade and corpse, and battered the dead man against the helms of other enemies advancing, toppling them from their ladders, until eventually the impaled body was shaken loose.

Bran was battling too, and Flagon-dry. Hakon fought superbly on that day. Though I saw him do nothing absolutely superhuman, he was plainly an artist with his short thrusting spear. He demonstrated a master's skill, making difficult and dangerous feats seem only simple tasks. He killed, he wounded, he disarmed and knocked back one attacker after another, meanwhile rallying his men with viking war cries.

But I spent little time in watching Hakon. Whenever Thrain/ Ivald came into my field of view, I could watch nothing else. I wondered whether I had fallen into the world of visions. I thought of magic, but if that was the explanation of this inhuman strength and ferocity, it was superior to any magic that I had ever seen or smelled before.

Again and again, despite the other fighting going on, my attention was forced back to this one man. When Ivald had blunted his first sword blade by carving tough leather shields, chopping hickory spear-shafts, hammering it on iron, and forcing it through chain, he cast it aside and instantly grabbed up another—spare weapons were now plentiful all along the wall. Raging back and forth along the parapet, arming himself with an ax when his captured spear was gone, then with a sword, grabbing up a new weapon every time one broke in his grasp or was torn free, slipping in his own and others' blood, he hacked off arms and heads, one blow to each, as Comorre's troops persisted in their mindless effort to climb into our stronghold from outside.

His breathing—most of the time I could hear it from where I watched—had settled into a hoarse sawing roar that cut like a battle cry through all the other noise.

Steadily attacked by shouting fighters, standing in the center of a hail of missiles, Ivald himself suffered a number of serious wounds, any one of which would have brought down any normal man in his tracks. I retain a vivid memory of the arrow stuck deep into the socket of his right eye. Other shafts protruded from his arms and legs. When one of these latter hampered him unduly, he spared a moment to grasp it and break it off. Then Thrain the Berserk fought on again, seemingly immune to injury.

Meanwhile, Hakon's men, inspired by their leader and by the bloody accomplishments of Thrain, fought well beside them. As I began to gain my first real understanding of combat, I perceived that once blades were drawn it was very often safer to fight bravely, facing the enemy and watching them, than to turn and run. And, when all was said and done, no real warrior wanted to die the straw death, struck down in bed by illness or old age, enemies one could never hit back.

The Northmen gave an excellent account of themselves, but Comorre's troops were hardly milksops either. They were approximately two hundred strong, and none was hanging back in idleness. As I heard the fighting described later, those in the rear put up flurries of arrows and flung spears, while those in front closed in. They took heavy losses and kept coming on—probably they counted their own lives as worthless anyway, and a long time later I learned that their leaders had promised them rape and pillage when they took the citadel, hinting at helpless virgins hidden inside who could be ravished. And they were encouraged when they realized how shorthanded the defenders really were.

Meanwhile the emissary of Vortigern, perhaps more experienced in these matters than me, or either of the women, did not need much time to realize that despite the berserk's superhuman power, and the bloody competence of the rest of the defenders, the fight at such odds was hopeless from the start. Guthorm began doing everything in his power to drag me farther away from the scene and toward the upper entrance of the cave.

Maud remained with the helmed druid and me—he could see that she was concerned about me, and he welcomed her presence. Meanwhile Bran had left the fighting and had run into the house to bring out Jandree and their infant.

Bran, emerging with Jandree at his side, looked up as he saw us and shouted an order to retreat to the cave.

When Hakon saw that Jandree was being led away, he called his remaining men from the wall to form a protective rear guard for the retreat.

* * *

Thrain/Ivald, of course, disregarded all orders to retreat. Stalking boldly back and forth along the wall, giving no indication that he was hurt at all, he growled and waved one weapon or another.

In another moment the attack surged forward again, Comorre's army a blind, sullen, hungry thing, like some great animal almost indifferent to its own loss of blood.

I caught one more quick glimpse of Thrain the Berserk, as he retreated past Wodan's chapel and toward the place of prophecy. I blinked my eyes in disbelief, for Thrain was moving surefootedly, steadily, though now his body bristled with arrows like quills upon a porcupine.

Hakon and the small number of his men who still survived leaped down inside the wall.

I continued to be enthralled by the fighting, especially by what I had seen of the berserk, but I was utterly horrified as well, and ready to retreat when I felt sure that we were going to lose. Though in my heart I felt sure that Old Merlin, silent at the moment, would have something to say about whether Comorre could seize and keep possession of these rocks.

And then I realized that I did not see Vivian anywhere, and I thought that Merlin was commanding me to look for her.

ᴪ Interlude ᴪ

Fisher got slowly to his feet, bracing himself awkwardly on his bad leg. Brushing his hands free of small white fragments of bone and other debris from the laboratory floor he took up his staff again and stood silently leaning on it, regarding the newcomers.

The tall, elegant woman in the doorway, a slender, commanding presence, ignored him totally, concentrating on Elaine.

"Dr. Brusen? My name is Morgan." The dark-haired woman's voice was honey, gliding over steel. "If you cooperate with me, we should have no difficulty in getting along." Briefly she held a hand extended, then let it fall when it was not accepted.

Elaine, standing, had a hard time pulling her eyes away from the giant cat, whose yellow eyes were giving a frightening impression of intelligence. Was the beast a leopard? she wondered. A lioness? Maybe, she thought, some rare species intermediate in size. A female, certainly.

Remembering very clearly Fisher's warning that these were dangerous people, Elaine cleared her throat and forced herself to meet the dark gaze of the latest intruder. "Ms. Morgan? Or is it Dr. Morgan?"

"I am both of those, and more." Morgan's eyes, once you looked at them closely, were more frightening than the cat's. "You should sit down."

The two men accompanying Morgan, both strong and capable looking, were standing by in stolid silence, like paid attendants or guards. Both were young and athletically large, one dark-skinned, one pale. Dressed in dull coveralls, the pair might easily have passed for maintenance or security people in any modern facility.

Elaine's growing fear momentarily yielded to anger. She made an ineffectual shooing gesture. "I must insist that you leave now, all of you. You have no legitimate business here!"

"Sit down, Dr. Brusen," repeated Morgan.

Elaine clenched her fists and defiantly remained standing.

The intruding woman snapped her fingers, and one of the men standing with her stepped to Elaine's side and roughly forced her into a chair.

She let out a faint cry, then turned to Fisher in silent appeal for help.

Fisher was standing aside with his arms folded. His staff was within easy reach, but he did not hold it. He shook his head and said: "Ms. Morgan is much more likely to compel my departure than I hers. But she doesn't really want to hurt either of us."

Looking from one to the other, Elaine choked off a new protest. Meanwhile part of her mind noticed, without comprehension, that a new verse had now appeared on the computer screens:

And moving thro' a mirror clear
That hangs before her all the year,

Shadows of the world appear.
There she sees the highway near
Winding down to Camelot:

Fisher, taking note of the direction of her gaze, murmured: "I had hoped it—the poetry—would give me a means of introducing you rather gently to the reality of the situation. Probably that approach was a mistake."

"Your whole intrusion here is a mistake." Dr. Brusen's voice was low and savage. "I wish you would remove yourself and your verses."

He smiled sympathetically. "When I can. At the moment, I must concentrate on other matters. Maybe I can do something that will be more helpful."

At a signal from Morgan, one of her aides began to carry several chairs into the room containing the hypostator and holostage. Then Morgan, with a word and a gesture, ordered everyone in there. Morgan's great cat followed.

Three chairs facing the central display were occupied by Elaine, Morgan, and Fisher. The uniformed men stood by.

Disregarding the holostage, on which the modeled shape of great stones on a grassy plain was steadily being refined in detail, the animal alternately lay and sat about. It watched Elaine alertly and almost continuously, adding to her nervous strain. Now and then the great cat yawned, showing long fangs as white as splintered bone, a red tongue, and black lips.

One of Morgan's men picked up some of the bone chips and brought them to her. Her inspection of the fragments left her as disappointed as Fisher had been.

Raising her eyes, she spoke to Fisher for the first time since entering the lab. Now her manner was that of one addressing a colleague. "Not *his* bones."

He was sitting apparently at ease, staff still at his side. "No. Definitely human, though. Maybe a planned deception."

With a gesture of contempt Morgan cast the fragments to the floor. The cat, suddenly interested, tasted them with a delicate pink tongue, and then looked about as if for more.

* * *

Switching her intense gaze suddenly to Elaine, Morgan demanded that the settings on the hypostator be changed, and gave new geographical coordinates; one of these was a negative number.

Elaine briefly considered refusing Morgan's orders. But she could see no way by which simply changing the settings on her machine, even to a mathematically nonsensical value, could do any harm. She thought she had better reserve her rebellion for something that counted. As calmly as she could, she arose from her chair and tuned the equipment to the coordinates provided by Morgan—including the nonsensical one. Maybe when craziness was proven not to work, reason could prevail.

The trouble was that the new settings, to Elaine's astonishment, quickly began to produce a solid-looking result upon the holostage. A new scene, on a seacoast, a rocky promontory crowned by a large manor house, fortified by a wall across the narrowest neck of land.

Elaine gasped as she realized that human figures were in the picture. Nothing as transient as people had appeared in any of the earlier experiments. Yet here they were. Men were fighting all along that wall, cutting one another down with antique weapons. An attack, moving in slow motion, was in deadly progress.

One of Morgan's people, addressing her with a title appropriate to royalty, urged an immediate attempt at intervention.

But the queen herself rejected the idea.

Elaine understood very little, at least at first, of the unfamiliar scene and activity now taking shape. This was the first time she had seen living creatures, let alone human beings, in any of the constructions produced on the stage.

Wherever the scene before her was actually taking place, what she saw of the carnage had the matter-of-fact horror of a combat documentary. Elaine was sickened at the sight and looked away. But her uninvited visitors, including Fisher, were much less easily upset, observing the battle with what appeared to be professional interest.

"A true berserk!" one of the men commented. "Look at that!"

"It does appear that Wodan may be taking a hand," was Morgan's dry response.

Only the great cat continued to ignore what was happening on the holostage, and stared unblinkingly at Elaine.

Fisher joined in the conversation from time to time. According to what they said, all four of Elaine's human visitors were excited at the prospect of somehow confirming the whereabouts of Merlin's Bones. Fisher and Morgan bickered on the subject in enigmatic terms.

Now Morgan said something about having spotted Merlin's library, and wondered whether they could establish a connection.

Elaine looked up, jolted out of fearful self-absorption by the sudden realization that for the last minute, more or less, she had been able to understand what Morgan and her aides were saying to each other. For several moments she had unthinkingly assumed that the intruders had suddenly switched to modern English—but now she realized that wasn't it at all.

Morgan at the moment was conferring privately with her two men. Elaine looked at Fisher, and he casually raised one finger to his lips, signaling her to be quiet. It dawned on Elaine that Fisher might not be as totally helpless as he had suggested. Again she listened carefully to what Morgan and her men were saying. No, they *weren't* speaking English, nor Russian, nor any language Elaine had ever studied even briefly. And yet she understood them perfectly. She felt confident that she could have joined in their conversation, had she wished.

Fisher's sardonic gaze seemed to assure her that he could tell what she was thinking. *Yes, I have given you this gift,* his manner silently confirmed. He had been able to provide Elaine—somehow—with the ability to understand and even speak the alien tongue. And Elaine understood that he had managed this so secretly and cleverly that Morgan was, at least for the time being, unaware that Elaine could understand what she overheard.

Morgan, evidently struck by some new idea, turned back to Elaine and demanded in English: "Conduct me to your library—your room of information storage."

Silently Elaine stood up and led the way, out of the holostage room and across the darkened corridor, into the familiar library—officially called the media/information center. The great cat came padding swiftly after her, and Morgan and the others were close behind. As in a number of other rooms in the building, lights came on automatically whenever someone entered.

The library of the Antrobus Foundation was of course largely devoted to electronic storage. Machines and screens stood in every corner, but relatively inconspicuously. There was still a maze of tall shelves, with tables and lamps and stools scattered about.

The wooden floor, possibly as old as the building itself, was worn but polished. The library was well lighted, with a gray carpet, burgundy upholstered furniture, and several kinds of viewing and listening machines scattered around.

But something in the room, Elaine realized as soon as the lights came on—something had *changed*. There was simply more space in it, for one thing, as hard as that was to credit. And that wasn't all.

There was a kind of connection perceptible, to another room, or more than one room, that in the ordinary sense was very distant indeed.

✍ Amby ✍

Just as I was being dragged away from the house, well on the way to the cave, I ducked to avoid a missile and tripped. Sprawling on the ground, I found myself looking into the dim mirror-surface of a puddle. And from that muddy mirror the face of Merlin, distorted by swift ripples, was looking back at me.

Sharply his silent voice commanded me to go into the house, find Vivian, and get her out to safety.

Breaking away from my companions, I ran back inside, screaming Vivian's name. There was no answer in any of the common rooms on the ground floor.

Scrambling frantically upstairs, I passed the door of Merlin's library, caught some kind of clue as I passed, then turned back and plunged into that strange chamber. At the far end, through a wall as of thick glass, I could see strange people doing incomprehensible things in an even stranger, distant place. Beyond a barrier I did not know how to pass, there were strange shapes of glass and metal to be seen, humming with unfamiliar energy.

Small fragments of material were flying past the barrier now in both directions. It was as if a door had opened, and then almost immediately closed again.

Before the portal in the rear of the library closed again, I caught a quick glimpse of the Jeweled Lady, standing beyond that barrier, in flesh that looked as solid as my own, and peering out in my direction.

Retreating from the library to the corridor, I ran into Vivian, who had been frantically searching the house for me. Together we ran for the stairs.

Back on the ground floor of Merlin's house, I took note in passing of other things that had suddenly and inexplicably changed in the minutes since I had last seen them. The double doors whose knobs were lion's heads with great rings in their mouths had somehow closed up tight.

Beyond those doors, my inward, mystic vision showed me the hidden Table and its surrounding chairs in the Circular Hall as suddenly fraught with great significance. A noble company of men and women had been, or would be, gathered in that chamber, which had become a place of strange distances and strange perspectives.

The house around me was now so full of magic that for a moment I thought that the clouds were smoke. Overcome by visions, seeking Merlin's help, I pulled out the little jade-rimmed mirror I had wheedled from Vivian, and in a moment saw his reassuring countenance in the glass.

Vivian was pulling at my arm. Together we scrambled out of the house, while the war cries of the attackers surged up outside.

I could see, if not understand, that new forces were intervening in the struggle. The house and its immediate vicinity were filled with magical darkness and confusion, which offered us the chance we needed to get away.

THIRTEEN

Hakon's retreat with his handful of surviving men was excellently timed and masterfully conducted. The enemy outside, bloodied and wary, half stunned by the ferocity of our resistance, did not come pouring over the wall shouting victory on the heels of the retiring Northmen. Instead, Comorre and his officers were content to order a professionally cautious advance. Thrain, as well as a growing sense of powerful magic in the house behind the wall, had made them wary.

This time fewer ladders had to be erected, because the last assault had created stairs of a particularly gruesome kind: at a couple of places the piled bodies of the invaders' dead now brought the top of the unfinished wall within easy reach of the next wave of attackers.

This deliberation on the part of the enemy afforded the survivors on our side time to seek shelter.

Bran's people had all survived the fight, and now we were heading at a good pace for the upper entrance to the cave. Soon we had formed a single file and were descending the path that led down into the earth past the Old Man in his rocks.

I suppose that even as we started down, the fact loomed large in all our thoughts that only the two small boats in the cave below were at all seaworthy, and that together they were far too small to carry anything like our total number of refugees. I could hear Jandree and Bran discussing the same subject in low voices as we walked.

Hakon's four surviving shipmates, whether following some prearrangement to rally at the cave, or compelled by some instinct to seek out boats and water, would quickly have got ahead of the rest of us, had not their leader barked orders for the Northmen to stay behind us as a rear guard, in case the enemy should be quick to penetrate the cave.

None of us had yet explored all the branching underground passages of the cavern. But Hakon and his men, during their first long hours within that sanctuary, had investigated sufficiently to be able to inform us that on the lower levels they made a formidable labyrinth.

Bran and Jandree, the latter fiercely clutching her blanketed infant, slowed the rest of us in our descent, but as there was no immediate pursuit, that did not seem to matter. In the faint greenish light that infiltrated from below, I caught a glimpse of Bran carrying his wife over a particularly difficult place, refusing aid offered by the leader of the Northmen. Jandree was still unable to walk far, or to climb.

Less than half of Hakon's original crew, only four men besides himself, had survived the fighting. As we were descending through semidarkness, I overheard a few laconic words of conversation, which told me that those badly wounded had been efficiently dispatched by their comrades—who if necessary would have wanted the same done for them—to prevent their being captured alive.

The handful of Northmen still on their feet had to be exhausted, but they moved with purpose and determination, their bloodied weapons firmly in hand, the fire of combat still in their eyes. Several of them, including Hakon, had suffered wounds, which they bound up as soon as they had a moment's respite, and then appeared to disregard totally. Indiscriminately they gulped down wine or mead and water, and proclaimed themselves ready to continue fighting if required.

Though young, these were all veterans, and I was astounded to see how calmly and philosophically they accepted their situation, stoically ignoring the loss of their comrades. They appeared not to have any sharp regrets over the losing fight they had been required to make, but were not anxious to prolong it. I heard one say: "Not much profit to be made in fighting just to stay alive."

Vivian was still making an effort to look out for me.

We had retreated some eighty or a hundred feet along the passage that wound its way down through Merlin's rocks when we suddenly heard the voices of our pursuers as they discovered the cave mouth and halted just outside.

We paused in our descent to listen to those alien voices being channeled downward through the tunnel.

"They must be wondering where we've got to," Hakon commented in a low voice.

Bran nodded. "Sounds like they're disputing over whether or not it would be wise to enter the cave."

"And who will go first if they do. From the way they sound, they are not exactly elbowing one another to get the place of honor. We stung them pretty well."

And abruptly a new and more clamorous sound came down. I closed my eyes as I recognized the wordless, inhuman utterance of Thrain/Ivald and pictured him leaping out for his last assault upon the enemy, in the amphitheater of the oracle. Listening from below we heard the last cries of the berserk, and those of his final victims.

We went on down.

As we reached the narrow side passage whose stones seemed saturated, dripping with magic, I yearned to speak to the Old Man again. And simultaneously I became aware that he was once more silently calling me to him.

Quickly I darted aside, heading for a private conference in the most secret portion of the buried and convoluted rocks.

The druid, taken by surprise, shouted after me, crying out with such urgency that his fellows thought we were being ambushed. The Horned One seemed to think, naturally enough, that I was trying to escape, or perhaps was worried that I might simply vanish. He called after me again, and grabbed for me with a thin arm—his long, soft fingers, but little used to physical effort, came clawing toward me in the darkness of the side passage. But he was just too late to get a solid grip, and there was nothing he could do.

The others were not waiting for either Guthorm or me. Vivian had gone ahead, and did not realize I had delayed. They went on down, while he remained at the place where the ways branched. Standing there, he continued to call my name, first wrathfully then sweetly, evidently in an attempt to charm me back, as if he thought I were no more than five years old.

But a moment later I heard him muttering, quietly but savagely, and the hair rose on the back of my neck with the knowledge that the druid was employing magic in an attempt to force me to return to him at once—but then I was cheered by the realization that whatever spells he might be uttering, I experienced not the least effect from them. Later I understood that the rocks surrounding me at that point were permeated with the presence that lay ahead. They absorbed and negated any spell that man was capable of casting, as the ocean absorbs rain.

In darkness, as on my earlier visit to this—this temple?—I groped my way forward.

The elder presence in the rocks gave me wordless greetings as I approached and was identified. Then more words came, with silent clarity.

Merlin first wanted to know whether my mission to the library, in search of Vivian, had succeeded.

"She's all right, sir. She's down deep in the cave now with the others."

Excellent. And the window leading out of the room of books is closed? The window opening on far places?

"I don't know, sir. I could see through it."

I was still carrying Vivian's small mirror, and by this time I had realized that some sort of mirror was essential for me to see this old man at all clearly. What I beheld now in the little glass was frightening. The old man's features were as I had first seen them in a large mirror in the house, but now underlain by what seemed a truer vision, that of a mere skull beneath the skin.

The lipless mouth seemed to be moving. *Have you told anyone that I am here?*

I was talking in a whisper, not wanting the lurking Guthorm to hear. "Yes sir. In a way, I have. I've told my friends." And briefly I blurted out the tale of how, on a sudden impulse, I had proclaimed the oracle as that of Merlin's Bones.

"And also," I added, "Comorre knows that you're here. He already knew, somehow, before he talked to us."

You told them my name?

"Yes." I thought that Merlin understood how that had happened. And truly he did not seem angered, only startled, as if my words had unexpectedly reminded him of something vital.

The skull-face in my small mirror turned to face me more directly; the hollow eye sockets seemed attentive. *You told them that Camelot is to be rebuilt?*

"No sir." The fact was that, with my own problems to think about, I had forgotten that.

Good! Good. You've done as well as could be expected. Now you must tell . . .

"Tell what, sir?" I waited, alone and answerless. "Tell who?"

Great God, if only I could remember properly . . . I must! And waves of Merlin's mental anguish swirled round me again, like hot wind blowing through the rocks.

"What is it that you want to remember, sir?"

The face in the mirror had flesh again, and it was very tired. *Never mind . . . you have been in the library?*

"Yes sir." I was shocked that the old man did not remember what I had told him in detail only moments ago.

There was a pause, in which I had the feeling that the Old One's attention was refocusing on me. To my relief, he did not seem particularly angry. He said, as if musing: *Now you must go . . . yes, I remember now. You are about to depart. Now you are on your way to the camp of the king called Vortigern.*

The reference to remembering things that were about to happen puzzled me, but I let that pass. "I don't want to go there, sir.

The druid wants to take me, and so does Hakon. But I don't want to go."

Why is it that bodiless I can remember so little? Now, when wisdom is essential . . . I fail to recall what you want, what you feel . . . can you read?

"Only a little." I was shivering. Suddenly it seemed very cold, in among the rocks.

You must soon learn to read. And write . . . what do you want to do?

I understood that I was being asked the question in a large sense. What did I want to happen to my life? "I don't know." But then I did know, after a pause for thought. "I want to go back to the way things were. With Bran, and the rest, traveling in the wagon. Everything was all right then."

Everything is never all right. Not then or now. It never is. And it is necessary for you to go to Vortigern. What the druid and the Northman may want counts for nothing, but your going is my will as well. What must be done in Vortigern's camp will be important for your future, so important that you have no choice.

I had no answer.

Prepare to be an adult, Amby.

Still I could say nothing. At the moment I suppose all I could think of was that being a grown man might mean one day having to take up a spear, like Bran and Flagon-dry, and face a hail of arrows, to stand firm against a line of charging murderers brandishing sharp-edged weapons.

And it seemed that Merlin could read my thoughts and my fears. *I will send my power with you. You will face danger in the camp of the dead king, but that is unavoidable. My protective power will be with you, and there will be moments when I will see with your eyes, and speak with your voice.*

"I know." By which I meant I knew there would be danger, which was the only part of Merlin's last statement that I understood. My attitude and tone were hangdog.

You do not know yet. But you will learn. Be guided by my magic and you will come safely through the danger. And I will see to it that you return to . . . to where you ought to be.

"Yes sir. Sir? Are you my father?" I realized even as I asked the question that it had been growing for some time in the back of my mind.

I am not. The answer was swift and decisive.

Then Merlin asked me a question that surprised me, because I had begun to assume that he knew everything. Of course I ought to have been prepared, since I had heard him protest his failing memory.

The question was: *Is Vivian to be brought along with you to Vortigern? I cannot remember . . .*

"Yes sir. She is."

Tell Vivian—remember, this is important—tell her that she will be protected, too.

"Is Vivian important, then?"

No more important than life itself.

A strange answer, offering a frightened boy no satisfaction. Still I wanted, if at all possible, to avoid going to the court of this king who had been dead for fifty years, and I mumbled some rebellious words to that effect.

But Merlin repeated that my going could not be avoided. Would I prefer, he asked me, to stay here alone in the cave, with the upper entrance open to Comorre's troops?

Then the old man showed me, in my borrowed mirror, adding some words of explanation, the place where I could pick up a certain cloak or cape that he insisted I must bring with me to the camp of Vortigern. The garment now lay crumpled and crammed into a nearby crevice in the rock.

Still feeling the need for reassurance, I repeated my earlier question: "And you are really Merlin? King Arthur's magician?"

I am.

"Then you are not dead. Somehow I didn't think you were."

He repeated his assurances that I would not go alone to Vortigern, and warned me again that I and my companions would there face certain dangers. Neither the druid nor King Vortigern were my friends. But then Merlin once more emphasized that I had reason to be of good heart; if I followed his orders I would come safely through the disturbing events I was about to experience.

"What are your orders, sir?"

They will be made known to you in good time, as they are needed. Keep my cloak and wear it, use it. Now go, and rejoin the one who waits for you.

Coming out of the narrow tunnel into the broader and better-lighted way of the main passage, I wore Merlin's cloak wrapped around my shoulders. It was a worn, dull-looking garment, lacking any clasp or button, frayed and stained, by its appearance hardly worth anyone's trouble to steal. The woven pattern, only visible if you looked closely, was a crude representation of oak trees and leaves.

I found the Horned One sitting on a rock with his face in his hands, the picture of dejection and despair. Vivian, having missed me down below, was standing uncertainly a little farther down the passage. The druid jumped up at a slight noise that I made, and at the sight of me his face became a study in the conflict between anger and relief. He halfway raised a hand to strike me, but thought better of it before he launched the blow. Once more I shook free of his attempted grip, and without offering any explanation for my delay, marched ahead of him down the path to the lower cave.

In the press of things to worry about, no one, not even Vivian, took any notice at all of my new garment. In the deep cave, the surviving Northmen and the spurious servants of the oracle alike felt safe from Comorre—at least until he and his men should nerve themselves to begin the serious exploration of what must have seemed to them the sacred precincts of the oracle. Somehow Merlin's reassurances helped more than I had expected they would, and it did not greatly bother me that the horned druid was now looking at me with the expression of a man who has just come into possession of a good slave—or a choice horse, or cow, or unspoiled side of beef—but is quietly desperate lest his prize be somehow snatched away from him. Listening to the talk that passed between Hakon and this man, I quickly decided that Merlin's warning had been accurate: The druid and the Northman must have concluded some further agreement determining my fate, and Hakon expected to make a profit of some kind by delivering me to Vortigern.

The small but heavy sacks of gold and silver taken from the house had already been hidden away in a secret recess of the lower cave, and there they would have to stay. One of the small boats would carry Guthorm and Hakon, Vivian and myself. The other would do for Hakon's four surviving men. Bran and the rest of our old troupe would have to remain behind. But Hakon assured them that the fact that he and his men were leaving their treasure here was the best evidence that they intended to come back.

Taking the first opportunity to be alone with Vivian, I whispered to her that Merlin had promised me that she would be protected.

"He did? That's nice." Vivian was skeptical at first. Then, gradually becoming more curious about the Old Man in the Rocks, she asked me questions about him.

She also wondered why Vortigern—whoever it was that the Horned One meant when he used that name—was going to all this trouble to get his hands on me, a child he'd never seen.

The emissary, treating with somewhat chilly professional courtesy the woman he supposed to be a seeress, told Vivian that Vortigern only wanted me, and possibly her, to give a prediction.

When Vivian pressed him further, Guthorm shrugged and told us outright that Vortigern was having trouble erecting a certain building—the work that was done during the day tended to collapse or disappear during the night, and against this magical disruption progress was slow or nonexistent. The king's druids had told him that a certain fatherless boy must be located, who would provide the answer.

Hakon, demonstrating great resilience, had had a couple of slight wounds bound up, and seemed already to be putting his recent bloody defeat behind him. Now he was waxing enthusiastic about bringing me to Vortigern. The druid was promising a substantial reward indeed, telling Hakon that this represented his only chance to claim some success out of his so-far disastrous viking voyage.

Hakon—after a false start or two in finding the way—guided Bran and Jandree to another branch of the lower cave to seek out a relatively remote chamber that the vikings had discovered in their first hours of exploration. With a few rocks rearranged, there was a good chance that Comorre's searchers, if and when he sent them down, would miss the hidden room entirely. There the Northman bade farewell to Jandree—and to Bran, of course, but that was something of an afterthought.

Hakon said he deeply regretted that he could not offer the family a passage in his boat—but unfortunately *Short Serpent* was still gravely in need of repairs.

Bran, who to judge by his demeanor did not entirely trust Hakon, quickly established his little family in the cul-de-sac Bran thought he could seal with a temporary barrier of loose rocks, so that they should have a good chance of remaining undiscovered when the enemy came down searching. There was very little light in this remote portion of the cave, and an ominous sound of dripping water. Bran and Jandree had some food with them, stuff they had grabbed up from the kitchen, along with flasks of water.

Maud and Flagon-dry had taken a hint from Bran and Jandree's cave, and had themselves gone to earth in a very similar little chamber, only a few yards distant.

I heard some of Hakon's men worrying aloud about the possibility that the people we were leaving behind would try to get away with the gold and silver while the Northmen were gone. Hakon, with a solemn wink, warned those remaining not to do so.

"There might be room for just one more," he added, as if in afterthought. And he looked meaningfully at Bran's wife, and at Bran.

I suppose that anyway, "one more" was not counting the baby. But whatever the Northman meant, exactly, Jandree refused to go anywhere without her husband. And Bran obviously did not want her to leave with Hakon. The Northman considered the situation silently, then shrugged and went on about his business.

The remaining hours of daylight passed. While remaining concealed down near sea level, we could hear, from time to time, Comorre's men calling to one another from somewhere near the cave's upper entrance, but to judge by the sounds they still seemed to be making no determined attempt to plumb its depths. Perhaps, since they didn't know we were the mountebanks they had been hunting, they did not care that a few people had escaped them, or were even glad to let the seer and seeress get away, and leave the oracle itself untouched. Meanwhile we waited. One or more of Hakon's sturdy spearmen was always standing watch a little way up the descending path, ready to give an alarm and strike at any hunters who might finally grow adventurous enough to come down into the cave.

Gradually the green light dimmed, became even more eerie, then seemed to go out altogether. Shortly after nightfall we shoved off our two small boats from the ruined dock and paddled away.

═══ FOURTEEN ═══

s we began to paddle, Hakon barked out orders, once more charging those we were leaving behind to guard his and his men's treasure as enthusiastically as they cared for their own lives.

Guthorm swore that by means of his magic he could guide Hakon and the rest of us to Vortigern in only two or three days. And he pledged that from Vortigern's camp an expedition could be, would be, dispatched at once to aid the survivors at Merlin's Rock. There seemed a very good chance that they would be able to endure until then, hidden as they were in the deep recesses of the cave. And Hakon and his men would come with the expedition, to reclaim their treasure.

Thus it was that I, along with Vivian, Guthorm, and Hakon in one small boat, and four other Northmen in another craft that was a little smaller, set out upon a journey that was to prove far stranger than any of us could have imagined.

As our journey began, both Guthorm and Hakon were keeping a close eye on me, as if they half expected me to try to leap out of the boat and swim away. Hakon had alerted his surviving men to watch me, too. But since my last conference with Merlin, I had no intention of separating myself from this expedition. My head was buzzing with things the Old Man had forced silently into my mind during our most recent meeting. By the time we were a hundred yards from shore, and changing course to follow the coastline, my mental state had gone well beyond a mere grudging agreement with Merlin's dictates. Though I did not fully realize the fact for several hours afterward, a sense of purpose had been instilled in me, and formidable powers had been placed at my disposal.

Our craft were only simple boats of hides stretched across wooden ribs, something like umiaks, slow in speed and clumsy in maneuver, but very hard to tip. But they should suffice, as the Horned One repeatedly assured us, because we had no need to cross any stretch of open ocean, only to make our way along the coast and then up a river.

As we paddled out of the cave into the gentle surf, we could see that fires had sprung up atop the rock, making a great beacon. I thought the conquerors of the oracle must have put the torch to at least some of the outbuildings, if not to the main house. Perhaps they intended to honor Wodan, in celebration of their victory.

Evidently it was only after the process of cremation had been started that Comorre decided the day's dead were too numerous to be efficiently disposed of in that way, short of setting the whole manor house ablaze. By the time of our departure he had a disposal crew at work heaving bodies over the cliffs, industriously feeding the fish, and we were briefly in some danger of being struck by falling corpses. One or two splashed heavily into the water as we passed.

The cliff-top blazes gave so much light that for a time we felt some concern that Comorre and his men would see our departing boats and set out in pursuit. We were not discovered by Comorre, but other difficulties soon arose.

From the very start of our journey, the guidance Merlin had promised me went into effect. My frequent unspoken questions as to which way we should go were met with effective though unspoken answers. When I pulled the shabby cloak around me, and closed or even half closed my eyes, our proper route at once became apparent. The visual signals were of the same general type as those that I had recently seen in a mirror in the house.

I found I could see the visions more clearly if I used the small hand-mirror borrowed from Vivian.

Vivian, on seeing me do this, repeatedly tried using the mirror to see the old man too, or to accomplish some other trick, but had no real success. So Vivian, who was keen on learning all she could about magic, could do little but look on enviously.

Plainly her curiosity about Merlin was still not satisfied. She continued to ask me questions at intervals during our journey: What had the Old Man looked like, when I glimpsed him in the mirror? I could give no very clear description. What had he said to me? That I repeated to the best of my ability.

"Amby, do you believe that he was really Merlin?"

"Yes. Not was. And it's not just what I believe. He *is*."

There was another point to which Vivian kept returning. "And Merlin mentioned me? Why me?"

I gave the equivalent of a shrug.

Her greenish eyes were gradually growing round. After three or four repetitions of question and answer maybe she was beginning to believe me. "Amby, what'd you ask him, to make him mention me?"

"Nothing, Viv. He just . . . he just started talking about you."

Sometimes when I held the glass and turned my thoughts to our best course, I beheld little images of Bran and my other friends, smiling encouragingly, ahead of me. However fast we went, we got no closer to them. Sometimes they seemed to be standing in the upper entrance to the cave of Merlin's Rock, or at the front door of the manor, and beckoning me on. But I now felt sure that the best way, the only satisfactory way, for me to return to Merlin's Rock and rejoin my friends, was to push on ahead, in what common sense insisted was the exactly wrong direction.

I was now fully convinced that the Old Man under the Rock was frightening not only in his power, but also in his emotions, which I did not understand. I believed him when he denied that he was my father. Yet it was no longer possible for me to question that my survival and my welfare were of paramount importance to him, and it was deeply comforting that through his cloak we remained in contact.

We had not been a quarter of an hour in the boat before I fell asleep, worn out by the terror of death and fighting, to be awakened several hours later by seagulls, screaming as they dove for fish. Morning had overtaken us, and our little boat still labored on. The seacoast, with its plants and birds and rocks, was beautiful beneath a morning sky still rimmed with the colors of sunrise.

"What river are we looking for?" I asked the question aloud of my new companion the druid when I heard him muttering something to Hakon about trying to reach a river. While Vivian and I took our turns at paddling, or watched the sail, and the second boat stayed close behind us, the two of them were crouched in our stern and seemed to be trying to draw a crude map upon a curved wooden thwart, using smears of grease from somewhere in our meager food supply.

He turned his horned head my way at once. His eyes were intent as usual upon my every move. "The Avon."

"I'll know the Avon when we come to it," I assured him, glancing into my little mirror. "We're going in the right direction now."

"You have seen this stream before, child?"

"I don't know if I've seen it before or not. But I'll recognize it this time."

Guthorm insisted on examining the little mirror that I was using. But he found it nothing but ordinary glass. For a moment I feared that the druid would toss it overboard, but he returned the glass to me instead.

The Horned One looked at me dubiously after I had promised accurate navigation, and so did Hakon, and Guthorm continued to manage the navigation himself. I did not protest, because I could see that he had us on the proper course.

During the night we had made several miles along the coast. The beauty of early morning was soon dulled in clouds of sullen gray.

In an hour or so the fog had knotted itself so thickly about us that ordinary sight became all but useless, and some thought we were in peril of being carried right out to sea. Calmly and unhesitatingly I pointed the way to shore.

Our second boat was no longer right behind us, but Hakon was not immediately concerned.

We paddled ashore and made camp on a likely looking stretch of beach, where the mouth of a small stream offered fresh water. Guthorm was prudently in the habit of carrying flint and steel, and we made a fire, with the thought of guiding Hakon's four missing shipmates to us. Then we ate a portion of the food we had brought with us. Everyone ate sparingly, because we knew that when our scanty supplies were gone, our only sustenance would be whatever we could kill or catch or steal or gather.

The fog dispersed almost as quickly as it had formed, but Hakon's four men and their boat were still nowhere to be seen. The Northman muttered curses, but there was nothing to do but set up a small cairn to indicate which way we were going next and get on with our journey.

This was new country to all of us, except perhaps the druid. The leader of the Northmen harangued Guthorm and tried to learn how far away the mysterious Vortigern was now—but Hakon had no success.

And so we proceeded, for the next several days—I will soon explain why I am uncertain about the time—while the world steadily became stranger around us.

The great oddity overtook us almost imperceptibly. It had begun in that first morning's heavy fog, so that at first none of us understood its nature. But as we traveled, all of us gradually became aware of the fact that time was becoming confused. There was no other explanation. The changes came in abrupt, disorienting jumps. While our location in space changed only slowly, weather and vegetation suddenly turned autumnal—there were nuts and berries to be harvested—then on the next day properly springlike. But after almost a full day of what seemed normal spring, the night turned bitter cold, ending in heavy snow—our teeth chattered, and without a fire I suppose we might have frozen to death. But before such a fate became a serious threat, the snow suddenly vanished, rather than melting, and daylight found us engulfed in green-leafed summer.

All four of us were frightened by the realization that in four days we had passed through at least as many seasons: summer, fall, winter, and spring, but not following their proper alternation. I had the feeling also that no two of the seasons that we encountered had properly belonged to the same year. Rather, I thought, they were segments of four years, separated by decades.

As we went on, the uncanny process accelerated, until we entered an epoch in which we beheld several alternations of light and dark during one brief rest stop—and from that the sky progressed to a mere flickering, days and nights coming and going so quickly that we could not distinguish one from another. The ground at times became no more than an uneven blur beneath our feet, a gray uncertain floor vibrating in a rapid hum that fortunately we could not hear; the water of streams and ponds when we approached them seemed to be churning at an invisible speed, its level uncertain, its substance varying somewhere between steam and ice. When I put my hand into water in this state I snatched it back at once, with the feeling that it was burning.

The druid admitted that he had experienced similar phenomena in his lone wanderings, before he had fallen in with Hakon and his men. He still, with deep satisfaction, attributed them to his own magic, which he also credited with his success in finding first Hakon, and then me.

Child that I was, I had already seen too much to believe that. In wisdom I was small indeed, but the range of my perception had become gigantic. Those days of cramped boat travel brought me many and strange visions, and very little of what I saw in them was comprehensible to me. But clearly, though indirectly, I now perceived a certain truth regarding the Horned One: around us far greater forces were contending than any Guthorm could possibly have bent to his will. Thinking himself steeped in wisdom, powerful in magic, he was in truth no more than an infant who had toddled out by accident upon a field of combat, whereon charging warhorses were carrying their armored masters thundering toward a clash.

And if this grave, learned druid, with forty or fifty years' experience in life and magic—if he was only an ignorant child, in danger of being trampled like an infant—then what was I?

On that question the little images in my mirror could give me no reassurance.

That night I needed Vivian's motherly embrace to let me fall asleep.

Driven by the strength of mundane human muscles exerted upon paddles, sometimes pushed forward by the wind even though it lacked a sail, our little vessel conveyed us across some narrow arm of the sea, and then for something like twenty miles up a river, which I could tell was the stream we were looking for as soon as it came into sight.

At our first encampment on the gently sloping bank of the Avon, we fell asleep snuggled in blankets beside a fire. I remember Vivian huddling against me (I suppose her purpose was partly to keep Hakon, or the druid, at a distance), and after enduring the fluttering passage of another thousand days and nights awoke to a warm morning in spring. And I remember clearly that a notable tree, at a certain point on the riverbank, which when we retired had been a mighty oak, had shrunken when we awoke to only a sapling.

Now and again in the course of our journey we caught glimpses of people, onshore or in other boats—unfortunately never that of our lost companions—and animals, whose movements were flickering passages at frightening rates of speed—obviously the time in which these beasts and humans lived and moved was not quite synchronized with our frame of duration, and we could not tell if they were aware of us at all. I, at least, was convinced that I could see plants growing and decaying before my eyes. Boats and wagons and ridden horses, even cows and sheep, shot past like arrows.

All surviving members of our party had accepted the fact that time for us was changing strangely, but in fact we seldom talked about this oddity. The druid's magic, such as it was, was apparently telling him to trust me. Meanwhile Merlin's vastly greater power, operating through me, guided us all steadily toward our mysterious goal.

As our journey progressed, the attitude of Vortigern's agent toward me changed. From time to time the druid, growing jealous of Merlin's authority, irritated at what he took to be my insolence, disputed with me over what course we should be following, and announced that from now on he would be the one to determine our proper route. But each time he did this he lost his way within an hour. The strange alternation of days and nights and seasons was held in abeyance whenever the druid chose our path, but on those occasions cold mist soon closed in, and unnatural darkness. It was soon plain that none of us, the Horned One included, knew where we were. Only I, with distant Merlin's guidance, had any idea of which way to go.

Three or four times Guthorm took my little mirror from me and tried to use it, but the glass proved useless in his hands, no matter how he muttered and gestured, making spells. After several such attempts the druid gave up and allowed me to take complete charge of navigation.

I knew—everything I saw and felt afforded me certainty, amounting to an obsession—that I must go forward. Merlin himself, whom I was now forced to trust absolutely, had told me that my destiny was to confront the man named Vortigern who had died decades before my birth, who called himself a king and had spent half his life trying to become one. This feeling was accompanied by a conviction that, though many dangers threatened me, at least when I should actually stand in Vortigern's presence I need not be afraid.

Whenever I made an effort to discover the proper direction, whether in fog or sun or dark of night, guidance was provided. In the most common form of the vision, I glimpsed a doorway ahead of me in the mist. Within the doorway stood a tall man—he was not the Old Man of my earlier vision, but someone entirely different, a regal figure I had never seen before. He was wrapped in a rich cloak and wore what passed in those days for a royal diadem, a copper circlet with a single jewel upon his brow. I knew, in the way one knows about things in dreams, that I was seeing Vortigern, who on the day I was born had already been dead for half a century.

And in the vision beyond Vortigern stood my friends, Bran's people who were my only living family, beckoning to me. There were Bran and Jandree, the young woman holding her infant. There was Vivian in the image—even as her living body continued to occupy the boat with me—and Flagon-dry and Maud. This visionary portal in the air was not before me continually; it did not obtrude itself like some mundane tree or rock. But when I sought the Old Man's guidance, it was always there.

For days now—for what seemed to us in the troubled flow of Time like many days—it had been obvious that neither the druid nor Hakon really considered themselves my captors any longer, and there were moments, when I saw those men looking at me with the beginnings of fear, that I felt that they had become my prisoners—though they were certainly not going to admit the fact as yet. There was no satisfaction for me in the thought.

FIFTEEN

After spending an indeterminate number of days en route—I have never been sure how many—our small party emerged from the insane cycle of flickering suns and moons and seasons, into an epoch where Time again wore a countenance—perhaps I should say a mask—of sober consistency. We had arrived at a place some forty miles from the sea, a pleasant river valley currently greening with spring growth, where the Horned One at last felt at home. No doubt he observed certain details about the land that reassured him that he had come back to his proper year as well. Smiling, he now informed us, in a voice that had regained its confidence, that our journey was almost over. The fact came as no news to me.

On a warm cloudy morning we used our paddles to pole our boat ashore through muddy shallows, then abandoned it among a collection of other small craft at a landing place. Grabbing our handful of belongings, we set foot upon an ancient and well-worn road. The four of us were gaped at by shepherds, who no doubt thought our clothing and speech outlandish and who were driving their sizable flocks in the same direction. We followed the road on its climb along one side of the gentle valley for a mile or two. At that point, on topping a gentle rise and emerging from a grove of pines, we found ourselves within half a mile of the monumental construction known to most of my readers as Stonehenge, standing in the midst of what is now called Salisbury Plain.

The monument stood—I have seen, in this much later time in which I write, a portion of it still standing—upon a broad, gentle swelling of the earth, so that in every direction the horizon of forests and fields was at least a mile way. This cleared expanse made easier the sightings and the calculation of the risings and settings of Sun and Moon, and the prediction of eclipses.

Never before had I—or Vivian, or Hakon—beheld anything remotely like this strange, sprawling, gigantic construction. And seldom in all the time elapsed since then have I beheld the like.

Vivian had heard stories of the Dance of the Giants (which was even then an ancient name for the collection of standing stones that dominate that place of power), though I had not; she recounted to me several of the tales. I listened, and doubted, and thought I would try to see for myself before accepting any account of how the wonderful construction had come to be.

Stones weighing, by modern measurement, as much as fifty tons had been erected in a closely calculated arrangement of trilithons, lintels, and uprights making square arches more than twenty feet in height. Surrounding the massive central stonework were three concentric circles, none of them quite complete, of wooden posts, some six feet high, which to judge by the twigs and leaves still attached to some were mostly or entirely oak. The outer circle of wooden construction was again enclosed by a bank of startlingly white chalk, some six feet high, constructed of blocks cut neatly out of the surrounding land.

The druid observed our astonishment with satisfaction. I am sure his shaken morale was boosted by seeing us country yokels gape at this great metropolitan enterprise.

As we drew closer to the center of activity, the road disappeared in a maze of muddy, rutted tracks. These ran everywhere, and had been made over a period of many months, perhaps years, by burdened animals and wagons engaged in a heavy, almost continuous traffic of building materials and other supplies. Improvised latrines and garbage dumps defaced the scene, as in the vicinity of any large settlement of the time. Partially surrounding the circle of enormous stones was the encampment of an army several times

larger than Comorre's—who of course, in this epoch of Vortigern's power, was not yet born. There were long rows of tents, most
of them dull brown or black, and enough fires to make the now-
autumnal air smoky for half a mile downwind. I suppose that on
the day of our arrival there may have been a thousand fighting
men, who doubled as workers, encamped around the monument—a vast horde of an army for that time and place—and half
again as many dependents and merchants, prostitutes, priests of
half a dozen gods and goddesses, farriers and dealers in livestock,
all manner of hangers-on.

The outer sentries of this encampment knew our druid by
sight and saluted him with respect as they passed us through without delay.

Near the center of the monument a hundred men and more,
whether free or slave I could not tell, were laboring with axes and
mattocks, ropes and sledges. An enormous construction project
was in progress. Quickly I realized that this current work had
nothing to do with the placing of the monumental stones themselves; the verdant earth had long since healed around them, and
they had not moved for centuries. But a less impressive though
actually more extensive work, of smaller stones and timbers, was
being thrown up over them and around them. The concentric circles of oaken posts were being incorporated into this new construction.

The more closely we approached the ancient circles of mighty
stones, the better I could see them. The obvious questions, that
the old stories pretended to answer, rose up at once: Who had put
them where they were, and when and why? There were dozens,
scores, of mighty blocks, and I tried to count them, which simple
process was made well-nigh impossible not only by the new construction, but by the thickness of distracting magic that overlay
the site like heavy fog—and was of course invisible to most folk,
to all but the few who possessed the necessary special vision. Alternately letting my eyelids close, and staring into Vivian's little
glass, I tried to see who had put the greatest monoliths, the uprights and lintels in their places, and how. But that proved a diffi-

cult seeing, and I could tell that success would require long effort and preparation.

Still I marveled greatly at the sight. Nowhere in all the broad expanse of the Giants' Dance was the glow of magic quite as intense as it had been in the few cubic yards at the center of Merlin's Rock, but here the display was more widespread, covering acres of land.

Shortly after our arrival we were taken to a kind of mess hall, a longhouse built of small logs about a hundred yards from the center of the monument. There we were well fed, while soldiers and minor officials at nearby tables inspected us with great curiosity.

Some men at the next table were discussing a ceremony shortly scheduled to take place. They were badly worried, because the gods were not smiling on Vortigern's great building project.

Looking back now at their conversation, it seems to me they must have been planning for dawn on Midsummer's Day, often considered the most important highlight of the ritual year. They said there were to be some preliminary human sacrifices, and my inner vision horrified me with images of one victim after another being held down upon a stone, and gashed and stabbed with a ritual knife of flint or bone. Sometimes a body would be entirely dismembered, to make it easier to spread the blood around. Then the blood of victims was sprinkled into a pit where the foundations of new construction were to be laid—again. Before the warm red drops were dry, the construction workers once more came trooping forward, carrying tools and timbers, the next attempt at building getting under way.

❧ Interlude ❧

Having been marched back from the library to the hypostator room, Elaine was once more confined by threats and orders to her chair. Meanwhile Morgan and her people again became intensely absorbed in their observations on the holostage of what was happening at Merlin's Rock.

Soon Morgan demanded that the machine's settings be

changed, to nearly the same as had earlier evoked the shape of Stonehenge on the stage. She was now convinced, through some magic of her own, that something of great importance was about to happen there.

Once more Elaine obediently adjusted dials and punched in new digits on the hypostator. She moved from one set of controls to another, from cabinet to computer console and back again, shifting the focus of her equipment back almost to the original geographical coordinates, with a slight adjustment in a variable that Morgan assured her influenced Time.

When the scientist had made the required changes she stood back, and suddenly became aware of the absence of Fisher's staff. Only moments ago the oaken stick had been in plain view, leaning against a nearby computer console. Elaine looked hastily around for Fisher himself—somehow that man's presence had become no longer a threat, but reassuring—and discovered that the man in the dark suit had quietly disappeared. He'd had been in the library with them a few moments ago, hadn't he? And surely he'd come back here, too. But now . . .

Morgan, absorbed in magic and other matters, needed a few moments longer to notice the departure. Then she turned her head sharply to demand of her assistants where Fisher had got to—Morgan called him by some other name, one that Elaine did not hear clearly.

Morgan cursed her aides for letting him get away. Elaine saw one of the powerful men turn pale.

Morgan then sent one of her people running out of the room to search for Fisher. She warned the man as he left to be careful.

Then, switching to English, she warned Elaine to behave herself, or she would be physically confined, actually tied into her chair.

"It seems I have no choice but to follow orders."

"That's an intelligent response. Mr. Fisher spoke the truth about one thing: Do what I tell you, and no harm will come to you, or your equipment."

Meanwhile the giant cat, indifferent to anyone else, continued to guard Elaine, to make sure she stayed in her chair unless

Morgan ordered her to get up. The cat's unwavering stare continued to convey a suggestion of intelligence.

With Stonehenge solidly back onstage, Morgan was soon satisfied that she had discovered the true source of the bone fragments that had been propelled into Elaine's laboratory.

"It's only Vortigern, making human sacrifice."

Elaine, shifting her gaze, could see that the verse on the screens now read:

> *And sometimes thro' the mirror blue*
> *The knights come riding two and two;*
> *She hath no loyal knight and true,*
> *The Lady of Shalott.*

For a moment Elaine had to fight down an impulse to ask this woman whether King Arthur had come with her in an ambulance.

Then she concentrated on listening, wondering if there was something wrong with her new linguistic talent, after all. What she could overhear of her captors' discussion suggested that Morgan was now determined to go, to force her way through physically somehow to Vortigern's camp. If Elaine understood her correctly, she was saying something about traveling between libraries. Or was she only speaking of communication between such facilities?

"Somehow," Morgan was telling her confederates, "the library passage seems to have been closed at Merlin's end. But I think the one at Vortigern's may very well be worth a try. The druids are in charge there, and they tend to be a trifle careless."

Elaine stared at the holographic model of the monument on Salisbury Plain. According to what Morgan was saying now, they were seeing Stonehenge not as it existed in the twenty-first century, but as it had been around the fourth or fifth—King Arthur's time, "or even a little earlier." It did seem to Elaine that more stones were standing upright than what she could remember of how the modern conformation ought to look—and what was all that extraneous construction? Wooden palisades, in concentric circles . . . and who in the world were all the swarming people?

The more of her captors' conversation she absorbed, the more Elaine understood that according to Morgan the hypostator required magical help, provided of course by Morgan herself, to give her visitors the view of the true past that they desired. It seemed that in this as in other matters, only magic and science working together could be strong enough to achieve the desired result.

Only a few minutes ago, Elaine had been completely convinced that the whole mysterious collection of intruders who had forced their way into her laboratory were quite insane. After all, when people came talking seriously of King Arthur . . . But Dr. Brusen was slowly being forced to modify that opinion. It was being challenged by the coherence of their thought, and by the strange abilities they demonstrated, among them that of successfully predicting, at least some of the time, what was going to happen next.

A complicated madness, if madness it truly was, and with a disconcerting measure of method in it.

Once more the holostage erupted, ejecting dust and chips of various materials. Madness or not, fragments of human bone were being hurled about. If this was madness, Elaine had to believe now that she was sharing in it.

ᴊᴘ Amby ᴊᴘ

Within an hour of our arrival at Stonehenge, before we had completely finished our meal in the mess hall, Hakon and Vivian and I were approached by a delegation of important-looking men, most of them druids, who surrounded us and escorted us into the presence of the chieftain or king called Vortigern.

Our druid Guthorm marched proudly just ahead of us, ready to display me as his prize catch. We were brought into a roomy hall, a long, low building with thick drystone walls—a different stone from that of the Giants' Dance—and a thatched roof. This building also contained Vortigern's own quarters. Fire smoldered in a stone hearth at one end. At the moment of our entry, the flames were discolored and half choked by exotic substances that had just been thrown on to make an impressive effect, if not actually to aid in magic. The long hall was full of smoke that made me cough, and already crowded with men, warriors and wizards, among them a sprinkling of women, wives and servants and an occasional respected seeress.

I caught one startling glimpse, out of the corner of my eye, of a face that I had seen before, but under circumstances so different that for long moments I could not think where in my memory it belonged. But then recognition came with a shock, and I turned my head and would have cried out, but I did not know what to say. My Jeweled Lady, once glimpsed through a wooden door, dark-eyed Morgan, her dark curls almost hidden in a monkish cowl, was here, unnoticed by others in the crowd. As we passed she nodded her head slightly, and favored me with a glance in which amusement and respect seemed blended. This time I thought she had emerged from a certain house-sized log building near the stone structure we were now in. The building from which the lady had emerged, as I much later discovered, served the druids as temple, research facility, and library.

In fact we were now led through this Stonehenge library on our way to see Vortigern in a kind of conference room in the rear. I was not especially astonished by this fact—to me, at the time, all libraries were about equally surprising. Vortigern's magicians had established a kind of research facility here, with a collection of scrolls, and even some ancient clay tablets. Here there were more trunks and chests than high shelves, and the floor was not as smooth, but the overall effect was almost the same.

On a large central table, crudely built but solid and level, stood a model showing how the new temple was to take shape according to the plans of Vortigern, so that in the end his building would entirely surround and encompass the ancient monument.

Something about Hakon irritated the senior druids, Guthorm's superiors. Sharp orders were issued, and Hakon was outraged to find himself suddenly a prisoner, instead of an honored visitor, an ally with payment owed him. Though he made efforts to control his temper, he was bold and impressive as usual as he began forcefully insisting that Guthorm's pledges of help be honored.

In a minute he had grown too insistent for his own good. One of Vortigern's guards clubbed Hakon on the side of the head, and when he staggered and would have fought back, several others seized his arms. By the time the Northman regained his senses fully, he had been disarmed and searched for weapons and his hands bound behind him.

Now it was clear, from the conversation taking place among Guthorm, his superiors among the king's advisers, and the king himself that Vortigern's original intention, following the advice of his druids, had been to use me and probably my companions as well in a blood sacrifice. But the king wanted to question me first, to try to learn the sources of my supposed magical virtue, before I was consumed.

Before our conversation, the men in charge took time out for a preliminary ritual, in which half a dozen other prisoners, strangers to us, were wiped out in human sacrifice. Women and children, appearing to be drugged, went willingly. Men fought fiercely but uselessly for their lives. I could not see that the killings really accomplished anything at all in the way of magic.

Vortigern's conversation with the Horned One revealed that by his royal reckoning only about a month had passed since he had dispatched his emissaries to find me and bring me back—only one druid, Guthorm, had survived out of several he and his chief advisers had dispatched. It was too bad, the king was saying in effect, that only one of his most favored counselors had survived the journey, but that was the way things were. The others were no doubt proud to have given their lives in the most glorious cause imaginable.

The druid emissary who had succeeded in finding me for the king, and had been fortunate enough to return alive, seemed at best reluctant to try to explain to King Vortigern, or even to his own senior colleagues in the druid craft, the full weirdness of the journey. Or the fact that in its later stages he had been forced to rely upon his prisoner for its completion. But actually there had been no harm in that, because—here we were.

Another man, a more impressive druid than he who had been with us on the journey, and more impressively tattooed and costumed, asked me my father's name.

I faced this new questioner without fear, and without hesitation gave voice to the flow of words that were coming to me, somehow, from far away for me. The power of the distant Old Man reached from under his rock to hold me, support me, as solidly as the mailed fist of some invisible giant.

I said: "My mother always told me that I had none."

There was a murmuring among the men and women who heard me speak. I am sure they were more surprised by my clear, commanding tone and by my attitude than by my words. Without turning my head, I was vaguely aware that both Vivian and Hakon were staring at me with rounded eyes.

Among the distant figures in the back of the long room, I now and then glimpsed the cowled head of the Lady of Jewels, her dark eyes always turned my way.

I could see that the senior druid was determined not to allow himself to be impressed by anything I said or did. "And by that, what did your mother mean? Something stranger than that you were simply a bastard?"

"I cannot tell you with any certainty what she meant, but only what she said." Again, my tone was haughty.

Too much so, evidently, to be endured. My interrogator turned his head slightly to speak to a subordinate, while his eyes stayed fixed on me. "Let the brat be taught his manners, as to how he should speak to those far above him."

Old Merlin's threadbare cloak lay warm and comforting around my shoulders, and I clutched it to me firmly with both hands.

I said: "I have been taught to speak by one greater than you." My voice was shrill, but with childhood not with fear, and it carried such undiminished confidence that now caution came into the eyes of all the old men, wariness enough to quell their growing outrage. One who had stepped forward to punish me held back the open-handed blow he had been about to aim at my head.

In that dangerous moment Vortigern spoke up, his voice biting like teeth at the robed men, establishing his authority—certainly he did so when the druids would have silenced me.

The top of my head scarcely reached the shoulder of the shortest of the white-robed men who glared at me. But inwardly I felt myself towering above men like these, looking down on them with confidence and great contempt.

I said: "I speak respectfully to your king, but not to you, who have lied to him. Not even a sprinkling of my blood would be of any benefit to the unstable foundations of your work."

The druids looked outraged, and again they would have punished me, or perhaps killed me on the spot, but the king intervened. Obviously he was not altogether happy with the results he had so far obtained from these eminent counselors.

Vortigern himself took over the interrogation. After glowering at me for a few moments—probably he was surprised that I could meet his gaze serenely—he asked me: "Where did you come from?"

I chose to give the question the only interpretation that allowed me to answer it. "From Merlin's Rock, Your Majesty."

That left the tall man at a loss. "Whose rock? The name is unfamiliar."

"Sir, I speak of Merlin, King Arthur's wizard."

The king frowned, and turned his head this way and that, vainly seeking enlightenment from his advisers. "Is there a king called Arthur, anywhere?"

A scribe was brought forward, a balding, toothless man of many years, who from memory recited a lengthy list of claimants to royalty—there were a great many such in our island at that time. But there was no Arthur in the list. It had become obvious that no one in this time and place had heard of either Merlin or the as-yet-unborn (or at least unknown) Arthur—unless as the subjects of some prophecy yet to be fulfilled.

Vivian and Hakon and I exchanged wondering looks.

The Horned One could tell his contemporaries only a little about Arthur: that one by that name had been a famous ruler among the people where he had discovered me, but had been deceased by the time of Guthorm's arrival among us.

King Vortigern soon brought the discussion back to his own immediate problem, and to me: How was I, the Fatherless Boy, supposed to bring him to a solution?

Driven by the demonic arrogance that had possessed me, I broke into an argument and challenged the king and his druids to dig deeper into the soil where they would have based their new construction, and I predicted what they would find when they dug there—because I had already been granted, through visions, some awareness of Elaine and her efforts in the far future.

Also I assured the men who held me captive that they were not going to find what they were seeking.

There followed a long argument, most of which I could not follow. At the end of it our captors herded us out of the building and through the outlying new construction into the open field beside the monument.

There they commanded a team of workers to dig again. The men reluctantly obeyed, taking up their tools only when bows were drawn at them. The mighty original stones of the Giants' Dance endured—even this could not unsettle them—but around their roots the earth erupted in new turmoil. This was like and yet unlike the confusion of our time-traveling journey; now it was space that seemed to have turned unstable, with alternate versions of reality contending for the same location, with loss of life and other damage, for which the druids wanted to blame me.

Proceedings were delayed while Vortigern talked to certain military scouts, who had just arrived bringing reports of an unknown army, sighted only a few miles away.

Eventually, while the dispute continued to rage among Vortigern's counselors, Vivian and Hakon and I were removed from this unedifying spectacle and taken back to the rooms in one of the temporary buildings, where we were kept under guard.

The three of us were removed from the king's presence and thrown into a single, strongly constructed room, with one small high window and a thick and solid door. It was next to the druids' library.

Outside, the activity of the camp went on, unheeding, a thousand people intent on their own lives.

We discussed our situation among ourselves. Hakon swore bitter oaths of vengeance upon the druid Guthorm and on this murderous king as well.

I had to admit that on the surface things seemed to be going very badly for us. Yet, as I continued to clutch Merlin's old cloak about me, I still felt confident that he would honor his pledge to me and protect us somehow.

Or so I told myself. Disturbing doubts had begun to creep in. Hadn't the Old Man's memory seemed to fail him at times, even when I was talking to him?

Time passed, and I fell asleep. I suppose that Vivian and even Hakon eventually did the same.

Several hours later, I was awakened by someone's voice, half mad, half mocking: "Merlin, Merlin, Merlin. Where is little Merlin?"

I came erect, stumbling, rubbing sleep from my eyes, and clutching the well-worn cloak about me. I protested: "No, I am not Merlin." But any attempt at explanation seemed hopeless. My unseen tormentor continued to chant the name, louder and faster than ever after he saw that this behavior bothered me.

Another hour or so passed, then we were roughly conducted back into the king's presence. On entering the long building, we saw our fate in his eyes, and in the triumphant gaze of the high-ranking druids who had made themselves our enemies, before we heard it from the king's mouth. Great Vortigern had yielded to their dark counsels after all, and had ordered yet more sacrifice. I was to be killed and my blood sprinkled into the foundations of his new structure, the great building that was to bring him all essential power, to inscribe his name indelibly on the short list of the greatest rulers of the earth.

SIXTEEN

I saw that the elder druids and their white-robed acolytes had begun elaborate preparation for the sacrifice that seemed certain to take my life, and Vivian and Hakon's, too.

The early stages of this ceremony included a ritual beating of wooden shields with spear shafts by Vortigern's massed warriors, who also chanted, hundreds of arms and voices producing a sea of sound orchestrated by the magicians.

My wrists were seized and held as I was dragged about. But still Merlin's old cloak—no one but I seemed to notice that it was suddenly shrunken to no more than a tattered scarf—clung to my shoulders and wrapped itself protectively around my neck as the men dragged us out of doors and to the center of the monument. There, as we stood surrounded by the churned earth and other evidences of Vortigern's failed construction, half a dozen of the magicians who meant to kill us went into action, chanting and gesturing. Their swaying, stamping dance encircled an ancient stone the size of a kitchen table, whose flat top was encrusted with dark and ugly stains.

Vortigern had been told by his wizards that some foreign material placed under the monument by his enemies prevented the Giants' Dance being integrated into his plan. And that material had to be found and removed before his work could go forward.

Until I, along with my two companions, was dragged into the

middle of the monument, I had been given no chance to make anything like a thorough study of the phenomenon now called Stonehenge. But by the time the ceremony began my perception of the magic underlying the whole area had been enhanced. When fear, horror at the sight of the first preliminary sacrifice, made me pull Merlin's diminished cloak tightly over my face and close my eyes, I was able to perceive certain things that were still invisible to others. And now I began to gain insight into the reasons for the difficulties encountered by King Vortigern's planners and builders.

The turmoil of strange forces in the middle of Stonehenge, swelling like an onrushing thunderstorm, had created an environment whose peculiarity resembled the strangeness of our journey. Here, too, among the tremendous stones of the Giants' Dance, the ordinary course of Time had been perturbed, even as it had been while we were traveling. Indeed, the upheaval under Stonehenge had been far more drastic, the gulf of the distortion was far greater than a mere fifty or sixty years. Powers from the far future were here at work, in some way interfering with, opposing, the work ordained by Vortigern.

The king and a small knot of his close advisers were standing near enough for us to hear their conversation. It became apparent that Vortigern's ultimate goal, which had been urged on him by the more fanatic of his druid counselors, was to incorporate the ancient construction into a new temple for Wodan. This projected temple, supposedly greater than any ever built, was to be a structure containing and incorporating the great stone blocks of the Giants' Dance, thus co-opting the psychic power of the ancients into his own service. But from the start, Vortigern's overseers and workmen had found themselves faced with enormous difficulties in carrying out their master's commands.

Being prodded along, so that we remained within a few feet of the king when he went to inspect the new work at close range, we discovered that Vortigern had gone so far as having his name carved on some of the blocks. He had even planned to have one of the great blocks sculpted into his likeness, an attempt at imperial portraiture harking back to Roman times, and that job had got under way as well—but the work done by day at his command was repeatedly wiped away at night, by unknown forces.

Certain arrogant elements among the druid leadership, a faction that seemed to include Guthorm, were not willing to concede that any power of magic could keep them from accomplishing their goal.

To judge by the conversation I overheard, and what I could see and hear of the actual work, it was plain that part of Vortigern's plan had been—and, in his stubbornness, still remained—to erect an oaken stockade all the way around Stonehenge. Thus he meant to lay claim to the place and all its tradition and its power, trying to make it his private temple and palace and oracle.

ᴥ *Interlude* ᴥ

In operation the hypostator was, as usual, almost totally silent, except for a barely audible murmur of moving air produced by cooling fans in the equipment cabinets. Before the eyes of Elaine and her unwelcome guests, the image on the holostage, as convincing as the life-sized mirror image of a solid, real-world scene, was changing. The hypostator was fabricating on the holostage a panoramic window opening upon a version of Stonehenge slightly altered from the one it had earlier displayed. This time the viewers in the future were looking at the monument as if from the darkened interior of a building, at a distance of about a hundred yards.

Or was the machine only discovering a domain of physical reality that already existed, at some indeterminate distance from the laboratory in space and time? Until today such questions had been purely philosophical, but now matters had taken a different turn.

Morgan, too excited to remain seated, was up and pacing, slender legs in dark trousers carrying her back and forth in front of the chair in which her unwilling hostess was still confined. At the moment the arrogant intruder was explaining to Elaine in condescending English that the hypostator itself was a partial cause of the turmoil in the scene.

Elaine protested, and demanded explanations.

Morgan obliged. The exchanges of energy between the con-flicting domains of space and time became so intense that steam geysers or even volcanic eruptions threatened. Not only the lives of the small handful of people now watching from the laboratory were at risk; the danger extended over square miles of the sur-rounding countryside.

"We must all share some of the risks." Morgan smiled, and announced that she was determined to go to Vortigern's camp. "There is one there who must be saved, and if Merlin cannot or will not do so, I must. Then it should be possible to learn some-thing from the wretched boy regarding the whereabouts of Mer-lin's Bones."

One of Morgan's assistants excitedly called her attention to some new appearance in the holostage display. Elaine, gazing anxiously into the display, could not tell what the others thought so important.

Whatever it was, it suggested to Morgan and her people that the rescue was going to be impossible to accomplish. Some gigan-tic power, called Wodan by Morgan (who appeared to be awed in spite of herself), had at last taken the field against Merlin, and was determined that no rescue should be made.

"Should we change our plan, Highness?" asked one of Mor-gan's aides in a hushed voice. The question was spoken in the alien tongue that Elaine now so clearly understood.

Morgan answered in the same language: "Nevertheless I am going through."

Morgan explained to Elaine something about the Bones. The power inherent in such a magician's relics would probably be strong enough to do almost anything—short of forcing a passage for Arthur farther into the future. Help from the hypostator, or something like it, was needed to do that. Somewhere in the fu-ture, Morgan was confident, she could find some beneficent, healing power with the will and the ability to cure her fallen brother at last of his wound.

"To force one's way into the future, instead of waiting for it to arrive in the course of nature is not easy, child. But saving Arthur is all that counts. All! To save him I would burn the bones of a thousand old men who have already lived too long."

Morgan was now standing with one booted foot on the central dais, as if she were about to plunge into the holographic display that filled space only an arm's length in front of her. With the attitude of one making final preparations, she began examining the contents of a pouch at her waist.

Elaine impulsively cried out a warning. Physically entering the scene produced by the hypostator would almost certainly be deadly dangerous, futile as a means of transportation, and damaging to the machine as well.

Morgan ignored the warning totally. Arms half extended before her, as if to pounce and grasp, she seemed on the verge of leaping into the display.

Looking away, unable to force herself to watch what she supposed would be Morgan's self-destruction, Elaine noticed that on the nearby screens yet another verse had blinked into existence:

> *But in her web she still delights*
> *To weave the mirror's magic sights,*
> *For often thro' the silent nights*
> *A funeral, with plumes and lights*
> *And music, went to Camelot:*
> *Or when the moon was overhead,*
> *Came two young lovers lately wed;*
> *'I am half sick of shadows,' said*
> *The Lady of Shallot.*

And just as Elaine's eyes fell on that last word, it seemed that the holostage blew up. Her gaze averted, she did not see the violence caused by Morgan's leaping entrance into the display. But she could feel it.

In the turmoil resulting from the eruption of violence in Vortigern's camp, more debris came drifting, bouncing, clattering through into the lab. Meanwhile material from inside the lab, papers, odd pieces of equipment, was being torn loose, whirled into the vortex on the holostage.

In the next moment there came a rush of force, a roaring wind that grazed Elaine, as if great solid objects had almost crushed her, leaving her dazed momentarily. There was a violent reaction, a greater disturbance than before.

A moment later her head cleared, and she saw that Morgan had disappeared. Both men were looking into the display after their mistress, and for once even the great cat was distracted.

Elaine, nerves already tensed to the limit, acted on instinct, giving herself no more time to think. Catapulting herself out of her chair, she scrambled for the door leading out into the corridor. Her back muscles were tensed against the tearing strike of great feline claws, or some even more terrible impact that would strike her down. But no blow fell. Nothing stopped her as she cleared the laboratory door and ran for freedom.

She pounded down the darkened hall, then down the stairs, three or four steps at a time, in the back of her mind the giddy wish that she had taken more time from work for exercise. Her goal was not to get completely away from the building, not yet. What was going on now in the lab was obviously deadly dangerous, and it was also beyond her comprehension. Elaine had decided that it must be stopped. If she could only manage to shut off the power . . . on the ground floor was a room where effective action should be possible.

Amby

Hakon whispered to Vivian and me that it was as if we had sailed all the way to Iceland. Hot mud and steam came bubbling up out of the gurgling earth, even as the beams and planks and rubble of the new construction were sucked, drawn, down into the ground. At the center of the disturbance the once-solid earth was churning slowly, apparently completely liquefied.

Those workers who were within a few yards of the disturbance threw down their tools and fled. But some of the men standing even closer, partially stunned or injured by the first eruption, were too slow to get out of the way. While Vivian and Hakon and I watched, along with Vortigern and many of his advisers, we saw several people drawn into the vortex, at least one of the victims screaming horribly.

Guthorm was one of the men who was too slow.

Unexpectedly I caught another glimpse of the Lady of Jewels, standing in the background. She was dressed very much the same as in my earlier vision, and wearing the same jewels.

She was trying hard to communicate with me at this point. To get me apart from the others somehow, make me a promise that she would help me get away if I would help her.

I could hear only a few words of this, only enough to let me guess the overall meaning; Morgan was prevented from carrying her effort through.

Still Hakon, while well aware of the churning earth, seemed totally oblivious to the waves of occult force crashing like surf around us. How could any adult, any human, be so blind and deaf? I yelled at him that evil magic threatened us, and tried to help him get away. My comparatively feeble effort was enough to tip the balance and pull him back. Meanwhile the king and his druids had not been particular about displaying their valor, and precipitously retreated.

But soon the paroxysm ceased for the moment, and space and time seemed quiet once more. I walked slowly forward, my feet sinking into the soft, newly opened, and still slowly moving earth.

I was in fact the very first to approach the spot after the upheaval had subsided, for my companions and my enemies alike were stunned, and my visions led me there.

The churned and cratered area, which looked as if it were being stirred by giant invisible spoons, was now about thirty yards across, and still expanding slowly at the edges. At the rim of solid ground, clods of earth, as if hacked free by invisible spades, continued to slide forward and down, going beneath the churning mass of loose dirt and the objects it contained. Within the region of disturbance, which was centered on one of the great trilithons, no leaf, no worm or blade of grass, survived. Later, when I was once more able to survey the whole area of the monument, I could see that the disaster had followed a pattern. Where there had been a determined effort to incorporate the old blocks of bluestone and sarsen into the new construction the worst of these disturbances had burst forth.

While the massive construction of the ancients stubbornly remained in place—no doubt Vortigern's diggers and builders had made every effort to leave the ancient footings undisturbed—all of the surrounding land was once more breaking into turmoil. The erupting earth spewed out bits of ceramic tile, wood, and plaster—all more or less familiar materials. But quickly there followed stranger stuff, fragments of bright, strange metal, and other material less easily identifiable.

On impulse I bent, my knees swaying with the shaking of the earth, and picked up one of the little pieces of foreign matter. The unbroken sides and edges displayed a smoothness and precision that seemed at first glance magical, but actually were not.

Hakon, perhaps partly motivated by a warrior's determination not to be outdone by a mere child, moved forward to stand beside me. Vivian ran to us, tugging at us both to move us back out of the steaming earth, which was now showing signs of splitting open in a chasm.

This time neither Vortigern nor his counselors had approached the region of convulsing earth as closely as I and my two fellow prisoners had done. But the king and his entourage had been standing close enough to get a good look, and were now caught up in a very serious discussion. All agreed that the loss of more workers had to be considered a bad omen.

It was obvious from the angry voices of certain officers, from the protests they were now daring to speak openly, that there had been, and still was, great uneasiness in the army at Vortigern's persistence in these matters.

✍ Interlude ✍

At last the laboratory was quiet once more, and on the surface peaceful.

Morgan's two assistants were now the only people in the room, which was strewn with the debris of centuries past. Both men were once more concentrating intently upon the scene at ancient Stonehenge, at the moment seeking anxiously for some confirmation that their mistress had made the transition between worlds safely and successfully.

"Yes! She's there!" one jubilantly announced at last. "Still alive . . . unhurt, I think . . . she's trying to signal us, but I can't quite make it out . . ."

The hypostator was still faithfully producing a three-dimensional model on the stage. But only occasional glimpses of the model now came through, between long intervals of fog and turmoil. The duel between the dead/alive old wizard and the power called Wodan was creating interference, making observation almost impossible for Morgan's two men in the twenty-first-century laboratory.

Murmuring between themselves, the men agreed that it was lucky for them that Morgan had departed without realizing that Dr. Brusen as well as Fisher had escaped their supervision in the laboratory. Morgan cared little about where Fisher went, but the scientist was another matter.

"When she gets back, she'll have our heads." From the man's voice and expression, Elaine doubted that he was speaking metaphorically.

"Maybe by then we'll be able to recapture the runaway. She can't have got far without help."

"Let's send the cat out to bring the woman back."

"I don't know . . . all right, we'll try it." The animal was silently given orders and dispatched.

Then, joining his comrade at the display, one of Morgan's aides made a strong argument that Merlin would not have chosen such a place to hide his bones—or alternatively, that the mysterious Nimue would not have chosen such a place to immure the old man whose unwelcome attentions had gone from amusing her to boring her to provoking her serious hatred.

They could only hope that their Lady Morgan was going to survive the fight in Vortigern's camp, whether or not she was able to accomplish what she wanted there.

On the darkened ground floor of what had been the Antrobus mansion, Elaine, still gasping for breath after her desperate run, had taken temporary shelter behind a tall vending machine.

But after a moment's respite she was running again, heading for the power lines and generators. Panic struck when she heard the swift clatter of the great cat's claws upon the marble stairs. In desperation she opened the nearest door and jumped inside, realizing only after the door was shut again that she had entered a lightless maintenance closet.

Cowering in darkness, pulling steadily on the knob to keep the lockless door closed against a possible tug from outside, she did her best to think.

If only she could turn the power off the hypostator . . .

The power lines entered the building in the same room containing the emergency generators, on the ground floor, no more than some thirty strides away down the dark hallway, and around a corner—in a dark house populated with a giant cat and dangerous, possibly murderous, humans.

If only the cat wouldn't—but her heart sank as the sound of claws on a hard floor stopped just outside the closet, and there sounded a faint, ingratiating whine.

The only way to defend herself against the cat was to keep a closed door between herself and it. Trying to reach the power room would have to wait.

Time passed. It was too dark to see her watch. Why hadn't she bought one with a luminous dial? She hadn't heard the cat for a while, and if she could count slowly to a hundred before hearing it again, perhaps she ought to dare—

She had to act while Morgan and her people were distracted. If she moved boldly, she had a chance of being able to shut down the whole experiment. A sudden power loss might wreak havoc on her work, but probably nothing that couldn't be put right in a day or two . . .

Suddenly Elaine's thoughts were interrupted by the unexpected sound of the opening of one of the building's doors leading to the outside. This was followed by a murmur of new voices, and a faint draft of chill air, perceptible even in her closet.

Gloriously welcome! Somehow the police had been alerted . . . but the night's events thus far had taught Dr. Brusen caution. She was going to have to make very sure of these new arrivals before she ran to welcome them.

The door she had heard opening slammed shut again, and in half a minute the voices came closer, borne on careless feet that sounded as if they were shod in boots. Marching down the hallway, right past Elaine's closet.

Her spirits soared. She could hope that the police, in some form, had arrived, though as far as she knew they had not been summoned.

So far it was only a hope.

When the latest intruders had trooped past, she opened her closet door very carefully, just in time to catch a glimpse of four or five men and women, vague figures in the darkened hallway, their backs to her and walking away. Glints of metal on belts and shoulders suggested that some of them at least were bearing arms. None was uniformed, though.

There was no reason to think they were police.

SEVENTEEN

✑ Amby ✑

Even in the thick of the danger and excitement, I sensed that the late Horned One's surviving colleagues viewed me as potentially a very dangerous rival in their profession of prophecy and magic. In this they were of course absolutely correct. Their vision made them all the more determined to carry out their original plan of sacrifice; but Vortigern now forbade their doing so. He insisted that he must at least question me further before I could be killed, and that the final decision regarding my fate must still be his.

I caught a second glimpse of the Jeweled Lady, and then a third. Again she was standing cloaked and hooded among the onlookers, and invisible to them all—or at least unnoticed by anyone save me. Again, from a distance, she favored me with a wickedly amused smile. I thought that she was probably waiting for a chance to get close to me again.

I with my special vision could see, without understanding very much of what I saw, that a group of powerful wizards dwelling in the distant future were somehow focusing on Stonehenge, and were employing powers that to me seemed as magical as anything Old Merlin could accomplish.

I recoiled in horror from the vision of the mangled body parts, the bone chips and the blood, of the Stonehenge sacrifices arriving there in the future.

Boldly I repeated to the king my claim that I could at least explain his problem, if not solve it. The trouble was that other powerful people, whom I assumed must be magicians, and who were not of his time or place, were contesting with him and with each other for this territory, the keystone of an arch of mighty forces.

Solemnly I warned Vortigern that he had no chance of succeeding in his attempt to transform the Giants' Dance into a personal shrine or temple.

Before he could reply, the king was distracted by the arrival of a messenger. More reports were now coming in to Vortigern of an unfriendly army, thought to be Saxons, only a few miles away.

After a few moments of intense conversation, Vortigern dismissed the messenger and turned back to me, demanding that I explain to him exactly what my warning meant.

I told him that I saw great forces in violent opposition to one another, putting him in danger of being crushed between them. The symbols by which Old Merlin let me see them were a red dragon and a white, two powers contending in mortal combat, though there were really more than two components to the struggle.

Fortified by an essential faith in the truth of what my visions showed me, given confidence by my recent success in navigating, I dared once more to dispute, this time in deadly earnest, with the very druids who had advised Vortigern to seek me out.

In this place of great magic, the invisible hand that gripped me, representing my support from Merlin, did not fail. The truth, as seen and proclaimed by the greatest wizard in the world, overtook me and spoke through me. When Merlin's words rang from my lips I was no longer a child. What made the experience terrible was the fear that I was no longer anyone at all.

What I most emphasized in my speech was a warning that this digging, the willful continuation of Vortigern's construction project, would certainly provoke an even greater outburst of violence.

When I strove repeatedly for a clearer vision of the twentieth-century interference, what I saw still took the form of red dragon and white. Then the image was that of a subterranean spring, threatening to burst forth, to wash away the foundations of the great blocks of Stonehenge.

❧ Interlude ❧

Elaine, struggling not to make a sound, trying to control her own breathing, was listening intently, crouching in a painfully awkward position with her right ear against the inside of the door of the maintenance closet. She had firmly shut the door again after her single glimpse of the latest band of invaders. Whoever they might be, one look had been enough to dash her hopes that they were police.

There was one bright spot in her situation: at least the scratching sound of the great cat's claws had not returned, nor the querulous whining that issued from the animal's throat.

Unmeasured time dragged on. Very soon Elaine reached a point where she thought that confinement in this closet for another handful of seconds was going to drive her mad. Drawing a deep breath, she quietly, gradually, eased the door open yet again.

Still darkness and silence reigned in the big building. But no. When she listened carefully, there was some kind of noise, disturbance, maybe even violence—but far away, somewhere upstairs.

A moment later Elaine had left the closet, and was running with as light a step as possible down the dim corridor in the direction of the Security office. In a matter of seconds she had reached the door she wanted, gasping a whispered prayer that she would find it unlocked.

Her wish was granted. The lights in the windowless Security office came on automatically as she entered the room. Or maybe they were always on; she couldn't remember. Her gaze took in the wall clock, without really registering the fact that the time was now approaching midnight.

After making sure both doors leading into the room were locked from the inside—though her confidence in locks was much diminished, given the intruders' evident contempt for such devices—she grabbed up a Security phone and tried again to communicate with the outside world, hoping that this dedicated line might have escaped interdiction. She was chagrined but by no means surprised to find this instrument as useless as all the others.

Here inside the blessed sanctuary of Security, all was quiet. She could take comfort in the fact that none of her enemies seemed to be actively pursuing her. But a dark suspicion immediately formed that she was currently protected only by the fact that Morgan and her men, and their fanged beast, were very busy with matters they considered more important.

The building's surveillance television was controlled from here in Security; pressing switches at a console, Elaine was soon able to peer unnoticed into her own laboratory.

Her newest fears and suspicions were confirmed. The latest set of villains (certainly *not* police; their motley clothing and their very faces, Elaine thought, precluded that) were now in possession, while Morgan's people had disappeared.

Three men in nondescript modern street clothing, but with heavy pistols holstered at their belts, were in view on the screen. Two were sitting in chairs in front of keyboards and consoles, while one sat alone, farther back against a wall. The man in the chair nearest the center of the screen was the only one clearly visible just now. He looked about thirty, with an arresting face, fair hair and beard both with a tendency to curl, and pale haunted eyes.

With all the building's telephones seemingly inoperable, Elaine turned to one of the computer systems to try to reach someone outside the building.

Several minutes of effort along that line brought no success.

Exhausted, and with a perhaps illusory feeling of security in the quiet office, Elaine came near falling asleep in the comfortable chair, waiting for some kind of answer.

Then she jerked awake, to see the useless response on the screen:

A bow-shot from her bower-eaves,
He rode between the barley-sheaves,
The sun came dazzling thro' the leaves,
And flamed upon the brazen greaves
Of bold Sir Lancelot.

In Elaine's growing desperation she conceded to herself that the time might be fast approaching when she would want a physical weapon, could absolutely need one to defend her life.

To keep awake, she got to her feet and moved about, searching drawers and cabinets. In a lower drawer in the chief's commodious desk, she came upon a silvery automatic pistol.

✌ Amby ✌

As the strings and volumes of local spacetime rearranged themselves, gaining a new equilibrium, there was yet another episode of violence, crashing death, mass panic. All around us, diggers and priests and spear-carrying soldiers were running away. A large part of Vortigern's army seemed to be near rebellion or in flight.

The Jeweled Lady persisted in trying to confront me. Still I had not the least idea of her name, or of her true relationship to Arthur and to Merlin. She was trying to tell me her name now, and that she was very curious about me, and my role in this great enterprise of magic.

From the few garbled words I was able to understand, I got the impression that the Jeweled Lady wanted to take me away from this place and bring me to where her own power was strongest.

But then the lady and I were separated, by some unknown force, exerted by one of her rivals.

In terror I turned away from her and tried to run, but I could get nowhere because I promptly became lost in visions. I saw again the bloodied altar stone, fresh red flowing over the old, dark stains. The sharp flint knife.

I was also forced, by my own largely uncontrollable powers, to look beyond the curving wall of Time into the future, to see what sort of death this Vortigern was fated to suffer. Only the time of his death was withheld from me. I saw him burned alive in a wooden tower—much like the one his workmen were even now struggling to build as part of the defenses of his great stockade.

When I emerged from my seizure and told the king what my most recent visions were, he glared at me in murderous silence.

And Merlin's grip upon me made me say: "What I see is not a certainty, Your Majesty. It may come to pass, or it may not . . . but I think that it will come to pass."

Only much later did I learn that my prophecy had been fulfilled. The king's doom came upon him even before the end of the very day on which I had arrived at Stonehenge, and had foretold his end. Even as I had foreseen, Vortigern's enemies defeated him. The Saxons attacked and a portion of Vortigern's own army rebelled, and his dreams of glory were crushed and trampled into the dust.

But as swiftly as those events followed, they came too late to be of any benefit to Vivian and Hakon and myself. When Vortigern had heard my bitter prophecy, he became more amenable to the plans for more sacrifice put forward by his advisers. Hakon and Vivian and I were dragged away from the building site and thrown again into a stone-walled cell, until the proper time for the sacrifice should come.

Vortigern had allowed his instinctive willingness to listen to me and heed my warnings to be overcome by the angry insistence of his druids. My two companions had been stripped of everything that looked valuable, Hakon losing a couple of armbands and Vivian some of her clothing. But I had nothing that appeared worth stealing, and I still clutched to me Merlin's old cloak.

Vivian huddled in a corner of the cell, praying earnestly to her Christian god—this time penitently excluding other deities from her prayers. When she would have hugged me in fear and sympathy, I shook her off impatiently, and continued to sit with my eyes closed; I was concentrating intently upon the wordless instructions being provided in a series of images by the cloak.

A soft rain had begun to fall. The roof of our dismal prison was dripping, but our solid bodies could not pass out where water came in; the stout thorny timbers above barred us in as effectively as the stone walls on every side.

Vivian was weeping softly, but Hakon was determined to make one more fight for life. Vivian and I helped him get his hands free. As a Northman he held it vitally important that he should die fighting, and not as a passive victim.

Hakon began to try to dig his way out, using only his hands at first, then bits of chalky stone pried with his fingers out of the hard floor. Yielding to a sudden impulse, letting myself be driven by images proceeding from the cloak, I snatched up one of the chalk fragments and began to sketch the outline of a boat, almost full-sized, on the dark, damp stone wall. It was a small craft, a river-boat much like the one we had used to come up the Avon, which had carried us away from Merlin's Rock. But this river-boat, the one I was compelled to draw, mounted a small mast, and therefore would need a sail.

To make my vision clearer, I looked into my little mirror, which I had kept hidden in a pocket, and Merlin's face appeared briefly, giving me comfort and reassurance, followed by the plan I needed.

In obedience to this vision, I spread the cloak on the floor away from the place where Hakon had been digging and stretched out one hand to each of my companions. When they reached out uncertainly to take my hands, I pulled them both toward me, and crouched down, so that we were all three huddled together on Merlin's cloak. What was about to happen I did not know, but I could feel some tremendous transformation coming, the feeling of a great wind about to strike.

When we heard someone approaching the door of our cell, Hakon released my hand and quickly sat down in a corner of our cell, head hanging as if in defeat, his hands behind him as if they were still bound.

As soon as a guard came in, the Northman sprang up and seized a dagger from a sheath on the belt of the careless man.

Hakon now fought off guards while I finished the outline drawing of my boat.

* * *

As if to mock my efforts, a light wind indeed arose, a wet breeze that came in, first murmuring, then howling, through the chinks of the door, and the cracks in the walls . . . but now, where *were* the walls? Not where they were supposed to be, not nearly as solid as they had been.

The swelling breeze lifted the frayed edges of Merlin's cloak and sent little waves under and across its fabric. I could even feel the waves beneath me, though it was only a breeze . . . and then abruptly it turned to a strong, real wind.

The cloak slid from beneath us and leaped up to become a sail, attached to a suddenly real and solid mast. Somehow the packed earth of our cell's floor had turned to wood.

The pair of guards who a moment earlier had been at the door, taunting Hakon with his little blade and looking forward to some sport, had ceased laughing, and disappeared. Exactly what those watchers saw and felt I do not know, or what they reported to their masters, but in the sudden shrieking of Merlin's wind their laughter had turned abruptly to alarm.

The folds of what had been a threadbare cloak, now grown to the size and thickness of a small boat's sail, snapped in the wind from nowhere, whipping and driving the men before it, forcing them out of the way.

Out of our way. Our small boat pitched and tossed in waves.

The stone walls of the cell were receding, slowly at first, then faster and faster. The ceiling had already climbed far out of sight. A deeper darkness than before had been sucked in from somewhere to fill the empty space.

Both of my companions were murmuring and marveling. I continued to grip each of them by one hand, and by this means I brought them along with me.

For a timeless epoch we rode together, Vivian and Hakon and I, rocked and cradled safely in the cloak-boat, which by imperceptible degrees had turned into a real and solid vessel. The wooden sides of our magic craft had come to be painted red, but she was otherwise as dull looking and mundane as that of any fisherman. We were certainly out of doors, afloat in a real stream somewhere, though our surroundings were mostly hidden in the darkness of the night. My two companions eventually let go of my hands, and when the boat lurched as if we were capsizing, they clutched at the thwarts and mast and tiller that had suddenly come into being. We were riding smoothly, and in no danger of capsizing or sinking, but Hakon and Vivian were staring at me in intense silence, and I realized that both of them were violently afraid.

The world seemed cleansed, and drained of power, as if in the aftermath of a mighty thunderstorm. For the time being I could sense no hint of magic anywhere.

Less than an hour passed before our craft drifted to a halt, upon a muddy shore, on the verge of a salt marsh. I got out immediately and looked around. Most of the horizon was lost in clouds and dusk, whether of sunset or of early morning we could not at first be sure, but trees made a tall mass of shadow just inland. For the time being my visions had deserted me. Still I knew that I should go on with Hakon and Vivian for a time, at least long enough to make sure that they were going to reach some place of relative safety. When the time came, I would be told what Merlin wanted me to do next.

I had survived my encounter with Vortigern by virtue of a strength that ought not to have been accessible to me, that certainly did not belong to any ten-year-old—and yet it had become my own.

Certainly that saving power had come from the Old Man Under the Rock—and it was equally certain that a strong connection existed between Merlin and myself.

By whatever strange channel the power had come to me, I had learned that I was now on my way to becoming a great magician—not that I could have done the great feats involved in our escape without the help I had been granted through the Old Man's cloak.

But the knowledge of vast and ruthless power, the foretaste of still greater perils to be borne, and things to be accomplished, was bleak, bringing me no comfort. For that almost godlike power was mine and yet not mine, and I did not know which fate, losing it or being engulfed by it, was more to be dreaded.

When at last I had the perception that Time was once more settling safely into a steady channel, comfortable and dependable, I was relieved to revert temporarily to the status of a child, following what Vivian and Hakon wanted me to do. The cloak was currently providing me with a picture that I considered to be no help at all. It showed me myself handing the magical garment over to Vivian, then turning away from her and walking into a forest.

When I persisted in trying to extract more information from Merlin's gift, it began to give me worse than nothing, only frightening, terrible images. With a cry I crumpled up the useless cloth and hurled it from me, out of the boat.

Vivian screamed a protest. Hastily grabbing for the cloak, she succeeded in retrieving it. Then, handling the old fabric gingerly, she wrung out the water and tried to smooth the garment into shape.

All my visions, even those in Vivian's little mirror, had been taken away from me, for the time being at least. And I knew, with a certainty that I could not explain, that I was going to be separated, soon, and for a long time, from my companions.

There were no sounds of pursuit, no trace in the newly visible water or land or sky of the terrible turmoil and madness that had engulfed Vortigern's camp even as we were being swept away to safety. Moving slowly, we made a fireless camp right on the shore, and rested there.

There in the dark night, with Time again (but for what length of Time would sanity endure?) flowing quite naturally around us, I wept and was fearful, while Vivian held me and rocked me, as she would have comforted an infant.

EIGHTEEN

◌ Hakon ◌

I have long believed that a man can get used to anything that does not kill him. Toward the end of the fantastic boat ride that swept the three of us away from the camp of Vortigern, I was holding firm with all my determination to this belief, doing my best to accustom myself to living with an extravagance of magic. But in the long run—as you will see—my effort turned out to be about as successful as that of some dweller on the seashore who determines to set up housekeeping on a beach in heavy surf, or some mountain farmer who adopts a nonchalant attitude about riding the avalanche.

Well, perhaps I did a little better than either of those unfortunates. After our first hour afloat in the magic boat, I ceased to devote much energy to marveling at the miraculous way in which our rude prison cell had been dissolved, our torments relieved, our bodies transported safely, our captors utterly confounded. Nor did I spend much mental effort considering how our transportation to the peaceful seashore was being so effectively managed. But the strength of our salvific power was staggeringly impressive, and I was determined to make certain of the identity of the wizard—or god—who had provided young Amby with the wondrous cloak.

"An old man gave me the cloak." That was all the lad would say when I first questioned him on the subject. This was on the morning after our wonderful escape, when it became possible to see, in gloriously natural sunlight, how brightly painted red our little boat was, and how neatly it had come ashore on marsh grass, overlooking an ocean bay, with woods beginning just inland. It was a fine morning, one of those times when the mundane world is strong, and it is almost possible to believe that no such things as wizards and magic and human sacrifice exist.

Stubbornly I persisted with my questioning. "He's an old man, you say?"

"Yes."

"And also a great magician, obviously."

"Yes."

"And this is the famous Old Man in the Rocks, whose house we were trying to defend. And he is truly Merlin? King Arthur's Merlin?"

"Yes. He is." Amby was looking me straight in the eye.

"I've heard you both talking about Merlin, for several days"—I included Vivian in my gaze—"as if he were alive. But in all the stories I've ever heard, King Arthur's Merlin has been dead for years, or at least imprisoned in such a way that he can never get out."

It was the boy who answered: "King Vortigern was supposed to be dead, too."

I ignored the tone of insolence. "Well, considering the power of the magic that we have just seen, I am ready to be convinced. This old man—Merlin—is to be found somewhere down among the rocks below the oracle? About halfway between the upper and lower entrances of the cave?"

"Yes."

It seemed that Vivian's curiosity on the subject at least matched my own, which rather surprised me, since at that time I had no doubt that she was a priestess of the oracle and ought to know as much about it as anyone could know. When I hesitated, she took up the questioning.

"Amby, I want to know. Are you saying that Merlin is a living, breathing, solid old man with flesh and bones, who lives there in a secret room inside the cave?"

Amby shook his head. "There's no secret room down there. None big enough for a man to live in, anyway." Then he paused, seeming troubled, trying to find the proper explanation. "He's alive, all right, and there are bones." Another pause. "Maybe no flesh."

I took a turn again at asking questions. "You mean some kind of a walking skeleton, then? You've seen this monster?"

"No, not a monster. Not really a skeleton." The lad drew a deep breath. "I need a mirror to see him, and even then I can't see him very well. I think maybe his bones are all . . . I think they've been there for years, kind of mashed into the ground. As if a lot of heavy rocks had fallen on him."

Vivian made a sympathetic sound, of indrawn breath. "If all you can see are mashed-up bones," I persisted, "how do you know they are those of an old man?"

The boy shook his head again. "I don't see Merlin, or the bones, or anything in there, the way I see you. Only in visions. I see a face, with skin and hair and everything."

"Then how do you know that what you see is real?"

He looked back at me levelly. "My visions are the truest things I see. They got us away from that crazy Vortigern, didn't they?" He paused, letting the point sink in. "And there's another reason I'm sure about the bones being there: Because people keep talking to me about them."

I let that pass, for the time being. "But I still want to know: What makes you so positive, my lad, that this old man, this magician, is really King Arthur's Merlin?"

Amby only shrugged again. It seemed he had gone into the subject about as deeply as he cared to go. Vivian put a sheltering arm around him. "Let the boy alone," she told me, with the authority of a seeress in her voice.

"Very well." Whatever powers might be working through the lad, I had seen enough of what they could do to keep me from wanting to provoke their anger. Evidently the Old Man in the Rocks was thoroughly alive and active, in some sense. And whether he was really Merlin or someone—or something—else, I had no wish to make myself his enemy. But it occurred to me to wonder why this Old Man, whoever or whatever he might be, should have chosen a mere child as his medium, or apprentice.

Why should such a supreme wizard have wanted that brat, or any ten-year-old, to be his spokesman against the druids, when he might have picked an experienced warrior like myself? Or, if aptitude for magic was required, why had he not chosen Vivian, the pythoness (as at that time I believed her to be) and presumably a faithful servant of his own oracle?

But, as I have said, I had not much time to spare for marveling. Our escape had been accomplished, but, as usual, as soon as one serious problem had been solved we were faced by others, new questions that required practical answers.

We had been resting on the shore for no more than an hour when young Amby suddenly got to his feet and announced in a steady voice that the time had come for him to take leave of Vivian and me.

At that point, almost nothing could have surprised me, and I was not minded to argue the point with him. But Vivian was concerned. "Why do you say that you must leave us, Amby? Where are you going?"

The boy shrugged. He looked pale and ill used, somewhat bruised and tattered, as no doubt we all did after our narrow escape. But he had recovered from his spell of weeping.

He said: "I'll go where *he* wants me to go. It won't be very far from here, I think." And he looked doubtfully over his shoulder, into the green woods.

" 'He'?" Plainly the girl had not much more understanding than I did of what was going on. "Merlin is still communicating with you somehow?"

"Who else?" I interpolated, with a kind of sighing grunt. Both of my companions looked at me.

"Yes," said Amby. "Merlin, of course." I got the impression that his feelings, when he thought of that individual, were becoming those of a youth toward a respected but annoying parent.

"We wish you well," I told the lad, honestly enough. But I made no attempt to argue him out of going. Grateful as I was for the help that Merlin—or the power claiming Merlin's name—had provided through him, I preferred then—and still do—to conduct my life as much as possible well out of the heavy surf, not to say avalanche, of occult forces that seemed to accompany Amby wherever he might be.

"Thank you," he responded solemnly, and came over to shake my hand by way of parting. Then he and Vivian exchanged a final embrace.

"I am certainly going to see you again," I heard his small voice murmuring into her ear. "Old Merlin says so."

"When?" she asked him anxiously.

Amby shrugged, bit his lip, turned away, and started walking.

"Amby!" Vivian called after him. "You've left the magic cloak!" Uncertainly she held out the ragged cloth.

He turned to look back at us over his shoulder. His shrill voice piped: "The Old Man says you should keep it. I won't need it now, and it will guide you back."

"Wait!" It was my turn to call. "Back where? Are we to take the boat again?"

"I don't know. I can't tell, now. You'll see."

"You mean the cloak will guide us wherever we want to go?"

The lad did not answer that, but only waved once more, and a moment later had passed out of sight among the trees. Briefly I considered giving chase, insisting on a proper reply to my last question. But my memories of the powers by which the boy was defended were still vividly fresh. When things of magic are concerned, it is no shame in a warrior to be cautious.

When Amby's small figure had disappeared from view, Vivian and I looked at each other.

The girl spoke first. "Where do you want to go, Hakon?"

There rose up before me, unbidden but demanding, a vision of soft blue eyes and yellow hair.

"Why," I answered, "assuming that the magic of the Old Man—or whoever is really in charge of these miracles—allows us a choice, I would like to go back to the seat of your oracle, by all means." Jandree was there, whom I thought was already bound to me by some mystic bond of fate, and there was such of my treasure as might still be salvageable. And my shipmates, if any of them still survived.

I added: "And if the Time in which we move is going to continue to be as shapeless and changeable as water, flowing backward and forward like the tides, I would like to arrive as soon as possible after the hour at which we left."

Vivian nodded thoughtfully. "I too wish to return to Merlin's rocks," she remarked as she smoothed and folded the cloak, then opened it again and tried it round her own shoulders.

"I assumed you would." I paused. "You ought to know the truth about the oracle, Vivian, if anyone does. And I think that I have earned the right to know it, too. Does Arthur's Merlin really lie there? Or his bones at least? Dead, or under some great enchantment?"

She hesitated momentarily, then nodded.

"Dead or enchanted, which?"

"I don't know, Hakon. Enchanted, I think. Not a ghost."

"It seems very strange to me that you, a priestess of the oracle, should be so uncertain about the power you serve."

She only looked at me.

I shrugged. "However that may be, let us return there, as quickly as we can."

Given the magnificent authority with which our escape had been accomplished, and the disarray and destruction evident in the enemy camp on our departure, I was not really concerned about pursuit. But it seemed that an inventory of our assets was in order before we resumed our journey. Vivian and I possessed almost nothing but the tattered clothing we had worn coming out of our prison cell. We stood in drastic need of food and weapons.

When I remarked on this fact, the seeress made some effort to obtain these necessities by means of Merlin's gift, rubbing the cloak and chanting and muttering over it. At first nothing happened, but a change in tactics produced a better result. Vivian, with the cloak pulled tight around her shoulders, as Amby had been wont to wear it, murmured in a delighted voice that now she could see behind her closed lids a good supply of food and fire, furs and weapons.

I gestured fatalistically. "Lead on, then, seeress."

A slight frown creased her forehead. "Hakon, there are three men in the vision as well. They are standing amid all the things we need—but they look fierce."

"The world is full of fierce-looking men. Does that mean we should hide under a rock like worms? Lead on!"

It seemed that we were not to take the boat again, and though I would have preferred boating to hiking I had little choice. In any case there were now only two of us to paddle.

Vivian turned inland and set out walking, stopping every now and then to close her eyes and concentrate. I followed.

On an impulse I turned, having walked a hundred yards or so, and looked back, just in time to see our little magic boat putting out to sea of itself. A leafy branch had somehow been provided, the butt end stuck somehow into the bottom of the boat to serve as a crude sail—crude but adequate, when magic served as the real motive power anyway.

I called Vivian's attention to this sight, but she had no comment. What was one more wonder at this stage of our adventures?

Our magic piece of fabric guided us through the night-dark countryside, to a place where the smell of wood smoke indicated a sheltered fire somewhere not far away. Vivian walked in darkness, surefooted even with her eyes closed, whispering that Merlin's cloak allowed her to see the path ahead as clearly as if it were high noon, and indeed we passed through the forest almost without noise, I following her closely and sometimes allowing her to lead me by the hand.

Pressing on a little farther, we came in sight of tall trees whose branches were limned by the glow of a small fire underneath, the flames themselves being sheltered out of sight on the ground.

For the time being the cloak had ceased to give guidance. A careful, methodical reconnaissance soon discovered an encampment of three men, all armed and of warlike appearance.

One of them, the smallest and most active looking, was cooking something, or half burning it at least, producing an appetizing smell. Meanwhile the others were sitting nearby, arguing in low voices about something while they waited hungrily for the meal in prospect. For the moment all of them had forgotten to be alert. After stealthily working my way to within twenty yards of their fire, I had a chance to look at each of them and estimate their several capabilities in combat—always a tricky and uncertain undertaking. Also I took note of the disposition of weapons on their persons and around the camp.

The biggest of the three men, he who seemed to be the leader, was also the most talkative. He gestured frequently and forcefully, and his voice rumbled, though it never became loud enough for me to hear it clearly.

After studying this trio for a bit, seeing and hearing nothing to indicate that there might be a fourth or fifth roaming about in the darkness nearby, I came to the conclusion that they were almost certainly bandits, though, the world being what it is, that type is not always easy to distinguish from honorable men-at-arms. In this case I was soon aided in making the distinction by the fact that their argument flared louder, and we could hear that it was over the division of loot from some recent robbery.

The food these villains had begun to cook, meat roasting on a stick, and some kind of cakes baking on a flat rock, likely also stolen from their latest victims, smelt very good. I was reminded forcibly that although we had been well fed upon our arrival at Vortigern's camp, from then on, during the last day or so of our imprisonment, we had eaten poorly or not at all.

Withdrawing a few yards from our advanced observation post, my companion and I found a spot well out of the firelight in which to hold a whispered conference. Vivian told me that, with or without the cloak, she did not have confidence in her ability to gain for us by magic what we needed.

"The cloak?"

She tried once more, then shook her head. The visions provided by the magic garment had ceased, or were showing her nothing relevant to our immediate situation.

"Then we will acquire what we must have by other means," I whispered back.

"But there are three of them. And they are armed, and you are not!"

"Another inequality that must be rectified."

Magic having done all it could for us, the responsibility for further planning and action devolved on me. Strictly speaking, I cannot claim that the deed of valor that followed was a solo attack, for Vivian bravely played an important part. We hastily devised a plan in which she would distract our victims while I came at them from behind.

Vivian removed several of her garments—there were not many—then hesitated and pulled off the last stitch. She stood shivering for the minute I needed to get silently into position on the opposite side of the fire. My brave comrade then approached the small encampment, in the character of a helpless woman, clad in nothing more than her long, red-gold hair.

For the essential few seconds, the deception was a complete success. Speechless the men all got to their feet, all of them staring in the same direction. Vivian, wearing a tentative smile, gazed back.

At this moment I sprang over a fallen log, and into their midst from behind. My first two blows, one to the kidneys and one to the head of the bandit leader, were struck with a thick burning brand of wood, snatched from their campfire in the instant of my arrival, when all their backs were turned—there were no sizable pieces of firewood, or other weapons, immediately available outside the fire.

My second swing with the burning log put down the biggest of my opponents, with an explosion of sparks and ashes on his skull. Before his bewildered fellows could react to any purpose, I had armed myself with his blade.

Once I had a real weapon in my hands, the rest was comparatively easy, though by this time my enemies had grabbed up weapons, too. The task was made even less burdensome by the fact that my companion was not content with her diversionary role, but grabbed up an ax as it became available, and took an active part. In moments the last of the bandits had ceased to cry out.

After Vivian had regained her clothing and what she was able to recover of her modesty, and had helped me drag the bandits' bodies outside the circle of firelight, we ate the food they had been preparing for themselves. Some meat had fallen into the fire, but fortunately the fight was over before it had charred into inedibility.

Once we had the situation well in hand, Vivian attempted a healing spell on a finger I had blistered when snatching my first blazing weapon out of the fire. I thought perhaps her magic helped a little, but no more than that, and again my doubts grew stronger.

After letting go my hand, Vivian prayed over the fallen—invoking several gods this time—I suppose the situation seemed unchristian—and also recited certain spells, in case their spirits should be inclined to restlessness. Then the girl and I moved to set up our own camp half a mile away from theirs, just in case the bandit trio had been expecting any comrades to join them.

As we were moving on to establish our camp, Vivian as we journeyed kept turning her head over her shoulder to look back. When I told her, reassuringly, that the three men we had felled were not likely to have friends who would pursue us, she told me that she was not worried about that, but rather still concerned over what might have happened to Amby. But there was nothing to be done about the boy now, and my companion was sensible enough to realize the fact; as we hiked on she looked back less and less frequently.

Nor did she need any urging to maintain a good pace. She seemed as determined as I was to get back to Merlin's Rock as soon as possible, saying she wished to learn magic from the master there. Also I think it was because Amby had urged her to do so.

I too was eager to confront Merlin—if that was truly the Old Man's name—again, to see if he might be the worthy lord I wished for. If not, perhaps he could advise me where to find him. Also the truth was that I had nowhere else to go.

ᴇᴊ *Interlude* ᴇᴊ

Elaine had hoisted the weight of the automatic pistol out of the drawer and set it on the desk. In her eyes it was an awkward thing, ugly and dangerous, but perhaps it was essential. Now, racked by fear and tension even as she huddled in the Security supervisor's comfortable chair, she watched with horror on the small screen of the surveillance television as the blond-bearded man and his small gang of followers settled into their occupation of the lab. Apparently the latest set of intruders still had not noticed the unobtrusive little television cameras in the upper corners of the room they occupied, or perhaps they were so confident in their own powers that they felt they could afford to be indifferent.

Now that Elaine was looking at the screen more carefully, she could see, lying in a corner of her lab, a body she recognized as that of one of Morgan's people. The man—or the body—was quite motionless, in what looked like an extremely uncomfortable position, and the newest set of invaders was ignoring him completely; the conclusion was inescapable that he was dead. Presently Elaine made out that Morgan's other man was in the same condition, lying in such a position that his body was almost completely out of sight of either of the room's surveillance cameras. All the hidden observer could see of this second man was the toe of one of his black boots.

Mordred—yes, that was what his subordinates were calling him—Mordred himself, the blond-bearded one with haunted eyes, continued to occupy the central chair, while one or two of his aides stood stiffly at one side of the room, coming and going now and then on obscure errands. Another was gingerly fingering the controls of the hypostator, and Elaine had to repress an impulse to shout at the woman to stop.

These newest conquerors of the laboratory were not speaking to each other in English, nor even in the same nameless language that Morgan and her crew had used. The sound of this tongue was quite different, but Elaine found she could still understand it effortlessly.

Yet another of Mordred's aides, who usually sat against the

wall and only occasionally appeared on-screen, was a middle-sized blondish man missing one arm below the elbow. He appeared to be wearing one of the newer model artificial hands. Mordred called this man Thrain, and Thrain was wearing a holstered gun, on the same side of his body as his real hand, as well as a long, sheathed knife. The strangest thing about him, and he and his comrades all amazingly ignored the fact, was that Thrain was dripping blood, at a gradually slowing rate, from great furrows plowed, as if by savage claws, in his arms and torso. These had left his clothing shredded, too.

Every one of the little gang addressed their leader as Lord Mordred, sometimes as Majesty.

The hidden watcher shuddered.

Switching to a different camera, Elaine was shocked (even after seeing the two dead men) to discover that Morgan's great cat was now lying dead in the farthest corner of the room. The beast's head lay at an odd angle, as if some power that outclassed the beast in strength and ferocity had wrung its neck. The body showed stab wounds also.

Thrain had now gone back to sit motionless in his corner, still dripping blood on furniture and floor.

"Poor kitty." That was Mordred's remark, sounding like an idle comment. And for a moment he did look sad, turning his head to glance briefly at the slaughtered beast.

Next, Mordred was wondering aloud where Fisher was.

Elaine, reminded of her own attempts to communicate with her first strange visitor, turned her head to look about. She noted that the content of the computer screens nearby had changed. The latest lines of poetry had been replaced—thank God!—by a single word:

ELAINE?

Hastening to the keyboard, Elaine typed in a quick response: FISHER? WHERE ARE YOU?

YES, FISHER HERE. IN HIDING, LIKE YOU. LET ME HELP YOU. USE YOUR KEYBOARD. ITS EASIER TO KEEP PRIVATE.

On the surveillance screen Elaine could see that Mordred was now fiddling with a keyboard himself, but it was impossible to tell what he was doing. She thought desperately. How to make certain that it was really Fisher at the other end of her own communication?

In a moment she typed: WHEN YOU FIRST ARRIVED YOU TOLD ME SOMETHING ABOUT SOMEONE BEING SOMEWHERE AND I DIDN'T BELIEVE YOU. WHO? WHERE?

CONGRATULATIONS ON THINKING OF A GOOD TEST. THE ANSWERS ARE: KING ARTHUR, IN THE AMBULANCE.

Elaine let out held breath in a long sigh. ALL RIGHT. HELP ME, PLEASE, IF YOU CAN.

SOON. MEANWHILE, ANY QUESTIONS?

There were so many she didn't know where to start. WHY IS ARTHUR HERE?

WAITING.

FOR WHAT? WHY WAIT HERE?

FOR A CHANCE TO BE HEALED. ARTHUR IS NOT THE ONLY ONE IN NEED OF HEALING.

I DONT UNDERSTAND. THIS IS NOT A HOSPITAL.

IT MAY BE THE DOOR TO ONE. HOLD ON TO YOUR COURAGE, I WILL TRY TO HELP.

Elaine went back to the surveillance screen. She soon learned that Mordred and his people were perfectly well aware that Morgan had actually traveled through the holostage to Vortigern's camp. They were uncertain of what had happened to her after that, but Mordred thought it likely that she had gone on to some place called Logres (it sounded like *log-race*), where she could try to defend herself successfully in her own castle.

Fisher's image appeared on Mordred's screen.

Mordred was a commanding presence. Even protesting that he was not such a bad fellow after all, he frightened Fisher. Elaine, watching screen-on-screen, could tell.

Mordred: "I suspect that getting rid of you would cause me more problems than it solved."

Fisher's image on-screen bowed lightly.

"A question for you," Mordred offered. He rubbed both hands through his fine curling hair, like a man preparing for mental concentration. "What has happened to all the people who normally work here, in this building?"

"Queen Morgan seems to have disposed of them, in one way or another."

"Oh? My sources suggest that there might have been one left over. The lady who normally works in this room where I am now. An expert on the use of this machinery."

"I suppose Morgan might have disposed of one person too many."

"I suppose. Or it's possible that this young woman has got away somehow. She might be hiding out or trying to hide out somewhere in the building. You wouldn't know anything about that, would you, Fisher?"

"Possibly she has even got clean away."

"Unlikely." Mordred rubbed his head again. "Now I must decide how much time and energy to devote to searching for her. How much is she worth?"

Elaine, feeling temporarily unable to listen and watch any more, turned away.

Once more she gingerly picked up the pistol and examined it, careful to keep the muzzle pointed away from her. She noted what appeared to be an electronic sight. Wasn't there supposed to be some kind of safety catch or something, so the damned thing wouldn't go off accidentally? Actually there were a number of knobs and things protruding everywhere. Carefully she packed it into the personal pouch at her belt, then checked the surveillance screen. The conversation between Mordred and Fisher was over.

Elaine went to the keyboard to consult Fisher again. Fortunately her adviser was still in contact. He counseled her to look for a kind of miniature trigger on the side of the weapon. PULL IT BACK, AS YOU WOULD PULL THE TRIGGER BACK.

She did so. And typed in: ALL RIGHT, IVE DONE THAT. NOW YOU ARE READY TO FIRE.

Hastily she pushed the safety forward once again.

Now, she supposed, she was as ready as she was ever going to be. The keys in the Security rack were all neatly labeled. Selecting the one for the inside entrance to the power room, she made another dash, frightened but successful, down a dark corridor and into the humming generator room.

✒ Hakon ✒

I have said that I wasted little time in marveling at Merlin's magic; yet the power and skill exercised on my behalf had not failed to make a strong impression on me. The conviction began to grow upon me inescapably that fate, or some mighty god, or some such overriding power, intended that I should play a much more important part in the world than I had been able to do so far. I began to wonder whether even such devastating blows as the loss of my men, and of my boat, could be parts of a great plan, leading me to success and glory in the end.

As Vivian and I resumed our journey by mundane means, I came near apologizing for carrying her almost by force to Vortigern and thus putting her in danger, along with the boy she was concerned about; my pride kept me from doing that.

Certainly I was angry at Vortigern for his having cheated me, as I saw it, out of my promised reward. But there was nothing to be done about that now, and now I had good reason to think that king had paid for his misdeeds.

I wondered what we were going to find when we reached our destination. I was grateful to the Old Man of the Oracle for having arranged our escape with such magical success; still, I thought I was due the best help he could give, fitting compensation for my having risked my life and squandered the lives of my crew in attempting to defend his house and territory.

Despite my spoken wish that we might regain the cave within an hour of our departure, I had never seriously expected that to happen, nor doubted that some days would have passed at Merlin's Rock by the time we got back. Nor that we would find Comorre or at least a small garrison of his troops still in possession of the house and grounds. I also took it for granted that by this time they had probably nerved themselves to explore the cave.

Beyond that point my imagination was reluctant to proceed. The question that really nagged at me was: What had happened to Jandree? And to the treasure? But it was mainly the yellow hair and blue eyes of the high priest's wife (as I still believed her to be) that kept intruding themselves before me. Such visions undeniably possess a certain magic, one that has nothing to do with spells cast by old men buried under rocks.

Having experienced Old Merlin's power, exercised at a great distance and through a mere child as intermediary, I could well imagine that Bran, as the high priest of such an oracle, had at his call a formidable capacity with which to punish any intrusion on his domestic life. Yet of course these matters are rarely as simple as a man might think. Another vexing question naturally came up: Why had the fount of such great magic been forced to tolerate Comorre's invasion?

As Vivian and I traveled, my brain still reeled from an excess of magic. Naturally I was grateful to have survived, but I now found myself in a new situation, a man with neither followers nor any lord to whom I owed allegiance. Having lost my men and the *Short Serpent*, I was quite thoroughly cut off from my own land and people.

In this situation, I considered it was time for me to choose some god and offer him my fealty—at first the most likely candidate seemed to be Thor. In the past the sturdy Hammer-swinger had always seemed to me likely to be understanding of the difficulties a man got into by simply being a man.

But then I thought that perhaps I ought to consider bestowing my loyalty upon another god, since it seemed Thor had had nothing to do with my recent miraculous escape.

In temporal terms our journey from Vortigern's encampment back to Merlin's Rock soon became every bit as confusing as the earlier trip in the opposite direction. Subjectively it seemed to occupy about the same number of days, perhaps three or four. I cannot be more precise because, just as on our outward journey, counting days became meaningless when daylight and darkness followed each other in irregular alternation. As one in a high fever may lose track of time, so too the matter stood with us.

Having completed, with the cloak's guidance, a long overland portage between streams, we found the magic boat, tree-branch sail and all, awaiting us at the shore of the next stream we reached.

Whenever weariness or hunger signaled that some rough equivalent of another day's travel had been completed, we stopped and made camp—provided the opportunity, in the form of a stable landscape, presented itself. Building fires was possible, and sometimes we were able to gather food; whatever local material we captured in our hands became part of our travelers' time frame.

Vivian wondered aloud what happened to the ashes of the fires we left behind us.

I growled that we seemed to have more important things to worry about.

Now and again, as we traveled or rested, I began to tell Vivian (who I still believed to be a priestess, and not a mere erotic dancer—who had once apprenticed as a Christian holy woman!), of my lifelong conviction that I was destined for greatness. She agreed, and listened dutifully, but it was easy to see that her thoughts were often elsewhere.

At night, in close proximity beside our small fire, I certainly felt an urge to lie with Vivian. As I watched her move about, there came before my mind's eye the image of her unclothed, in those long seconds when she had startled and distracted the unfortunate bandits. The wrecking of the *Short Serpent* on Merlin's

Rock had been preceded by a long, cold voyage, in the course of which women had been notable only by their absence. Still I was somewhat concerned by my companion's presumed dedication as a priestess, perhaps as a holy virgin.

When I asked whether she had taken a vow to remain a virgin, she paused, then answered thoughtfully: "Once I did."

But after considering me a moment longer, she demurely amended that statement, saying that really the vow she had taken had not been final.

I had no doubt—have none now—that Vivian found me attractive. I was not boasting in those days when I said of women that they almost always did. But still, like many other females, she was of two minds. In Vivian's case these doubts took the form of more hesitation, of murmuring that such blanket matters would be certain to interfere with her magic. Magic was certainly important to her, and more often than not it seemed to be her chief concern.

"I think it is not your magic that guides us, but Merlin's."

In this matter she did not consult Merlin's cloak, but folded that enchanted garment and put it away from her.

Then, after giving me another long appraising look, she let me have my way, stretching herself out on the ground beside our fire, murmuring that she certainly wanted to keep peace between us.

I was not much interested in what arguments and reasonings the attractive young woman found convincing, so that they led her to the conclusion I desired. Nor was I much distracted, at the time, by the discovery that she seemed to be no virgin after all.

A minute later I found myself closing my eyes, imagining that the soft body moving and moaning so pleasantly beneath me was Jandree's.

NINETEEN

Our passion spent, Vivian and I fell asleep still locked in a close embrace. Hours later, we were simultaneously awakened beside the ashes of our fire by a small intruding sound, in fact the click of a wooden paddle against the side of a boat. Twice this noise came sharply through the mists of early morning, and was closely followed by a faint splash and a murmur of human voices. A small boat, an umiak containing several people, was approaching.

The leafy nest wherein we two were snuggled offered as much concealment as we were likely to obtain anywhere nearby. I raised my head and gripped my weapon but otherwise did not move, except to make sure, with a quick pressure of my hand, that my companion was also awake and silent. Vivian turned carefully to look in the direction I was staring. Quiet as the dead we lay, wrapped in our captured blankets, and presently were able to watch the passing of our earlier selves.

Vivian and I saw ourselves as two of the four people heading for the meeting with doomed Vortigern, and the other two were very familiar also. When we realized what we were seeing, we were too paralyzed with wonder to move or hide. But no one in the passing boat took notice of us. At one point Vivian drew breath loudly, as if she would have cried out to the apparition. And a moment later I found my voice and, perhaps foolishly, called out in a bold challenge. But for some reason neither our passing selves nor the versions of Amby and Guthorm with them could see us or hear us.

Frozen in shock, we lay contemplating the passage of that phantasmal party. As the boat moved on upstream and out of sight, and for some little time afterward, we remained in our leafy nest, watching and marveling.

"It was you, and I!"

"And the druid," she breathed. "And Amby."

And for hours after the boat had passed on, I knew fear for having seen dead Guthorm's ghost. And a deeper fear that I was going to see him again—but like most fears, that one has never been realized.

In a way I was more shaken by that vision than by any of the terrors and marvels we had encountered in the camp of Vortigern. Death and sacrifice were nothing new to me, but such an apparition was. There was my earlier self, confident that King Vortigern could be made to pay me gold for bringing him the magical boy. And confident that events lying ahead of him in Time were still to be decided; while I who watched knew better, or I thought I did.

One of the strangest sights a man can ever see is his own life-like image, not in a mirror.

Perturbed by the experience, Vivian and I arose and resumed our journey. We pressed on through several more days of travel, facing nothing worse than the usual routine discomforts of any long trip. Still our journeying was anything but tedious. We ate what we could gather, berries and fruit and sometimes mushrooms, in the summer and autumn sections of our route. We hurried without sleep through the wintry segments of our passage, resting as little as possible to keep from freezing.

One night, when I would have lain again with Vivian, she put me off, saying that now the cloak advised against it and was punishing her with horrible visions for having given in to me before. For the moment I was irritated. But in a few hours, as the prospect of once more seeing Jandree grew more immediate, Vivian's attraction was proportionally diminished.

At length my companion and I reached the sea again. By command of the visions Merlin's cloak provided, we beached our most recently acquired boat upon a narrow strand that looked familiar. The season was early spring.

What we saw gradually confirmed the extent of the marvel. As the cloud shapes and colors slowly altered, it seemed to me that I could remember the forms they were assuming; I was frightened (no warrior need be ashamed of fearing things of magic and of spirits) as I realized that this was the very same sunset whose fading embers had vaguely lighted our departure, now giving illumination for our return.

Then my spirits bounded up. If Merlin's magic, by some incomprehensible spinning back of the days and hours, had indeed brought us back on the very night of our departure, then the chance was greatly increased that my treasure was safe, and that Jandree—and the others who had been with her—were still undiscovered in the cave.

My excitement grew. Still following the cloak's magical guidance, Vivian and I put out a little before sunset, to paddle along the shore, in a borrowed boat even smaller than the one we'd ridden on the way out. After about an hour of riding the currents through gentle surf the two of us found ourselves, our clothes ragged and worn from journeying and struggle, our bellies once more empty, back at Merlin's Rock. We paddled through the low entry and into the watery cave only an hour, or even less, after our departure. The tide had not yet come in enough to fill the passage, which was hard to see from more than a few yards off, particularly at night.

Immediately on our entrance we were challenged by Flagondry, taking a turn as sentry. As we pulled in he gaped in astonishment, a reaction followed in a moment by disappointment.

Moments after we stepped ashore, the others we had left behind came crowding out of their hidey-holes to greet us. I saw the silent figure of Jandree, waiting with a blanket round her shoulders. Somehow she looked heavier and not quite as alluring as I remembered her.

"Were you spotted, getting away?" she demanded. "Is that why you came back?"

Bran, his face taut with worry, had come out of a dark stony recess to question us. "How is it you return in a different boat? And what happened to Amby and Guthorm, and the men in the other boat who went with you?"

Vivian and I looked at each other, then began to give two different explanations, then put them off until later.

The questioners were distracted by Vivian's letting out a little shriek. Merlin's cloak at this point seemed to move upon her shoulders, and then turned into a garland of flowers. I looked at the blooms closely, as did Vivian, but they seemed only natural leaves and petals, emptied of all magic.

Everything we found inside the cave confirmed the fact that we were returning to Merlin's Rock only an hour or so after we'd left. A candle, which, as I remembered now, had been burning on a natural table in the cave, was still not consumed.

Atop the highest layer of the rocks in which Old Merlin's bones supposedly lay buried, the large fires that had lighted our leave-taking were still alight, making a good beacon out to sea. As we had approached the lower entrance of the cave, we had heard from atop the high cliff the same sounds of drunken celebration that had accompanied our departure.

At the time of our departure it had crossed my mind that the conqueror might be intending to burn down the house. But now, looking at the scene with a different perspective as it were, I thought that was not so, the fires were only by nature of a celebration. Or perhaps Comorre and his magicians had a better idea than I realized of what marvels lay below them, and the blazes were only watch fires, meant to keep the Old Man in his cave and his darkness at arm's length.

More excitingly, as we soon discovered, Comorre had not yet searched the deepest recesses of the cave, he and his men being still engaged in examining the wonderful things to be discovered in and about the house. As we were soon to learn, it was the library that especially engaged the Cursed One's attention.

Later, also, one of our people who had overheard certain talk among Comorre's men told me that a rumor had spread among them that there were ravishable virgins, servants of the oracle, hiding in terror in the buildings.

Bran and Jandree, and Maud and Flagon-dry, had scarcely had time to grow bored with the confinement of their deep isolated hiding places. In our absence, so brief by their reckoning, they had been clinging to the forlorn hope that they had been forgotten by the Cursed One, or would not be noticed or discovered before Comorre and his troops moved on. And my hasty inspection confirmed that the sacks of gold and silver still lay packed in the deep hole, covered with small rocks, where my men had left them.

Comorre's men, disappointed in their expectation of numerous dedicated virgins to ravish inside the buildings of the oracle, had decided to wait until morning to search the cave, where they assumed their quarry must be hiding.

Whatever we were going to do, it would not be another escape by sea. The boat in which Vivian and I had returned was too small to hold more than two or three people, and now no other was available.

Bran was doing his best to devise some other plan, but it seemed to me that all our hopes depended on the Old Man. And I had made up my mind to confront him—or his ghost, if that proved necessary.

Freely I confess that now, when the opportunity of doing so at last lay within my grasp, I felt a certain reluctance to approach the Old Man who, in some mysterious way, dwelt under the rock, here at this isolated meeting place of land and sea and sky. Still, I felt that I ought to give him thanks, at least. And once I had properly expressed my gratitude, I was determined to do my best to find out certain things that I thought he alone could tell me.

* * *

Vivian did not offer to come with me to see Merlin, and I thought this an odd attitude for the seeress to adopt.

Presently I took a supply of candles and found my way halfway up the passage leading to the surface, and into the side passage where Amby had darted away.

Yesterday, by local reckoning—what an incomprehensibly long time ago that seemed!—I had made an estimate of the size of the passage when Amby had darted into it, and had promptly concluded that it would be a waste of time to send a grown man in pursuit. But now, on actually making the attempt myself, candle in hand, I was somehow able to slide much farther in than I had expected. It was as if in some eerie way the rocks were quietly accommodating themselves to my greater bulk.

I supposed, even while doing my best not to dwell on the matter, that great magic must now lie coiled about me, thick as smoke, but I have never had much sensitivity to such matters, a lack that is sometimes an advantage but more often not. Unless the power were to manifest itself openly, I knew I would not be consciously aware that it was there.

When I had found the narrow way, and had advanced as far as I could along it without doing serious damage to my clothes and skin, I stopped.

After listening in silence for a few moments to my own breath, and my own heart, I said in a soft voice: "Old Man, I am Hakon, and I have come to thank you. If you are really there . . . are you there?"

For a moment I felt foolish, whispering words aloud to rocks. But for a moment only, and then the sense of foolishness was replaced by awe and fear.

Amby had told me that he needed a mirror to see Merlin, but I had no particular wish to behold the speaking Bones. In fact, I realized that my eyes were closed. Still I began to form a mental image of the face behind the voice that spoke to me. It was an old man's face, and stern, but not horrible.

I know who you are. I am here. The reply came in the form of a grating whisper, and I had the impression that it reached my ears through the hard rock itself, and not the air of the narrow passage.

I am here, warrior, the voiceless utterance repeated. *What do you want of me?*

"First I want to thank you for my life. In Vortigern's camp they were ready to kill all three of us."

Your gratitude is accepted. What else? As the conversation went on, I realized that the words were not coming to me through my ears at all. Not traversing either rock or air, but simply growing in my mind. And their tone, which was conveyed as plainly as if I heard them normally, was harsh and abrupt.

It had been in the back of my mind that at some point in this meeting with Merlin, honor and self-interest could require me to haggle over payment for services I had already rendered, and for my shipmates' lives lost in the process. But now, deep underground and surrounded by silence and magic—caught up in a flow of time, that of the rocks themselves, so endless that it seemed there was no time at all—now such bargaining seemed churlish. Even enmity or friendship would have to wait. Greater and more fundamental questions had first to be settled.

"I wish to know whether you are really Merlin," I demanded boldly, and in a somewhat louder voice.

I am he. What else do you want?

I had the impression that Merlin was coldly furious with me, and I could think of no reason why this should be so. "If I have done or said anything to offend you, Lord Merlin, I am sorry. If I could relieve you of your imprisonment, I would do so."

That cannot be done.

"I am sorry." Then on an impulse I told him: "Lord Merlin, in the camp of King Vortigern the three of us encountered strange people, powerful magicians."

I know that.

"These powerful magicians came, I think, from some other, distant world. I heard them talking to the boy Amby. And they said they were seeking . . . your bones."

I had the impression that this news came as no surprise. *They must not be allowed to get them. The villains must be driven forth.* Pause. *Has Amby told you that I plan to rebuild Camelot?*

This was a great surprise. "No."

Have you seen the library?

"Yes, lord. The book-room in your house here. But it did not mean much to me, because I can read only a few words."

It is also a window to other places. And as such it must be guarded.

"I will do what I can, sir, at your command. You know I am not skilled in magic."

At that there was a pause in our conversation, lasting long enough for me to draw half a dozen breaths. The rocks were so quiet around me that I could easily hear my own unforced breathing. No other set of lungs was active. Somewhere in the distance, water dripped, a hollow, plopping sound.

Have you any other reason, besides gratitude, to come pushing in here, now, today, inside my walls of stone? the sharp voice probed at last.

"I seek some worthy lord—a king, a queen, a god—whom I may honorably serve. If I could see you, great wizard, Merlin, face-to-face, then I . . ."

Do not expect to see me so. It may not be. The anger—I was sure now that it was anger, and directed at me—was not abating. But grudgingly it was being mastered.

To my mind came an image, sudden and unbidden, of dry bones, a human skeleton, being slowly crushed to powder beneath great rocks. In the background somewhere sounded a woman's voice, and I thought that she was laughing. When I have such visions, I know they are the result only of imagination, not of magic, and I did my best to put this one from me.

"If your King Arthur still lived," I said on sudden impulse, "I would be glad to offer fealty to him."

Arthur is gone, Merlin responded slowly, flatly.

After those words, a silence once more began to stretch between us, and I thought desperately of what to say next. At last I drew a breath and hazarded: "If all the stories describing how well and nobly King Arthur ruled were true—no, I suppose if only half of them were more than mere tales and moonshine—then I would be honored to sit at his Round Table."

There was another pause, seeming much longer than before,

and I thought a faint breeze came whispering through the enclosed passage.

But Merlin's voice still came to me as if it were being squeezed out of rock. Again I thought his anger was less apparent, though we were very far from cordiality. *You would be honored more than you imagine, pirate. You do not comprehend the magnitude of what you speak about so lightly. Still, in my own name I accept your offer of service. It may be that you will yet earn the right to sit at the Round Table.*

"I thank you, sir. I am ready to be tested, to earn the right, as you put it."

No reply.

"Sir, you say King Arthur is gone. But is he really still alive, somewhere?"

Do not waste time worrying and wondering about one who is gone. If Camelot is to be rebuilt, there are practical matters requiring your attention.

That was fine with me; what I wanted was a practical job, clearly defined tasks suitable for a fighting man, and though I said no more upon the subject at the time, I fully expected the powerful lord wizard in whose service I was now enrolled to reward me handsomely for all that I accomplished.

Merlin, evidently satisfied that I was now properly engaged in his service, wasted no time explaining to me my first assignment: *There are certain things in the house that must be protected from such lackwit villains as Comorre and his men. The Round Table is in the house. And the library—whether that room means anything to you or not, it must be defended. So far the vital things are safe—but that may change.*

"Arthur's Round Table," I whispered, marveling.

You have seen it, in the dark hall.

"That one. Yes, I saw it." But I scarcely remembered what it looked like. "But it was . . . it looked like just a table. Big, but otherwise like any other." I paused. "Some of the chairs were covered with a cloth."

Not like any other. And one of its chairs is not here—that is the Siege Perilous.

"Forgive my ignorance, Lord Merlin, but what might that be?"

A seat wherein only a pure and perfect knight may rest, else great harm may result. Merlin paused, and then went on. *Harm to the whole realm. I suppose the Siege Perilous was a mistake . . . sometimes great works of magic once accomplished are impossible to change.*

"Like those spells that keep you imprisoned, sir, here in the rocks." In my heart I was not ready to believe that anything was really impossible.

Merlin was evidently not of a mind to discuss his personal situation. *First, the vital things in the house, the Table and its chairs, and my library, are to be protected. Then Comorre and his rabble must be driven off, and without any further waste of time.* Old Merlin spoke with a calm determination that struck a responsive chord in my own heart.

He spoke of the feat of driving off an army as if it were an easy thing, and I wondered, if it were so, why Comorre and his rabble had been allowed to kill my men and invade the manor in the first place. But for the moment I raised no objection. One point in our favor occurred to me: Comorre was still in his first flush of triumphant occupation. "As long as he is certain he has won, it may well be possible for us to catch him off guard."

Excellent! To earn a place at the Table, a warrior must be capable of making aggressive plans.

"But, Lord Merlin, if I am to drive out a whole army," I pointed out, "I will need a substantial number of men to lead. If I had even a hundred Northmen, half of Comorre's strength, I could undertake the job with confidence."

Just over my head a rock cracked, as if it had been broken by some giant's hammer, making me flinch involuntarily. Merlin's anger surged again.

Curse your timidity! You will not have a hundred Norsemen! Or even ten. And even as Merlin finished speaking, crack! went the nearby rocks again, as if two loose boulders had been hurled together, or the whole pile were about to come down upon my head.

But my face was burning with the accusation of timidity, and this time I refused to flinch. "What force am I to lead, then?" I demanded, in a voice turned disrespectful.

Merlin would not respond directly to that question, only telling me that there was someone else I had better meet before we attempted any action.

"Who is it, my lord?"

But Merlin only informed me of where and when I might expect to encounter this newcomer, who would soon arrive at the manor. He did not try to tell me whom I should expect. I can see now that this reticence was a good idea. Even though I had begun to accustom myself to marvels, and had pledged my loyalty, had the Old Man given me that information I would never have believed him.

TWENTY

D awn, on the morning following our return to Merlin's Rock, found me wide awake after only a few hours' sleep and out again in the open air. None of the enemy was on hand when I emerged from the upper entrance to the cave, and I cautiously made my way to a pile of rocks just a few paces distant, from which modest elevation I could look down at the house, a long stone's throw away. Whether it was sheer chance that caused me to choose this spot, or whether I was led to it by some subtle influence, I was in an excellent position to witness the arrival of the very individual Merlin had told me to expect.

It was a lean and dark and twisted figure that came limping boldly and energetically through the gateway and set about the task of begging alms from some unlikely donors. With the house now in Comorre's control, this portal had been left standing open as confidently—or perhaps as foolishly—as by the mysterious earlier proprietors. An angled surface of the oaken gate's bronze sheathing caught the rays of the newly risen sun and hurled them glinting up toward me.

Logically I had no way of being sure that this perhaps demented stranger was the person I had been told to expect, and yet, somehow, I knew. My eye was drawn back again and again to this impudent suppliant, who boldly accosted soldiers and hangers-on alike as he moved among them, leaning on a wooden staff and holding out a mendicant's frayed cap. Whether he actually received any contribution from our enemies I could not tell. The thin and crooked figure walked slowly around the house, and seemingly even dared to go inside, disappearing for a time from my view, only to reappear among the rocks halfway up the hill, much closer to me.

A small sound behind me caused me to spin around, hand on hilt; it was only Vivian, who had also come up out of the cave. She joined me in silence, and we stood together, looking cautiously over the rocks toward the house.

Meanwhile, several of Comorre's soldiers, either feeling sadistic or simply playful, had tried to delay the beggar's progress by making sport of him, but we could see that something had happened to change their minds. Exactly what had happened was not clear. Watching, I had the feeling that as soon as the mendicant's figure disappeared from their sight, they promptly forgot that they had ever seen him in their midst.

After he had gone around the house, with a general air of one casually looking a situation over, his course was generally toward us. When he moved among some of the soldiers, it seemed that they stepped out of his way without looking at him, or being consciously aware that he was there.

The misshapen beggar looked our way once, and I would have withdrawn to the cave, but Vivian's hand on my arm held me in place. As she watched the approaching man, her face took on a peculiar expression.

As he advanced, leaning on his staff, he glanced again in our direction, and I thought he smiled. Without pausing he came limping on to meet Vivian and myself, and while still some twenty yards away indicated with a forceful gesture that we should move back to the upper entrance of the cave.

I started to challenge this strange arrival, but before the words had left my mouth the figure altered drastically before my eyes. Beside me I heard Vivian's soft gasp of surprise.

How much of the disguise was magical, and how much of it achieved by mere mundane cleverness, was not immediately apparent, at least to me. But with the likeness of a repulsive, probably leprous beggar stripped away, this newcomer appeared as a blue-eyed beardless youth, of average height and strongly built, who rested his large left hand, one finger bearing a golden ring, in an intimate and companionable way on the rocks a hundred feet or so above the place where the Old Man was encapsulated. There were familiar things about this youth, a way of moving, a look about the eyes, which I could not immediately identify, and then the strange truth dawned on me.

His eyes locked with Vivian's, and it was soon evident that neither of the two was readily able to look away from the other.

"Do you know me, Vivian?" The youth—for such he was, still beardless—had a deep voice. He was standing straight now, and pushed back a hood to reveal a pallid face, not quite handsome. None of its features was truly irregular, but the whole was rather out of the ordinary. His countenance was certainly not that of a warrior or peasant, but rather of one who might be priest or scholar, living much sheltered from the sun. Dark thick hair grew in a slight curl over the middle of his forehead.

When she did not answer, the stranger took hold of a thong that looped around his neck inside his robe and pulled up the small object that hung on it. His amulet was a small cross, of horn or darkened ivory, and it seemed to me that I had seen it somewhere before.

The girl's eyes widened, and for a moment she could not say what she was thinking. But then it burst out: "*Amby?*"

He nodded soberly. "That's what you used to call me. No one has called me by that name for years, but you can still do so, if you like."

I, with Merlin's enigmatic warning fresh in my mind, was perhaps not as surprised as Vivian. She was amazed to the point of incoherence, and needed a full minute at least to convince herself that a close connection existed between the ten-year-old she'd parted from such a short time ago—only a day, by our reckoning—and this young man of her own age.

In her astonishment Vivian forgot to try to make any impression at all. "But—but—but you—but how . . . ?"

"I can't explain, really. I can't begin to explain." The pale youth sat down with her and, after an almost imperceptible hesitation, took up and held her sunburnt, roughened hand. Again I noted a gold ring on the little finger of his large, pale hand. "I've lived through five years since I saw you last."

I was more quickly convinced than Vivian was that this was Amby five years later. I had more experience of the world than she, though less of magic, and I was readier than she to believe that someone I had known could be so thoroughly transformed.

To make sure I had as firm a grasp on the facts as possible, I asked the newcomer: "Is this what you really look like?"

No doubt, since we had just witnessed one transformation, that question might have been interpreted in more ways than one. But the youth grasped my meaning at once, and seemed grateful for my understanding. "Yes, this is what I really look like now. Only a few days ago—measuring by your time—I was really a small boy."

"And by what name," I asked, "should we call you now?"

Before he could reply, Vivian in her flustered state interrupted to ask: "Where have you been?"

That seemed to be a hard one to answer. After struggling with it for a few moments, the young man said: "For the most part, I have been not far from the time and place where I said good-bye to you and Hakon. I seem to remember telling you that things would work out that way."

Once more the girl seemed speechless, and the questioning was up to me. "You mean that since we parted, you've been living . . . in the time of Vortigern?"

"Yes . . . in or near that time for most of my five years. If you understand me, Hakon."

"I don't know if I do, but I'm making an effort. What have you been doing there?"

"Chiefly learning. There is so very much to learn. . . ." Quickly tired of looking at me, he turned to our companion. "Oh, Viv, the world is so much greater than any of us ever knew! Greater than any of us could ever begin to imagine, when we were roaming the land with Bran, singing songs and doing tricks!"

On hearing this, I frowned at them both, but for the moment neither of the young people was paying any attention to me.

Vivian was still marveling. "You've . . . changed so much!"

He shrugged helplessly.

But I was ready to believe. "What would you expect," I asked, "if the lad is five years older?"

At this point Bran and Flagon-dry came up out of the cave to join our little gathering. Both men needed a little time to recognize the newcomer.

"Amby's back!" Vivian rejoiced at them.

And both were totally bewildered to be told that this stalwart youth who had come down into the cave with us was Amby.

Amby promised confidently that he would see what the Old Man had to say on the matter of dealing with Comorre, and what plans if any he had for the survivors in the cave. And then Amby took leave of us for a time, saying it was necessary for him to have his own private conference with Merlin.

I said I would come with him part of the way at least. As we descended the now-familiar path, I told him of my arrangement with Merlin. Amby seemed not that much surprised. He cautiously expressed approval, as if some responsibility in the matter lay with him.

In his turn, he talked hesitantly of Vivian, and of other matters. He asked me hesitantly if anything important had happened to Vivian and me on our return to Merlin's Rock from Stonehenge.

"We managed to keep ourselves alive, though facing several dangers. That was an achievement of some importance. Thank you for the cloak, by the way. It was a considerable help."

He made a gesture brushing this aside. "Thank the Old Man."

"I have done so. But I think he has no love for me."

The youth blinked at me, and offered no comment. We parted at the branching of the ways, and Amby, looking determined, turned down the small passage leading to the Old Man. In the dim greenish light it seemed to me that the rocks parted slightly to let him slide between them.

When he was out of sight, I went on down to the bottom of the cave, to wait for orders. Every time I saw Bran's wife I wanted to see her again. And this time I had hopes of being able to see her without her husband being present.

I was pleased to find Jandree alone. She greeted me with her usual calm friendliness and assured me that she was well—and so were her husband and her infant. By their measurement of time, Vivian and Amby and I had been absent from the rock only a short time, hardly long enough for the people left behind to begin to deplete the few stores they'd taken into their hideaway.

"There is that between us, Lady Jandree, of which we have not yet spoken."

She blushed and drew her eyes away, but could not deny what I had said, and would not pretend she did not know my meaning. Soon her eyes came back to mine.

"I am a married woman, Hakon. With a small child who must be cared for." She jiggled the baby at her breast, calling my attention to its presence. Then she added defiantly: "My husband is a good man, and I love him."

"I know that all these things are true, my lady. But when I look at you they make no difference. When you look at me, as you did just now, I forget about them entirely." As I spoke the words, I found myself believing them.

"I forget all those things, too," she whispered.

In another moment I would have taken her in my arms, but already I could hear her husband and others coming back.

"We did get away," I informed Bran's people as they gathered round, asking for an explanation of what seemed to them our aborted expedition to the camp of Vortigern. "Now we've come back."

Obviously Bran and Jandree did not understand, but at the moment I did not feel like attempting an explanation.

They asked what had happened to the Horned One.

"I can guarantee—if anything can be guaranteed in this morass of magic—that the druid's not coming back."

"And Amby? This young man who just arrived is really the same as—as—"

"He is indeed. Right now he's conferring with the Old Man in among the rocks. If you want more of an explanation, ask one of them. I can't give one."

Bran looked at me and shook his head and sighed. "Wherever you and Vivian were, I don't suppose you were able to bring back a usable boat?"

"If what Old Merlin down in the rocks tells me is true—and I'm inclined to believe him—we'll have no need of boats."

Amby's private conference with the Old Man lasted for what seemed to me an ominously long time. He came back to us pale but determined, with the outline of a plan, and a confident attitude about being able to get rid of Comorre. He wanted to talk to all of us, to Bran especially.

Presently we were joined by Flagon-dry, who had not yet seen nearly as much magic as I had—and who, as far as I knew, had never tried to squeeze his bulk into the narrow passage leading to Merlin's Bones. Flagon-dry had therefore started to develop a theory that the one who appeared to us as the Old Man—whether the genuine Merlin or an impostor—was indeed hidden in among the rocks, but that he was still very much in the flesh, cunningly concealed, by magic or simply by some physical trick, in some inner portion of the underground labyrinth.

Amby with an air of calm confidence announced to our small assembly that we were now going to drive Comorre's army out of the manor and its grounds. Getting rid of them was necessary, to protect Arthur's Round Table and Merlin's library, both of which were in the house.

All of us of course were pleased at the idea of driving Comorre and his army from the stronghold. Our trouble was in believing that we could do so. Of course I had no fighting men left with which to attempt such a cleansing. I thought that if I could manage to come to grips with Comorre, man to man, I could soon settle the matter one way or another, but that was an unlikely possibility to say the least.

Still, orders were orders, and fundamentally I trusted Merlin. I discarded the inferior sword and knife I had captured in the bandits' camp—the blade of the knife was starting to loosen in the handle, and both blades were already badly nicked—and went searching among the collection of available weapons, picking out the armament I wanted. There was an excellent selection. As I moved about I could feel the growth within me of a great sullen rage, directed at Comorre and his troops. And in my mind's eye I could see Ivald, and other berserks I had seen in the Northland. What I saw did not add to the rage I felt, but rather helped me to contain it.

I had sincerely accepted Old Merlin as my liege lord, but in my own mind and heart, though I did not realize it at the time, I was still searching for something more—a god. Something in me clung stubbornly to the idea that gods ought to be more reliable and not simply more powerful than men. I wanted one who would serve me as well as I was willing to serve him. My objective was to choose a god for his utility, as I chose a weapon.

If Wodan wished to claim me as a worshiper . . .

Such a claiming, such acceptance, would of course be a magnificent honor, one for which many warriors, in the North and elsewhere, would be ready to kill—or die. That offer was not made to everyone.

Men often talked loosely about berserkers. When a duel or a battle was in prospect, some men acted a good show, grimacing, gnashing their teeth and groaning like animals, trying to terrify their opponents into flight or helplessness. But despite that, the true berserk madness was not often seen.

By all the gods, one thing I could be sure of was that Ivald had not been acting when he took part in the fight along the wall.

In imagination I found myself dreaming—folk looking at me do not often take me for a dreamer, but the tendency is there—dreaming of bards someday composing sagas detailing the exploits of Hakon the Proud. The Brave.

Hakon the Berserk? Almost silently, I mouthed the words. Like glamorous women of ill repute, that phrase carried a dark attraction, and at the same time the certainty of unhappiness to come.

Meanwhile Bran, who still had had no intimate contact with the Old Man, was going on making independent plans, as if the welfare of his followers still depended on him. He was making his plans aloud—fortunately or not, that was a habit to which he was addicted, as if it was only natural that people not obviously attached to any other service, and not far above his station in life, were going to accept his leadership.

He also asked my advice, as if he considered me an expert on the subject, about the best way to get his small family to a place of safety.

I wondered how much Bran suspected of what I felt when I looked at Jandree—who, I thought again, was surely far from looking her best now, having so recently given birth. But her breasts were large and filled with milk, and my imagination, unbidden, restored her to virginal vitality and grace.

Once or twice while I was in the presence of both of them I turned, suddenly and sharply, to look at Bran—but whether he was looking at me or not, there was no sign in his face that he suspected anything of my feelings for his wife.

Amby and Vivian and I convinced Bran that there was no safety to be had, other than by winning the fight that Merlin wanted us to make and driving the enemy away from the stronghold.

Bran and Flagon-dry and I were going to hack at the enemy in traditional mundane style, with weapons borrowed from the house's substantial armory. Meanwhile, Merlin's beardless young assistant would fight beside us, armed with powers of enchantment that I assumed were largely or entirely borrowed from the Old Man. Amby told us that his intention was to send strange and powerful visions against the intruding soldiers, thereby distracting and terrifying them. After having seen what I had seen, I was ready to take the Old Man's word that any attempt he made to terrify would be successful.

But Flagon-dry did not seem much impressed. Of course he had not seen the truly miraculous events that effected our escape from Vortigern's camp, and I doubt that he really believed that the youth before him was Amby. "Visions, young one? They'll have to be strong visions to frighten those men who drove us off the wall."

The pale youth nodded calmly. "They will be."

"If we could not withstand Comorre's army then," said Flagon-dry, reasonably enough, "with almost twenty men and the advantage of position, how can we beat them now, with only four?"

"We now have the advantage of surprise," I responded. "But more importantly, Lord Merlin is with us."

"Merlin, Merlin," the stout man said in irritation. Then he thought better of expressing his irritation, and cast a glance over his shoulder. "Not that I intend any disrespect. But . . ."

"Have faith," I advised him, "in the Old Man in the Rocks. In an uncertain world, it has been demonstrated that one may securely have faith in Merlin's Bones."

"Hakon speaks wisely," Amby commented. "Besides, I was only a child yesterday, when Comorre defeated us here and fought his way in over the wall. Today, I am much more."

"You were only a child when you managed our escape from Vortigern," I put in.

"I did not manage that, Hakon. I was only a channel for the Old Man's power."

"And now you are something more?"

"Now I can be more, as long as he does not take part."

I blinked at him. "I don't understand."

Flagon-dry, totally out of his depth and for once at a loss for words, was gazing openmouthed from one of us to the other.

The youth was regarding me with a certain respect but yet with doubt. Then he visibly came to a decision; he was going to attempt an explanation.

"Hakon, you can accept that I, and the small boy you called Amby, are the same person?"

I nodded slowly. "After all that I have seen, I cannot very well doubt that fact, strange as it seems. Small boys do grow up. It is only, in your case, the speed that is amazing. By the way, I asked you a little while ago, by what name should I call you now? Your child-name no longer seems to fit."

"In a moment, Hakon, we can speak of names. But first—I beg you, have patience—first, what if I told you that the Old Man in the Rocks, who is Merlin indeed, exists also in other shapes, other bodies?"

"I know not the limits of what such a wizard may accomplish."

"Yes, of course." For a moment the youth chewed on his beardless lower lip in thought. "What I am trying to explain is that while all of these active bodies are Merlin, at different ages in his life, and that they may travel in strange ways through time, no two of them can ever be in the same place at the same time. At least they had better not come together, because it would be very dangerous. In fact it is even dangerous for two of Merlin's bodies to approach within a mile, or an hour, of each other, because . . . because very bad things would happen if they did."

Such understanding as I had thought was beginning to dawn upon me was quenched in abysmal darkness. My countenance, by this time, must have taken on the same lackwit expression as Flagon-dry's.

Reluctantly Amby took note of this fact, and sighed. But he was not ready to give up. "The hidden, buried bones, which also constitute the presence of Merlin . . . they are safer. Their possibilities of action are quite limited. The hold they offer Merlin on life in this world is very tenuous. Therefore, Merlin's more active bodies can—one at a time—approach the bones. In that sense, Merlin can meet and talk to himself."

"Yes?"

He looked into my face and his own face fell. He sighed. "Hakon, I can't explain it all to you now."

Vivian, in her character of seeress, now joined our discussion, to raise the question of why the Old Man never called her in for a private talk.

She said: "I know he's there, I can feel his presence. And I am supposed to serve him. And I would like to learn magic from him. But I never have a chance to talk to him."

"You will, Viv," said Amby.

"I will? How do you know?"

"From my own talks with him."

"Really?"

"Yes."

The young woman was still doubtful. "*When* will he see me? Or teach me something?"

He sighed. "Not yet. Not for some time, I think."

"First things first," I said. "When does Merlin want us to undertake this liberating battle?"

Amby looked at me soberly. "Soon, Sir Hakon, very soon. Within a few hours."

"And how long does Merlin think our glorious attack will take?"

"A quarter of an hour should be quite long enough for the battle," the youth who had been Amby assured me with confidence. "If everything goes smoothly."

"Or even if it does not," I answered. If the least little thing went wrong, even a small detachment of Comorre's army ought to be able to kill four men in much less time than that.

TWENTY ONE

Three able-bodied men, Bran, Flagon-dry, and myself, comprised the force that was about to launch a surprise attack with sword and spear against Comorre's victorious army. Naturally, adolescent Amby was going to fight on our side too, and we depended totally on him for our success, but his efforts would be confined to a different plane, that of magic and illusion.

Still I had not yet had a real answer to the question of why, with such powerful magic on our side, any physical attack at all was necessary, but I considered that I had good reason to trust Lord Merlin. And my two armed colleagues were desperate enough to trust him too, for lack of any better plan.

I had already rearmed myself, but now I belted my newly chosen sword at my side, and from the casual assembly of weapons carried down into the cave in our retreat picked out a thrusting spear to go with it. My two comrades, who were also dependent on mundane weapons, still had to make sure, by smoky torchlight and the green underground reflection of the sea, that their blades and armor were as ready as they could be. I looked forward to having the fine armory in the house once more available; meanwhile I sat with my new comrades-in-arms on rocks in one of the dank and dim-lit chambers of the lower cave, and while waiting for the signal to attack we naturally began a discussion of warlike matters.

As this proceeded, I confirmed an impression I had formed earlier when fighting to defend the wall: the High Priest Bran seemed quite competent to put on a mail shirt without puzzling over whether to put his head or his arms in first, and he gripped and examined both sword and spear as if he might know what to do with them. He had taken a worthy part in that earlier fight, and though I had been too busy then to observe him, obviously he had survived without serious hurt. But of course many men can manage that much, given a little luck.

I think it was at that moment that my conscious doubts concerning the servants of the oracle first grew strong. Bran seemed very young to be in charge of any such important shrine. And he and Vivian were both quite unlike any other occult practitioners that I had ever known.

Flagon-dry was taking test swings with a battle-ax, against a chunk of timber that had once been part of the subterranean dock. Meanwhile he delivered a would-be learned discourse on the value of Roman blades.

Interrupting this lecture, I did now what I ought to have done before, and asked Bran straight out: "High Priest of the Oracle, have you had training in arms?"

"I have. When I was very young." He sighted along a blade, and spoke in a glum tone of voice. "You will find me no champion in strength or skill, but no helpless novice, either."

I dealt him a hard cuff on the shoulder, meant as reassurance. "Cheer up! I expect to die in combat some day, Bran. But I think it will not be this morning or this afternoon."

He raised his sandy eyebrows. "Only three of us—"

"In this case, a sufficient number to do the job. So says the Old Man. And I, having had firsthand experience of what the One in the Rocks can do, am ready to believe him."

"If three men aided by Merlin's magic are enough to beat an army, I don't see why Merlin can't do the job without any help at all."

"I suppose the Old Man has his reasons."

Bran picked up the sword he'd used in our first battle. He looked doubtfully at the dented blade, and set it down again.

"Have we all given all our lives over into his care? Maybe we have, but I don't want it to be by accident. Perhaps I'd better have a talk with him myself."

Now Flagon-dry, his doubts reinforced, also looked at me doubtfully, and grunted something noncommittal. Folding my arms, I looked from one of my companions to the other, returning their gaze in kind. The more I saw of Bran, and of Flagon-dry, the less likely either of them seemed as priests of any oracle—not that I had had much previous experience with such.

"Bran."

"What is it, Hakon?"

"Tell me truthfully—are you really the high priest of anything?"

Flagon-dry attempted to generate a derisive laugh at the question. But Bran looked at me closely, and gave the answer I was now expecting. "You deserve the truth, Hakon. No, I am no priest, no magician. Never have been. Though, as you can see, the oracle and its treasures are real enough."

"Oh, I admit they're genuine." I paused, looking around me. "Where is the high priest, or priestess, then? And he or she must have had assistants, servants—?"

"I don't know!" He made a helpless gesture. "Believe it or not, friend Hakon. We came here, Jandree and Flagon-dry and myself, running for our lives, along with Maud and Amby and Vivian—and Ivald. We found the house, the cave, the whole place, completely uninhabited."

"I see," I answered after a pause. More bizarre events, I had no doubt, that could be laid at Merlin's door. Matters he'd arranged somehow, for some purpose of his own. "You mentioned Vivian—?"

"No more a priestess than I am a priest. I think she has real ability in magic, or will when she can find a teacher. Not as much as Amby, but—"

At that moment Amby put his head into our little improvised armory, and announced that the time to attack was drawing near.

Bran declined to be hurried, and was growing more and more stubbornly determined to have his own private conference with

Merlin. On our way up out of the cave, I walked with him, and when we came to the little side passage I pointed it out to him. "There's where you'll have to go."

He shook his head. "What are you telling me? That's much too narrow. Not even a ten-year-old could squeeze through there."

"Nevertheless, there it is." When he looked at me as if trying to make up his mind to challenge my truthfulness, I added: "It's Merlin's doing, of course, like almost everything else around here. This is the only real side passage anywhere along the route, until you reach the labyrinth at the bottom. Examine the way for yourself, if you have doubts."

Carefully Bran studied the passage I had indicated, and tried to push himself in between the rocks, but whatever magic was in them would not yield an inch for him. After one more attempt he gave up.

As we were about to advance upon the enemy, I confronted our adolescent leader once again.

"Now that we are going into a fight, we must be clear about who is in command."

The youth answered without hesitation. "On the field of battle, Hakon, you are. Of course I hope you will be open to advice from time to time."

"Am I really in command? Then I say it is time now for true names." My voice sounded awkwardly respectful. "You once were Amby, but you are no longer."

"Very well, Sir Hakon. Call me Ambrosius now, if that suits you better."

"Ambrosius, then. But perhaps I should say Lord Ambrosius. Because I think you have a greater name than that, even if you are reluctant to pronounce it."

He looked at me closely, then sighed, as if with relief. "I'm glad you understand . . . at least partly. You see, I am far from comprehending this business completely yet myself—I mean that of my own strange and twisted life."

"I don't understand a thing!" This was Flagon-dry, squinting from one of us to the other, his mouth open again.

"You will, in time, my friend," Ambrosius muttered to him, and then turned back to me. "Hakon, I have not yet earned the name you have in mind. That is why I will not use it."

"Then let your name be Ambrosius, for now. And you tell me I am in command?"

He gave a nod that was almost a little bow. "Lead on." In effect ordering me to do so.

Presently Bran and Flagon-dry and I, all three of us armed, helmed, and shielded, having received the blessings and well wishes of Maud and Jandree, climbed with Amby to the upper entrance of the cave, Vivian tagging along to see us off.

As we were about to start I asked Ambrosius if he was going into battle wearing beggar's garb (it seemed to me that even—or, perhaps, especially—a wizard ought to dress up for the occasion, given the opportunity to do so).

"It will not much matter, Hakon. I expect the enemy will be unable to see me anyway."

"What will they see?"

"What they will not like. But your eyes will be spared."

My two armed companions and myself, looking curiously at the beardless youth, and then at what seemed empty air beside him, could not at first see the visionary creatures he had somehow conjured into being and was now herding forward with economical gestures of his staff. But Vivian, who had come up with us as far as the cave entrance, clutched my arm and murmured that she could see them, like transparent reflections, distorted by an uneven surface of thin glass. Before we started our actual advance, she reported to us in an awed whisper that there were half a dozen creatures in all, each looming taller than a man: two dragons, and four even stranger monsters, standing near the young man.

"There is one like a . . . like a dragon disfigured by some loathsome disease, and with three heads. And there is another, the worst one, with no head at all . . ."

"Ambrosius."

"Yes, Hakon?"

"I suggest that it might be well for your visionary creatures to be visible to your comrades in arms. It will help us anticipate the enemy's probable reaction to them, and his movements."

After a little reluctance, he agreed. He made no gestures, spoke no words that I could hear, but from that moment the six horror-creatures took shape, though their bodies remained for us as transparent as the mist. Bran on my right hand, and Flagon-dry on my left, uttered small, unmanly sounds.

Now that I had seen what Merlin could devise when he wanted to be frightening, I considered changing my mind about having the things visible. But then I thought it would be cowardly to shudder at mere phantoms.

And so it came to pass that we three fighting men, and one young wizard, took one last cautious look around, and then marched forth.

Our first objective was to drive the intruders from the house—Old Merlin had evidently emphasized to Amby, even more than to me, the importance of protecting the Round Table and the library. According to Amby it was vital above all to make sure that Comorre could not carry the Table or any of its chairs away.

Ambrosius as we began our advance was wearing no armor and carrying no physical weapons, unless one counted his wooden staff as such. It was crooked at the upper end, like something a shepherd might find useful, and about as tall as a man.

At some time after our most recent foray on the surface, Comorre had posted sentries at the mouth of the cave—perhaps because one or more of us had been seen in that area. And these two unfortunate men were the first victims of our counterattack. My spear point went easily through the throat of one, and Flagon-dry's battle-ax almost severed the other's head from his shoulders—the first skirmish was over before Merlin's magic monsters even took the field.

Shield on my left arm, spear at the ready, I moved forward among the rocks, with Bran on my right hand and Flagon-dry on my left, following the little path toward the house. We marched in silence, at a steady and unhurried pace. Ambrosius was some-where close behind us, and the ghostly forms of our terrible inhu-man escort paced silently on our flanks.

As we drew within a few yards of the first outbuildings, the first of our enemies came in sight among them. These men caught sight of us, and simultaneously of the phantom beasts that marched at Merlin's orders. From the way that some of the sol-diers dropped their spears and ran, it was evident that they per-ceived the phantom dragons in full, heart-stopping solidity. Doubtless they heard the crunching of their huge feet, and smelled their breath. The rest of Comorre's men froze in panic, could not tear their eyes away from the magical monsters long enough to notice that they were about to be cut down by real men with real iron in hand.

Our blades now thoroughly bloodied, we marched unhesitat-ingly forward, kicking open the doors of outbuildings along the way to the main house, and cleaning out a small handful of amazed villains from these sheds. Some of Comorre's soldiers dropped their weapons before they ran, some carried them along, but only a small handful stood their ground and tried to fight. A couple of the enemy spilled their blood upon the old stains in the chapel, and one more died in the privy.

In a minute or two we had finished a successful harrowing of the stable and were entering the main house through the kitchen. It was as if no one in the house had heard the shouting or the clash of arms outside, for we achieved complete surprise. A few of the slaves and hangers-on of Comorre's army were busy about the stoves and ovens. These ran out screaming as we entered, and a moment later the big room was filled with steam and smoke from pots overturned on floor and stove top.

Ignoring the wretched slaves and scullions who fled from us in panic, we marched on.

Passing through the central hall on the ground floor, we entered the Hall of the Round Table through doors already standing open, only to find it deserted. The heavy wooden chairs, elabo-rately carved, were not arranged in any orderly fashion, but stood every which way, one or two of them even on top of others, one even sitting on the tabletop. We shoved chairs unceremoniously aside when they got in the way of our search for cowering foemen. There was no sign that Comorre or any of his people had yet realized the true nature of this furniture, though they certainly must have gone through the room looking for portable treasure.

Our visionary monsters came with us, stamping and drooling, bending their necks where the ceilings were low, some dragging thick, misshapen tails.

Our next stop was the armory, both because we thought it likely to find some of the enemy there, and because all three of us wished to at least partially reequip ourselves.

After hastily rearming ourselves with some of the finer weapons there available, we made our way up a small stair in the rear of the house, and by this means approached the library.

The door of the library was tight shut, but as we approached, in response to a commanding gesture by the staff in the hands of Ambrosius, it burst open for us.

Half a dozen magicians who served Comorre were present. Some of them were women, some men, a couple of the latter druids to judge by their tattoos and clothes. All of them looked up startled and (how reassuring it was to see!) frightened from their work at shelves and tables. But in the next moment Merlin's staff, in the hands of its youthful wielder, scattered them as a broom in a housewife's hands might scatter dust.

Two or three soldiers who had been with the magicians fled with them, and two more who were not so quick went down before our blades. Once inside the library, I paused to look around. A few of the shelves had been swept clean by Comorre's intruders, and now scrolls and flat-bound books, along with some stranger objects I could not understand, lay scattered about everywhere, on tables and on the floor. I thought we had interrupted a systematic attempt at vandalism. Curly ashes on the nearest hearth suggested that a few of the scrolls had already been burned.

"Come, look at this!"

The room had changed since my previous visit. Now it narrowed, I thought unnaturally, as it went back; bookshelves grew closer together, until there was barely room to move between them, and in the very rear the convoluted chamber terminated in a wall of what looked like solid glass. Visible in a distorted way beyond this wall was another room, seemingly far distant, and inhabited by strangely clothed people.

I could not see any of the people plainly enough to have recognized them, had I known them, but I thought that Ambrosius could.

When I marveled at these strange sights, Ambrosius muttered to me: "All libraries are the same place, Hakon. Destruction in one may spread to others."

Then he explained that one of the objectives Merlin had set for our raiding party was to seal this passage off. Ambrosius hastily set us to work constructing a barricade, by moving whole shelves of books. One shelf, with Flagon-dry and myself straining at it, collapsed with a majestic roar like that of falling masonry, seemingly inappropriate for the small material weights that moved and toppled.

It seemed to take a long time, but eventually our labors were complete. The otherworldly light that had been flickering through from beyond the glassy wall winked out, and presently Merlin's library was once more only a room in a house, albeit a strange room indeed.

Marching out of the library again, after doing what we could to secure it from any destructive incursions from afar, we descended the main stair to the central dining hall. There a handful of officers and troopers, belatedly alerted to our invasion, were waiting for us.

They came at us, armed and bellowing outlandish war cries, from around both ends of the long refectory table, and we fought our most serious skirmish yet. In this room our three sharp blades, and the vaporous monsters that came oozing with us, scraping their insubstantial heads on the high ceiling, were pitted against almost a dozen of the foe. But that was only at the very start. Half of our opponents screamed as witlessly as had the kitchen slaves when they beheld what young Ambrosius wanted them to see, and broke and ran. Even the three who showed some fight could not help but be fatally distracted by the horrendous visions sent against them; when we had cut down the last opponent in the hall, I looked around for Comorre himself, hoping he had nerved himself to join his officers, and was disappointed not to discover him.

Moving out of the house again, we fought another skirmish in the paved yard just outside the front door. There young Ambrosius's shadow-monsters proved themselves capable of a formidable solidity, when one or two of our more courageous enemies actually raised their swords against them. The arms and armor of Comorre's men were smashed, the men's flesh torn, by invisible talons and teeth. When the monsters became thus solid, they also turned more fully visible to all present. When the thing with no head capered before me, I confess that for a moment I came near dropping my own weapon and turning tail.

It is customary for the winners in any fight to boast. But the action we saw that day was not truly a battle, or even much of a fight, but a plain rout. As such, it was not nearly as bloody as the long struggle on the wall had been.

When at last we had cleared the foe from house and courtyard and were able to look out over the wall again, we saw no bodies—evidently a grave-digging detail of Comorre's men had been prompt about clearing away those who had died in the earlier fight.

Most of my comrades who had followed me from the Northland of course had fallen here. Briefly I looked forward to meeting them in Valhalla someday—very likely, I thought, someday soon.

But probably not today. Not with the one who called himself Ambrosius fighting at my side.

When, after a pause to catch our breath, our counterattack burst out of the front door of the house, scattering men before it in raw panic, Comorre was standing atop the wall, conferring with his officers over something, and the Cursed One was able to leap on a horse and get away when he decided that there was no use trying to stem the panic among his troops.

We might have overtaken some of those who were running away on foot, but we did not chase them far. I saw no fame or honor, and certainly no booty, to be won in cutting down men who'd thrown their weapons away and turned their backs.

"Come, look at this!"

To the great horror and astonishment of my comrades in arms, we found their former associate Ivald/Thrain tied down to a bench in the courtyard, where he had evidently been tortured, cut, and burned, by Comorre's own hand or at his orders. When the body fastened to the improvised torture rack twitched in movement, and made a noise, we realized that it still, incredibly, retained a spark of life. Fresh blood still dripped, with the regularity of a pulse, to a dark puddle.

I could see now that one of the berserk's eyes had indeed been lost to an arrow—the arrowhead and a stump of broken shaft were still lodged in his skull. The trickling blood from the socket was still fresh.

Young Ambrosius, looking paler than ever, in horror and revulsion said that his magic could do nothing in this case.

The man on the rack had words to whisper to us. Given his condition, they were hard to understand. But when he had repeated them I realized with amazement that they were not a plea for death, but rather to be given a weapon.

I stood back, shaking my head. The poor wretch was no longer capable of holding a weapon, and anyway the enemy was out of sight. There was but little left of Ivald, and indeed we could be certain of his identity only because of the old arm stump. Little of his face was left, his manhood had been mangled, as if with a dull knife, and his one hand no longer had any fingers. I did not hesitate to do my former comrade in arms the only favor possible in the circumstances, administering a finishing stroke with my spear into his heart.

When his now-breathless body at last lay still, we unfastened it from the improvised torture rack and arranged it decently on a half-completed course of masonry, with his eye sockets covered by pebbles (I still had bags of gold and silver loot, but not a single coin about me), and what was left of his one hand on his breast. I remarked to my comrades who were with me that we would carry the corpse to be burned with those of our own fallen shipmates when we had had time to find them all—certainly no warrior had ever fought with more bravery or strength.

One of Comorre's large watch fires were still burning, and we, with some magical help as in other matters of housekeeping, had stoked one with wood from the supply for the house and converted it to the cremation of fallen enemies and comrades.

On returning to the site of the torture rack half an hour or so later, in the course of the essential work of disposing of the dead, I noticed that Thrain/Ivald's body had disappeared. Naturally I assumed that some of my new comrades in arms had already taken it to the pyre.

═══ TWENTY-TWO ═══

S hortly after the last of Comorre's people disappeared from view, the staff Ambrosius had been carrying, that occult weapon none of our enemies (even including those magicians in the library) had been able to resist, caught fire spontaneously and burned quickly to a handful of ash.

I got the impression that the youth had decided on this destruction and managed it himself, without consulting the Old Man in the Rocks.

When we were thoroughly convinced that no more of Comorre's people were lurking about, and I as commander had given Bran his formal discharge from the ranks, he immediately unbelted his sword and hastened back down into the cave, a man clearly obsessed with concern for his family. This time I declined to go with him, deciding that I would make no particular effort to see Jandree again until I could manage a visit in her husband's absence.

Of course they were only entertainers. Well, like the great majority of Northmen, I respected ability more than birth or caste; whenever I could find a sympathetic listener I related with some pride the story of how my own grandfather had begun life as a slave. He had been captured as a child in some intertribal raid in Iceland, and by his own efforts had risen to freeman status and beyond, an achievement remarkable but not at all incredible in his time and place.

*   *   *

To Jandree, on the first chance I had to talk with her alone, I said: "I was totally convinced that you were the high priestess."

"I know you were, Hakon. I am sorry. We had to pretend to be the people of the oracle, when we thought our lives depended on keeping Comorre outside the gate. And would you have fought to defend people who belonged to a carnival?"

"I would have fought for you, my lady, and for your good name, whatever you were said to be."

Her fair cheeks colored, and she dropped her eyes from mine. But then her eyes came back, as if they could not help themselves. She gestured the helplessness she felt. "The truth is that none of us is what we seem."

"I think that I am. I try to be no more and no less than what I seem, and I have not lied to you about my wealth, or my name."

And there we were, with her baby crying in her arms.

And nothing happened. As I later came to understand, Jandree was not really thinking about me. She was simply caught up in envious dreams of what the life of a queen, or a great lady, must be like, and in me she saw some possibilities along that line that seemed totally absent from her present life.

In truth, when I had time to think about it, the aspect of the deception that irked me most had to do with Vivian. She, who with me had worn such an air of pride, and sometimes condescension, was nothing but, or little more than, a common slut.

Was I tempted to punish Vivian for deceiving me thus? Well, I felt a momentary impulse along that line, but it was easily resisted.

The fact was that I had lost nothing because of Vivian's deceptive behavior—but I wondered what attitude Amby (or young Merlin) was going to take, when he found out. But then I smiled mockingly at my own slow-wittedness. Of course he must have known the truth before I did.

Soon I began to wonder why Old Merlin in our private talks had never revealed to me the truth about Bran and his companions. I could not prove or remember that the Old Man in the Rocks had lied to me. But it seemed there were some important questions I had never asked.

Patrolling again on the surface with young Ambrosius, looking around to make sure that no straggler remnants of the Cursed One's force remained, we came to the ruined chapel. I stepped inside, and found myself making a fumbling attempt at choosing a god to whom to pray. At least that is what I now think I was doing then. But it is perfectly possible that I simply stood there without any conscious purpose at all, gazing at the symbols on the walls, and the still-unshattered glass. Little had changed inside those broken walls since I had spoken to Ivald there—had that only been a day ago? Two days? I was finding it well-nigh impossible to keep track of time.

The Christian symbols carved into stone or wood still stubbornly clung to their existence—and so did those that were mere stainings of fragile glass.

Merlin's youthful self came to stand beside me in the chapel. The aftermath of battle found Ambrosius in a melancholy mood, exhausted by his efforts with the phantasmal monsters.

"Are they worth anything, Hakon? Any of the gods?"

"Perhaps you should know that better than I." Strolling in front of the image of the suffering Jesus, I told Ambrosius I wanted someone to explain the Christian god to me. There he was, by all accounts some kind of rebellious Jew, crushed by the power of Rome, hanging like Thrain upon his torture rack. It was a mystery to me how such a poor defeated victim could attract followers, even though I knew he was supposed to have been brought back to life by his divine Father. I thought there must be part of the story I had not yet heard, or had failed to understand.

Ambrosius thought it over. "Vivian may be the best one to give you an explanation. She was in a Christian convent for a time."

"I'll ask her."

It may have been an hour later, and I was walking alone behind the house, trying to locate Vivian, with the idea of asking her some questions about the god called Christ, when I happened to overhear her voice and another's, coming from some secluded place invisible to me among the nearby rocks.

Soon I heard another voice, that of Ambrosius, coming from the same place.

I had not set out to eavesdrop, but there was an intensity in their voices that compelled attention. Under ordinary conditions either of them, skilled as they were in magic, might have easily detected my presence, or found a way to conceal themselves from observation. But at the moment all of their senses were focused on each other.

There came the small sound of a clasp or button being undone, and then a faint rustle of clothing.

"I love you, Amby."

When he spoke again his voice was so tight that for a moment I was sure another man was talking: "I have never done these things before, with anyone."

And Vivian answered, in a passionate whisper: "Come, do them with me."

Descending into the cave again, I once more braved the mystery of the side passage leading to the core of magic. I took note of how foolish it was to suggest that a man might be physically hidden among these flattened and contorted rocks.

This time Old Merlin was more welcoming when I approached his sanctuary. He even asked if I would prefer to see him, and when I assented, a ghostly, wraithlike figure appeared, the transparent image of an old man outlined, like a reflection in wavy glass, against a blank wall of rock. Quite a different face, coarser and more haggard, than the one I had been imagining.

Now that I thought I knew what to look for, I tried without success to see in this aged face some resemblance to Ambrosius.

After an exchange of greetings, Merlin, or his wraith, congratulated me, with what I considered notable restraint, on the victory over Comorre. My impression was reinforced that the Old Man, for whatever reason, did not like me.

You have done well, Sir Hakon. The library, and the Table, and the Dangerous Chair, are all secure for the moment.

"Thank you, sir."

Merlin went on to question me in detail about our sealing of the magic window in the rear wall of his library. He also wanted to know what conditions I had observed in the rest of the house.

Then he returned to a discussion of the status of the library, whether its doors had been sealed shut when we got there, and who and how many of the enemy had been inside. And how much damage the contents of the shelves had appeared to suffer, or whether any of those contents seemed to have been removed.

I gave the Old Man what information I could, and assured him that Ambrosius had seemed satisfied with the library's condition when we left.

To my dismay, there were moments during this interview when the Old Man sounded confused and uncertain. He asked me the same question more than once, as if forgetting that I had answered it.

And the library . . . we must take serious thought, Hakon, about what ought to be done to secure the library—the whole house—against another invasion.

"Yes sir."

But in truth your fight against Comorre, this time, was much easier than it might have been. Wodan fought against me in the camp of Vortigern, but chose not to do so here. None of the powerful ones who seek my bones entered the struggle here. I must try to make sure of what this means.

"And who are they, Lord Merlin? These enemies who seek your bones?" My interest was intensified by my recent experience in facing and fighting against some of them.

I was somewhat surprised to get, this time, what sounded like a practical answer: *There are three with whom we must be immediately concerned. One is Morgan le Fay, Arthur's half-sister. The second is Mordred, Arthur's bastard. The third—not an open enemy yet, but one we must not trust—is the Fisher King.*

"Of that last one, sir, I have never heard."

Merlin for once seemed ready to provide information—unfortunately I found most of it too esoteric to be useful. He explained to me—or tried to explain—something about the Grail—but only gave me fresh cause for worry. Because he revealed in the process that even he, Merlin himself, could not be completely sure just what the Grail was. Perhaps, I gathered from his rambling discourse, the Grail was more than Christ's cup from his last meal before his death—though it might be that. Perhaps it had begun as some kind of pagan ritual cauldron far older than Christianity. But I could determine nothing in this matter with any certainty.

Mordred's name, of course, was familiar to everyone who knew the common stories. As for Morgan, I knew little more than her name, as a woman, and enchantress, who figured in some of the stories about Arthur. Generally she was called his sister, or his half-sister as Merlin had said, and in some stories she was Arthur's enemy, in others his friend.

I remembered Morgan as the Jeweled Lady Amby had mentioned when we were adventuring in Vortigern's camp. Merlin now assured me that she and Morgan le Fay were one and the same.

"And is she still a living, breathing woman?"

Living and breathing lustily enough. As you will perhaps discover for yourself. I should warn you, if you still mean to sit one day at Arthur's Table, that tasks lie ahead much harder than what you have already accomplished here.

It was at this meeting, too, that Old Merlin first broached to me his plan to eventually establish a new Camelot, ruled by a new king.

This was news indeed. "A new Arthur, sir? Then the original is really dead, and cannot be restored?"

Merlin ignoring my question for the time being, told me that the manor house was (among other things) the first stage in the reconstruction—he would build it into a suitably great castle.

Vast size is not required. Arthur's Camelot was not vast, as towns and castles are measured, and it was not lack of size and numbers that brought it down.

. . . and the new Camelot, when it was completed, would stand right here. Even the landscape could be magically altered to some degree to achieve the configuration Merlin wanted.

And in accordance with the wishes of the new monarch, when that choice too has been made.

The past cannot be undone. A new monarch must be crowned, to sit in Arthur's seat.

"But who is it to be?"

A ruler honorable and brave. Yet there must be more to king or queen than courage and honor.

"I know that." Then I added on a thoughtless impulse: "If I were ever to become a king . . ."

What then, friend Hakon? If you became a king, what then?

"I would—I would seek out wise counsel. And I would try very hard never to dishonor the special position that I held."

Would you, indeed? Perhaps it is foolish to expect more than that from any mortal man or woman.

And our talk quickly returned to more practical matters. But the seed of an idea, which at first seemed utterly fantastic, had been planted in me. Gradually—very gradually at first—over the following hours and days, I became secretly intrigued with the idea that I was, or might be, destined to be that chosen king.

In the course of our discussion the old man expressed his opinion that the original Arthur had been not quite up to the demands of his role—no more than Lancelot had really succeeded at his.

Lancelot, who had served and cuckolded the recent Arthur, had, as most of the stories told, retired to a monastery about the time Arthur was killed.

I said that I would have liked to have met them both.

Arthur, as I have said, is gone. But very likely you will meet Lancelot.

This was news indeed. "When, sir?"

Soon, I trust. For I intend to send you to find him and bring him back.

And I was left to puzzle such meaning as I could out of that reply.

As I stood there in an awkward half-crouch, wedged into that deep hidden place, with the sharp edges of rock seeming to grow sharper against my knees and forehead, I heard the Old Man, abruptly querulous, demand to know whether I was still ready to serve him faithfully.

"I have sworn allegiance, and I do not break my oath. Even if I wanted to do so, which I do not, you have so far kept your part of the bargain, and we are bound together."

When, an hour or so later, I next saw adolescent Ambrosius, he told me that he was soon going to leave us again—for how long he could not say. He said he would have to depart as soon as he had finished putting the library to rights as thoroughly as possible. And he confirmed the most shocking thing that Old Merlin had said to me: that we were all to somehow assist the Old Man in a great project he had determined to accomplish—nothing less than the reconstruction of Camelot.

Vivian was listening. "When will you be back?"

"I don't know, Vivian. As soon as possible. It might be only a few days, in your scale of time."

"But it might be much longer."

"Yes."

"Years!"

"Possibly."

A new fear was growing in Vivian's green eyes. The more she thought about the possibilities, the more frightened she became. "Will you come back—will you come back changed, as you did last time? Years older, a—a different man entirely?"

"Again, I don't know. All I can tell you is, I don't know. But I do love you very much. More than I can say. I always will!"

The youth was trying to explain this to Vivian, but she was thrown into a panic at the prospect of losing him and was unable to hear anything beyond that. Soon she flared out at him angrily, provoked a quarrel, and ran away in tears.

I thought of mentioning to Ambrosius my concern about the

uncertainty and confusion that Merlin sometimes displayed, but decided that I had better await a more propitious moment.

Before Ambrosius departed, he and I walked through the house once more, and he tried to show me some of the marvels of the library, which was now being magically restored. I could not deny the power that lay in books, though like magic it was closed to me.

We also discussed Merlin's plans, and the difficulties of renewing Camelot. If that was what the Old Man wanted to do, Ambrosius said, then that was what we must all try to bring about.

"We will restore Arthur to his throne?"

"I doubt it, Sir Hakon." Ambrosius shook his head. "Bringing back the old Camelot would be beyond even Merlin's powers; there is never any true going back for any of us, much less for the world."

And then he urgently pressed me to promise to keep a certain secret from Vivian. "Do not tell her, Hakon, that I am Merlin. Or that I am going to be Merlin, if you want to look at it that way. She doesn't realize yet, that what I must one day become is that Old Man down in the Rocks; worn and decaying and wrinkled—if he had any skin left he would be wrinkled . . . and babbling, sometimes. He doesn't always make sense, you know, when he talks."

"I have sworn to serve him," I responded stiffly. I wished I could refute the description, but could not.

"You are loyal, Hakon. I hope that any god who can reward you does so."

"Thank you, Ambrosius." I hesitated. "How will you—how was the Old Man sealed in the rocks, really? Is it true that nothing can be done to get him out?"

"Nothing can be done." The youth sighed fiercely. "As far as I can make out, the stories we all have heard are true. He began—that is, I will begin when I am old—to dote on some young woman—named Nimue, whoever she will be—and she tricked him—she will trick me, when I am old . . ."

Ambrosius shook his head and looked as confused as any

youth of his age might appear to be when pondering the ways of women and the intricacies of life.

Though somewhat older than this version of the great magician, and perhaps wiser in some ways, I could readily sympathize. "I will tell Vivian nothing about who you are—who you are going to be."

"Thank you, Hakon. She loves me as I am, and I desperately love her."

We talked some more. He told me, and I could well believe it, that there were tremendous difficulties in accomplishing the goal of renewing Camelot, because of the opposition of Morgan and others.

Ambrosius told me also how Morgan and Old Merlin were in opposition because she was determined to restore the original Arthur to his throne. The Old Man, on the other hand, had had enough of Arthur and his inconsistent behavior before his fall.

Ambrosius before leaving took Bran and myself into the Circular Hall.

"Why are we here, Ambrosius?"

"I thought it would be good if you could see something of what Camelot was like—and what it may be like again."

We remained in the Room of the Round Table for only a few minutes. I had been there before, of course, and nothing very remarkable had happened. But this time there were moments when I thought myself standing in what seemed a different place altogether, a hall of many mirrors, so strange were the perspectives. Yet whenever I looked closely at my surroundings, there was not a single mirror to be seen anywhere. No glassy images of myself. Only the stone walls and silken tapestries, one after another after another, diminishing into darkness, into an unreachable distance.

The linen cloths had been undraped from the chairs now, but it seemed that one chair was missing.

* * *

Again the Old Man summoned me to a conference and confirmed the details of my mission to find Lancelot. He informed me also that he was sending Ambrosius on quite a different quest—and Bran and his people on a third.

After thinking it over, I decided not to raise with Old Merlin the subject of my latest conversation with Ambrosius.

But the chief subject of my talk with Merlin was my mission to find Lancelot and persuade him to come back. *Tell him that Merlin requires his help.*

"And if he asks me about Arthur?"

If Lancelot asks about anyone, it will likely be Queen Guinevere.

"And what shall I tell him on that score?"

All you know on the subject. Which will be nothing.

"Ah."

I think you will find him perhaps not as tired of fighting as he thought he was when he chose to enter a monastery. He has languished there among priests long enough. Perhaps by now he is tired of religion. There followed a peculiar utterance that I eventually realized must be the Old Man's laughter. *But at least he will listen with some respect to a fighting man like you.*

Old Merlin also mentioned, casually in passing, that in the course of this coming adventure I would encounter trolls, and perhaps even giants or other monsters who were seldom or never found outside the borders of Logres.

As far as I was concerned, trolls were mythical creatures. But they certainly existed in a number of stories, and if the Old Man said they were to be taken as sober fact, who was I to argue? I would deal with them when the time came.

"Lord Merlin—when your New Camelot has been established, will it be my home?"

You will have many homes, and none.

It seemed I was going to learn no more details regarding my status in the new world that was to be. "Is anyone coming with me on my search for Lancelot?"

Whom do you wish to take?

"From the way you spoke, sir, I assumed there is to be fighting.

If so, I will naturally do better with the help of some good fighting men."

Find Lancelot, before you begin your fighting. He will supply all the help you need.

"If you say so, sir. But it seems to me that the great, legendary Lancelot must be very old by now."

Lancelot in mundane terms is in his fifties. Elderly for a warrior. But in his case not so ancient as you might think. And he will help you recruit other fighting men. His name and his presence will draw them. Enough will join you when the time is ripe—if you are worthy.

I considered. "I'd like to see that Bran—and his family—are taken care of. Well, all his crew from the oracle here. Maybe it doesn't matter so much whether they are really seers and servants of an oracle, or only mountebanks. Maybe there is not so much difference."

Sometimes you show the beginnings of wisdom, Hakon.

Bran, more than anyone else, continued to worry over the fact that none of us had ever found out who had occupied the house, who had presumably served or controlled the oracle, before he and his troupe arrived, nor what had happened to those people.

Bran confronted Ambrosius and demanded to see and speak to the Old Man.

The youth was doubtful. "Why do you want to speak to him?"

"I would rather explain it to him. You and he are not identical, I believe."

"No, we are not. But in this, Bran, I can speak for him."

Bran looked about at me, and at his followers, as if he might be appealing for help, but Merlin was my lord, and in any case I had no help to give.

And with that Merlin, the elder wizard, began to speak through the body of his younger self—as had happened in the camp of Vortigern. I could hear the difference in the voice of Ambrosius, and see it in his face. He told Bran, while the others and I listened:

"The cave of the oracle stood empty for many years, before I, Merlin, came here and chose it for my own. The house and wall are new. You and your people are here by invitation. This house and cave are not to be entered, this promontory not trodden by human feet, or even seen with human eyes, save by my permission."

"Comorre and his army had your permission to invade?"

"I was too tired then to keep them out."

Bran was showing more daring now than I think our one-sided sword fight had required. He pursued Merlin with a relentless courage I could not help but respect. "Who sustained the fires in all the hearths? Whose clothes are we wearing, whose pigs and chickens and eggs have we been eating? Who owns the bottles of wine that we have emptied?"

Ambrosius nodded. The voice of aged Merlin came from his lips. "All were, and are, my gifts to you. All furnished by my art. Long, long ago I knew that you were coming here, and when."

"Who sat in those two tall chairs in the great hall, before we came?"

For a moment I thought that Merlin/Ambrosius had actually been flustered by that question. "It seems those chairs were premature. They were meant for a couple who never came to claim the place of honor."

And Bran pursued: "Old Man, I have the feeling that this house and the wall protecting it are ancient, maybe even older than you. Even though they appear unfinished. I have seen moss growing on some of their stones."

"The foundations of Old Camelot persist. But the upper wall as you see it now, and the house as it stands today, were built for you. My purpose was to create a place of refuge for the seven of you who were coming in darkness seeking sanctuary."

"You knew, then, that we were coming."

"I have said so."

There was a long pause before Bran went on, now much more humbly: "Why are we so important to you, Lord Merlin?"

No reply.

Bran persisted: "I want to know. It seems to me I have a right to know. Why do you think we are important?"

The face of Ambrosius had changed again, and it was once more only a young face, strong but vulnerable. Bran's last question received no answer, except the faint howling of the wind.

TWENTY-THREE

✎ *Interlude* ✎

Elaine's original concern about the mysterious Fisher, and even her fear of the more awful Morgan, had now virtually disappeared, swallowed up in her deep terror of the brutal killer and his gang who had now taken over her laboratory.

The killer's name was definitely Mordred. Or at least, in keeping with the prevailing Arthurian lunacy, his followers continually called him by that name, and he was willing to answer to it.

What little Elaine could remember about Mordred from Arthurian legend was anything but reassuring.

Looking over the console in front of her, she saw that pressing a couple of handy switches ought to start some security equipment recording what the surveillance screen displayed, as well as whatever sound could be picked up in the room under observation. Elaine reached for the proper switches, intending to preserve on laser disk the faces and speech of the murderers, as well as solid evidence of their crimes.

A few minutes later, in the interest of thoroughness, she checked the disk—and discovered that nothing at all was being recorded. There was no obvious reason for the failure. She fiddled with the equipment for a little while, but couldn't find out. And right now she had more pressing problems to think about.

When Elaine considered her current situation as coolly as possible, she realized that the feeling of relative safety provided by the solid walls and extra-heavy doorlocks of the Security room was probably an illusion. But the feeling remained real nevertheless. Fear had eased enough to allow her to be hungry, and suddenly she was ravenous, having missed more meals than she had eaten over the last two days. Fortunately there was food of sorts available. In one corner of the large room stood a small refrigerator, where people on duty had kept their lunches or snacks, and everything had not been eaten.

Mordred. She remembered the fundamentals of the character as portrayed in the traditional King Arthur stories, and she was anything but reassured.

But for the moment Elaine remained unmolested. Chewing on a stale half-sandwich, she tried to think of what to attempt next.

In the power room, the electronic circuit-breakers had been inaccessible even with her key from Security. And the big manual knife-switches had been immovable. And nothing else worked. The knife-switches, when she had looked at them closely, appeared to have been welded in the ON position. Great arcing sparks might have somehow accomplished such a feat, Elaine supposed; at least that was the only half-logical idea she could come up with by way of explanation. If she were to try greater violence directly against such power, she thought she might well kill herself in the attempt, and she was far from ready to contemplate suicide.

While Elaine continued to puzzle over what her next move ought to be, a nearby screen suddenly came alight.

FISHER HERE, said the neat lettering, black on cream. SUGGEST YOU LOOK AT THE AMBULANCE AGAIN. YES, ITS STILL THE AMBULANCE.

What on earth did that mean? She found it difficult even to remember that Fisher had once seemed threatening. She had now accepted him gratefully as an ally, even though she was still conscious of doubts as to whether he could be trusted.

She typed a brief acknowledgment of his message, and then, since the room she now occupied was windowless, she used remote controls to swing one of the outdoor surveillance cameras around to let her study the current population of the parking lot. There was Fisher's car, and there was her own—unfortunately hers was the farthest of any from the building. And there was a new vehicle, doubtless the one in which Mordred and his crew of killers had arrived. And there, closest to the building, just where it had been . . . but certainly the van now occupying the space where the ambulance had been was quite a different vehicle. No longer an ambulance, even though Fisher had just called it that.

Zooming in on the machine with a telescopic security lens, Elaine studied it intently. Though the markings, and even the overall color, had been radically changed, there were certain things about it that at least suggested it might really be the same vehicle. For one thing, the general size and shape corresponded. For another, it seemed to be parked in exactly the same careless way, at just the same slight angle to the painted outline of parking spaces, and occupying parts of three of them. Whether the license plate had changed or not was more than Elaine could say. But most familiar was a minor dent in one of the doors on the side of the van turned toward the building.

The machine was now painted and externally equipped as a van belonging to the Antrobus Foundation. Naturally the organization did own a few vehicles, including at least one van, for maintenance and business trips, shuttling into town and to the airport. But Elaine had thought the company's only large van— quite a different model from this one—was currently parked in the garage, a modest building sheltered by bushes and reached by a short drive from the rear of the parking lot.

Back at the keyboard, she typed: IVE LOOKED.

YOU SHOULD GET INTO THE DRIVERS SEAT, AS SOON AS POSSIBLE, AND DRIVE IT OUT OF HERE. NOT YOUR CAR, WHICH IS NOT ARMORED.

Right now the prospect of leaving here by any means at all seemed glorious. Quickly she responded: WHERE ARE THE KEYS?

Fisher's answer came back at once. IN THE AMBULANCE. Then those words disappeared. The computer screens, still evidently somehow programmed with the poetry supplied by Fisher hours ago, were not being helpful.

> *All in the blue unclouded weather*
> *Thick-jewell'd shone the saddle-leather,*
> *The helmet and the helmet-feather*
> *Burn'd like one burning flame together,*
> *As he rode down to Camelot.*

Yes, unhelpful, to say the least. The necessity loomed of trusting Fisher, though Elaine's intelligence warned her that she had no proof he could be trusted.

Verse once more vanished, and Fisher's dialogue was back. THE AMBULANCE MUST BE DRIVEN AWAY. MORGAN CANNOT DO IT, AND HER MEN ARE DEAD.

I KNOW, Elaine typed back. I CAN SEE THEIR BODIES.

I CANT DO IT EITHER. THEY COULD LOCATE ME IF I TRIED TO MOVE. YOUR MOVEMENTS ARE NOT OF GREAT CONCERN TO THEM.

WHY ME? she queried instinctively.

BECAUSE THERE IS NO ONE ELSE. After a pause, the unseen typist added: YOU KNOW WHAT IS AT STAKE.

By this time Elaine thought that she knew at least what Fisher would claim. King Arthur's very life, and kingdom, were hanging in the balance.

Well. There was certainly her own life to be considered, not to mention Fisher's.

Whatever the truth about Arthur might be, Elaine found it easy enough to believe that anyone in the mysteriously transformed vehicle was truly in great peril, and would continue to be so as long as it stayed in the parking lot, in reach of Mordred and his crew. They too believed in Arthur, strongly enough to kill on the strength of their convictions.

While pondering her chances of getting out into the parking lot and to the van, or even to her own more distant car, and driving away, Elaine tried to determine where all of Mordred's people were; rarely if ever did they all seem to be in her lab.

Fisher was still at his hidden keyboard, and seemed to be growing impatient. ELAINE? CAN YOU REACH THE AMBU-LANCE?

DONT RUSH ME. WHERE ARE MORDREDS PEOPLE? WHAT IS THIS ALL ABOUT?

There was a pause, as if Fisher were trying to think up some convincing explanation—or perhaps just mastering his anger at this young woman who did not immediately jump to obey orders, but instead insisted on asking questions.

Then there came an answer: MERLINS BONES. WIZARDS LAST REMAINS ARE ITEMS OF GREAT MAGICAL PO-WER. BELIEVE ME. MORDRED WANTS TO GET THEM OUT OF ROCKS AND INTO HIS CONTROL. MORGAN LIKEWISE. ME TOO, BUT I HAVE A GOOD PURPOSE.

Well.

While she mulled that answer over, Elaine quickly looked in on her lab again. Mordred and some of his people were deep in a private discussion that the security microphone was not sensitive enough to pick up.

On the other screen, at Elaine's elbow, Fisher started nagging her again. NOW IS A GOOD TIME TO RUN FOR THE AM-BULANCE. THE MORE YOU DELAY THE WORSE YOUR CHANCES WILL BE.

Unhelpful, totally unhelpful. Chewing fingernails again, Elaine stared through an agony of indecision into her old, once-familiar lab, now become the home of monsters. From time to time in the hypostator room, additional bits of matter, in obedience to some laws of physics (or of magic? or was there a differ-ence?) that Dr. Brusen had not begun to understand, were coming through from whatever other world the new display had touched.

Every time she looked, Elaine shuddered. She couldn't help it. Debris of ancient bone chips and fresh though ancient blood was falling upon the twenty-first-century dead men on her floor. Mor-dred and his people, moving around on booted feet, stepped over corpses in their way. Imagination and shock made additional mangled human body parts out of twigs and leaves and lumps of dark earth.

* * *

ELAINE. DOCTOR BRUSEN. GET TO THE AMBULANCE
NOW, WHILE YOU STILL CAN. DRIVE IT AWAY.

"Shut up!" she screamed, suddenly on the edge of total panic.
Hammering her fists on the arms of her soft, comfortable chair.
"Shut up shut up shut up!"

Fisher would not shut up. He persisted in his silent bullying,
entering sentence after sentence on-screen, urging Elaine to drive
the ambulance away. He said he would do something to distract
the enemy while she ran out and got into the vehicle.

ARE THE DOORS OF THE VAN UNLOCKED?

THEY WILL BE WHEN YOU REACH IT. KEYS ARE IN-
SIDE.

Her final look around inside the Security room showed her
that Fisher's last words had been replaced by:

> *She left the web, she left the loom,*
> *She made three paces thro' the room,*
> *She saw the water-lily bloom,*
> *She saw the helmet and the plume,*
> *She look'd down to Camelot.*

At last, hardly knowing what she was doing, but thinking that
she was accomplishing nothing by staying where she was, Elaine
made it out of Security and through the darkened hallways again.

Then out of the building somehow, through a door that
seemed to make a great noise when she pushed it open, and into
the parking lot, where she felt nakedly exposed in what seemed a
terrific glare of light.

There was her own car, but nightmarishly far away. And, as
Fisher had ominously warned, her car wasn't armored. And she
would never be able to run that far before . . . and the van was
near, and reassuringly large and solid.

In the midst of Elaine's frightened, gasping run she looked up
at her lab windows, lonely lights in the dark wall of the building,
like something on the cover of a Gothic video or holodisk.

Running with all her strength, feelingly hideously exposed,

she sprinted at last behind the van, reaching for the handle of the driver's door. Here no one looking out from the building could see her.

Just as she turned the corner, she cast one more look back and up, and saw the outline of a man's figure, Mordred or one of his murderous assistants, in one of her own windows.

Startlingly, the door to the building from which she had just emerged now slammed again. Feet, those of a heavy man moving at a hard run, pounded on the pavement, coming after her.

Sobbing, almost blinded, Elaine felt her fingers close on the door handle. It was hard to see anything, peering in through the tinted, rain-smeared windows of the vehicle, even as she almost fell against it. For just a moment she thought that there were shadowy human figures in there, as if of attendants, and in the next moment she was not sure.

She pulled open a door, gasping with relief to find that Fisher had spoken truly and it was not locked. She hurled herself into the darkened interior, slammed the door, and pushed down the latch that ought to lock up everything.

From somewhere in the rear came a dim glow: there was of course an onboard computer screen.

Out flew the web and floated wide;
The mirror crack'd from side to side;
'The curse is come upon me,' cried
The Lady of Shalott.

Outside, the single pair of running feet were pounding closer. The figure loomed up, crossing the illuminated spaces. It was the heavy, one-armed man, the one Mordred had called Thrain.

The keys were in the ignition, as Fisher had promised. The engine, thank God, leapt into life at once. Without bothering about such nonsense as seatbelts or lights, Elaine put her foot down hard on the accelerator, and the van leaped forward—there seemed to be engine power worthy of an ambulance at her command.

Thrain, his pale-faced stocky figure almost right in front of the van, leaped sideways to avoid it, at the same time drawing something from a holster at his belt. A moment later, smashing impacts battered the van, but hidden armor kept the projectiles from penetrating the interior. Elaine drove in a circle, trying to get a clear look at the familiar exit. There it was. In desperation she drove straight at it, ignoring the fact that the horizontal arm of the exit gate was down.

The arm jumped up as if by magic, when Elaine drove straight at it, hoping to break out violently if no other way was possible.

The unmanned guard post shot past.

And now the Antrobus Foundation and, she could hope, the whole night of madness and murder, were behind her.

Abruptly, with the jolt of nightmare reasserting itself, another large vehicle, looking like the twin of the one in which Mordred and his people had arrived, loomed ahead, pulling out directly across the road, blocking the only passage, and her escape.

Even as Elaine's foot was moving instinctively for the brake, Fisher—or some greater power—intervened on Elaine's behalf. One moment her headlights showed the familiar drive, blocked by the triumphant enemy—and in the next the road ahead was clear, but unpaved and utterly unfamiliar. Large rocks and uneven ruts jarred beneath the tires.

Her right foot completed its motion to the brake pedal. She slowed down, but kept going, the vehicle lurching violently on uneven ground.

Looking behind her through the large side mirrors, she saw the unpaved road, or track, on which she drove disappearing into deep night. There was no trace of lighted laboratory or parking lot, or indeed of any lights at all.

But light ahead was growing. A kind of daylight, low in the sky. Elaine kept driving. In another ten minutes she had emerged into a different world, a vicinage all twilight green and shadowy, a land prodigally supplied with tall green trees, into the mass of which the curving road ahead soon disappeared.

Elaine took her foot from the accelerator and applied the brake, turning a little off the road before the vehicle came to a full stop.

When it had done so, she turned in the driver's seat and looked around. The night was silent, except for a jarringly out-of-season racketing of summer insects.

No pursuit. But in a moment Elaine knew with certainty that she was not alone—she got up and made her way back into the rear of the ambulance. Two beds, or berths, were there, one on each side of a narrow central aisle, and one berth was occupied. Yes, there really was a patient, reclining on his back, an unconscious sandy-haired man of about fifty whose head above his eyebrows was bandaged heavily.

══ TWENTY-FOUR ══

✑ Hakon ✑

hree days after Ambrosius's most recent departure, I looked
up from my midday seat of contemplation in the chapel to
see a dark-haired, middle-sized young man of twenty-five or so
standing at one open end of the ruined space, regarding me with a
kind of hopeful uncertainty. This newcomer had a good start on a
beard, but his face had not changed that much, and to recognize
him I did not need to take note of his exotic clothing or his lack
of visible weapons.

Respectfully I got to my feet. "Greetings, Ambrosius—if that
is still your name."

"Greetings, Hakon." His face brightened, and he waved one
hand in a disarmingly awkward gesture. "I am glad you know me.
Yes, the name of Ambrosius will still serve me well. The Old Man
would like to see you, down in his sanctuary."

"Then I'd best go to him at once." I got to my feet, stretching.

"Just a moment, Hakon. Have you seen Vivian? Where is she
now?"

I shook my head, smiling. "Somewhere around here, pining
for her missing lover. She will be pleased."

A quarter of an hour later, the Ancient One and I were alone
down in the deep rocks. This time the cave looked and felt differ-

ent to me, somehow more hospitable. It was as if the very shapes of the rocks were smoother, the colors livelier.

Merlin began by putting more questions to me, particularly about Vivian. I told him she seemed to be preparing to spend her life with his younger self, a statement on which he made no comment. When I had answered his other questions as well as I was able, I was ordered to proceed on the quest that Merlin had warned me would be very difficult, but also absolutely essential to the success of his great enterprise: to reach Lancelot in his monastery. I was to carry certain things to him, material objects as well as words. And—without fail—I was to enlist him in the cause of Camelot's renewal.

Naturally enough, I asked Merlin how I would recognize King Arthur's famous warrior when I saw him.

You will know him.

Merlin went on to admit that my comrade-in-arms-to-be was now somewhat elderly for a warrior. When the great wizard helpfully provided a preliminary vision, I saw a face shockingly old in appearance.

"Where is this monastery?"

Somewhere in the kingdom of Logres. I need not give you precise, mundane directions. Travel in Logres is not like travel elsewhere.

"I have already noticed that, my lord."

But the Old Man at least gave me certain hints on how to find the place.

I was to depart, alone, on the next morning. By Lord Merlin's bounty I would be well armed, mounted, and supplied. I was to bring to Lancelot, as a gift from Merlin, a magnificent warhorse—a stallion, as snowy white as my own mount, otherwise its equal, was coal black. A pack mule was also provided, to carry to the famous knight a suit, just his size, of the marvelous armor from the manor's armory. Merlin assured me that Lancelot had worn the same type of armor often enough before, and would be perfectly familiar with its use.

"Never, Lord Merlin, have *I* seen the like before."

Certainly you have not; such armor will not be made for almost a thousand years.

Vivian was startled on encountering the bearded man who had approached me in the chapel, and for a few moments her reaction was uncertain, but the man of twenty-five evidently had enough in common with the lad of ten years younger that she could quickly recognize her lover.

Immediately she became entranced again. The pair went off somewhere to be alone, and no doubt enjoyed another day or so of glorious happiness before he told her that he must leave her yet again, be off on his own mysterious and vitally important business. This time, I heard him assure her later, he had a plan that would enable them to spend their lives together.

That evening it was at last Bran's turn to be summoned to a conference with the Old Man in the deep rocks.

The meeting took only a few minutes. Bran, on emerging from this confrontation with Merlin's Bones, called his old associates about him. He welcomed my presence when I joined them, out of curiosity.

Flagon-dry, Maud, and Jandree anxiously awaited what he was going to tell them.

The message Bran passed on to his remaining followers was that Merlin wanted them to take to the road again.

Before anyone could comment, Vivian and the young adult Merlin joined us—she kept looking up at him as if her life depended on him—and he presented the former minstrels with a choice. He offered it as a serious and important decision: whether they wished to remain here in New Camelot, as it would come to be, or resume their old nomadic life.

Bran himself said that if allowed a choice, he preferred to return to the entertainment business rather than stay here. As for taking part in the reconstruction of Camelot, he felt that life at court, any court, was not for him.

* * *

Vivian left it to the latest, oldest, and most dazzling version of her lover as to whether she would stay where the new king's court would eventually be located—especially if her lover could be expected to return to her here in any reasonable time—or go with Bran and his diminished troupe.

The youthful adult Merlin, standing with his arm round Vivian, told her lovingly that he meant to send her as soon as possible to some special place, keep her safe in the difficult and dangerous times that he foresaw ahead for all the rest of us.

Maud and Flagon-dry looked at each other, and announced that they were content to let Bran do the deciding for them. Bran had a magnetic quality of leadership, and Flagon-dry in his critical pride was already rumbling ominous predictions about the way the new court was likely to be organized.

Jandree was not at all satisfied with simply going back to the life of a traveling entertainer. But at the moment she seemed to have little choice. She still had a child, which she was perhaps beginning to view as a great encumbrance.

I thought that she looked at me with a silent appeal, but I felt less and less inclined to form an attachment with this woman who carried about and nursed another man's baby. Besides, I was about to set out on a difficult and dangerous mission. And I seemed to remember Old Merlin telling me that he meant to send these people on a mission of their own, for him. Now he appeared to be offering them a choice. I said nothing about the apparent contradiction, though it perturbed me somewhat.

"What will happen here?" Maud was demanding of Bran, and Merlin, or of anyone else who wanted to answer her.

"It will be Camelot," Bran assured her.

"What?"

"I said, this place is going to become Camelot."

"Have you gone daft?"

Bran controlled his temper. He looked around for Merlin and Vivian, but they had disappeared. When his remaining followers tried to demand assurances and explanations, he admitted being uncertain as to whether Merlin had really said this was the place that was really going to become Camelot. But the name had definitely been mentioned. And the manor house was expected to become a castle, and some kind of town would appear nearby, and would eventually be filled with people.

In the morning, making my final preparations for departure, I found that some unseen agency had already packed the mule with the objects it was to carry. Lancelot's suit of armor—and, as I discovered, a similar outfit tailored to fit me—had been disassembled into so many different pieces, of many different shapes, that it was not only heavy but somewhat awkward to pack and carry. Bound in two bundles on the mule's back the metal pieces rattled and jangled, as if enough armor for a whole longboat full of Northmen were being shaken.

With the arguments still going on among Bran and his people, I took my leave.

Departing uneventfully from Merlin's Rock, I traveled for some days alone through a green and pleasant countryside. After all the time-shifting I had experienced on my last journey, I was no longer at all confident as to what season of the year I might encounter in the next hour, or even the next minute. But I accepted fine weather gratefully, as I accepted the mount and the fine equipment that Merlin had provided. My horses, though mettlesome and strong—I took turns at riding each of them—gently tolerated the control of a relatively inexperienced rider.

Most of all I was thankful that on this quest I was spared any drastic shifts in time. Night followed day, and vice versa, in the traditional and logical progression. After riding for several days, I arrived one morning in the middle of a summery forest, where in a pleasant glade divided by a murmuring stream I found the establishment I sought. It was only a simple hut with a couple of small outbuildings, but I could distinguish this place from an ordinary small farm by the fact that a few yards from the central dwelling stood a small chapel surmounted by a crude wooden cross.

A man came out of the chapel and stood watching me with an anxious expression. He was short and stout, dressed in a gray robe, clean-shaven and with a tonsured head.

"Father Gregory?" I inquired.

His face cleared. "I am he."

He carried in his right hand a green bushy twig, and at his belt of beads a small flask of holy water. He was, as I soon learned, much given to splashing everything and everyone with holy water. Dipping twig into flask, he sprinkled me with crystal drops as I approached, then watched closely to see what the effect on me might be.

I did not care much for this spattering, but after the magical buffeting I had already survived, I did not want to be in the position of flinching at a joke or trifle. "What wizardry is this?"

"No wizardry, young man, but rather the blessing of Almighty God."

"In that case I accept it."

"You had better do so! Have you come far?" Gregory inquired.

"Far enough. From the spot where Camelot once stood." I said nothing, for the moment, about its standing there again.

My original Northman's clothing had long since been replaced, and my present outfit probably suggested that I came from Merlin. But when Father Gregory heard me talk he knew my origins.

The fact that I was a Northman suggested to the abbot that I was an unregenerate heathen, and he began to express great concern about my soul.

The stout man demanded sternly: "Have you been baptized in the name of Jesus?"

"Not yet. But I have not entirely ruled out the possibility."

The abbot's eyes were suddenly alight with hope. "Then you know that God's Son was made man, and dwelt among us?"

"I would like to hear the details of that story, sometime. But that is not why I have come here."

"Ah."

"I have come looking for Sir Lancelot."

The priest's eyes considered me warily. "No member of our little community bears any such worldly title."

Merlin had warned me about this, among other things. "I am

told that the man I seek may now be using a different name. Once he was Sir Lancelot, the right hand of King Arthur."

"Aha." The rotund priest clasped his hands so that the long sleeves of his habit swallowed them both, along with his sprinkling-twig. "And what do you want with such a man?"

"I bear a message to him, from Lord Merlin."

"Ah." Gregory raised his eyebrows, but he did not sound much surprised. "Only a message?" He looked meaningfully at my two horses, and the burdened mule.

"There are gifts also, if he will accept them. And also a princely donation for any church—or parish or monastery—whose abbot or Father Superior is cooperative."

"Ah." Gregory did not appear shocked by the prospect of worldly wealth, but neither was he overcome with greed.

"Tell me, most holy reverend, where will I find this man, who once was Lancelot?"

Somewhat to my surprise, Gregory did not insist on knowing first what I wanted of Lancelot. Nor did he attempt to answer for him, or forbid me to see him. Merlin, who knew much, had told me that Lancelot's not having taken final vows would simplify matters.

"Back in the days when Arthur ruled, I, too, once wanted to be a knight," said Father Gregory wistfully. His faded blue eyes looked far into the distance. "But it was not to be. Then for a time my dearest wish was to be a chaplain in King Arthur's court." As he said this he gazed at me hopefully.

"You knew King Arthur, then?"

The abbot's hands twitched in their sleeves, as if he might be repressing an urge to sprinkle something. He answered glumly. "Alas, no, I was never granted such a privilege. Nor have I ever met Lord Merlin—" His gaze sharpened. "For years now, as is widely known, Merlin has been confined in a kind of living tomb, by magic beyond even his power to countermand. How can you bring a message from him?"

"I understand that you have received certain signs that a true messenger is on his way to you. I am he."

"Merlin, yes." He rubbed his chin, then actually shivered.

"When we consider it is Merlin . . . yes, I suppose we all ought to have realized that no mere spell of an enchantress could succeed in holding . . ." He let the thought die away unfinished.

Gregory continued to ponder silently for a moment, then turned away, wordlessly beckoning me. I followed, with our two horses and the mule.

═══ TWENTY-FIVE ═══

L ancelot, clad like Gregory in a monk's habit of simple farmer's homespun, was working in a fair-sized garden when I first saw him, his big hands gripping the handle of a hoe. I have little knowledge of gardens, but I thought that this one showed evidence of care and skill. Surrounding the retired knight and working with him were a dozen other monks and novices, of all ages from beardless to bald, but his gray cowl towered above the others, and from my first glimpse I had no doubt of which man I was seeking.

The abbot and I had hardly come into view when Lancelot caught sight of us, and I suppose he might have hoped that we had not yet seen him. Be that as it may, when the man I had come to find looked up and saw a well-dressed stranger approaching with a small caravan of laden animals, he reacted with a champion's sure instinct for quick action, dropping his hoe and running swiftly on big sandaled feet into a nearby patch of woods. One glance at me had evidently told him where I came from, and his quick wit may have divined my mission.

Father Gregory and I followed. A little persistence on our part was necessary. He who had been the foremost knight of Camelot at first refused to come out of the woods when his ecclesiastical superior called after him, almost as if summoning a naughty child.

After delaying momentarily to sprinkle the garden and its work-ers from his flask, Father Gregory, muttering in irritation, led me in a patient, persistent pursuit into the grove. After Gregory sternly appealed to his honor, Lancelot at last emerged gloomily from behind a screen of bushes that had failed to adequately con-ceal him.

I suppose he might have retreated farther instead of coming out, except that he was well aware of the futility of trying to run away from a mounted man.

Father Gregory introduced me to the old knight as Sir Hakon, and said I had come with a message for him trom the great Lord Merlin. Then the priest, muttering something about wanting an-other look at the garden, withdrew politely to give Lancelot a chance to speak with me in private.

I had of course expected to meet a man no longer young, and Merlin had even granted me a brief preliminary vision, but still Lancelot's appearance in the flesh was something of a shock. The great champion's face was wrinkled now, his fringe of unevenly tonsured hair was gray and scant. The knuckles of his large hands were even larger than they should have been, beginning to swell with what must have been painful age. His right cheek was scarred, and some of his teeth, including a majority of those on the right side of his mouth, were missing, doubtless knocked out years ago in some deadly combat or friendly joust. Great Lance-lot's once magnificent frame had begun to collapse in upon itself, and it required no magical command of the future to see that if this man stayed a peaceful monk the straw death waited for him in no very great number of years.

I dismounted and shook his hand. His hooded, gray-blue eyes looked levelly into mine; he was one of the few men tall enough to do that.

He might be old, and beginning to bend, but the grip of his swollen knuckles was still strong, his hand steady. I remembered the speed with which I had seen him run out of the garden. I won-dered also whether before the fall of Camelot the champion might have had some magical help from Merlin in maintaining his youth—it seemed to me that Merlin had vaguely alluded to some such thing. If there ever had been such magical support, no doubt it had been withdrawn, or renounced as part of entering the religious life.

I told Lancelot succinctly what Lord Merlin wanted. I showed him the armor and the sword.

So far King Arthur's hero had hardly spoken a word to me. Absently he stroked the white stallion's neck. It was plain that he admired the animal, yet his real thoughts were elsewhere.

At last, in a surprisingly high-pitched, gentle voice, he asked about Arthur—calling him only "the king"—and I could do no better than relay the unsatisfactory answers Merlin had provided.

The gray head nodded. "Yes, that is always Merlin's way. To give ambiguous answers, or none at all."

"Sir Lancelot, I serve Lord Merlin. Are you ready to do so, too?"

There was a long pause before Lancelot answered. "I have found peace here, at last, and I am loath to leave. Yet it may be that my duty requires it. Merlin was never good King Arthur's enemy. Or mine."

The old knight had many questions for me, once he had got started asking them. Had I actually seen Arthur? Or anyone else from the court? How much truth was there in the stories telling how some young enchantress had charmed Merlin's best powers from him and entombed the old man alive? I answered to the best of my ability, explaining as best I could what I knew of the Old Man who dwelt in the deep rocks.

The man I had come to find, the knight on whom Merlin seemed to think our cause depended, listened morosely. Now and then he brightened with a small smile, but in general he retained an expression of deepening gloom.

Merlin had strongly hinted to me that Lancelot, whether he admitted the fact or not, would be still obsessed with Guinevere, that the possibility of being able to meet Guinevere again might be the only thing that could draw the old warrior-knight back into action. But so far neither Lancelot nor I had mentioned that name.

* * *

Father Gregory, who had not really retreated very far, eagerly rejoined us the moment Lancelot beckoned him back.

The abbot, his plump chest swelling, obviously was pleased to receive an emissary from Merlin. He envied Lancelot his opportunity to return to a life of glory, his chance to serve God by heroic deeds. How glorious to be offered a career of smiting evildoers, overturning false gods, defeating evil spirits and sending their willing human tools to join them in the Christian hell! Plainly Father Gregory was vaguely surprised and somewhat disappointed that Lancelot did not view the prospect with the same enthusiasm.

As Lancelot's hesitation seemed to be growing greater rather than less, the more he thought the matter over, Gregory became visibly displeased. He began to deliver a stern lecture, telling the elderly monk that his God-given gifts and duty lay in the direction of worldly, military service. The abbot also reminded his elderly novice of certain oaths of obedience that he had sworn.

But Lancelot continued to listen to our encouragements with a gloomy expression. He was not at all eager to go anywhere with me. He did not seem sure of where his duty or his salvation lay. But one thing he knew without having to ponder the matter, and said repeatedly: he was going to regret giving up his peaceful tilling of the soil. Once or twice he even spoke wistfully of fishing in the small nearby stream.

I was still quite a young man at that time, and basically shared Gregory's view of the situation. I did my best to persuade Lancelot to give up his monkish life and take up arms again.

"Lord Merlin bade me tell you that his enemies now press him sorely, and that the life of King Arthur hangs in the balance."

Lancelot seemed to take this information very seriously, but for the moment he made no comment.

I insisted the old warrior take a close look at the horse and armor Merlin had sent him. Actually the ploy was somewhat successful in stirring up old fires. Lancelot put his hand on the hilt of the new sword, then on the butt of the new lance, and stood for what seemed a long time in contemplation. It seemed to me that a certain spark had been reborn, deep in the gray-blue eyes.

I could hear the abbot's impatient breathing.

At last Lancelot, stroking the neck of his new warhorse, commented that they could certainly use such a strong beast in the fields.

The abbot and I were both becoming somewhat angered by this attitude. But we assured the old knight that he could retire again after he had helped Merlin.

"When must we leave?" he asked at last.

"The sooner the better."

Lancelot courteously bade farewell to each of his companions in the fields, who had been watching all these proceedings from a distance with open, silent mouths. Then he accepted a bundle of clothing from me and walked away; when he rejoined us ten minutes later, he had replaced his monkish habit with the garments Merlin had thoughtfully provided.

Gregory sent gaping novices scrambling about on errands. He hastened to provide us with some provisions, sprinkled all our equipment thoroughly, enviously waved farewell, and shouted blessings after us till we were out of sight.

❧ *Bran* ❧

I had not realized how attached Jandree had grown to the physical comforts of life in Merlin's manor. But as the appointed deadline for our departure drew near, she hemmed and hawed about leaving this place of magic, thought up and wanted to debate new difficulties.

I felt it necessary to prompt her: "He wants us to go, since that was our choice, and he has established a deadline for our departure."

"But now you want to leave early." She jiggled our still-nameless baby in her arms, and looked at our son as if commiserating with him on his father's obstinacy and general wrongheadedness.

The current weather was threatening, if not quite forbidding. "Perhaps not necessarily today. But tomorrow is the deadline."

Meanwhile Maud and Flagon-dry, for all their continual arguing and debating, were basically content to allow me to decide things for them. Once I had decided to return to the road, they began to look forward to the prospect.

"Merlin says he'll give us a new wagon—*two* new wagons—and see to it that we have success. That was how he put it."

This discussion took place while we all sat round the ordinary rectangular dining table in the front hall, with a wan sun lancing in through high narrow windows.

At this moment, to the general surprise of the assembled company, a rat suddenly appeared, as if from nowhere, and went scurrying along the base of the wall. Another small furry shape soon followed. The house, so warm and inviting when I first saw it, was becoming gradually less hospitable.

The two women—three at the times when Vivian was on hand—whose holiday from kitchen work had now evidently ended, reported that not only had the magical preparation and preservation of food come to an end, but the larder was starting to run short of supplies.

When the question arose as to exactly when we should leave Merlin's house, the others deferred (in Jandree's case reluctantly) to me. And I was ready to leave at any time, the sooner the better.

❧ *Hakon* ❧

Lancelot and I discussed all manner of things between us as we rode side by side. Now that he had agreed to accompany me, my irritation had evaporated. And gradually his gloom was lifting. The weather was fine, and his stallion, as I have said, was a magnificent animal. Heartened by his courtesy, I began to feel more than ever that I might really make a successful king, if some great power appreciated my virtues sufficiently to give me a chance.

In the midst of our discussions Lancelot asked me: "Hakon, in what ways do you believe kings are above the ordinary?"

I frowned. This was one of those difficult questions that a man may have settled to his own satisfaction, in his own mind, and yet the answer is difficult to put into words.

"I think," I said at last, "that a great king like Arthur—or a queen, like old Boadicea—would be great whether or not anyone had ever adorned their heads with golden ornaments. On the other hand, there are many who wear crowns, or want them badly enough to kill for them, who are strong in nothing but ambition and arrogance. Such are not worth a simple honest warrior, or even a peasant. But they can be very dangerous."

৵ Interlude ৵

The beds, or berths, inside the ambulance were built about waist-high to a person standing in the narrow aisle between. The berth on the left was wide enough to have held two adult bodies side by side. On the right side, Arthur—or whoever the comatose man might really be—pretty well filled the narrower, single bunk. His sizable frame was clad in a white shirt or robe, under a blue sheet.

Elaine again tried speaking to the unconscious man, tried touching his arm, then gently holding his muscular hand, on which, she now noticed, were two jeweled rings of impressive beauty. But the eyelids with their fair lashes remained closed, and beyond those gentle attempts at waking him she was afraid to go.

The ambulance's main onboard computer was in the rear, where anyone in the driver's seat would have to turn and strain to see it. The small screen now proclaimed:

> *Down she came and found a boat*
> *Beneath a willow left afloat,*
> *And round about the prow she wrote*
> *The Lady of Shalott . . .*

At the moment Elaine had no trouble ignoring one more screen filled with madness. She was enormously relieved at having got clear of the laboratory, away from Mordred and his killers. But she had not the faintest idea where she had landed. She was enormously grateful to Fisher for getting her away, but he had given no warning of anything like this.

Dr. Brusen thought she would be delighted to see again, or at least communicate with, Dr. Fisher, even if his on-screen verses were threatening to drive her mad. She wanted to make contact with him, and this time force him, or induce him, to tell her what was going on.

She drove on a little farther, then, feeling herself in the last stages of exhaustion—how long was it since she had really slept?—she pulled off the road, turned off the van's lights, and crawled fully clothed onto the bunk opposite King Arthur's. Her head had hardly touched the spartan pillow before she was asleep.

On awakening, to the brightness of midday sunlight filtered through high mist and falling on tinted window glass, she lay for a few moments thinking what a marvelous dream it had all been and wondering where she really was. Then outrageous reality intruded. She got up, checked the patient again, and observed no change.

After a brief trip outdoors—there was no onboard plumbing—she found some food, peanut butter and crackers, and an apple, in a small locker behind the driver's seat.

Yet another look at Arthur. No change—of course. Elaine once more left the vehicle and began an attempt at exploring this world on foot, but she was afraid to go more than a few paces from the ambulance, which represented not only shelter but a psychological connection with the world in which she had spent her life until yesterday, and which she thought of as reality.

A couple of deer looked at her from the edge of the woods, and then ran off. Otherwise this green and pleasant place seemed uninhabited.

The trees crowded around, if not in friendly fashion, still unthreatening. The road went forward and back, in both directions promptly vanishing among the trees. Birds sang. Bees hummed.

Well, she couldn't sit here indefinitely. It was not in Elaine's nature to wait passively for anything. The only alternative to sitting here was to drive on again.

Arthur still looked comfortable; he was leaving everything up
to her. The van's engine started promptly. When she had proceeded about a quarter of a mile, the figure of a man appeared at
roadside just at the next turn, fifty yards or so ahead, staff in hand,
making the traditional gesture of a hitchhiker. Elaine slowed,
crept forward anxiously, until she could see that it was Fisher.

Eagerly she pulled up and stopped to welcome him as he
limped aboard.

His first words, delivered in a worried tone, told her that she
reminded him somewhat of Tennyson's *Lady of Shallot*.

Dr. Brusen did not bother to reply to that. Her passenger
belted himself into the passenger seat, where he sat clutching his
staff. His first practical advice, given tersely and with a look over
his shoulder, was to keep on driving.

Elaine eased the van forward. She was surprised at how relieved she was to again be in touch with, and have the support of,
this man, who only a few hours ago had been a feared intruder. It
seemed to her that many days had passed since Fisher's first unexpected phone call.

"Maybe you can tell me where I am, at least. And give me
some real information about—the man in back."

Fisher looked concerned. "Is he all right?"

"I don't know. He's alive. There's what appears to be sophisticated medical gear hooked up to him, and he's breathing. Of
course I suppose he ought not to be here, riding around in this,
this . . ." She didn't know how to finish.

Fisher smiled. "And you and I aren't enjoying it that much
either. Well, we can try to bring him to where he'll get the help
he needs."

"Fine. So let me repeat my first question—where am I?"

"In Logres."

"*Where?*"

"It's difficult to be more specific. There's really no latitude
and longitude in Logres." He had to spell it for her. Still the word
meant nothing. "Distances are variable, but if you can keep your
destination firmly in mind, you can generally reach it."

She replied: "I don't know that story."

"Doubtless that's just as well. Look here, Dr. Brusen, are you coping? Have you had anything to eat?"

"Not much. But there are still some crackers left, and that's the least of my worries."

"I can't stay with you long. I will try to remain in communication, but it is really necessary that I should be somewhere else. I must try to draw the attention of the enemy away from you."

"You're leaving me again?"

"Yes, I'm afraid so."

"Maybe it would be better if I just went with you when you leave."

"No, it would not be better." For once Fisher looked quite grim. "You will be much more comfortable, and even safer, driving on—and if things work out properly, you won't have very far to go to find real help."

Fisher warned Elaine to look out for Morgan—but, since Mordred posed a much deadlier threat, the best move was to try to reach Morgan's castle and seek help. Fisher also assured Dr. Brusen that she would have enough fuel.

"A castle. All right," Elaine murmured, nodding. It occurred to her that if Fisher had told her to stop at the next crossroads and ask directions of a dragon, she would have agreed just as calmly.

Fisher described Morgan's flag. Elaine stopped the vehicle, and before Fisher got out the two of them went together to look yet again at the patient in the back.

Then Fisher, saying he thought it would be better if he did not visit Morgan's castle, got out and waved good-bye, and limped away into the woods.

Elaine hesitated for just a moment, then shouted and ran after him. But it was no use. Fisher had simply disappeared.

Arthur—she found herself compulsively thinking of the patient by that name—was still comatose, but still breathing, and still being monitored and cared for by the machines. Whatever the truth of that matter, she couldn't just sit here. Well, maybe she could try that tactic for a while. But she refused to.

* * *

Elaine drove on. There was no odometer, she realized suddenly, and she had no way to measure how far she had driven. She could only hope that Fisher had been right about the fuel, as he seemed to have been right on other matters. Certainly the dashboard lacked any conventional gauge.

The road curved, and curved, and then suddenly straightened into an unbranching vista, leading to the lowered drawbridge of a huge impressive castle, set a quarter of a mile away amid broad treeless fields. Fluttering from the highest tower were pennants of red and black that Elaine could now recognize as belonging to King Arthur's half-sister, the sorceress Morgan le Fay.

═══ TWENTY-SIX ═══

↬ *Bran* ↬

O ld Merlin's promise of largess to our once-shabby group of entertainers was kept in full measure as we made ready to set out upon our journey. In the courtyard, which was still littered with the ugly aftermath of war, we climbed aboard our two new wagons, with two big young oxen hitched to each. There were two spare mules for riding. None of this seemed magical, I thought. All of the equipment and animals were as solid and mundane as mud—or as the stone walls of the House of the Oracle—more so, because some of those walls had already begun to swell, practically before our eyes, into the walls of Camelot.

One wagon would have been enough to transport our diminished company, even had we all chosen to ride. But one of our new conveyances, as we soon discovered, was loaded with a variety of new musical and other equipment, all snugly packed away. These things, instruments and clever gadgets, were well and truly made, but possessed no magic powers that I could see—none of us had practiced music for many days, and we frequently hit sour notes when we tested the new instruments. So to hold everything two wagons were really necessary. Anyway, the new wheels and strong oxen made travel almost a pleasure.

Hour by hour, lately almost minute by minute, the house at Merlin's Oracle had been losing the magic that had made it so seduc-

tively pleasant to live in, becoming less welcoming and support-
ive to us all. It was as if Merlin meant to force us to move out for a
time, simply because the place would not be safe to live in, during
the coming transformation.

Still Jandree kept questioning the desirability of moving on.
She kept saying she wanted to delay the journey until she felt
stronger. I pointed out to my wife that the place had begun to get
downright inhospitable. Refuse now accumulated as it would
in any other house, and the spoiled inhabitants felt somehow
wronged by the fact. The fires in hearths and stoves went out if
they were left unattended—sometimes even if they were not—
and fresh unspoiled food no longer appeared in kitchen and refectory before we were aware we needed it.

Maud clothed her near-eagerness to leave in a kind of crabbed
reluctance. "Well—this business of sleeping in fine beds, eating
every day at the main table in the great hall—I suppose it's not
really for us. And a room that goes on and on, and has glass for a
rear wall—and all those books!"

She paused, looking at me. "You don't think he's angry with
us, though?"

I shook my head. "Merlin? No, not at all. Actually I get the
impression that he's well satisfied. Giving us a free choice as a
reward. Maybe the most valuable thing he could have given us."

To them it seemed only reasonable. "Shall we tell the Old
Man good-bye, sir? Or can you do that for us?"

"I can do it. But . . ."

"But what?"

"We don't really need to say good-bye. I think we'll be hearing from him again."

"Oh."

When we had all in readiness, we began our journey. Vivian
was no longer with us, which did not surprise me when I remembered that young Merlin wanted her with him. After a little debate over what was most fitting, we left the gate of the House on
the Rock open behind us, just as we had found it.

When we had gone a quarter of a mile or so, I turned back for
a last look. But although the place where we paused should have

been in sight of our starting point, the high rocks and the manor house and the wall had all disappeared, and the very coastline looked entirely different.

As the days of our renewed wandering passed, Jandree recovered rapidly from the wounds and stresses of childbirth. I was at least pleased at having been able to get Jandree away from the man who would have seduced her, and for all I knew had already done so.

Most of the days I spent riding on my new mule beside one of the new wagons. At night I stretched out to sleep, a little apart from the others—Jandree was of course not yet fully healed from giving birth, and in any case matters had turned decidedly cool between me and my wife.

Once we had left Merlin's Rock behind us, no further magical manifestations seemed to attend our progress. Except that, whenever there was any definite choice to be made, one road, one route, always seemed easier and more inviting than the others.

As soon as I had taken notice of this effect, I decided to test it one morning by deliberately choosing what seemed a more difficult turning. I did this without telling any of my comrades. Soon more choices arose, the differences between them more and more dramatic, until we had been brought back to the path Merlin really wanted us to take.

We visited a number of villages, and several lesser manors or strongholds in succession. In the first we recruited out of the audience, by happy accident as it seemed, a girl better at dancing and singing than Vivian had ever been. That girl left us at our next stop, but another joined us. Merlin's hand again, and we all realized it now. Despite what I thought were our diminished skills, our performances had never been more successful.

Hakon

Lancelot and I got on as well as I had hoped, and we made what seemed to me good time on our journey (as I thought) back to Merlin's Rock.

One may have a hard time finding the place one wants to reach in Logres, but all roads there lead to something interesting. Whatever the difficulties of living in that land, dullness and boredom have never been among them.

Presently my companion and I came to a river crossing where we found ourselves confronted by trolls, who barred our way.

Lancelot had met trolls before, and I was not, with Merlin's warnings in mind, greatly surprised at the sight of the monstrous creatures.

The trolls were grotesque half-human-looking monsters, disfigured by pointed heads and enormous ears, crudely armed with clubs and poles, who came out of the thickets of tall reeds growing rank along the riverbank and silently took up their positions squarely in the road.

If we were not to turn back—and of course that was out of the question—there appeared to be no way of avoiding combat. I was certainly no novice when it came to fighting, but against such opponents I found myself at a loss as to the best way to proceed.

"Disgusting creatures!" I observed.

Lancelot only nodded. They dropped their dung like animals, as if unconscious of the act, even as we stood looking at them. They called to us insultingly, or at least I took that to be the intention of the barking noises that they uttered. It seemed to me it would be a waste of time to call anything at all back to them. Lancelot agreed.

Adding to the uncertainty was that of the possible numbers of the enemy. There were three of the trolls in sight, all male, with thick, gray, almost hairless bodies, and mud-colored skin. One wore only a minimum of ragged clothing, while the other two wore none at all. Black hair coarse as that of any horse grew wild on their misshapen heads, and on their chins, and from under their knobby arms. On the body of the biggest troll the hair was turning gray. From a little distance they appeared no larger than men, and indeed they were no taller. They began a very slow advance, and when they had worked their way closer I could see not only their oddly bright green eyes, but how enormous were their hands and feet, and the muscles in their oddly shaped arms.

Lancelot, who if half the stories were true had faced a considerable number of exotic challenges during his active career, did not seem at all uncertain as to how to proceed against such fantastic creatures.

He dismounted, saying simply: "In the land of Logres they are not uncommon."

Looking at Lancelot's wrinkled face and stooped shoulders, I was struck by a sudden worry that I would not only have to fight three trolls, but also protect the old man at my side.

Lancelot had not yet tried on Merlin's armor. Nor had I, thinking that such clanking weight must be a wonderful hindrance to the actions that a man in combat is required to perform.

"What do you recommend, Sir Lancelot? Advance or retreat? I say we have a go at them." Though I did not relish the prospect, we really had no choice, if we were to follow the indicated road. The river was a real torrent, both above and below the ford; the landscape of Logres was always interesting to say the least.

"We will fight them." My companion's tone was reassuringly workmanlike. He was not giving an order, only stating a fact. I had wondered if the prospect of immediate combat would cheer him up, but it seemed to have no emotional impact at all. "We must fight. But it must be done properly."

"Do you suppose there may be more than three?"

"Of course, they may have reserves back in the thicket." The elder knight shot me an approving glance, well satisfied that I had thought of that. "But we can find out before the fight begins."

I murmured something to the effect that I supposed magical help against trolls was possible. My companion brusquely reminded me that we had no effective magician with us at the moment.

"I suppose I ought to have expected as much."

I had never actually encountered anything resembling such

monsters before. But then I thought of the creatures Merlin had herded before him with his staff, when we went to drive Comorre out of the manor, and I wondered whether these had had their origins in some similar, though opposing, magic.

"With armor," said Lancelot, untying the metal bundles from the mule, "we can defeat them easily."

I expressed a polite doubt that anyone could move effectively in such a mass of metal.

The old man showed the remnants of his teeth. I think it was the first time I had seen him really smile. He said in his calm, high voice: "More effectively than you seem to think. If the right man wears it."

Refusing further explanations for the time being, Lancelot got me to help him unpack the armor from the mule's back and lay it out on the muddy ground as if this were some tournament field and we had all the time in the world to make our preparations.

"For myself," I said, "I choose not to wear the armor."

My companion only nodded and smiled. Then, instead of putting on his own armor, his next move was to shoo our animals away from us, in the opposite direction from the enemy. The horses and mule were well trained—I suppose I ought to have realized that Merlin would have provided no other kind—and did not go far.

I had grave doubts about the wisdom of depriving ourselves of our horses' strength and speed, and it seemed to me that my concern was soon justified. Scarcely had we arranged the gleaming display when the trolls advanced with threatening displays, awkwardly and ineffectively hurling rocks and clods of dried mud, shouting unintelligible noises that must have been meant as threats and imprecations.

Lancelot immediately retreated on foot, toward where our animals waited, sharply ordering me to come with him. In this game I was glad to avoid the responsibilities of command.

The trolls, on coming up to where we had left the display of armor, stopped suddenly and began to investigate the bright strange objects. In a moment, they had been thoroughly distracted by it, and began to dispute over this prize among themselves.

They were clever enough to understand that the pieces were meant to be somehow strapped on and worn, and tried to fit them to their own inhuman bodies. Only the smallest troll had much success in fastening armor to his limbs or body; only the largest found his head a decent fit inside the helm.

In rage the creatures struggled on, trying to force the armor to fit their bodies, hobbling and entangling themselves with straps and unbending plates. Sometimes they could twist the gleaming greaves and breastplates in their bare hands when they strained; for the most part Merlin's armor was too strong for even trolls.

In another moment the trolls were quarreling and fighting among themselves over the bright metal, and one of them stunned another with a blow to the head from his wooden club.

"Now, Sir Hakon!" And Lancelot raised his sword and charged.

I followed that great warrior, and passed him on my younger legs, and fought, with my own short spear and sword. It turned out that, as my mentor had foreseen, we had no need for long lances, or well-trained horses.

Lancelot and I slew the monsters. Despite the fact that one of them was stunned before we attacked, and the other two were seriously hampered in their movements, they were still able to put up a considerable struggle, in which I suffered a couple of trifling wounds.

When wounded the trolls groveled on the ground, and this would have made it difficult to finish them off from horseback.

In my view Lancelot fought amazingly well, perhaps better than I did, for all his years. Once the combat started, he seemed visibly rejuvenated.

When the fight was over and we were resting, I learned from Sir Lancelot more concerning the skill and art of fighting monsters, trolls, and giants, and he discussed with me some of the fine points of fighting dragons, too.

He mentioned at least one other good system for troll-fighting, which I now pass along, for whatever it is worth: "You bait a giant, and get him to follow you to the ford or bridge, what-ever the place may be; and with any luck at all, your two enemies will contest the passage with each other."

✣ Bran ✣

Most of the towns and villages that our diminished troupe visited in our tour appeared quite ordinary, places such as we might have encountered in our travels before arriving at Merlin's Rock. But it became plainer and plainer to me that on leaving that locus of enchantment, we had not reentered the same land that we had traveled before we arrived there. We were in the land of Logres now, and we kept recruiting and losing talented girl dancers at practically every stop.

Some of the inhabitants of Logres, as of other lands, were na-tive born, while others, particularly the older residents, had mi-grated there from more mundane realms—as we had now done also.

In every town or manor that we visited, any entertainers at all were welcome, and any who made such a bright appearance as those of my entourage were well treated indeed, and urged to stay.

And still, whenever we were ready to move on, one way always looked the easiest and most promising. Merlin, I was increasingly sure, was not done with us yet. He had not given us these replace-ments for Vivian, these wagons and tools and animals, out of the sheer disinterested goodness of his heart. There was no doubt in my mind that he wanted something more from us. But what?

✣ Hakon ✣

Shortly after Lancelot and I had overcome the trolls and crossed the ford, we found our path crossed by a strange trail, as of out-sized wagon wheels evidently unaccompanied by the hoofprints of whatever beasts were pulling it. The road was soft enough that any feet must have left some tracks, yet there were none but the strange endless grooves.

My companion on studying this became positively jovial, and said he thought it signified the possibility of some great adventure, and that we would be but poor knights if we failed to investigate. I was half inclined to agree with him, and as I had but small idea of which way to go to get back to Merlin's Rock, I shrugged and went along.

Through swamps and thickets and over rocky outcroppings we followed the strange trail for half a day. Though I began to urge that we should return to Merlin and New Camelot as quickly as possible, Lancelot insisted on following up this adventure. Still, my arguments were deprived of much of their force by the fact that I had no idea which way we should go to find New Camelot. The road I had taken on departing thence had wound about in complex curves, and days of mist and fog had prevented my getting a good bearing on the sun.

And at last, worn and bewildered, but as far as we could tell no closer to overtaking the strange wagon than when we started, we reached a castle and sought shelter and hospitality for the night.

When the drawbridge came creaking down to let us ride into the courtyard, it was Morgan le Fay who greeted us, with the air of one who had been expecting our arrival. The enchantress, surrounded by her usual retinue of animals and a respectable number of human attendants, welcomed us into her own realm.

Lancelot and I rode in to find parked in Lady Morgan's courtyard the strange wagon that had left the mysterious trail. There, surrounded now by various workers, spear-carrying soldiers, and gaping attendants, stood one of the most amazing objects I had ever seen in a lifetime of adventuring: a closed conveyance of metal and glass, mounted on four black wheels, and evidently to be propelled by sorcery, for there was no provision for harnessing horse or mule or oxen to that smooth carriage.

And beside it, an unusual woman, dressed in outlandish clothing. When Lancelot first saw her I thought for a moment that his heart had stopped, and then he breathed something about how like this woman was to the young Guinevere.

And then the rear doors of the strange carriage were being opened, and suddenly the name of King Arthur was in the air; on every side, Morgan's soldiers and attendants were murmuring it with wonder.

TWENTY-SEVEN

I was pleased that the Lady Morgan had chosen to grant me something like equal status with the great Sir Lancelot. She had welcomed the two of us with the same cheer, and now we were alike her guests—both welcome visitors at the castle of Morgan le Fay, King Arthur's sister, and an enchantress whose power had been surpassed only by that of Merlin himself.

But my arrival and even Sir Lancelot's went almost unnoticed by most of the inhabitants of Morgan's castle. Their attention was still concentrated on the magic vehicle that had reached the castle only minutes before we had, driven by the woman who so resembled Queen Guinevere. But the truly important development, the fact that set everyone in the courtyard talking, was the fact that King Arthur himself lay grievously wounded inside this conveyance, which was said to come from the unknown future. His sister, Morgan, had looked in on him, and then had given orders that the king was not to be removed; there were magical devices inside that preserved his life. This, too, Morgan had evidently foreseen.

I had a great curiosity to see King Arthur but was unable to do so, because of the press of others in and about the wagon.

Lancelot continued to marvel at how closely the woman Elaine resembled Guinevere. Otherwise he accepted our situation with what I thought surprising calm. Earlier, as we rode side by side on our magnificent horses, he had told me stories confirming ideas I had heard in recent days from others, that Morgan le Fay was fanatically determined to see Arthur her brother healed of his near-fatal wound, and then restored to what she regarded as his rightful place upon the throne.

As soon as he heard the outcry about King Arthur being in the strange conveyance, Lancelot forced his way through the crowd, to the side of his former king and comrade. It seemed that he meant to stay there. Such loyalty was commendable, but it added a puzzling complication to my duties, because Lord Merlin had required me to bring Lancelot back to New Camelot.

Moments later the Lady Morgan, saying there were important matters she wished to discuss with me alone, dazzled me with an invitation to walk with her in an inner courtyard. There, amid masses of tall flowers whose perfumes made my senses swim, we strolled side by side in a beautiful (and, I have no doubt, enchanted) garden while two of her great cats padded beside us and stared at me solemnly with yellow eyes.

As the enchantress and I walked among these scenes and scents of beauty, she questioned me closely about Merlin. I saw no reason not to tell her the truth of my dealings with the Old Man in the Rocks, and she listened with great interest. Then the Lady Morgan admitted to me that she was suspicious of Merlin, to say the least. But that old man, as she called him, was not her biggest problem at the moment. She announced herself ready now to make common cause with Merlin, against the combined threat of Wodan, Mordred, and Comorre.

As a pledge of her good faith, the Lady Morgan said, she was now willing to restore, to Merlin's soon-to-be-rebuilt Camelot, the magic chair called the Siege Perilous.

"I have heard it mentioned, lady," I responded cautiously.

She moved beside me with a long stride, hands clasped behind her thoughtfully, pacing almost like a man. But nothing else seemed masculine about her. "As for Old Merlin himself . . . I cannot tell at this distance exactly how much life remains in those rock-crushed remnants of his bones. But I am sure that a great deal of magical virtue still resides in them . . . and you, Hakon, my honorable Northman, having been by your own admission down among those rocks, you could probably lead a determined seeker to the exact spot where Merlin's Bones are hidden." Her dark eyes flashed at me, and she offered a smile that stirred my manhood and at the same time sent a chill of apprehension down my spine.

"It is possible that I could do so, lady. But I—"

"Yes, yes, to be sure, you have pledged your loyalty to Merlin. Well, I require no treachery of you, but we shall see. When you and I are standing close together—near the place where his bones lie—then we shall see."

Indeed I still considered myself a loyal vassal of Lord Merlin, and had no intention of revealing anything to his enemies that would harm him. Still, it was not clear to me that Morgan was really Merlin's enemy. And she already knew that I had spent days on the site of what was going to become New Camelot, and that I had talked to the bones—or to the Old Man for whom those relics represented his last tenuous grasp on earthly life.

Linking her arm in mine, in a gesture that assumed we were close allies or even intimate friends, Morgan paced on, catlike. She led the conversation around to the attacks we could all very soon expect to endure from Mordred, who had now joined up with Comorre the Cursed, their combined forces being dangerously strong. I had heard something from Lancelot about Mordred, how he was really Arthur's bastard son, and how he had survived the battle in which his father was struck down. And how Lancelot feared that Mordred, sad to say, was still out to destroy his father.

Morgan's silver laughter mocked me when I incautiously admitted my suspicion that Merlin someday intended to make me, Hakon, the new king, replacing Arthur. The lady in turn promised me nothing. But somehow I came away from our conversation with the idea that she might someday consider making me lord of her domain—that a day might come when she herself would sit beside me as my wife and lady.

Morgan also told me that one day she would show me her library, and claimed that it rivaled Merlin's.

And the lady hinted that she knew and had used the secret of opening a path from one library to another. This made it a practical matter, and I had questions. Was there a certain minimum number of books required in each room, or possibly several copies of the same volume, or volumes? Were the opening and reading of books part of the ritual necessary to establish a connection? Alas, my questions received no solid answers.

As we continued walking in her garden, Morgan le Fay also gave me information (more than I could understand) about a subject on which Lancelot had, in passing, provided only a few tantalizing details. This concerned the head of the third powerful faction contending for Merlin's Bones—the Fisher King.

The enchantress assured me that this mysterious ruler, who suffered from an incurable wound in his thigh, was connected in some way with the Sangreal, or Holy Grail, the vessel used by Jesus of Nazareth at the Last Supper, which he shared with his disciples on the night before he was betrayed and slain.

Morgan told me that Lancelot himself had once, long years ago, been given an opportunity to discover the Grail, but he had failed bitterly, through some unspecified weakness on his part; the lady provided no details, and in such a matter I did not try to discover them.

Morgan, though she was certainly capable of ruthless deeds, spoke always warmly and lovingly of her brother, and impressed me as having King Arthur's welfare as her first objective. She at least did not seem to be the worst of those contending for the power inherent in Merlin's Bones.

My talk with the Lady Morgan was interrupted by a messenger, who brought news of the arrival of a troupe of traveling entertainers. From the description, I at once recognized Bran and his people. I quickly explained to the lady that I knew these folk, and that they had been with me at Merlin's Rock.

I think that Morgan was surprised, for once. But I could see that immediately some idea occurred to her of how she might make use of this development.

"See that they are given food and drink," she told her courtier. "But they are not to entertain us, or even unpack their wagons. Rather I have a little extra cargo for them to carry back to Merlin."

As I soon learned, her idea was to send the Siege Perilous on to Merlin with Bran and his people. There were apparently reasons why she now wished to be rid of the magic chair as soon as possible.

No sooner had the courtier left us than Lancelot appeared in the garden, having temporarily left his place at the side of his fallen king.

The old knight asked Morgan if he and I were her captives or her guests. Lancelot also remarked that it was not the first time that he had been Morgan's guest—or prisoner.

Seeing how Morgan looked at him, I wondered if they had once been lovers; but if so, it was soon plain, from the lady's behavior, that those days were past. She answered: "You are both my guests, brave knights—God forbid that I should ever detain either of you against your will. I only regret that both of your visits are going to be so extremely brief."

With that she turned her back on us and swirled away. Lancelot and I, exchanging helpless looks, hastened to follow the enchantress out of her garden, back to the courtyard where Arthur still lay hidden in his magical conveyance, surrounded now by attendants of every kind. Still I was unable to get near enough to see what the great king looked like. Well, I thought, I had witnessed marvels enough for one day.

Now standing near the king's magic conveyance were the two new wagons Merlin had provided for Bran's people. While the performers were being treated to a meal, one of their wagons had already been loaded with the new cargo Morgan had wanted placed aboard. And now she hastily gave orders that the entertainers should be hurried on their way—and in a seeming afterthought she declared that I, Hakon, should go with them.

This required a protest. "My lady, I have orders from my lord Merlin to bring Lancelot to him."

"I promise you, Sir Hakon, that I will see to it that Sir Lancelot goes to Merlin's Rock."

⚜ Interlude ⚜

Dr. Elaine Brusen sat, for the moment alone, at a table in the great hall of Morgan's castle, enjoying a good meal of exotic though nonmagical food. And attempting, as usual these days, to come to grips with everything that had happened to her. The man named Bran and a small group of his fellow entertainers had been in the same room for a while, dining at a lower table, but a moment ago a man had come to hurry them on their way—some plan of Morgan's.

Human servers came and went through the big, stone-walled room, like the rest of Morgan's retinue quite ordinary-looking people except for their Dark Age costumes.

Dr. Brusen, chewing on some truly tasty bread, thought that she had learned much over the past few hours. Now she believed she had gained some understanding of the basic facts about the magical struggle to recover Merlin's Bones and to put to use their massive magical potential.

Elaine soon returned to the courtyard where the ambulance still waited. There she rejoined Morgan and the older man who had been introduced to her as Sir Lancelot. Looking at him, Elaine found herself ready to believe it.

Lancelot proclaimed himself willing to fight for King Arthur's survival. And ready to risk his life, in order that King Arthur, his former lord, rival, and intimate companion, should at last be healed.

"And are you ready," Morgan demanded, "to risk your life that he may once again be king?"

"Lady, he is my king, I have no other." Lancelot paused before asking: "And where is my lady Guinevere, the queen? I have heard that when Arthur fell she went into a nunnery."

"That is true, noble knight." Before Morgan could say more,

she was interrupted by an outcry. Lookouts on the high walls were crying that Mordred's army had appeared, and was advancing rapidly.

Morgan took this news coolly. She told Elaine that as Arthur's sister she was pleased and grateful for Elaine's help, and that Elaine had earned a reward. But that would have to wait. An attack on the castle by Wodan's army was obviously imminent, and there was no guarantee that the defenses would hold. Morgan was therefore anxious to get the ambulance and its all-precious (as she saw it) cargo away to some place of greater safety.

The best hope she could come up with—any port in a storm—was the vicinity of Merlin's Rock. "There is much about the old man that I do not like, or trust—but at the moment we have little choice. Besides, from there the way may be still open to your world." She looked at Elaine. "And from there, the magic of machines that you are capable of working can carry him to where he may be healed."

Morgan was standing in front of the ambulance now, stroking the smooth metal of the hood as if to soothe a nervous animal. She said: "Lancelot is going with you." She smiled. "As your protector. I think that will work out well. Yes, that should be best for all concerned." And she smiled an enigmatic smile.

"In any case, my lady," said Lancelot, "I think I should have refused any order that required me to leave my king's side, as long as he remains in danger. But this command I will not refuse." And his hooded, gray-blue eyes stirred Elaine deeply when they looked at her.

The lady now climbed into the right-hand chair inside the front compartment of the magic vehicle, murmuring that she wanted to see what it was like. "Meanwhile," she continued, "I must stay here, to put up as strong a defense as possible, and delay any further pursuit. You must drive first, if you can, to Camelot— or to what was Camelot. Whether or not it may ever be so again. To Merlin's Rock." She twisted in her seat to frown at the computer screen. "What say those words, appearing on the glass? It seems that some enchantment prevents my reading them."

Elaine turned in the driver's seat to look, and read:

And down the river's dim expanse
Like some bold seër in a trance,
Seeing all his own mischance—
With a glassy countenance
Did she look to Camelot.

But before Elaine could attempt a rendering of Tennyson, Morgan had slid out of the ambulance again, and was standing beside it exchanging questions and answers with her military advisers. Meanwhile Fisher's face had now appeared upon the onboard screen. He began giving advice in his avuncular way, assuring Elaine that a passable road existed for the entire distance.

"And though Lady Morgan is personally unfamiliar with the ambulance, it is largely her creation—you might say it has been customized at her orders—and it can doubtless handle difficult terrain better than any mere twenty-first-century vehicle."

Morgan had turned back to face the van, and was making urgent motions. Elaine, already behind the wheel, muttered something in reply and faced forward again, fastening her seat belt. In another moment Sir Lancelot, looking grimly ready for this new experience, was strapped into the right front passenger seat, holding his weapons. He nodded his readiness for whatever was about to happen next. Elaine felt something solid and reassuring in his controlled ferocity.

More shouts came drifting down from high upon the battlements; the enemy force was powerful, and rapidly advancing.

In the next moment a huge rock, evidently propelled by some siege engine, came hurtling over walls to land in the courtyard with a crash. The screams of the wounded and terrified went up to the sky.

"Quickly! That way!" Morgan commanded fiercely, and stepped back, pointing. Elaine pressed her foot down on the accelerator, and the big van leaped forward.

The great gates in the high wall were flung apart by magic.

The attack of Wodan's army was threatening, about to burst

upon the castle's defenses, even as Elaine drove the ambulance roaring out, over a lowered drawbridge.

There flew the boar's-head banners of Comorre. Human men in armor, moving side by side with larger things that were not human, formed ragged ranks that at first sagged back before the accelerating van, then closed again, tighter than ever, as it hurtled straight toward them.

═══ TWENTY-EIGHT ═══

ഛ *Hakon* ഛ

Neither Bran nor I realized what was about to happen when we departed from Morgan's stronghold. But less than an hour was to pass before the army led by Mordred and Comorre arrived at the castle and fell upon its defenders in a furious attack.

No one in that army was aware of my absence from the scene, or Bran's. Nor did they know or care that we had recently been present under Morgan's roof. I, a single Northman, must have counted for nothing in Mordred's calculations, and certainly he must have valued a couple of wagonloads of minstrels and actors, with their equipment, at less than nothing, if that were possible. (The Cursed One, being what he was, no doubt still dreamed from time to time of skinning alive the poor comedian who had insulted him; but he realized that his private fantasies were of no importance to Mordred—and Mordred, next to the spirit of Wodan, was in command.)

I believe the little band of entertainers was pleased to have my company once more. Or most of them were—I thought Jandree was upset by my reappearance. But if my presence created any problems, all of Bran's people knew I was a stout and capable protector against certain kinds of difficulties.

When after several hours we stopped to rest the oxen, I took the opportunity to study the Siege Perilous, which was riding packed in the back of Bran's second wagon, covered loosely with a faded blanket. When I put the blanket aside, I thought the piece of furniture beneath it looked quite ordinary—at least no different from the other carven chairs I had seen encircling the Round Table in Merlin's manor, sporting a few dragons and other fanciful images.

I touched one of the wooden arms, and nothing happened. I stroked the polished wood. As usual, the presence of magic was imperceptible to me.

Bran had come to stand beside me and was also pondering the chair. "We must carry it back to Merlin," he said, frowning. "I hate being drawn into these games the great ones play among themselves. But what choice have we, when they insist upon our playing?" He paused, then added: "I think our best plan is to stop every day or so and give a performance somewhere, as usual. That way folk will be less likely to suspect that we are carrying anything out of the ordinary." Then he looked at me and smiled. "You will not perform, of course, Sir Hakon. We will be your servants— only your *entourage*."

I covered up the chair again, arranging the blanket with seeming carelessness, just as before, and we moved on. I walked for a while, leading my horse, beside the wagons. The new oxen were indeed young and strong. I wondered if Merlin's magic had created such creatures from nothing, or only brought them here into his service? They looked real and smelled real, and their heated backs drew flies, like any other beasts of burden, as they pulled the smoothly turning wheels forward at a good pace, almost equal to that of a brisk walk, despite the fact that today the whole troupe, or anyway most of its surviving members, were riding instead of walking. Even the roads, or at least the ones we found ourselves taking, were uncommonly smooth and level, passing neatly between hills to avoid steep climbs, and fording rivers and streams only at gentle crossings. I thought I would no longer have been greatly surprised to encounter trolls or giants, but nothing stranger than cows and cowherds crossed our path.

* * *

The war at Morgan's castle was hours behind us, and as far as we knew not getting any closer, when we made our first real stop, at a small village.

The visit to Morgan's castle had given me much to think about. Despite the lady's jeering, the idea that I might someday be crowned king by Merlin continued to exert a hold on my imagination. And now I thought the possibility had arisen that Morgan herself might someday want me as her consort. Had she not said as much?

As I tried to prepare myself mentally for some such high position, I thought that when I rose to power I could do worse than to try to enlist Bran as both counselor and spokesman. The showman might be of no higher birth than I, but he spoke much more smoothly than ever I could speak, and was infinitely better able to converse upon the subjects of books and poetry. I had seen him use a sword and spear, and while I thought he would not stand against me for a minute with such weapons—indeed, there were very few who could—yet there were many proclaiming themselves warriors who would not have been able to match him. He had the necessary cool nerve in the heat of battle, which counts for much more than any technique that can be trained or taught.

But I also realized that my attraction to Bran's wife had become more a burden than a joy. Well, I had always found plenty of fish in the sea. If I was going to be king, I would need a more queenly woman than her beside me. And if fate someday made me Morgan's consort . . . well.

Jandree went through the motions of trying to be a good mother—up to the limits of her interest, which in truth did not extend very far. And she did not dislike her husband, or want to treat him cruelly. But what really seemed important to her was the necessity of trying to rise above her station—I was sure she still dreamed of being a great lady or a queen.

Perhaps she felt wounded by my new attitude of indifference. We had only been on the road two days when she told me to bother her no longer. I was not bothering her, and had not done so for some time, but still my vanity was wounded.

We reached the seacoast, and began to travel along it. None of the landscape looked familiar to me, but Bran plodded steadily ahead, and I assumed that he knew, in the special way that people know in Logres, where he was going.

When our small cavalcade, consisting of one mounted knight and two ox-drawn wagons, at last came in sight of Merlin's Rock again, we were granted our first look at what the original Camelot must have been like—the humble construction that had occupied the site before Merlin arrived to put Arthur on his throne and to exalt the place with his great magic.

What we beheld was little more than a hill fort with thatched roofs, wooden palisades, rooting pigs and cackling geese nearby, and a minimum of masonry, the latter comprised in a couple of concentric dry-stone walls.

But the closer we approached, the more the scene changed. We were of course expecting Merlin's tricks, but still we marveled. By the time we had come within a hundred yards, we confronted a magic picture of what Old Camelot must have been: the great castle, standing, as had Merlin's manor, on a tongue of rocky land that climbed, and extended, out for a quarter of a mile or so into the sea.

And when we had advanced another twenty yards, Old Camelot had mostly been destroyed. We faced a towering, abandoned ruin.

I could picture the Round Table, one badly chipped and abused piece of furniture, now sitting somewhere amidst this wreckage, waiting for us to rescue it. In my imagination it seemed that low-born folk might have been carving their initials, and dirty pictures, in the oak. Again we moved on, wanting to be free of such a painful sight—and all such vaporous imaginings promptly vanished with the fact of our true arrival.

Bran's wagons rolled to a halt at the gate of what had been Merlin's manor, and people jumped down from their seats. I remained in my saddle a moment longer, marveling at how drastically the place had really changed since we had left it only a few days ago. The half-built wall that I recalled was gone. The power of Merlin had raised Camelot from its ruins and was now in the process of transforming it into a magnificent castle.

Then, getting down from my horse, I took it upon myself as the leader to be the first to approach the place, my weapons ready to hand.

Bran hesitated, then came with me, following a step behind on my right side.

Entering the outer courtyard, we stopped. The presence of numerous horses, mules, wagons, and attendants indicated that some important gathering must be taking place inside.

Heads turned toward me as I walked forward, Bran following a pace behind. The guard or sentry at the door looked at us as we advanced upon him, and then retreated speechlessly inside.

When the doors of the great hall swung open inward, I found myself facing the Round Table, and a noble company of men and women assembled round it.

To right and left the bases of the tall columns were grounded in everyday reality, but up toward the top their substance faded, became transparent as glass, as uncertain as a reflection in troubled water. Those uppermost stones and beams were still only half-things, like the fabulous beasts young Merlin had once conjured up to drive off Comorre's men. But these details of construction I only became aware of later.

At the moment I could only gaze in amazement at the distinguished company, perhaps some thirty folk in all, who until our entrance had been sitting round the Table, obviously enjoying a considerable feast. At our entrance they had begun to rise in awe. They stared and marveled, and their voices rose in an excited murmur.

"It is Arthur."

"It is Arthur, come again!"

"Our great king come again, in the full strength of his youth!"

And all of the noble knights, the highborn ladies, the bishops and merchants and noblemen who one after another pushed back their chairs and stood, who raised their voices and their arms in awe, who knelt in homage—they were not looking at me.

None of them had eyes for me at all. They gazed at Bran.

✌ Interlude ✌

Hour after hour Elaine pressed on, forcing the ambulance forward at as good a speed as the rutted ground allowed. Again she was following an unbranching road, though not the one by which she had approached Morgan's castle. She was obeying the crude directions given her by the enchantress. She didn't want to go too fast for fear of jouncing the tubed and wired Arthur out of his berth, or doing him some other harm.

Meanwhile Lancelot served as escort, lookout, conversational partner—and eventually as relief driver. Mostly he rode in the right front seat, wearing at least part of his armor all the time, his sheathed sword forever in his lap or within easy reach.

Right now the little onboard computer was treating driver and passenger to another verse from Tennyson:

> *And at the closing of the day*
> *She loosed the chain, and down she lay;*
> *The broad stream bore her far away,*
> *The Lady of Shalott.*

> *Lying, robed in snowy white*
> *That loosely flew to left and right—*
> *The leaves upon her falling light—*
> *Thro' the noises of the night*
> *She floated down to Camelot:*

Lancelot demonstrated that he was a competent reader, if a trifle slow. He was able to comprehend the verses as readily as if they had appeared in his own language. Elaine supposed that as far as he was concerned, they did. But Morgan le Fay hadn't been able to read the screen—there was something to ponder.

The reference to Camelot puzzled him, and respectfully he asked Elaine to explain. As she was struggling to comply, he interrupted—respectfully again—seeming overwhelmed with the need to tell her what an amazing resemblance she bore to Guinevere.

Somehow the conversation proceeded more easily after that. It turned out that Lancelot at the castle had overheard some interesting things. Hesitantly he alluded to the fact that Morgan and others were now convinced that Elaine was going to be Nimue—the young woman sorceress, coming from nowhere seemingly, who would somehow loop back in time to enchant Merlin and bring him low, put him under the rock.

Elaine protested fiercely. She had never met Merlin, and had no wish to do so. She could perform no sorcery, and had no intention of putting anyone under a rock.

Lancelot listened politely. He observed that he refused to believe that his fair companion could do no magic—the wagon in which they were riding was proof enough of that.

They were chatting on, Elaine feeling more at ease than she had at any time since . . . and suddenly rounded a curve to find that the road ahead was blocked by the huge bole, three or four feet thick, of a fallen tree. The ambulance lurched to a stop as Elaine was forced to apply the brakes.

Moments later, another tree fell across the road in the rear. This was a planned ambush.

A lone attacker appeared, dressed in rags, jumping on the log that blocked the road in front, shouting a challenge. He had only one arm.

"Wait! I've seen him before."

Lancelot peered with narrowed eyes. "I have not," he decided. "Who is he?"

"A man called Thrain," Elaine said slowly, peering at the capering, shouting figure. "I have seen him in my own country. Despite what he looks like, he's no cripple. He has the strength of a madman, and he works for Mordred."

Thrain bellowed and grumbled shouts and insults. These were largely unintelligible to Elaine, directed against his former comrades. Particularly he seemed to be incensed against Lancelot's companion Hakon, who had once tried to kill Thrain rather than let him go on fighting. Evidently Thrain had been trying to catch up with Hakon ever since.

Elaine failed to understand much of this, but Lancelot nodded. "Sir Hakon, when we rode together, told me something of this man. Like Hakon he came from the North. Once he was a peaceful farmer, then a one-armed juggler. Now he is a berserk, one of the worst kind. A grave-breaker brought back to life by Wodan."

"He is a *what?*" To Elaine the half-crippled dancing figure looked like the victim of some terrible accident or attack. There was something wrong with his one good hand, the fingers looked so swollen.

"Once," said Lancelot, starting to work himself into the rest of his armor, "once the fingers on his good arm were cut off by Comorre's torturers—so Hakon told me. Now I see they have grown back. But they look like troll fingers now—so that I now wonder whether trolls may be something like berserks."

"I'm sure I don't know," was all Elaine could think of. "I've seen him strangle a leopard." Actually she hadn't *seen* that, but . . . She was staring at Thrain, who now with his one hideous hand had picked up a log as thick as his leg, longer than his whole body, and was swinging it jauntily, like a walking stick. "What are you going to do?"

Instead of answering her directly, the old knight rolled a window down partway, and called out in a cheerful voice: "Sir Thrain, if you will not remove the obstacle so we can pass, I must come out to see that it is moved!"

Only an inhuman bellow answered him.

◆ Hakon ◆

When Bran and I entered the great hall, a feast, magically attended, had been in progress. The food and wine were now forgotten. All of King Arthur's old companions, his most loyal followers, were on their feet.

Some of them had been weeping at the things they saw in the half-made hall that reminded them of the destruction of the Old Camelot. And many more were entranced by the work that Merlin had already begun upon the new.

Some were eagerly receptive to any suggestion that Arthur might be restored to them. For the most part the men at the Table were grizzled, battle-scarred veterans, King Arthur's old companions.

Already on hand were Sir Tristram; Sir Percivale; Sir Kay, the Seneschal; Sir Gawain; Sir Bors; Sir Ector; and others. Sir Palomides, the dark-skinned Saracen, had been recruited from somewhere far away in time and space, by only his God-knew-what complexities of Merlinian magic.

And now Merlin, no vision from the rocks, but in an older body than any I had yet seen out of the cave, had come from somewhere and was standing at one side of the great table, looking solemn. He raised his hand for silence, and a hush quickly took possession of the great hall.

"You see before you Arthur's son," he said, when all was quiet, and he pointed impressively at Bran. "His true son, though a bastard, and it is time to crown him king."

A new murmuring broke out, a wave of approval that began to swell, but before it could quite reach the stage of acclamation, there came a new interruption.

The doorway through which Bran and I had entered was darkened once again. Morgan now burst on the scene, crying aloud that the army surrounding her castle had withdrawn, and that Mordred and Comorre were now marching on Camelot with all their power.

When the assembly would have reacted to that, she raised a hand imperiously for silence. "I bring you news still more important. Your good King Arthur is still alive, and he is still your king. At this moment he is also on his way to join us here at Camelot. To talk of crowning anyone else is not only premature, but treason!"

After another moment of hushed silence, the great hall exploded in loud accusation, appeal, and debate. A good part of the assembly were now bitterly resentful of what Merlin had suggested, and all were deeply suspicious of any suggestion that the original Arthur might be, or could be, supplanted by someone else.

Morgan, arguing, assured everyone who would listen that Comorre, Mordred, and others, now hurrying on with their massed forces from Morgan's castle to Merlin's Rock, would be greatly pleased to hear that Arthur now had a new rival, an upstart put forward by Merlin himself.

Merlin—mature, distinguished Merlin—had not moved. He calmly disagreed with Morgan. Arthur had been king once, and it was not beyond the bounds of possibility that he might be again—someday. But now he was incapable of being king—could his sister deny that? Another must be chosen, and who better than Arthur's son?

On and on the wizard spoke, his voice not loud, but ruthlessly hypnotic, utterly compelling.

When Merlin, beginning to feel confident, paused for the first time, many of the old warriors, Arthur's old henchmen, asked for word of Lancelot. Many seemed to have reached quick agreement among themselves that they were ready to be guided in their decision by what Lancelot should say.

I raised my voice to tell them that Lancelot was on his way; so Morgan had promised . . . and I looked around, but Morgan was no longer to be seen. It seemed that, sensing Merlin's victory, she had withdrawn.

In the high, cavernous Hall of the Round Table, torches, spaced in iron brackets round every quadrant of the high circular wall, were roaring, giving out light and heat in plenty. The room that had once been dim and dingy was now as bright as summer. The gloomy tapestries, covered with indistinguishable figures, had been drawn back to reveal high, clear, sunny windows.

All the old-timers kept remarking on the closeness of Bran's physical resemblance to the original Arthur.

Having spoken once to the assembly, I soon retreated. It appeared that in the argument and uproar I had been practically forgotten. My dream of sometime being king had turned into a hollow mockery. Whatever had Merlin actually said to me, to lead into such imaginings? I tried to remember, but could recall nothing meaningful. I supposed that if I were ever required to prove myself in this company, it would have to be by at least ritual combat.

If I could claim convincingly that Lancelot had knighted me on some field of combat, or had expressed his opinion that I should be knighted, that would add tremendously to my stature.

Seeking air, and open space, I moved to the great doors and out. Before me, almost around me, rose the half-built walls of the New Camelot. It was—would be, when finished—a great palace, a towering castle, a perfection of the medieval builder's art, standing next to the town that would support it. Later, much later, I came to understand that Merlin's work was sited outside the flow of normal Time, founded elsewhere than in the dimensions of ordinary space. New Camelot, firmly rooted in the kingdom of Logres, lay at the mouth of a river and next to the ocean—which is almost timeless and spaceless in itself. The castle and town were served by a small harbor. The landscape had altered drastically around the place we had called Merlin's Rock, but not so drastically that its chief features could not be recognized at all.

Within the castle walls, routine housekeeping chores were handled as they had been in the original manor house, as if by magic. Water gushed forth upon demand from taps and pipes, and roof cisterns were magically kept full. Ashes and other refuse somehow removed themselves, cows and chickens remained healthy and productive, and firewood and grain and meat and drink restocked themselves on shelves and in icehouses.

Inside the great hall, Merlin was speaking again. In his persuasive speech in favor of Bran's coronation, he boasted that he had reached out far indeed, seeking in the most remote and dangerous parts of the world, to find a source of powerful help for this production.

A population of a thousand people or more had already been assembled under the great magician's influence. Some were willing domestic servants, and magic aided them in their tasks. Others were genuine fisherfolk, armorers, merchants and artisans, travelers and scholars, some of them from the far reaches of the world.

Some common people, from various times and places around the world, had at least begun to occupy the dwellings of New Camelot apart from the castle itself. There was now a lack of distinction because of race or wealth, creed or birth. We spoke to some who had come seeking prophecies from Merlin and entreating Arthur's help against the oppressions of the world—and then had decided to join in the great effort to sustain Camelot.

And now in the debate, there arose the question of choosing a name by which Bran should be crowned. Here again, any long hesitation would not do.

King Bran the First? Arthur the Second? Even beyond the fact that the original was not completely dead, there were reasons, and for the wise reader I need not spell them out, why Bran's own voice was now raised for the first time, resisting that name fiercely, resisting with genuine fervor the idea that he should be a king at all. But the old retainers would now have things no other way; the only question being whether he should take his father's name.

Not quite the only question. Some, including Merlin, wanted a Christian ceremony of coronation—others were more in favor of the old gods. There was talk of a ritual with clergy of several religions taking part.

While this was going on indoors, my ear was caught by my own name, called in a soft whisper. Bran's two wagons still stood where they had stopped on our arrival, and Morgan, standing in the shadow of one, quite alone and unattended, was smiling invitingly in my direction, and beckoning.

In a moment I had joined her there. The wagons were now otherwise deserted, as the whole courtyard seemed to be, Bran's small original retinue having crowded into the great hall to see what all the excitement was about.

"It seems that I have lost," said Morgan wistfully. "Who can resist Merlin when he is at the peak of his powers, and so determined?"

"Who indeed? My lady, I am sorry—"

"Never mind, dear Sir Hakon. It is not your fault at all." She smiled, with sadness irresistible. Then it seemed that a bright thought occurred to her. "At least I can give the new king of Logres a coronation present—a peace offering. Dear Hakon, will you lift the Chair out of the wagon? It is heavy, and a bit beyond my strength to carry."

Eagerly I complied.

Then the enchantress frowned prettily. "Would you first set it down here, in the sunlight? Is that a scratch—?"

I set down the chair as commanded and bent and looked, and turned ready to say that I could see no scratch.

"Good-bye for now, dear," Morgan murmured, and pushed me with precise violence. I was taken totally off guard. The edge of the seat of the Siege Perilous caught me just behind the knees.

TWENTY-NINE

✤ Bran ✤

No, I did not see Morgan le Fay push Hakon into the Chair, nor hear the yell that I am sure he uttered. Minutes passed before I heard even a lying account of that event, and a considerably longer time before I understood the truth. But everyone within miles was aware of the immediate result. The presence of an unworthy occupant in the Siege Perilous turned the world of Logres dark, all in an instant, as if the switch of an electric light had been thrown. At the same moment the solid rocks encapsulating Merlin's Bones quivered and split beneath our feet. The disaster was compounded by the fact that only moments later the figure of Merlin that had so dominated our meeting disappeared without a moment's warning.

It seems to me that the logical place for me to begin my portion of this narrative is at the moment when, after entering the great hall a step behind Hakon, I was struck by the figurative thunderbolt, seized by the inwardly earthshaking awareness that I was the one Old Merlin had chosen to replace King Arthur.

Real thunderbolts were not far behind; they came, with storms, as an accompaniment to the literal earthshaking that now racked the world of Logres.

Merlin, just seconds before Morgan's devilish trickery caused him to vanish, had announced that the coronation ceremony must take place as quickly as possible, in a much grander hall than any the Old Camelot had boasted, even though the magical construction of the new castle was not yet complete, and the upper courses of stonework looked transparent.

Shocks in the earth began at the moment of Hakon's involuntary transgression, and continued for several minutes. Parts of the Hall of the Round Table's upper walls, along with the high beams and roof, were soon loosened, and began to fall with the quaking of the rocks beneath the manor. More pieces of masonry and timber were tumbling every moment, and the survivors inside New Camelot scrambled about, some shrieking in most unknightly fashion, trying to get outdoors before the remaining beams and stones and slates should bury them.

Morgan met us out of doors, under a sky turned suddenly as black as midnight with great scudding, writhing clouds. She was standing near our deserted wagons, and the empty Chair.

"And where is your great wizard now?" she screamed at us triumphantly. "Gone, is he?" She fastened her gaze on me. "Where is your crown now, little man?"

"I have no crown," I said. "And wanted none." But then my next words, with no planning on my part, came out in the form of a royal demand. "Explain this havoc you have caused. Where is Hakon?"

She paused, sudden rain washing dark hair down across her pale forehead, examining me with a new evaluation. "I will explain. Hakon was unworthy, and when he dared to take his place in the Siege Perilous, its magic hurled him to the greatest distance possible. And if you want to know where Merlin's gone, why, the earth has opened, exposing the old man's damned relics to the air, and this will have the effect of forcing all of his lively avatars to stay away."

"All this?" I demanded, suddenly only half articulate. Wildly I gestured at the ruin that now surrounded us. "You have done all this, killed, created havoc, simply so that my father can retain his crown?"

Moments earlier, I had been on the brink of being made king by acclamation. Thus it was only natural that many of those present would look to me for guidance in this emergency, only to be expected that Morgan and I were soon surrounded by men and women clamoring for help, demanding to be told what to do.

Morgan proved willing to let me assume temporary leadership, as long as there was no question of my coronation.

Plenty of urgent problems had to be dealt with. First there were the wounded and the dying, victims of falling beams and stones, to be attended to.

The tall rocks that had once hidden the upper entrance of the cave had fallen, and when after a few minutes the rain slackened and the clouds began to lighten, we could now see an ominous cloud of dust billowing slowly up out of the upper entrance to the cave, as well as from deep crevices in the earth.

"Merlin's Bones," someone near me murmured.

It seemed that those relics might now really have been ground into powder—along with anyone who might have been near them at the time.

✄ Interlude ✄

Looking out through the windshield Elaine caught a glimpse of people, off among the trees—it flashed across her mind that maybe they were woodcutters—running away in evident terror. Whether it had been the sight of a four-wheel-drive vehicle that so disturbed them, or the presence of Thrain, she could not tell.

Thrain had ducked out of sight momentarily, but in another moment the berserk reappeared. He approached the ambulance and began to bash the outside of it with a fresh piece of timber, this one only slightly bigger than an ordinary spear or lance. The vehicle rocked under the repeated impacts. Glass here and there broke in, metal dented, and the berth that cradled the unconscious king pitched and rolled with the tossing of the whole machine.

Lancelot remained cool, almost unperturbed. Courteously he requested Elaine's help in getting the last of his armor on. He explained that some of the fastenings were impossible for the knight himself to reach.

"Are you sure you want to go out? I mean, *look* at what that lunatic is doing . . ." Crash! "*Listen* to that!" The heavy vehicle rocked on its tires.

The knight might not have heard her. He closed his visor and opened the door on his side.

Lightly Sir Lancelot stepped down from the vehicle, sword ready in his right hand, shield—three diagonal red stripes on silver—on his left arm. His lips moved; Elaine could not hear exactly what the old knight was saying, but he seemed to be addressing a few courteous if angry words to his advancing foe.

Thrain advanced with raging confidence to meet the champion of Arthur and of Camelot.

Thrain, swinging his log one-handed, hit the old man in heavy armor before Lancelot could either step back or move in close enough to use his sword. The knight took the impact mostly on his shield, but still was staggered. Gamely he moved in again. Thrain battered him repeatedly.

Elaine screamed in terror. Lancelot was being mangled, and she was going to be left alone. She remembered the pistol in her personal pouch and got it out.

Lancelot was not mangled yet—not quite, though his shield was dented. He kept trying to move inside the roundhouse swings, but the berserk's crazed energy kept the log swinging back and forth with incredible rapidity. And now the knight in armor was knocked down.

Elaine opened the door on the driver's side and climbed out to try to help. As she raised the weapon in her hand, she was reminded that it incorporated an electronic sight—which of course she had not the least idea of how to operate.

With horror she saw that Lancelot could not get up. Or maybe he was deliberately crouching. Anyway he was close in front of Thrain, who still flailed with the timber. The clumsy-looking weapon was only a speeding blur, but the berserk seemed to lack the sense to realize that he was standing too near his target, so that most of the timber's impacts hit only the long-suffering earth.

Dr. Brusen remembered to make sure that the handgun's

safety was off, then did her best to aim at Thrain. She squeezed the trigger several times. Bark and wood flew from a tree trunk near the monster's head. Probably she was being overcautious, concentrating on not hitting Lancelot.

But Thrain had at least been distracted. His pale face, a mask of madness, turned in her direction.

His arm jerked in violent motion, and a moment later Elaine saw the long piece of timber come flying straight at her, turning end over end.

She screamed, and somehow lost her gun, and tried to duck but was knocked over by the missile. Fortunately the log had struck her only a glancing blow, on shoulder, back, and head, before it went on to spend most of its force against the side of the van.

Still, for a moment the world began to dissolve in gray half-consciousness. Then Elaine was aware of crawling on her hands and knees, close beside the ambulance. Her gun had fallen around here somewhere, and she could not find it, but she must—

Here was the timber that had struck her down. When an end of the log came under Elaine's close inspection, she saw, at first with lack of comprehension, that Thrain's twitching fist still gripped it. The hand had been sharply amputated, so that it presented to her numbed gaze the raw end once joined to the wrist.

Dazedly Elaine lifted her head to see what was happening in the fight. Lancelot was up on his feet again, though still in a half-crouch, his bloodied sword held forward.

Thrain, armless and weaponless, severed arteries in his fore-arm spouting gore, still raged and tried to find a way to carry on the battle. He kicked at his opponent, ineffectively.

Sir Lancelot, bright armor now crimsoned with his foeman's splashing blood, stepped in and with an easy-looking home run swing cut off Thrain's head. Elaine caught an ineradicable vision of the pale face, still rage-contorted, falling, trailing long fair hair, the loose head bouncing on the earth beside the collapsing body.

She was sitting on the ground, her screams beginning to trail off into mere groans, when a fierce clutch at her ankle made her jump and look. A new shriek burst from her throat.

Thrain's amputated hand had given up on trying to swing the log, and had come groping after her.

In a moment Lancelot was at her side. Dimly she was aware of his prying the troll-fingered member gently away, and carrying it out of her sight.

Presently her knight was back. She clutched at Lancelot to keep him from going away again. Tenderly he lifted her, still half-dazed, still tending to see creeping hands and fingers in every moving object. Lancelot carried her into the ambulance, and tucked her with amazing gentleness into the bunk across the aisle from Arthur's.

He spoke to her calmly about the necessity of unblocking the road, and asked her what tools were available. Somehow she found answers, suggestions of where to look. Then, though she cried for him to stay, he went away.

After what seemed a long time, she heard him getting into the driver's seat. Elaine heard the engine start, and felt the van start moving, before she allowed herself to slide into something that was like sleep.

Lancelot drove on for an hour or two, not stopping until darkness fell. Then he came back, still wearing partial armor, to stand beside Elaine as she lay in the wide berth listening to his movements. Somehow, she noticed, the curtain on the other berth had been drawn shut, cutting Arthur off from view.

Now Lancelot was holding Elaine by the hand, and telling her comforting things. Of course it was his presence that was really reassuring. He smelled heavily of sweat, and blood. Not his own blood, as far as she could see, and that was good. Actually he did not seem to be seriously hurt. She supposed that she smelled strongly, too.

From the expression on his face, she thought that he was about to tell her something else, something of great importance.

How strange, she thought. *I had thought that this man was old.* But now she could see how mistaken that idea was. He wasn't really old at all. Only . . . only mature.

"I need someone," was all she said.

Pieces of armor fell clanging in the aisle. And presently Lancelot had joined her in the wide berth, where there was room enough for two, if at least one of the two was too badly off to care—or if they were on good terms. Elaine was not too badly off to care.

She whispered: "Please draw the curtain shut."

✨ Bran ✨

Morgan had done her best to prevent my being crowned. But now she felt compelled, by her awareness of Mordred's advancing forces, to try once more to make an alliance with me, and those who would have made me king, against a greater evil.

Her scouts assured us that Mordred, leading Comorre's army, was trying to capture not only Arthur's unconscious body, but Merlin's Bones.

An unnatural darkness still covered Logres. The footing in the vicinity of Camelot was now uneven at best, and hazardous in many places. The layers of rock beneath the surface of the earth had been split by several devastating fissures, and a large part of Merlin's new construction had collapsed; what remained in place was sustained more by magic than physical support. The sea had rushed in where the cliffs were split, and at some great depth had evidently encountered hot or molten rock; the resulting steam-explosions made some fear that the fires of hell had been loosed upon the earth.

Shouting, I did my best to put down panic: "The fires of hell can have no power to burn us unless we welcome them."

Beyond trying to look calm, to set an example of resisting panic, there did not seem to be much that I could do. I, the king-to-be, went stumbling about through a radically changed land-scape, trying to be a leader of a people I scarcely knew at all, in a place that was utterly unfamiliar. Where now was the ruined chapel? Where were the other outbuildings of the old manor house?

It was Flagon-dry who reminded me: We had to find out what

had happened to the Bones. He said that Morgan le Fay was already down in the cave somewhere, looking.

ᴘ Interlude ᴘ

Awakening in the snug double berth, finding herself held solidly in Lancelot's formidable arms, Elaine took stock of her situation as best she could, then decided to go back to sleep.

She and her new lover had still many hours of driving between themselves and Merlin's Rock.

In the course of this last leg of their journey, Lancelot, a quick learner, took several shifts at the wheel.

Simply watching Elaine drive during the previous leg of their journey had enabled Lancelot to take over the task in an emergency, with sufficient skill to get the ambulance past Thrain's roadblock. Well, the controls were simple enough, and the new driver was not given to nervousness in the face of physical difficulties. There was, after all, practically no other traffic to contend with—and if any appeared, it might be something that it would be as well to hit as to avoid.

Getting the ambulance to Merlin's Rock, even driving by turns, took the couple several days, an effort interrupted only by a brief pause or two for food and sleep. They agreed that they must push on to Camelot; there, if anywhere, Merlin's power would be able to protect them and their helpless passenger.

Lancelot treated his companion with steadfast courtesy. It was almost as if their interval of lovemaking had never happened. He had proved to be a good and reliable companion. But it seemed to Elaine that now when he looked at her he remembered Guinevere, and was—if not exactly ashamed—afraid of what he and Elaine had done. For the remainder of their journey he never shared the berth with her, but simply stood guard or drove while Elaine slept.

And Arthur, continuously tended by machines and magic, slept on, oblivious to it all. Elaine when she looked at him could not help wondering if he dreamed, perhaps of the Round Table, and Guinevere faithful at his side.

In a more practical vein, she was beginning to suspect that the vehicle's fuel, or perhaps more properly its power supply, might at last be growing low. A previously blank spot on the padded dashboard had turned into some kind of indicator gauge—only a short, glowing line, not very informative, except that the short line was slowly growing shorter. Dr. Brusen hadn't attempted to look under the hood—what would be the point?—but by now she was firmly convinced that the engine therein must be more advanced than anything the early twenty-first century could build.

Maybe—why not?—it ran on magic.

And as the boat-head wound along
The willowy hills and fields among,
They heard her singing her last song,
The Lady of Shallot.

Heard a carol, mournful, holy,
Chanted loudly, chanted lowly,
Till her blood was frozen slowly,
And her eyes were darken'd wholly,
Turn'd to tower'd Camelot.

At last she screamed in English at the computer screen: "Fisher, I am not going to be your goddamned Lady of Shalott!"

Sir Lancelot, who happened to be driving at the moment, turned around to look at her in wonder.

The next time Elaine fell asleep she had a nightmare in which she and Lancelot and their helpless passenger were still trying to get out of Morgan's castle. Again and again in the dream, the van went roaring under a falling portcullis, over a drawbridge to freedom, blasting a gap for itself through the astonished ranks of Wodan's enveloping army.

She awakened to feel the earth shaking, and to see that a great mysterious darkness had come over the land.

* * *

The ambulance did not stall until she and Lancelot had regained the vicinity of Merlin's Rock, and then the engine quit while they were trying to negotiate a place where the road had been almost removed, by a great new earthquake crevice. It might have been impossible to drive farther in any case.

Lancelot told Elaine that he must stay, for the time being at least, with his unconscious king.

Elaine agreed, but announced that she was going to scout ahead. She made sure her pistol was in her pouch—Lancelot had picked it up for her, back at Thrain's roadblock—and set out.

Walking uphill through fog, over unfamiliar terrain, she soon encountered confused residents of what seemed to be a new town built nearby. And these folk, gossiping and marveling, in a few minutes brought Elaine up to date on all that had happened since Hakon and Bran's people arrived at Camelot.

The local folk had plenty to tell, all of it enthralling, but Elaine was mainly concerned with her own survival. Steadily she pushed on, and in fifteen minutes had reached what could only be the fresh ruins of New Camelot, which at the moment seemed entirely deserted. Soon she was making her way through tottering stone halls, climbing on gently swaying masonry, in hopes of locating the hypostator field. That, as far as she could see, represented her only possibility of ever getting home again. If only the field was still in place!

But where to look? There would probably be no obvious signs.

Then an idea came. If Morgan, and Mordred, had been obsessed with any particular place in this vicinity, it had been Merlin's library.

Elaine climbed on, precariously trying to reach the place that corresponded, as nearly as she could calculate, with the location of Merlin's library in the original manor, as she had glimpsed it from afar. Sometimes she found herself treading on transparent stones that threatened to fade to nothingness beneath her.

At last Elaine discovered the glassy, magic wall. Now what?

She had been playing games with books and scrolls, trying to pretend that she was not really doing magic, for some twenty minutes, before the recognizable face of Hakon appeared on the other side of the transparent wall. He seemed to be looking at Elaine from inside the hypostator room of her own laboratory.

Quickly they discovered that, if they spoke clearly and distinctly, they could hear each other. Communication established, Hakon, as eager to get back to his world as she was to hers, struggled to explain to Elaine how the Chair, into which he had been treacherously thrust by Morgan, had catapulted him to this strange place, seemingly an infinite distance from where he ought to be.

"It is a strange realm. You are right. I live there, and I know."

"What is this land called?"

"Its inhabitants know it by different names. But I think all of them would tell you they are living in the early twenty-first century."

ᴒᴒ Bran ᴒᴒ

I wonder if the authority who has requested this tale-telling realizes—or cares—how difficult it is going to be?

For many years I had strongly suspected that I was King Arthur's bastard son. Giving the reasons for that suspicion would require telling the story of my life, and that story will not be told here. But I had hoped never to involve myself in high affairs of state. As the thunderbolt of realization struck me, the false impression I had been given, that Merlin intended to put Hakon on the throne, was annihilated, exposed as only a misunderstanding or a pretense. All along the king's enchanter had known that I was Arthur's son, and had intended to elevate me. Of course I should have known, have guessed as much . . .

But in those heady moments before Morgan's earthquake struck, when those assembled warriors and wise men began to hail me by the name of Arthur—or, as some did, to call me Majesty—my surprise was genuinely total. To say that for the first time in my life I was struck dumb with astonishment may actually be to understate the case.

In shock I turned to meet the blue gaze of my wife, and saw

the transcendent joy that filled her eyes; then, silently as in a dream, I moved to accept the homage offered me. Yet it would be false to say that only because Jandree wanted to be a queen did I accept. I acquiesced in Merlin's offer of a crown because in my heart I wanted to become king. I suppose I had always wanted that.

In the courtyard of Morgan's castle I had learned that my father was still alive. Now I swore to myself that if circumstances required me to wear a crown, I would relinquish it again as soon as he was able to resume his rightful place.

Meanwhile, the army of Mordred and Comorre was laying siege to New Camelot. The attackers had been as much inconvenienced as the defenders by darkness, and convulsions in the earth, but now the rocky promontory was on the verge of being invaded.

ᴣᴘ Interlude ᴣᴘ

Morgan by her arts began working, from a distance, to restore function to the exhausted ambulance. It was still needed, to carry King Arthur on to the next stop in his long search for healing. But even more important now to Morgan was her search for Merlin's Bones.

THIRTY

For Vivian there came a time of awakening, or, more precisely, of being aroused to clear awareness. Whether or not she had been asleep, she had been enjoying a peaceful and pleasant and dreamlike existence, seemingly far removed from any conflict. But an urgent call had summoned her back into a very different realm, no less magical, but of sharply detailed reality. Unpleasantness had not yet raised its head, but now the possibility existed.

She felt no shock, no loss at being separated from the kindly folk and good companions who had shared her recent life—all that might have been a dream. She could not now remember the details of the people or the place, or exactly what she had been doing there. But the lack seemed unimportant.

Taking stock of her situation, she knew that she was no longer a girl, but a fully mature young woman. Whether the long epoch now ending had actually been one of sleep, or of dreaming, was more than she could have said. It seemed only another detail, not of much importance. What truly mattered was what was happening to her now. She was traveling, or rather was being carried, like a leaf on a pleasant wind, journeying through clouds of . . . well, clouds of something.

This was a strange passage, but she knew perfectly well that it was no dream.

Whatever the truth about her recent activities, they had occupied a goodly stretch of time. According to Vivian's best sense of the matter, a year or more must have passed since she had last seen her lover Merlin. And she missed him desperately.

She seemed to hang suspended in the air, while clouds flew by. The strangeness of it all reminded Vivian, irresistibly, of her experience years ago with little Amby—and with Hakon—when they had all been swept off to the court of Vortigern. The three of them had . . .

. . . now *that* was very odd. Vivian realized that she had almost entirely forgotten Hakon, even though he had once been her lover—or something close to that. And even now, when she recalled the fact of his existence, she could not quite remember what his face looked like.

She hoped devoutly that this whirlwind bearing her so gently on would take her soon to her lover Merlin . . .

. . . and that wish was granted.

This time their meeting took place in a cave. At first glance Vivian did not think this was the unforgettable cave at Merlin's Rock. The walls were rugged rock, the atmosphere one of damp and dimness that somehow brought a feeling of security, not of menace. People were the really dangerous elements in life, and just now all other people were very far away.

Barefoot, wearing a long, fine robe that might have been a queen's nightgown, she stood on damp rock awaiting her lover's arrival. These meetings between the two of them, these visits, were nothing new. But every time she met a somewhat different man. What would he look like this time?

And then all at once he was standing close before her. Vivian recognized Merlin instantly, and she was delighted as always when he appeared. But at each encounter he had been older, and she was alarmed that this time he stood before her as an old man, aged and infirm. The staff he leaned on seemed less a tool of power than a necessity to help him stand and walk.

Conflicting feelings raced through Vivian's heart. With a

surge of fierce loyalty she reminded herself that this, her lover, was *Merlin;* it was easy enough to convince herself that even age and time must yield before this man, that tomorrow or the day after he could once more stand before her as young and vital as on that day—how long ago it seemed!—when they had first made love.

But now when he put out his wrinkled hands to her, she saw that they were quivering.

Arm in arm, old man and young woman strolled together. Some kind of simple spell, an afterthought drawn from her lover's vast store of magic, illumined their way through the dark cave, made smooth and safe the rocks before their feet.

They talked, but spells of silence grew between them, each interval of quiet a little longer than the last. Neither mentioned his deteriorating condition, but obviously Merlin had something extraordinarily weighty on his mind. Vivian hoped it was not only his own decrepitude. Then she felt guilty for the thought.

She asked him: "Why are we in a cave? Would not a sunny field be pleasanter?"

"Yes, of course. But there is something we must do here."

"What?"

The old man thought about that seemingly simple question for a while, and when he answered it was with another question: "Vivian, my sweet. Do you know what year it is now, today, by the Christian reckoning of time?"

"I have no idea. Tell me." She was by now so familiar with her lover's tricks involving time that when his answer came it caused her no great astonishment. Only a trick, a joke, a paradox to find amusement in. "Then—let me see. Today I am a young girl, five or six years old, somewhere out there in the world beyond these stony walls. And you are—a baby? Actually five years younger than me! I wish that I could see you as a baby! But wait—are you even born as yet?"

"It is good that you have grasped that point, my love." Merlin's aged fingers patted hers. "As a matter of fact, your other self out there is not yet quite five years old, and *I am not yet born.*" The last five words bore a peculiar emphasis.

She tried to see the point, to derive whatever knowledge she was supposed to gain from the paradox. "But here I am, I certainly have been born, and years of my life have passed since I first met you—"

He shook his old gray head. "Not many years, not for you, my love. You are only a young girl still."

Vivian fought to repress the traitorous wish that he should not be quite so old. "But in all that time we have only managed to spend a few days together. Have you ever tried to count them up, to see how few the days have been? I have!"

"Viv, dear Viv. That is why I have brought you here to meet me now. Because there is something that must be done before I can be born. My life, our lives together, depend upon it utterly."

Listening to explanations that at first made no sense to her, Vivian thought to herself that after all this place did look quite a bit like the well-remembered cave of the oracle, at the place called Merlin's Rock—and as they strolled she observed signs of human activity, suggesting that this cave had been an oracle for many years. But still there was a different look and feel about this cave, so that Vivian doubted that it was the same.

Merlin kissed her—and she could not keep from shivering a little at his touch, because it might have been her grandfather kissing her, if she had ever had a grandfather. Then he told her that he had just come from an important conference with King Arthur. "In this year, you know, he is still king."

Her lover's failing body, if she had allowed herself to accept it as reality, might quickly have disgusted her. She told herself firmly that age was only a mask, a disguise, behind which her Merlin was temporarily forced to hide. "Oh, I want to see King Arthur, as he was in the days of his health and strength. Do let me see him!"

"That may not be."

She wished he would try at least not to *sound* like a grandfather. "I wish there were something useful I could do!"

Eagerly he took up that suggestion. "There is, my dear. More than merely useful. Vitally important. That's why I've brought you here today."

"Good! What is it?"

"A bit of magic. There are certain secret, powerful spells that I want you to master, and then to use. You are an apt pupil, and I think that today you can learn what you must learn in half an hour."

"You will trust me with important magic, then?"

"With this most terribly important magic I will trust no one else." His haunted eyes glowed at her from beneath his shaggy brows. "Because, as I have said, my life depends entirely upon it. And not only my life, but other matters much more important to the world." He paused. "You see, it is time now for Nimue to appear."

It took a moment for the significance of that name to register with Vivian. Then she looked around her wildly. "Where is she? What can we do to stop her?"

"She is here." And the old man continued to look lovingly straight at Vivian.

The next realization took another moment. Then she screamed, violently. "No!"

Merlin labored to explain. Inexorably he pressed the facts upon her.

For what seemed a long time Vivian was unable to understand. She was shocked, and violently refused to play the role of Nimue.

"But you are Nimue—the only Nimue who ever has been, or will be."

He repeated the statement, and explained again and again, lovingly, carefully: it was her duty to put him, the aged Merlin, under a rock. Only when that had been done could the infant Merlin, Amby, be safely born. This deliberately chosen immolation offered him his only means of surviving the strangely tangled loops of time that were his life till now, and projecting himself into the future.

Vivian gazed at her lover, in an agony of wanting to believe. And she heard what she wanted to hear. If he was right, there was a chance he could be young again, and strong, and they could be together.

Patiently, hypnotically, he repeated: There was no one else he dared entrust with Nimue's task, even assuming he would have time to teach someone else the necessary spells.

Vivian continued to be horrified at the thought of presiding over the virtual destruction of her lover's body, and sealing the remnants in what amounted to his tomb. But eventually the aged Merlin convinced her that no less drastic measures would allow him to survive.

"Old Merlin must go into the earth, before young Amby can be born." He told her more: how and where she was to wait for him, how to know when the time had come to work the counter-spells.

He offered hope, and Vivian consented. She and her lover shared a last embrace.

She wept as she recited the spells, performed the powerful rit-uals, which had the effect of putting her lover under the rocks. The rock seemed to be melting in her tears, glowing as if the sun had come down from the sky to enter it.

There were times, during her period of waiting afterward, when Vivian was able to contemplate the business almost calmly. Mer-lin had opened her mind to new ideas, explaining that his burial alive was rather in the nature of putting one's economic assets into a blind trust. He would never be able to extricate himself from the sealing he must undergo, but must depend on Vivian—or on someone to whom she might delegate the power—to get him out when the tangled time-loops of his life were safely in the past, when the risk of encountering any of his younger selves was at least greatly diminished.

And provided his bones, pressed in rock like flowers in a book, could be preserved, through the period of crisis, from those who had evil designs on them.

There were other moments in which Vivian nursed wild dreams, of putting herself to sleep under the rock with the man she loved. Or pondered mad schemes of how she might, without telling Merlin, put herself to sleep somewhere nearby, so that in some far, promised future the two of them could be together again.

But in her heart she knew such maneuvers were impossible. Vivian had to remain quick and alive, because only she could bring Merlin out of the rocks when the proper time had come.

❧ Interlude ❧

Years after the interment of Merlin's Bones, at the time and place of Mordred's attack upon New Camelot, contending groups of diggers, savagely exchanging blows and missiles when they met, were clambering in the shattered earth, striving to uncover and undo that magical sealing.

Men who wanted Bran to be their new king comprised one fighting expedition. Morgan's people formed another, which as the fighting went on became allied with the first. Mordred and Comorre were the leaders of the third group, still the strongest, though by now diminished by attrition to hardly more than a squad of frantically driven soldiers, burrowing frantically into the deep, broken rocks of the seaside cave. The knights of the Round Table and all their men at arms had bitterly opposed the entry here of Mordred's forces, and these temporarily victorious survivors were wounded and battle weary.

Their masters drove them mercilessly. "Find the Bones!"

And, having given that order yet again, Mordred raised his head and looked around him sharply, thinking he had heard an answering voice:

No one rules Logres, no one ever has. Many struggle for control.

By this time Elaine, up in Merlin's library on the second floor of the tottering castle, communicating with Hakon through the glass wall, had instructed him on how to adjust the hypostator controls to localize and intensify the field. Thus the way was opened for Elaine to return to her laboratory.

On emerging from the holostage, within those gloriously familiar walls, she found that Hakon had already encountered there some members of Mordred's gang, men Mordred had left to hold the place for him while he returned to Merlin's Rock to seek the Bones.

Dead men were no longer totally unexpected in Elaine Brusen's life, no longer a numbing shock. In her lab, new bodies lay beside the old. Hakon himself was unhurt; evidently his advantage of surprise had more than made up for the foe's superiority in weapons. Elaine discovered him absorbed in his examination of a captured handgun, which she managed to persuade him to put down before he shot himself.

All Hakon really wanted was a return trip through the hypostator field. He was seething with impatience to get back to the struggle around New Camelot, and there fight for his liege lord Merlin.

Arriving deep in Merlin's Rock, where what had been the inward parts of the cave now lay cleft open to the cloudy sky, Hakon joined the faction that was more or less commanded by Bran.

Hakon saluted the man Merlin had chosen to be king, and apologized for the trouble caused by his landing in the Siege Perilous.

Bran, delighted to see Hakon, grabbed him by the hand. "It wasn't your fault; forget it. Can you help us win this fight?"

"I'll do my best."

The digging and seeking went on, with intervals of combat flaring between the rival parties.

There were moments when each of the factions thought they had succeeded in uncovering Merlin's Bones. Those who did so were deceived. When the failure of any magic to result taught them the truth, some laughed bitterly, and others cursed the Old Man, who had plotted his defenses well.

He had plotted his own resurrection, too.

Just when it seemed that Mordred and Wodan were going to win, Vivian came to bring the Old Man back.

Recalled somewhat sooner than she had expected from her secret place of rest, now fully dressed for combat and adventure, she arrived on the scene knowing much better than anyone else just where to find the Bones. Forced to accept the fearful risk of revitalizing them prematurely, she soon had the relics up and walking on their own. No more than two good handfuls of white fragments, all that her spells could scrape together, they formed a kind of bony wraith, more empty space than solid, that shambled independently, and hurt her eyes and heart to look at.

Merlin, in need of a solid body as a matrix, to give him the ability to stalk or to avoid his enemies, and to help his friends, gave orders in his soundless whisper. He dispatched Vivian to commandeer one of the suits of full body armor still to be found in what was left of the manor house that had become New Camelot.

Comorre and Mordred's men, aided by the power of Wodan, eventually succeeded in driving Bran's faction and Morgan's from the field, and thought themselves now on the verge of being able to extract Merlin's Bones from the rock.

The proper place was now unmistakably identified, by Wodan's magic. But yet the prize was not easily grasped. Great rocks still had to be lifted, tossed aside, by elder magic. And hard physical digging was still necessary.

And when the burial place was opened, Merlin was already gone.

The would-be looters recoiled.

Comorre the Cursed, in sudden terror of something that he saw, went staggering back and raised a trembling, pointing arm. "He walks! *He walks!*"

And over the nearest bulge of rock, a gleaming helm appeared, the visor open to reveal what looked like emptiness within. An arm in armor came in sight, holding no lance, but a thunderbolt.

Haggard and hollow-eyed, slumped in a chair back in her ravaged lab, staring at a screen while her mind was elsewhere, Dr. Brusen read:

Who is this? and what is here?
And in the lighted palace near

Died the sound of royal cheer;
And they crossed themselves for fear,
All the knights at Camelot:

But Lancelot mused a little space;
He said, 'She has a lovely face;
God in his mercy lend her grace,
The Lady of Shalott.'

And meanwhile Lancelot, keeping his steadfast watch over his fallen monarch in the ambulance while battle raged nearby then faded, was puzzling over the same message on a much smaller screen. His own name had appeared, but he had a hard time determining the meaning of the context.

When the sounds of fighting had finally died away completely, Morgan came to praise his loyalty, and to enlighten him. Her plans to seize the Bones for her own purposes, and to prevent Bran's coronation, had been foiled. But victorious Merlin had not moved against her, and she, as bitterly determined as ever, promised that Arthur was going to return eventually and reclaim his throne.

She was still determined to carry her beloved brother to the far future, for his healing. But he, Lancelot, was going to have to stay behind.

Somewhat to Morgan's surprise, the old knight did not protest. Until Arthur should come back, Lancelot intended to return to his peaceful life in the small monastery.

Elaine came near despairing when she found that it was still deep night at the Antrobus Foundation, that now all the clocks in the building had stopped at different times, and that all her efforts to communicate with the outside world of her own time were still frustrated. The building and a small patch of land around it were cut off, just as completely as before.

She had a little time to wonder, now, just how that outside world of the twenty-first century might be experiencing these strange events—had the whole Antrobus property suddenly turned up missing? Her imagination raced on to construct fantastic scenarios—the laboratory building would be reported as having blown up, in the midst of processing exotic new forms of matter. The body of Dr. Elaine Brusen was never found. An investigation, several investigations, were launched into the reasons for her apparently having been working there alone when the accident took place. Was there a possibility of sabotage?

She was in the grip of half-crazed thoughts like these, and wondering what she might be able to do next, when she looked out the window and saw the ambulance, restored to its original appearance, back in the parking lot again. This time it was parked in a slightly different place.

Immediately she ran downstairs, and out of doors. Fisher was limping toward the building, coming, as he said, to say good-bye. He had insisted on making a brief stop here, for that purpose and to give Elaine some reassurance that her environment would be restored to normal. Arthur was being taken away again, to await another chance to reach the twenty-second century—and this time Fisher was lucky enough to be given the chance to go along.

The lights of the ambulance were on, and the vague forms of queenly attendants, Morgan among them, were visible.

When Fisher had embraced Elaine, and reassured her once more that her own world could be made right again, and had climbed into the ambulance again, it started into motion—and then it was simply no longer there. It disappeared before it reached the unattended gate.

✦ Bran ✦

In the aftermath of battle, with Merlin out of the rocks again, and Mordred driven from the field, the land of Logres no longer appeared so much like sunny medieval England. But there were certain signs offering hope that its appearance and nature would be restored.

Morgan had told Hakon that when she came back, as she

would in her own good time, she really did want him to sit beside her as her consort. But after that trick with the Siege Perilous, he was extremely wary.

Merlin—a luminous figure of adult size, now appearing young, now old—had successfully completed the process of his own reconstitution and effectively regained control of his life. Vivian was in loving attendance.

The achievement dearest to Merlin's mind and heart, as he eventually confided to me, was now to bring about the birth of Galahad, the perfect knight, who would be able to deal with the Siege Perilous, to find the Grail, to lead humanity where humanity should go.

Merlin's plans for a New Camelot now seemed to have a good chance of success. The plans for my coronation went on apace— but my own doubts about the matter were as strong as they had ever been.

Flagon-dry and Maud, having discussed the matter intensely between themselves, pointed out to me that if I really rejected the crown, the old-timer knights, who had already given up on getting Arthur back, would all lose heart. The barons and other nobility, the leaders in all fields, would once more go their separate ways, unless they were provided with some replacement for Arthur as a focal point—or unless they at least thought they had been favored with such a magnificent monarch.

I needed no one to warn me that if the same knights came to believe that the man they had already acclaimed as their great king was an impostor, they would almost certainly kill him.

"Once a king has been acclaimed—and they have already chosen you, having been persuaded that they cannot have Arthur back—death is really the only good way to depose him."

Another possibility, perhaps even more devastating, was that, if I wavered, or appeared to hesitate too long, some of these powerful men would still support me, and others would choose Lancelot, or hold out for Arthur, or some other candidate. At that point the chances of a ruinous civil war would become very great. Any such conflict would almost certainly destroy Merlin's remaining chances to rebuild Camelot.

Of course Flagon-dry and Maud probably foresaw comfortable posts for themselves, if I were king.

After much soul-searching, I reluctantly continued to play the part of the new king. In my own mind I thought that I was doing so only until a better leader should come along.

I had privately told Lancelot as much, before he resumed his interrupted retirement.

Merlin told me that he was aware of no man currently available who was likely to do better in the job. He also emphasized once more that it was my task, my duty, to somehow gather helpers, associates, to help him in the great task he had undertaken. In turn I pointed out, not for the first time, that a woman might also succeed admirably in the role—"Boadicea, who died centuries ago, presents a stellar example."

Merlin groaned, inaudibly, and heartily seconded the wish that Boadicea were available. But he had to work with the material at hand. Did I have some particular woman to suggest?

And I could think of no one, least of all Jandree.

Eventually—when both Logres and its surviving citizens had somewhat recovered—I was indeed crowned, the golden circlet placed on my head by a version of Merlin reassuringly solid but noticeably less elderly than the one who had vanished with the shaking of the earth. And in the presence of many happy old knights (and of some others who were not so happy) I sat in my father's chair at the Round Table.

And Jandree, who loved me in a way, and who certainly loved the idea of being queen, received her own crown from my hands. Then my wife sat beside me, in another tall chair no different from my own—or from any of the other chairs around the Table. I had ordered that a certain one of them should be securely draped with linen, as warning to anyone who might move inadvertently to sit in it.

* * *

The new king had, as you might imagine, several things to worry about.

Never could the knights who pledged their fealty to me have accepted as a leader any man who had once capered before them as a jester. But I had never appeared *before these men* as an entertainer.

When Morgan, or one of her agents, made sure my inglorious past was revealed to my new followers, several of them spontaneously came up with the most obvious explanation: that I had been living incognito, or under an evil or protective enchantment.

Other concerns were more subtle. I was fully aware, or at least I strongly suspected, that as monarch I was on probation, and that if I failed to satisfy Merlin's idea of what a king should be, he was quite ready to cast me ruthlessly aside and recruit someone else.

"Fine," I muttered to myself, confronting my patron in my imagination. "Go ahead, get someone else."

But there were good reasons why my abdication would not have been that simple.

Thus it came to pass that another king of Arthur's line took his seat—not on a throne, but at his place at the Round Table, amid a flawed but distinguished company of friends and supporters.

In order to get anything accomplished, I had to put on the manners of a king, and try to speak in royal words and tones, when men and women came looking for a new leader. An actor can play a king's role, of course. A good actor can do anything if he has some help.

But it was plain to all that neither king nor kingdom were what they had been before—not even Merlin's magic can ever put what is broken, what is past, back to what it was.

✒ Interlude ✒

With the final departure of the ambulance, normalcy was immediately restored at the foundation—just as Fisher had promised. Conditions snapped back with magical speed to what they had been just before the first arrival of Morgan's ambulance. Security people, unaware that anything out of the ordinary had taken place, were calmly back on duty, their own cars parked in the lot just where they had put them when they came to work.

Elaine was seated at the console where she had been when Fisher entered, dressed as she had been then. She noted with some perplexity how clean her hands were, and how relatively well fed she felt. After a few moments she retained only fleeting memories, jumbled and terrible and glorious, of the great adventure. Of Lancelot, and, and . . . well, mostly of Lancelot.

She wondered if overwork could be producing a tendency to hallucinate. She pondered fiercely on the nature of reality. That, after all, was the foundation's business.

She felt a stirring, deep inside her belly.

How curious.

A word formed in her mind. A name.

Galahad.